JUSTICE LEAGUE UNLIMITED
TIME AFTER TIME

CARLO BARBERI and **WALDEN WONG** collection cover artists

SUPERMAN created by **JERRY SIEGEL** and **JOE SHUSTER**
By special arrangement with the **Jerry Siegel** family

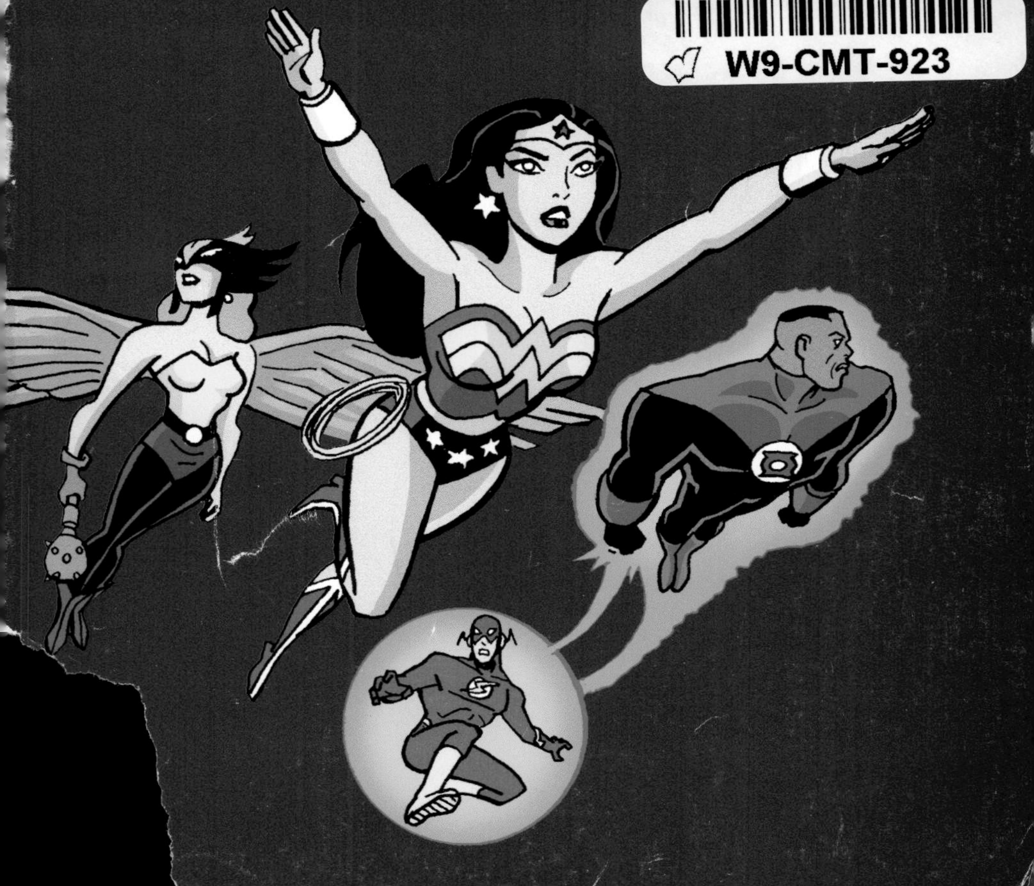

K.C. CARLSON
STEPHEN WACKER
TOM PALMER JR.
MICHAEL WRIGHT
Editors - Original Series

FRANK BERRIOS
JEANINE SCHAEFER
Assistant Editors - Original Series

JEB WOODARD
Group Editor - Collected Editions

SCOTT NYBAKKEN
Editor - Collected Edition

STEVE COOK
Design Director - Books

AMIE BROCKWAY-METCALF
Publication Design

KATE DURRÉ
Publication Production

BOB HARRAS
Senior VP - Editor-in-Chief, DC Comics

JIM LEE
Publisher & Chief Creative Officer

BOBBIE CHASE
VP - Global Publishing Initiatives & Digital Strategy

DON FALLETTI
VP - Manufacturing Operations & Workflow Management

LAWRENCE GANEM
VP - Talent Services

ALISON GILL
Senior VP - Manufacturing & Operations

HANK KANALZ
Senior VP - Publishing Strategy & Support Services

DAN MIRON
VP - Publishing Operations

NICK J. NAPOLITANO
VP - Manufacturing Administration & Design

NANCY SPEARS
VP - Sales

JONAH WEILAND
VP - Marketing & Creative Services

MICHELE R. WELLS
VP & Executive Editor, Young Reader

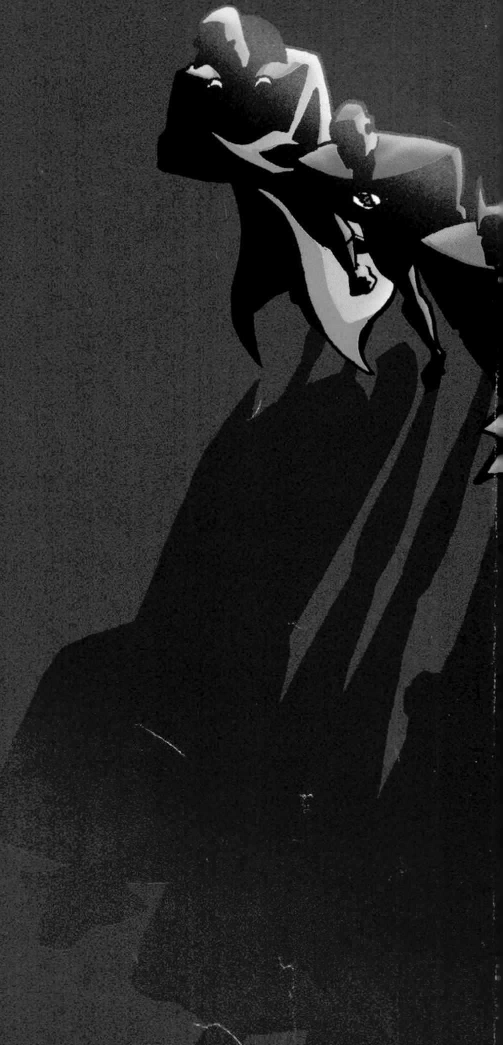

JUSTICE LEAGUE UNLIMITED: TIME AFTER TIME

DC Comics, 2900 West Alameda Ave., Burbank, CA 91505
Printed by LSC Communications, Crawfordsville, IN, USA. 9/25/20. First Printing.
ISBN: 978-1-77950-724-2
Library of Congress Cataloging-in-Publication Data is available.

CONTENTS

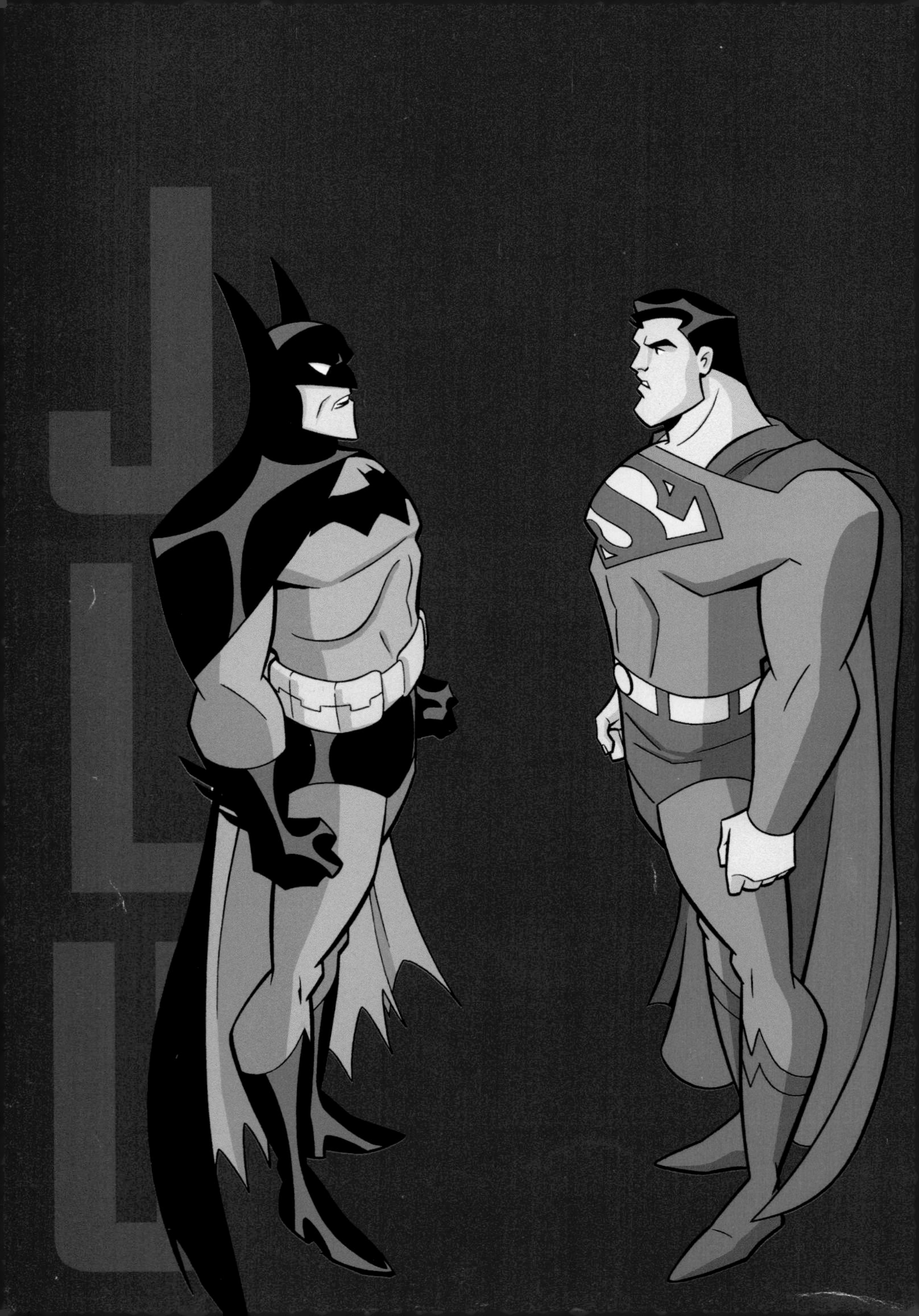

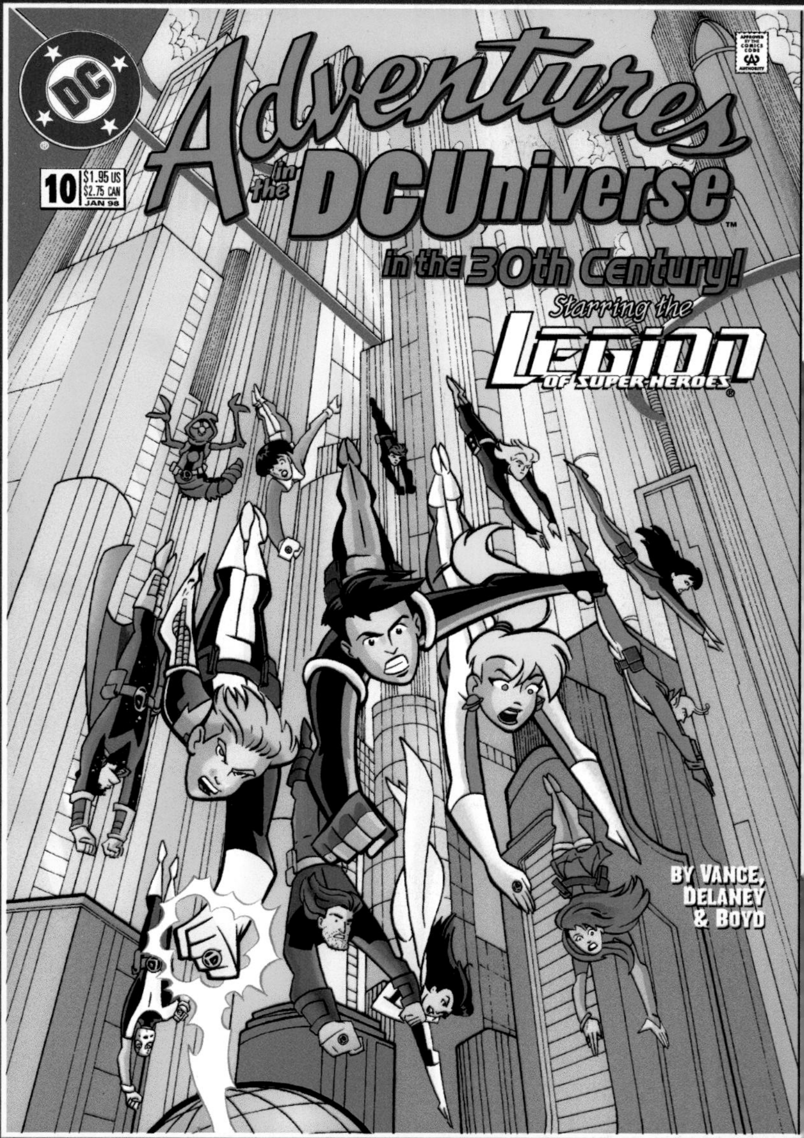
DC
10
$1.95 US
$2.75 CAN
JAN 98
Adventures in the DC Universe
in the 30th Century!
Starring the
Legion of Super-Heroes
BY VANCE, DELANEY & BOYD

CHAPTER 1: THE BLOBS

JUSTICE LEAGUE UNLIMITED

COVER ART BY JOHN DELANEY AND RON BOYD

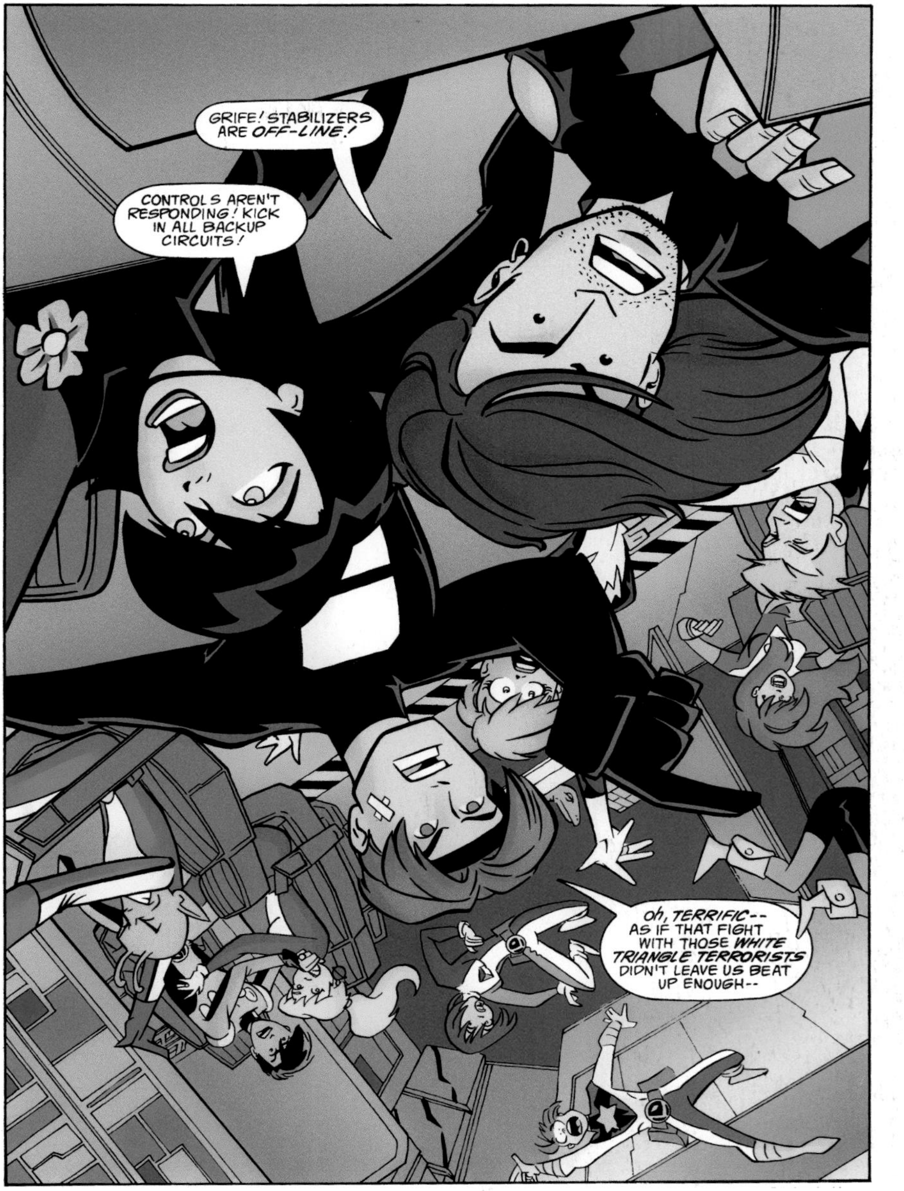
GRIFE! STABILIZERS ARE OFF-LINE!
CONTROLS AREN'T RESPONDING! KICK IN ALL BACKUP CIRCUITS!
oh, TERRIFIC-- AS IF THAT FIGHT WITH THOSE WHITE TRIANGLE TERRORISTS DIDN'T LEAVE US BEAT UP ENOUGH--

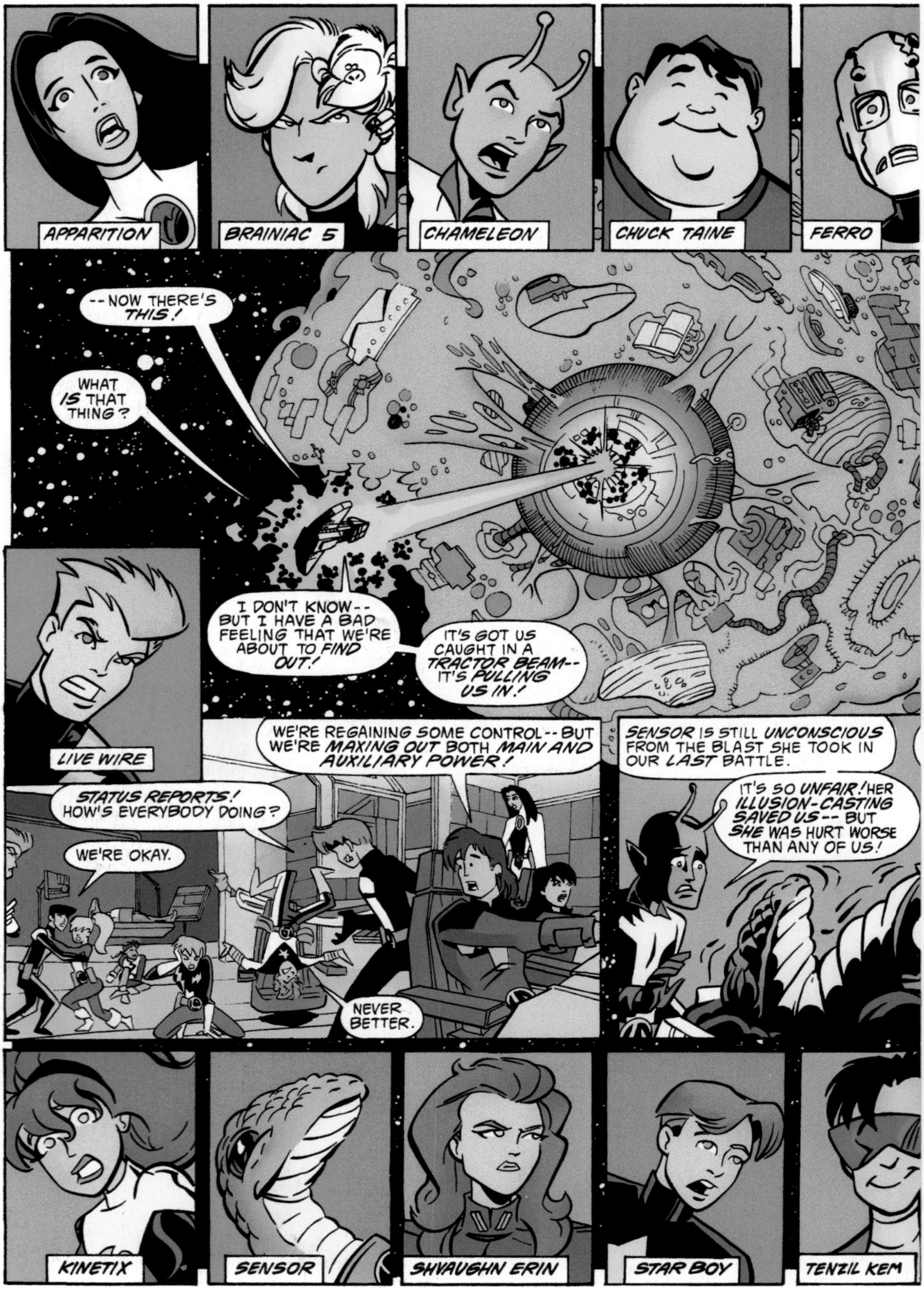
APPARITION
BRAINIAC 5
CHAMELEON
CHUCK TAINE
FERRO
--NOW THERE'S THIS!
WHAT IS THAT THING?
I DON'T KNOW-- BUT I HAVE A BAD FEELING THAT WE'RE ABOUT TO FIND OUT!
IT'S GOT US CAUGHT IN A TRACTOR BEAM-- IT'S PULLING US IN!
LIVE WIRE
WE'RE REGAINING SOME CONTROL-- BUT WE'RE MAXING OUT BOTH MAIN AND AUXILIARY POWER!
STATUS REPORTS! HOW'S EVERYBODY DOING?
WE'RE OKAY.
NEVER BETTER.
SENSOR IS STILL UNCONSCIOUS FROM THE BLAST SHE TOOK IN OUR LAST BATTLE.
IT'S SO UNFAIR! HER ILLUSION-CASTING SAVED US-- BUT SHE WAS HURT WORSE THAN ANY OF US!
KINETIX
SENSOR
SHVAUGHN ERIN
STAR BOY
TENZIL KEM

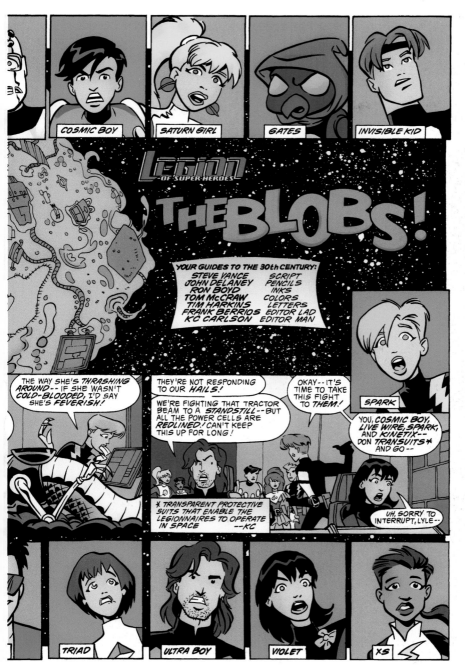

COSMIC BOY

SATURN GIRL

GATES

INVISIBLE KID

THE BLOBS!

YOUR GUIDES TO THE 30th CENTURY:

STEVE VANCE	SCRIPT
JOHN DELANEY	PENCILS
RON BOYD	INKS
TOM McCRAW	COLORS
TIM HARKINS	LETTERS
FRANK BERRIOS	EDITOR LAD
KC CARLSON	EDITOR MAN

SPARK

THE WAY SHE'S *THRASHING AROUND*-- IF SHE WASN'T *COLD-BLOODED*, I'D SAY SHE'S *FEVERISH!*

THEY'RE NOT RESPONDING TO OUR *HAILS!*

WE'RE FIGHTING THAT TRACTOR BEAM TO A *STANDSTILL*--BUT ALL THE POWER CELLS ARE *REDLINED!* CAN'T KEEP THIS UP FOR LONG!

OKAY--IT'S TIME TO TAKE THIS FIGHT TO *THEM!*

YOU, *COSMIC BOY, LIVE WIRE, SPARK,* AND *KINETIX*-- DON *TRANSUITS* ✱ AND GO--

✱ *TRANSPARENT PROTECTIVE SUITS THAT ENABLE THE LEGIONNAIRES TO OPERATE IN SPACE* --KC

UH, SORRY TO INTERRUPT, LYLE--

TRIAD

ULTRA BOY

VIOLET

XS

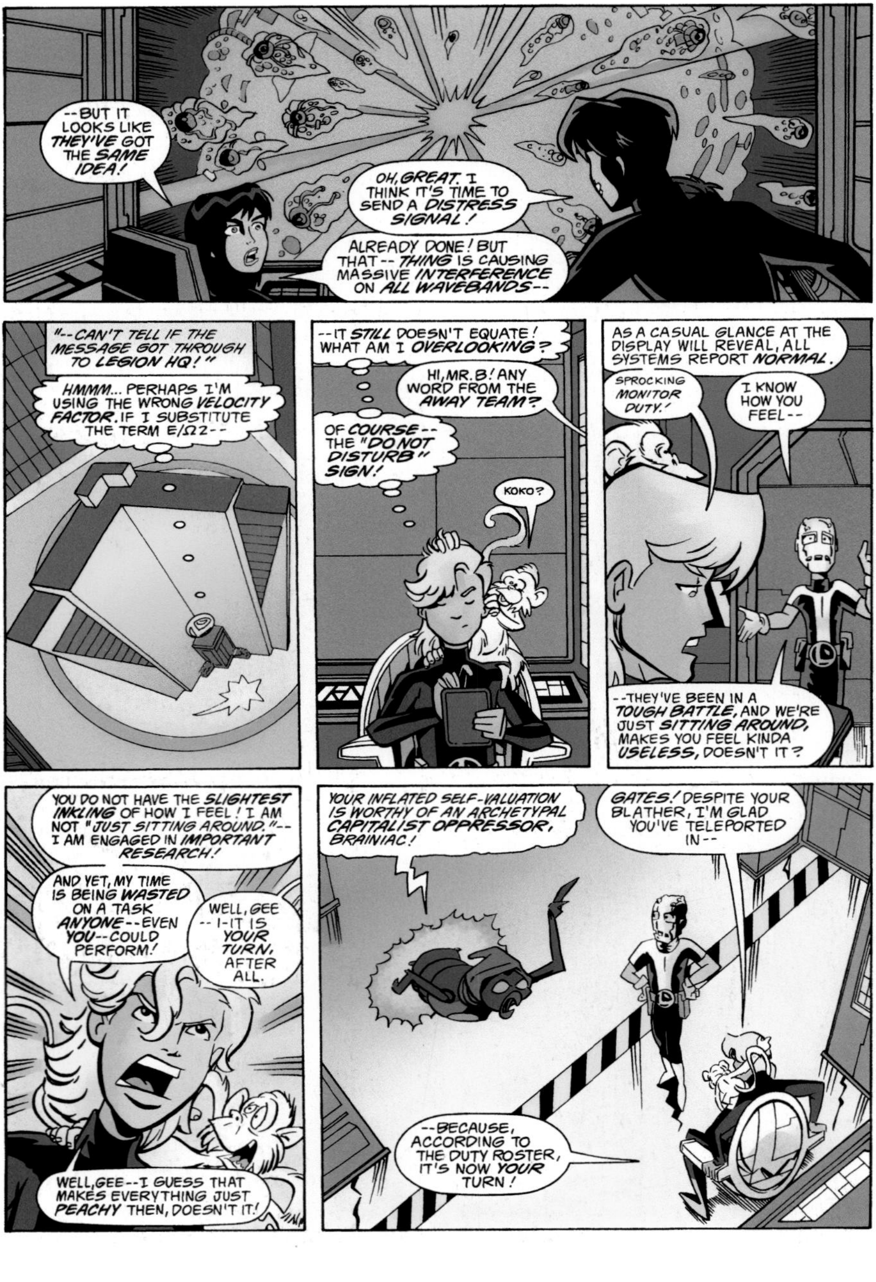
--BUT IT LOOKS LIKE THEY'VE GOT THE SAME IDEA!
OH, GREAT. I THINK IT'S TIME TO SEND A DISTRESS SIGNAL!
ALREADY DONE! BUT THAT--THING IS CAUSING MASSIVE INTERFERENCE ON ALL WAVEBANDS--
"--CAN'T TELL IF THE MESSAGE GOT THROUGH TO LEGION HQ!"
HMMM... PERHAPS I'M USING THE WRONG VELOCITY FACTOR. IF I SUBSTITUTE THE TERM E/Ω2--
--IT STILL DOESN'T EQUATE! WHAT AM I OVERLOOKING?
HI, MR. B! ANY WORD FROM THE AWAY TEAM?
OF COURSE--THE "DO NOT DISTURB" SIGN!
KOKO?
AS A CASUAL GLANCE AT THE DISPLAY WILL REVEAL, ALL SYSTEMS REPORT NORMAL.
SPROCKING MONITOR DUTY!
I KNOW HOW YOU FEEL--
--THEY'VE BEEN IN A TOUGH BATTLE, AND WE'RE JUST SITTING AROUND, MAKES YOU FEEL KINDA USELESS, DOESN'T IT?
YOU DO NOT HAVE THE SLIGHTEST INKLING OF HOW I FEEL! I AM NOT "JUST SITTING AROUND."--I AM ENGAGED IN IMPORTANT RESEARCH!
AND YET, MY TIME IS BEING WASTED ON A TASK ANYONE--EVEN YOU--COULD PERFORM!
WELL, GEE--I-IT IS YOUR TURN, AFTER ALL.
WELL, GEE--I GUESS THAT MAKES EVERYTHING JUST PEACHY THEN, DOESN'T IT!
YOUR INFLATED SELF-VALUATION IS WORTHY OF AN ARCHETYPAL CAPITALIST OPPRESSOR, BRAINIAC!
GATES! DESPITE YOUR BLATHER, I'M GLAD YOU'VE TELEPORTED IN--
--BECAUSE, ACCORDING TO THE DUTY ROSTER, IT'S NOW YOUR TURN!

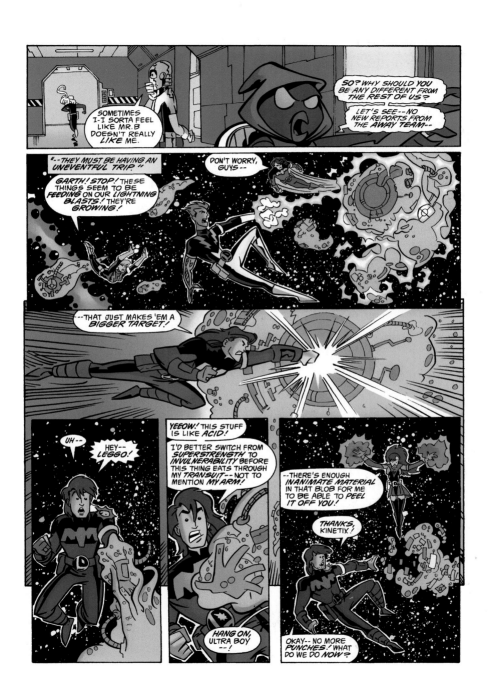

SOMETIMES I-I SORTA FEEL LIKE MR.B DOESN'T REALLY *LIKE* ME.

SO? WHY SHOULD YOU BE ANY *DIFFERENT* FROM THE *REST* OF US?

LET'S SEE-- NO NEW REPORTS FROM THE *AWAY TEAM*--

"--THEY MUST BE HAVING AN *UNEVENTFUL TRIP*."

DON'T WORRY, GUYS--

GARTH! STOP! THESE THINGS SEEM TO BE *FEEDING* ON OUR *LIGHTNING BLASTS!* THEY'RE *GROWING!*

--THAT JUST MAKES 'EM A *BIGGER TARGET!*

UH--

HEY-- *LEGGO!*

YEEOW! THIS STUFF IS LIKE *ACID!*

I'D BETTER SWITCH FROM *SUPERSTRENGTH* TO *INVULNERABILITY* BEFORE THIS THING EATS THROUGH MY *TRANSUIT*-- NOT TO MENTION *MY ARM!*

--THERE'S ENOUGH *INANIMATE* MATERIAL IN THAT BLOB FOR ME TO BE ABLE TO *PEEL* IT OFF YOU!

THANKS, *KINETIX!*

HANG ON, ULTRA BOY--!

OKAY-- NO MORE *PUNCHES!* WHAT DO WE DO *NOW*?

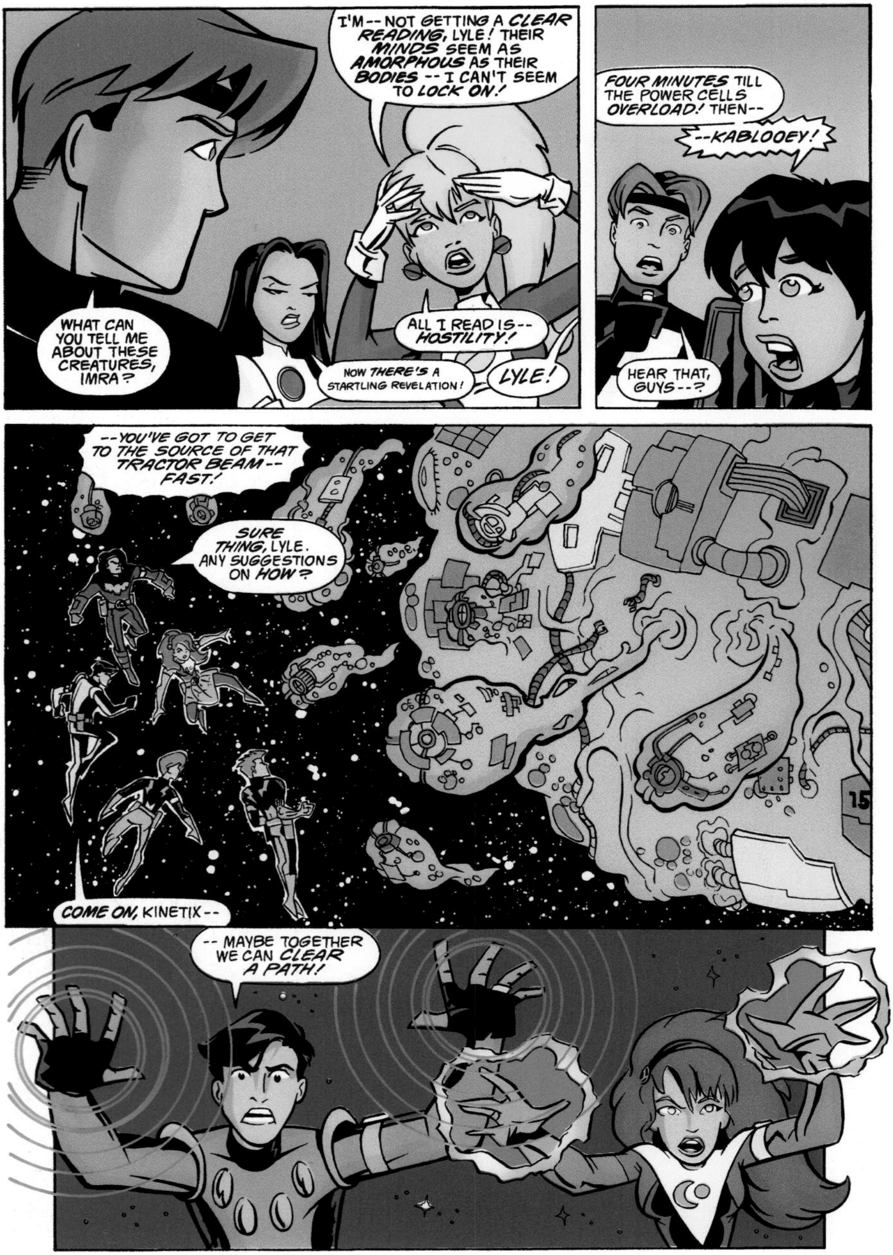
I'M -- NOT GETTING A CLEAR READING, LYLE! THEIR MINDS SEEM AS AMORPHOUS AS THEIR BODIES -- I CAN'T SEEM TO LOCK ON!
WHAT CAN YOU TELL ME ABOUT THESE CREATURES, IMRA?
ALL I READ IS -- HOSTILITY!
NOW THERE'S A STARTLING REVELATION!
LYLE!
FOUR MINUTES TILL THE POWER CELLS OVERLOAD! THEN--
--KABLOOEY!
HEAR THAT, GUYS--?
--YOU'VE GOT TO GET TO THE SOURCE OF THAT TRACTOR BEAM -- FAST!
SURE THING, LYLE. ANY SUGGESTIONS ON HOW?
COME ON, KINETIX--
-- MAYBE TOGETHER WE CAN CLEAR A PATH!

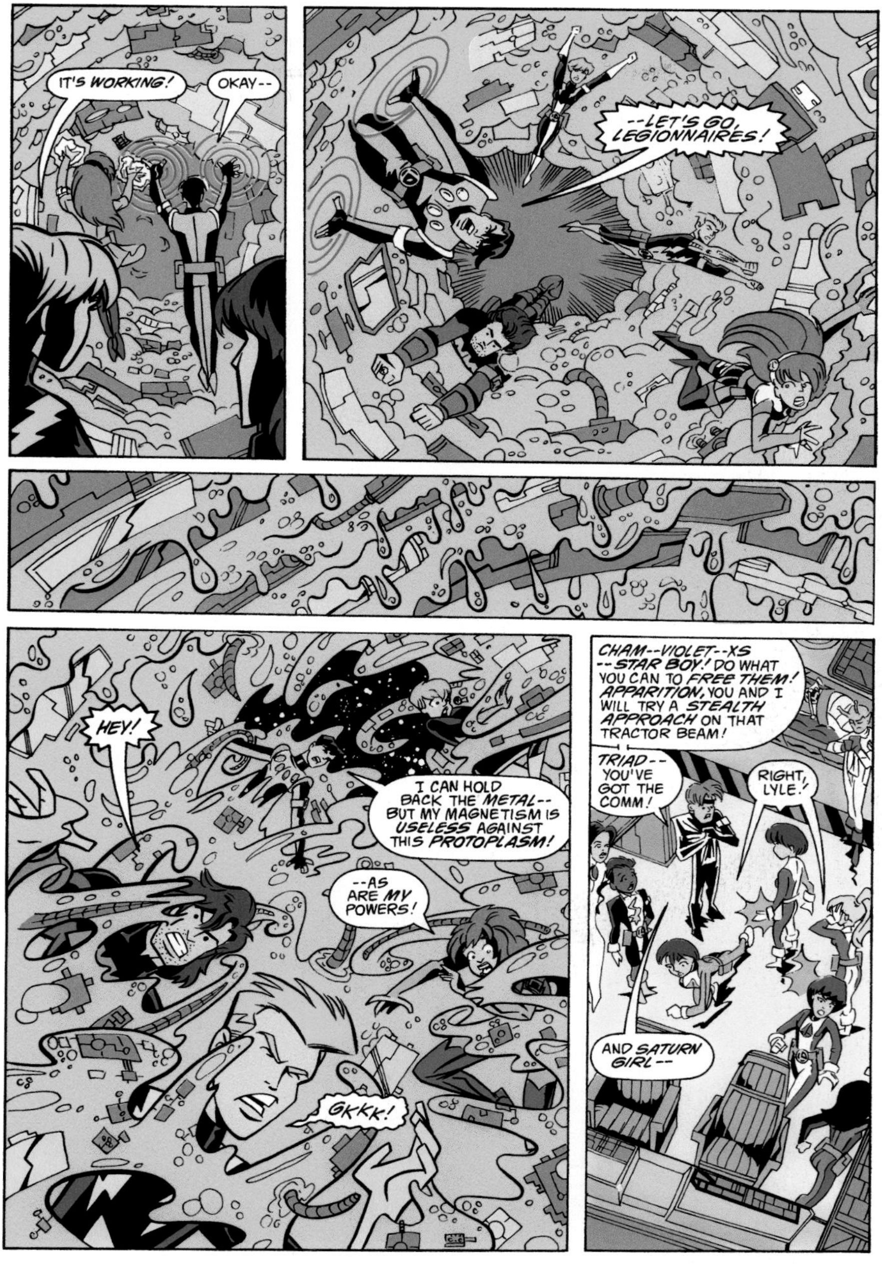
IT'S WORKING!
OKAY--
--LET'S GO, LEGIONNAIRES!
HEY!
I CAN HOLD BACK THE METAL--BUT MY MAGNETISM IS USELESS AGAINST THIS PROTOPLASM!
--AS ARE MY POWERS!
GKKK!
CHAM--VIOLET--XS--STAR BOY! DO WHAT YOU CAN TO FREE THEM! APPARITION, YOU AND I WILL TRY A STEALTH APPROACH ON THAT TRACTOR BEAM!
TRIAD--YOU'VE GOT THE COMM!
RIGHT, LYLE!
AND SATURN GIRL--

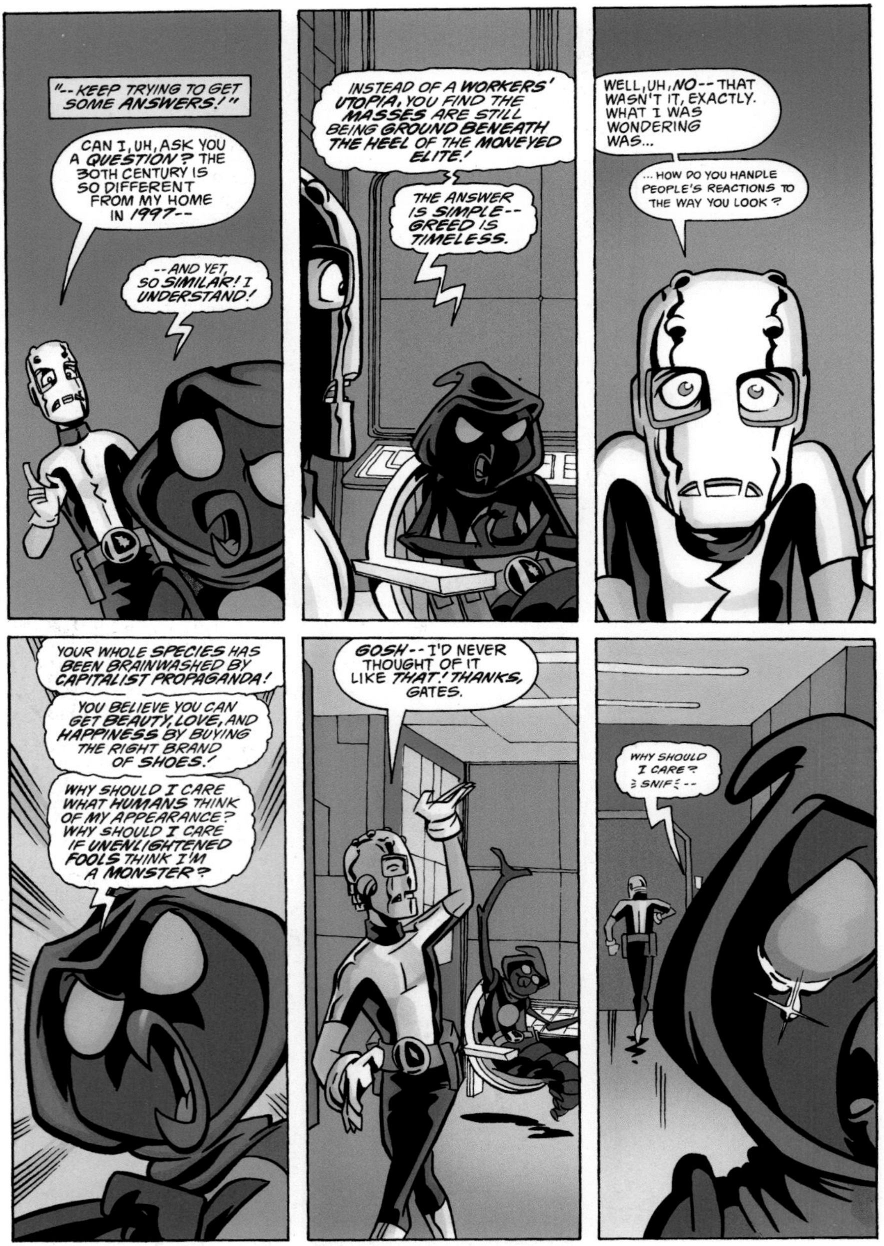
"--KEEP TRYING TO GET SOME ANSWERS!"
CAN I, UH, ASK YOU A QUESTION? THE 30TH CENTURY IS SO DIFFERENT FROM MY HOME IN 1997--
--AND YET, SO SIMILAR! I UNDERSTAND!
INSTEAD OF A WORKERS' UTOPIA, YOU FIND THE MASSES ARE STILL BEING GROUND BENEATH THE HEEL OF THE MONEYED ELITE!
THE ANSWER IS SIMPLE-- GREED IS TIMELESS.
WELL, UH, NO-- THAT WASN'T IT, EXACTLY. WHAT I WAS WONDERING WAS...
...HOW DO YOU HANDLE PEOPLE'S REACTIONS TO THE WAY YOU LOOK?
YOUR WHOLE SPECIES HAS BEEN BRAINWASHED BY CAPITALIST PROPAGANDA!
YOU BELIEVE YOU CAN GET BEAUTY, LOVE, AND HAPPINESS BY BUYING THE RIGHT BRAND OF SHOES!
WHY SHOULD I CARE WHAT HUMANS THINK OF MY APPEARANCE? WHY SHOULD I CARE IF UNENLIGHTENED FOOLS THINK I'M A MONSTER?
GOSH-- I'D NEVER THOUGHT OF IT LIKE THAT! THANKS, GATES.
WHY SHOULD I CARE? SNIF--

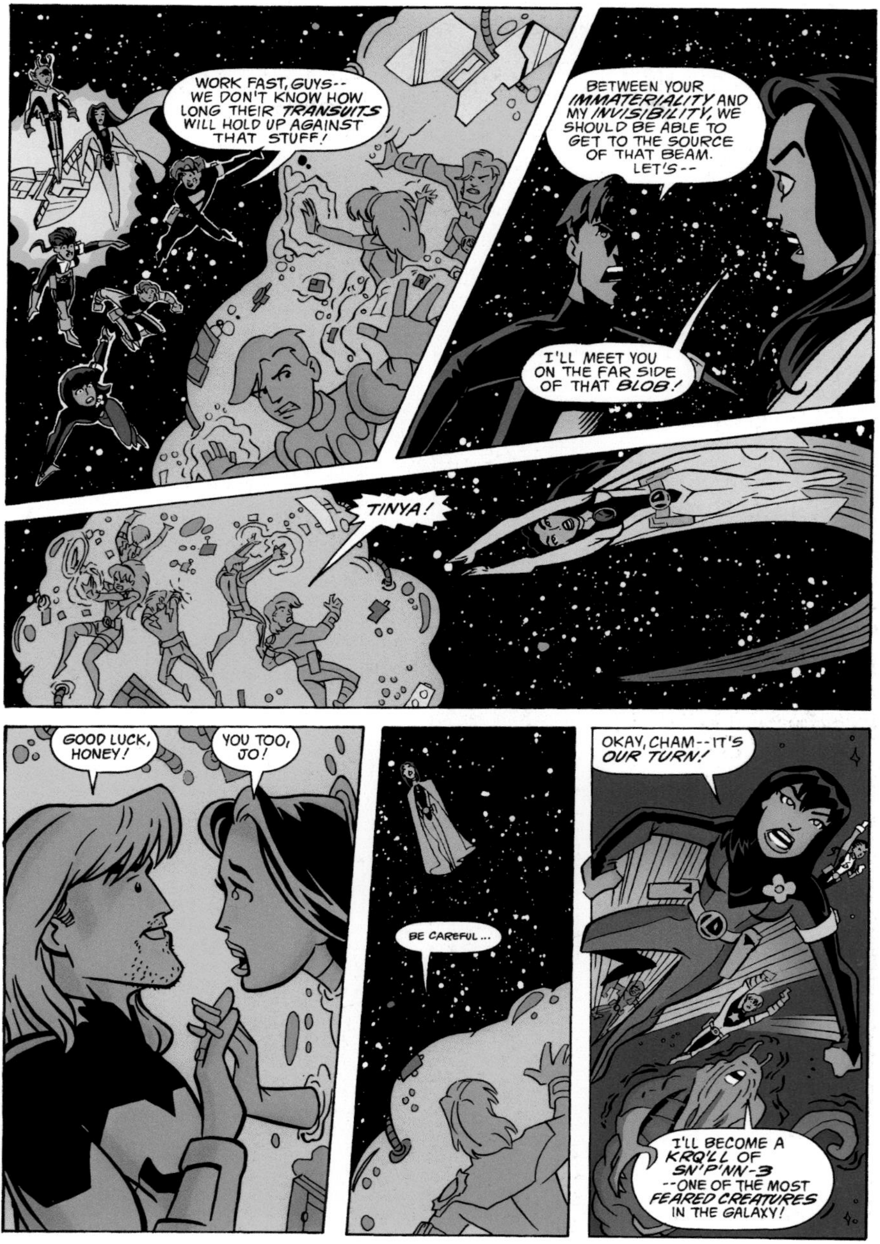
WORK FAST, GUYS-- WE DON'T KNOW HOW LONG THEIR TRANSUITS WILL HOLD UP AGAINST THAT STUFF!
BETWEEN YOUR IMMATERIALITY AND MY INVISIBILITY, WE SHOULD BE ABLE TO GET TO THE SOURCE OF THAT BEAM. LET'S--
I'LL MEET YOU ON THE FAR SIDE OF THAT BLOB!
TINYA!
GOOD LUCK, HONEY!
YOU TOO, JO!
BE CAREFUL...
OKAY, CHAM--IT'S OUR TURN!
I'LL BECOME A KRQ'LL OF SN'P'NN-3 --ONE OF THE MOST FEARED CREATURES IN THE GALAXY!

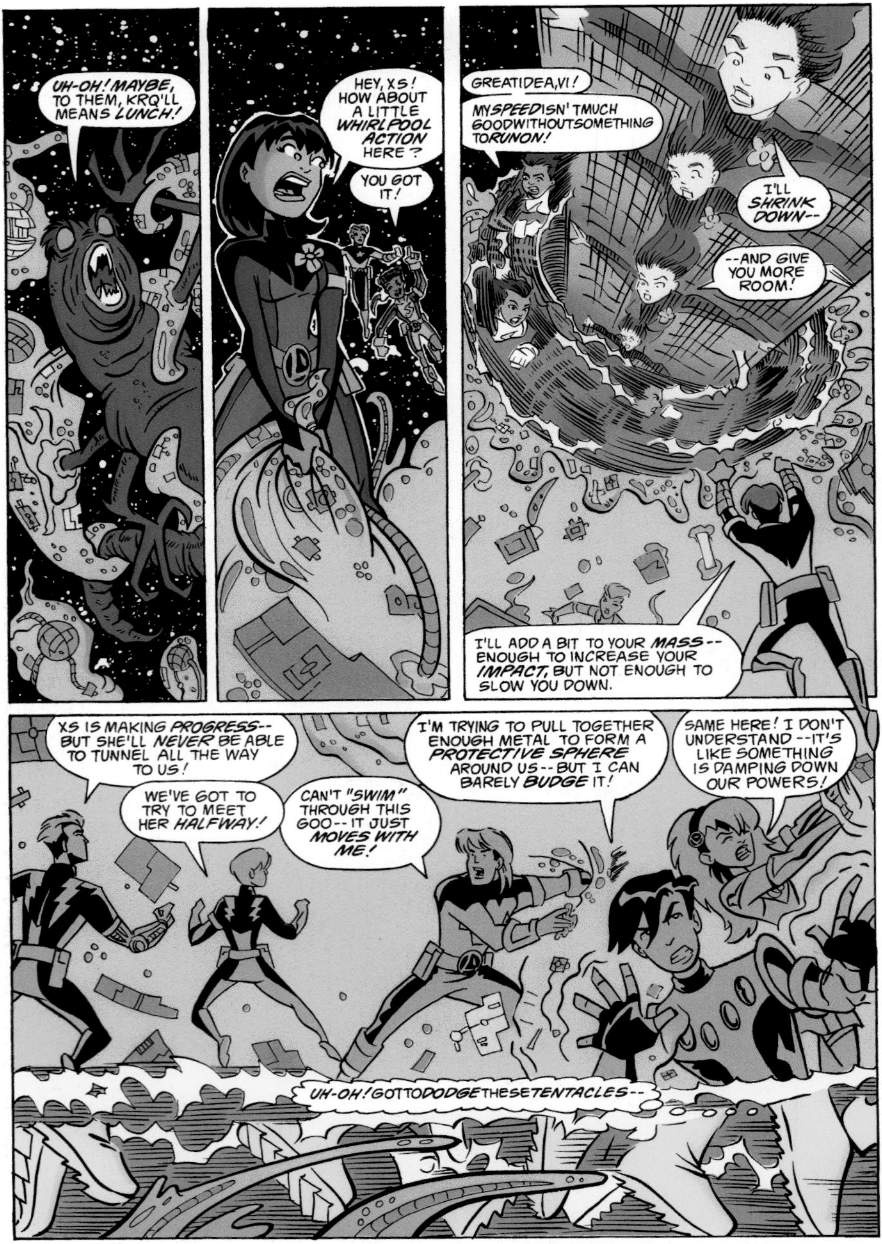
UH-OH! MAYBE, TO THEM, KRQ'LL MEANS LUNCH!
HEY, XS! HOW ABOUT A LITTLE WHIRLPOOL ACTION HERE?
YOU GOT IT!
GREAT IDEA, VI!
MY SPEED ISN'T MUCH GOOD WITHOUT SOMETHING TO RUN ON!
I'LL SHRINK DOWN--
--AND GIVE YOU MORE ROOM!
I'LL ADD A BIT TO YOUR MASS-- ENOUGH TO INCREASE YOUR IMPACT, BUT NOT ENOUGH TO SLOW YOU DOWN.
XS IS MAKING PROGRESS-- BUT SHE'LL NEVER BE ABLE TO TUNNEL ALL THE WAY TO US!
WE'VE GOT TO TRY TO MEET HER HALFWAY!
CAN'T "SWIM" THROUGH THIS GOO-- IT JUST MOVES WITH ME!
I'M TRYING TO PULL TOGETHER ENOUGH METAL TO FORM A PROTECTIVE SPHERE AROUND US-- BUT I CAN BARELY BUDGE IT!
SAME HERE! I DON'T UNDERSTAND --IT'S LIKE SOMETHING IS DAMPING DOWN OUR POWERS!
UH-OH! GOT TO DODGE THESE TENTACLES--

-- BUT THERE'S *TOO MANY OF THEM!*

NASS! THESE THINGS CAN *SHAPESHIFT* ALMOST AS FAST AS I CAN-- AND THEY'VE GOT ME *SERIOUSLY OUTNUMBERED!*

IT'S ONLY A MATTER OF *TIME* --

-- BEFORE THEY *DRAG ME DOWN!*

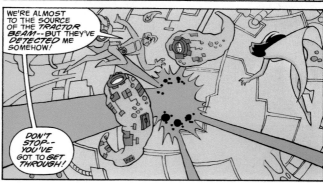

WE'RE ALMOST TO THE SOURCE OF THE *TRACTOR BEAM* -- BUT THEY'VE *DETECTED* ME SOMEHOW!

DON'T STOP-- YOU'VE GOT TO *GET THROUGH!*

I FEEL LIKE I'M *ABANDONING LYLE* -- BUT HE'S *RIGHT!*

BY PHASING THROUGH THE DEVICE THAT'S FIRING THE *TRACTOR BEAM,* I CAN *DISRUPT* THE *MECHANISM* AND *FREE* OUR CRUISER.

THEN MAYBE WE CAN FIGURE OUT HOW TO --

OH, NO!

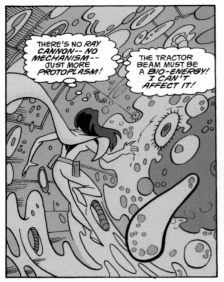

THERE'S NO *RAY CANNON*-- *NO MECHANISM*-- JUST MORE *PROTOPLASM!*

THE *TRACTOR BEAM* MUST BE A *BIO-ENERGY!* I CAN'T AFFECT IT!

TWO MINUTES TO *CRITICAL MASS!* AND THEN WE EITHER *ABANDON SHIP, SHUT DOWN* AND *SURRENDER*--

--OR *BLOW UP!*

HEY! I'M GETTING IT--!

I THINK I'M FINALLY BEGINNING TO UNDERSTAAAAAAAAA

AAAA!

IMRA!?

"IMRA--CAN YOU HEAR ME?"

SATURN GIRL?

HI, FERRO-- I DIDN'T HEAR YOU COME IN.

OH--EXCUSE ME, OFFICER ERIN. I THOUGHT THE LIBRARY WAS EMPTY.

THAT'S QUITE ALL RIGHT,--THERE'S ROOM FOR TWO!

AND PLEASE --CALL ME *SHVAUGHN.*

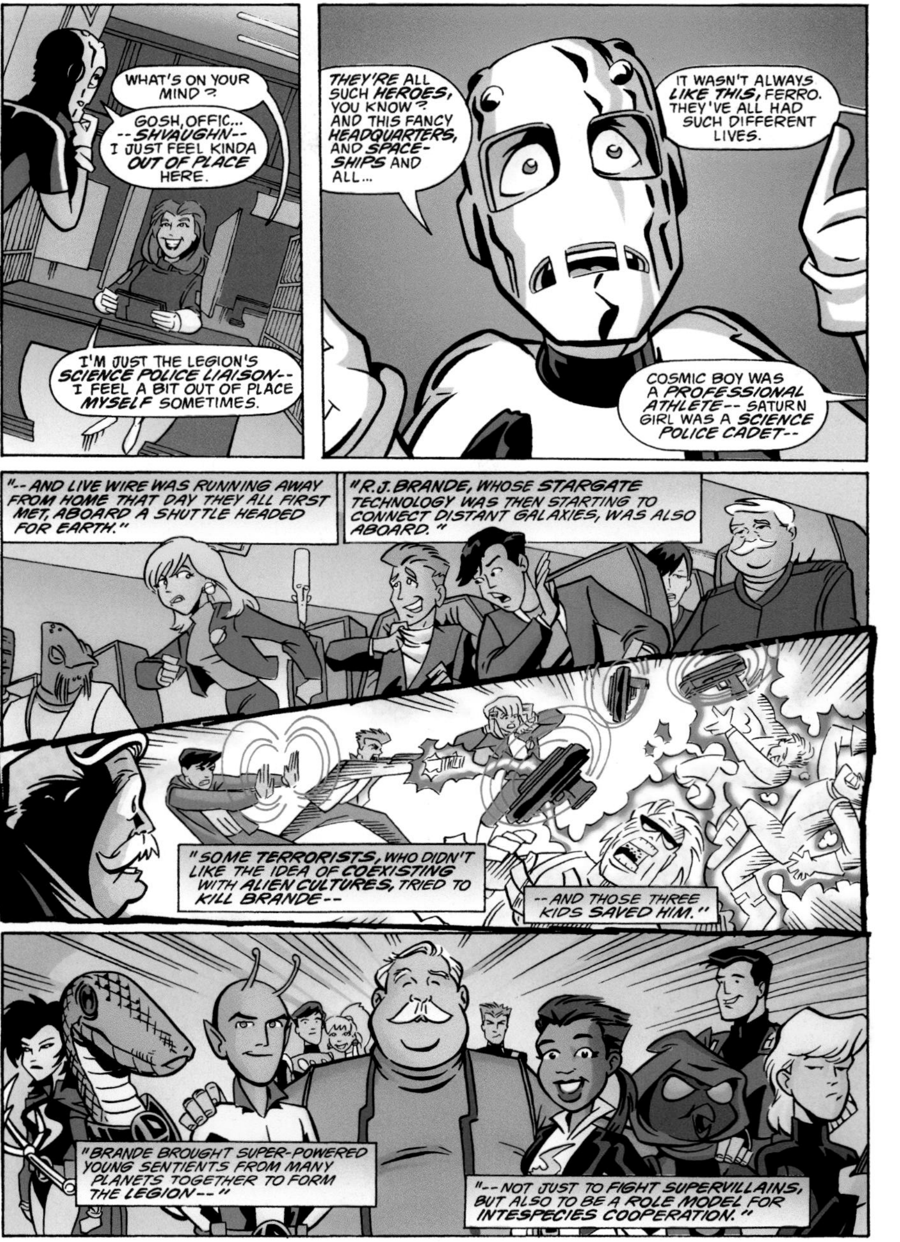
WHAT'S ON YOUR MIND?
GOSH, OFFIC... --SHVAUGHN-- I JUST FEEL KINDA OUT OF PLACE HERE.
I'M JUST THE LEGION'S SCIENCE POLICE LIAISON-- I FEEL A BIT OUT OF PLACE MYSELF SOMETIMES.
THEY'RE ALL SUCH HEROES, YOU KNOW? AND THIS FANCY HEADQUARTERS, AND SPACE-SHIPS AND ALL...
IT WASN'T ALWAYS LIKE THIS, FERRO. THEY'VE ALL HAD SUCH DIFFERENT LIVES.
COSMIC BOY WAS A PROFESSIONAL ATHLETE-- SATURN GIRL WAS A SCIENCE POLICE CADET--
"--AND LIVE WIRE WAS RUNNING AWAY FROM HOME THAT DAY THEY ALL FIRST MET, ABOARD A SHUTTLE HEADED FOR EARTH."
"R.J. BRANDE, WHOSE STARGATE TECHNOLOGY WAS THEN STARTING TO CONNECT DISTANT GALAXIES, WAS ALSO ABOARD."
"SOME TERRORISTS, WHO DIDN'T LIKE THE IDEA OF COEXISTING WITH ALIEN CULTURES, TRIED TO KILL BRANDE--
--AND THOSE THREE KIDS SAVED HIM."
"BRANDE BROUGHT SUPER-POWERED YOUNG SENTIENTS FROM MANY PLANETS TOGETHER TO FORM THE LEGION--"
"--NOT JUST TO FIGHT SUPERVILLAINS, BUT ALSO TO BE A ROLE MODEL FOR INTESPECIES COOPERATION."

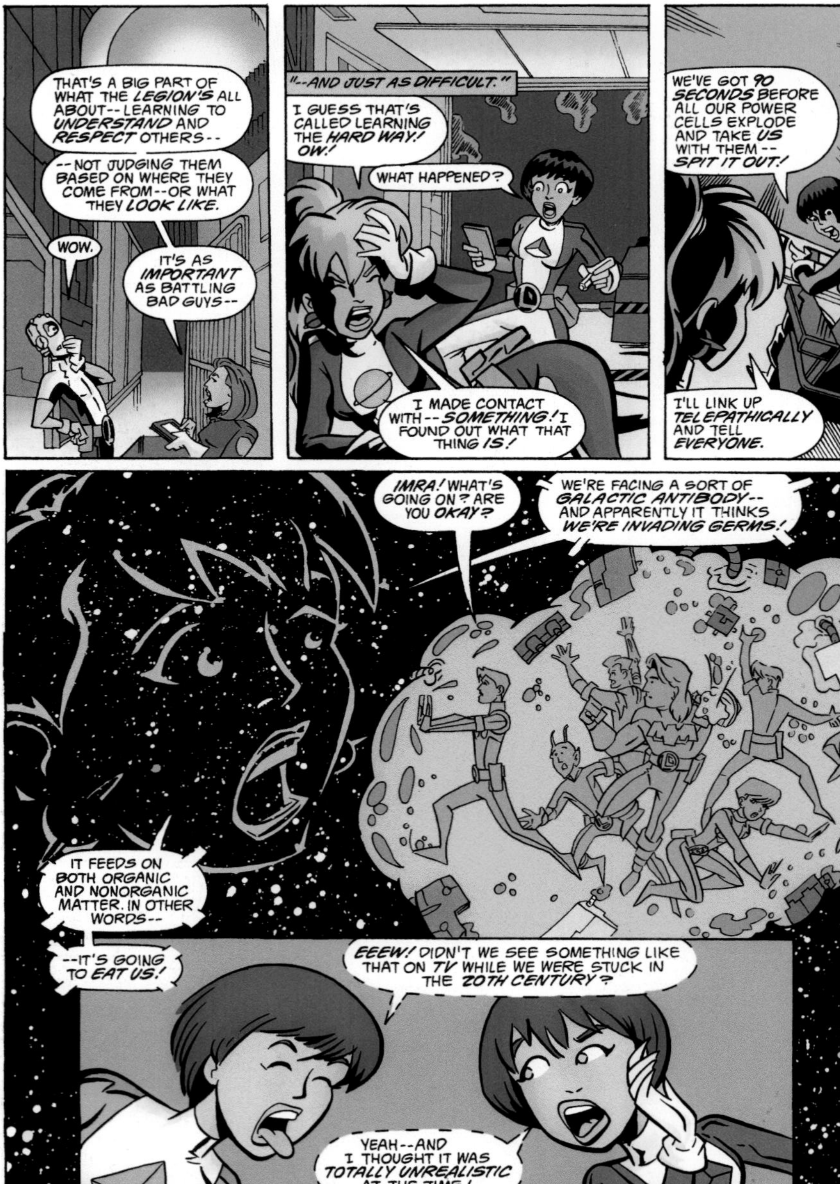
THAT'S A BIG PART OF WHAT THE LEGION'S ALL ABOUT--LEARNING TO UNDERSTAND AND RESPECT OTHERS--
--NOT JUDGING THEM BASED ON WHERE THEY COME FROM--OR WHAT THEY LOOK LIKE.
WOW.
IT'S AS IMPORTANT AS BATTLING BAD GUYS--
"--AND JUST AS DIFFICULT."
I GUESS THAT'S CALLED LEARNING THE HARD WAY! OW!
WHAT HAPPENED?
I MADE CONTACT WITH--SOMETHING! I FOUND OUT WHAT THAT THING IS!
WE'VE GOT 90 SECONDS BEFORE ALL OUR POWER CELLS EXPLODE AND TAKE US WITH THEM--SPIT IT OUT!
I'LL LINK UP TELEPATHICALLY AND TELL EVERYONE.
IMRA! WHAT'S GOING ON? ARE YOU OKAY?
WE'RE FACING A SORT OF GALACTIC ANTIBODY--AND APPARENTLY IT THINKS WE'RE INVADING GERMS!
IT FEEDS ON BOTH ORGANIC AND NONORGANIC MATTER. IN OTHER WORDS--
--IT'S GOING TO EAT US!
EEEW! DIDN'T WE SEE SOMETHING LIKE THAT ON TV WHILE WE WERE STUCK IN THE 20TH CENTURY?
YEAH--AND I THOUGHT IT WAS TOTALLY UNREALISTIC AT THE TIME!

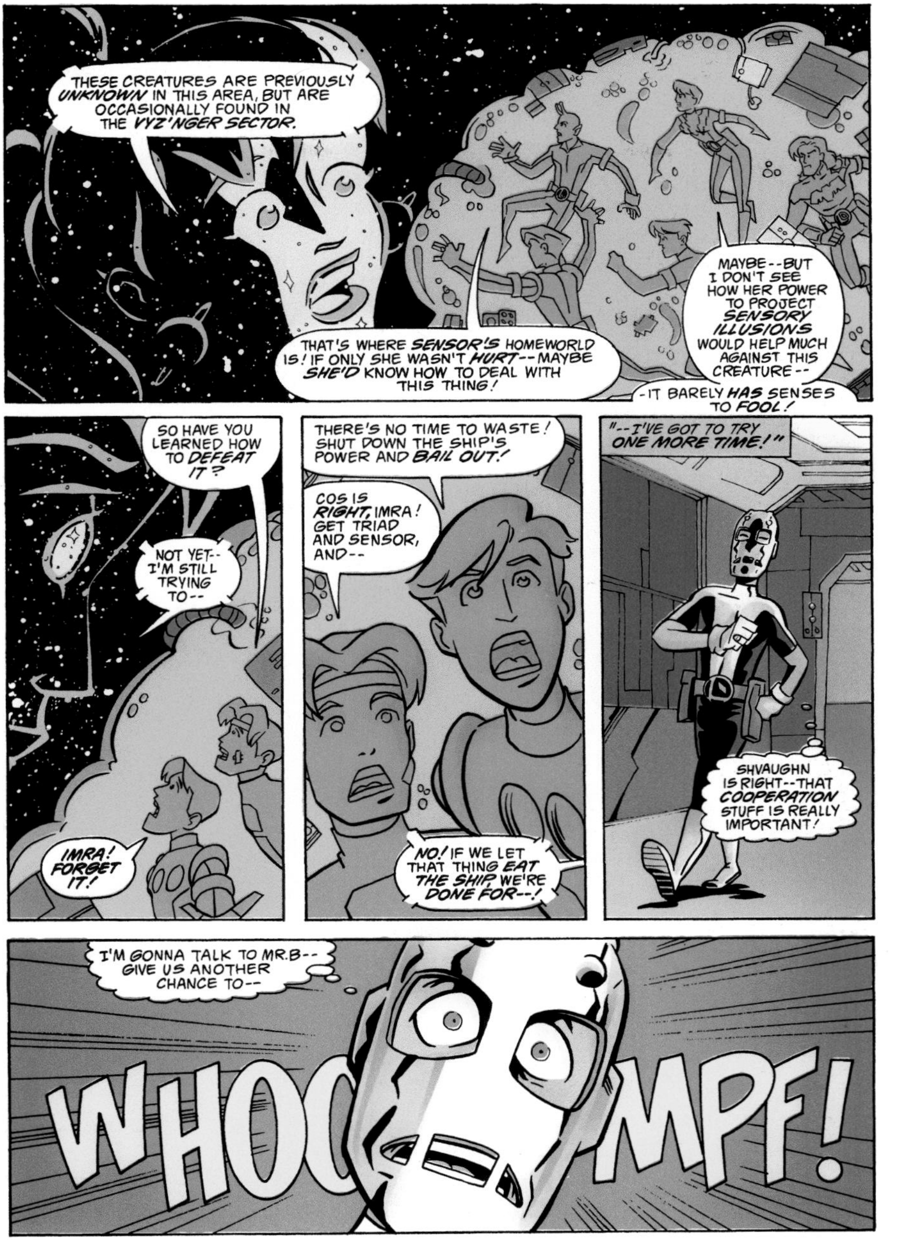
THESE CREATURES ARE PREVIOUSLY UNKNOWN IN THIS AREA, BUT ARE OCCASIONALLY FOUND IN THE VYZ'NGER SECTOR.
THAT'S WHERE SENSOR'S HOMEWORLD IS! IF ONLY SHE WASN'T HURT--MAYBE SHE'D KNOW HOW TO DEAL WITH THIS THING!
MAYBE--BUT I DON'T SEE HOW HER POWER TO PROJECT SENSORY ILLUSIONS WOULD HELP MUCH AGAINST THIS CREATURE--
-IT BARELY HAS SENSES TO FOOL!
SO HAVE YOU LEARNED HOW TO DEFEAT IT?
NOT YET--I'M STILL TRYING TO--
IMRA! FORGET IT!
THERE'S NO TIME TO WASTE! SHUT DOWN THE SHIP'S POWER AND BAIL OUT!
COS IS RIGHT, IMRA! GET TRIAD AND SENSOR, AND--
NO! IF WE LET THAT THING EAT THE SHIP, WE'RE DONE FOR--!
"--I'VE GOT TO TRY ONE MORE TIME!"
SHVAUGHN IS RIGHT--THAT COOPERATION STUFF IS REALLY IMPORTANT!
I'M GONNA TALK TO MR.B--GIVE US ANOTHER CHANCE TO--
WHOO MPF!

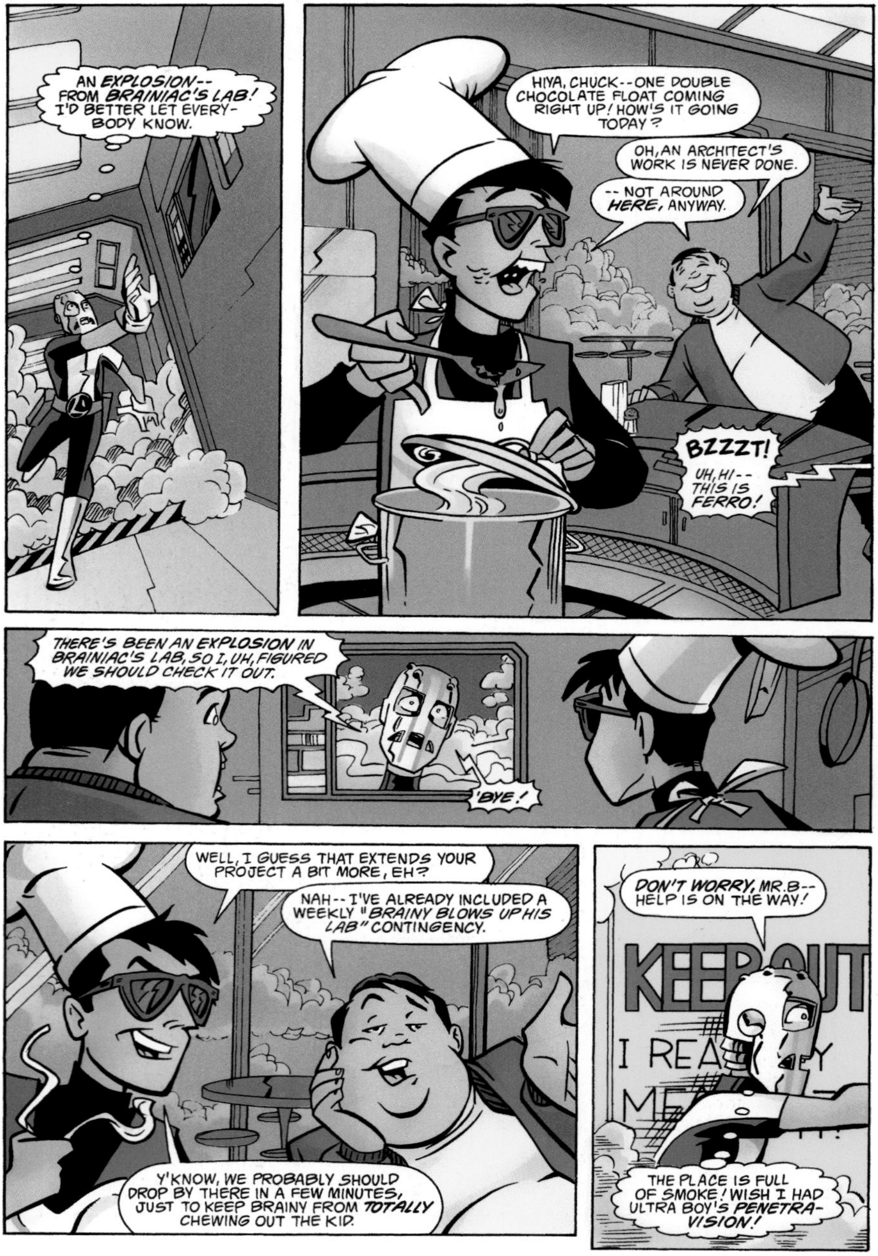

AN EXPLOSION-- FROM BRAINIAC'S LAB! I'D BETTER LET EVERY-BODY KNOW.
HIYA, CHUCK--ONE DOUBLE CHOCOLATE FLOAT COMING RIGHT UP! HOW'S IT GOING TODAY?
OH, AN ARCHITECT'S WORK IS NEVER DONE.
--NOT AROUND HERE, ANYWAY.
BZZZT!
UH, HI-- THIS IS FERRO!
THERE'S BEEN AN EXPLOSION IN BRAINIAC'S LAB, SO I, UH, FIGURED WE SHOULD CHECK IT OUT.
'BYE!
WELL, I GUESS THAT EXTENDS YOUR PROJECT A BIT MORE, EH?
NAH--I'VE ALREADY INCLUDED A WEEKLY "BRAINY BLOWS UP HIS LAB" CONTINGENCY.
Y'KNOW, WE PROBABLY SHOULD DROP BY THERE IN A FEW MINUTES, JUST TO KEEP BRAINY FROM TOTALLY CHEWING OUT THE KID.
DON'T WORRY, MR.B-- HELP IS ON THE WAY!
KEEP OUT
THE PLACE IS FULL OF SMOKE! WISH I HAD ULTRA BOY'S PENETRA-VISION!

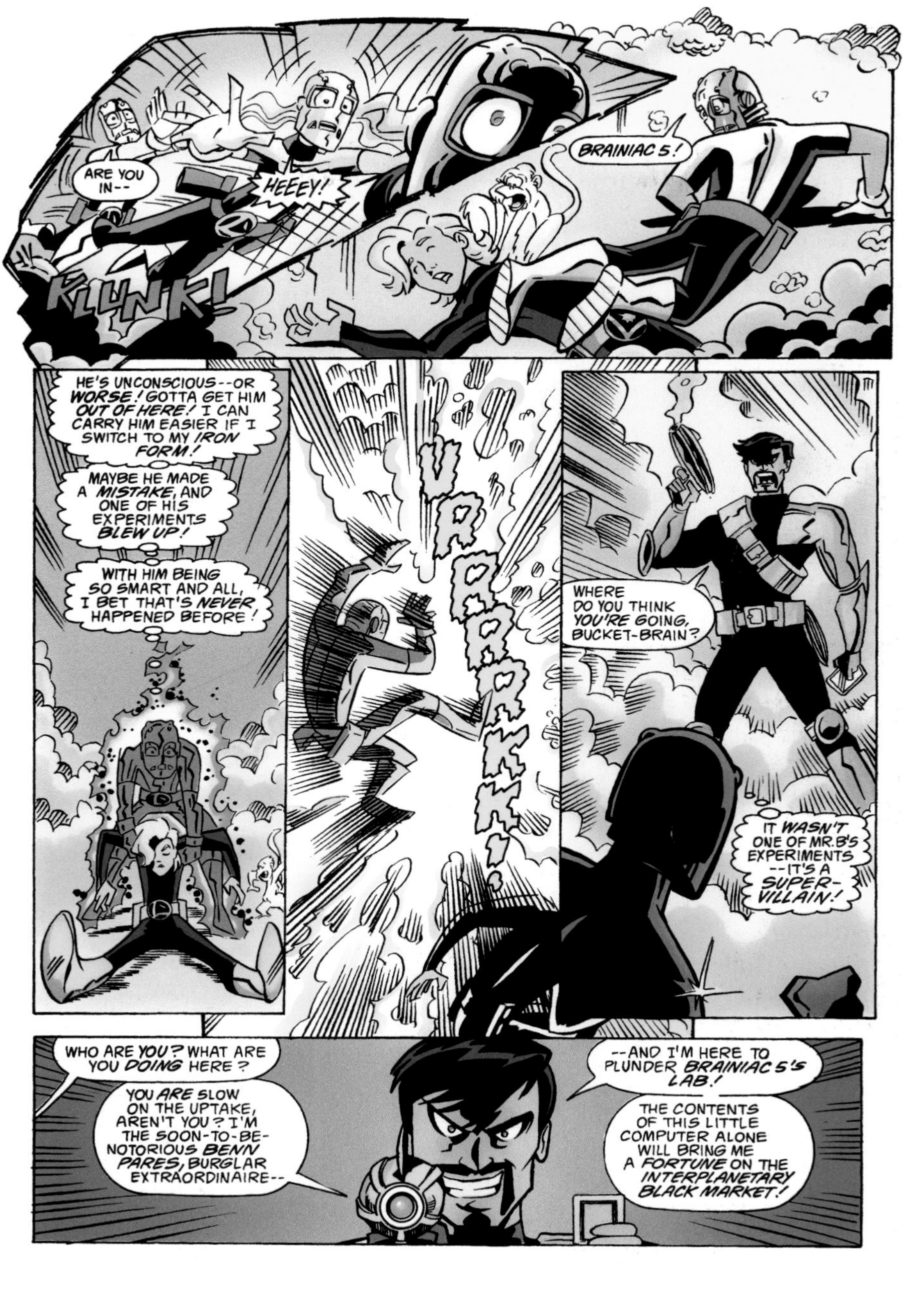
ARE YOU IN--
HEEEY!
KLUNK!
BRAINIAC 5!
HE'S UNCONSCIOUS--OR WORSE! GOTTA GET HIM OUT OF HERE! I CAN CARRY HIM EASIER IF I SWITCH TO MY IRON FORM!
MAYBE HE MADE A MISTAKE, AND ONE OF HIS EXPERIMENTS BLEW UP!
WITH HIM BEING SO SMART AND ALL, I BET THAT'S NEVER HAPPENED BEFORE!
VRARRKK!
WHERE DO YOU THINK YOU'RE GOING, BUCKET-BRAIN?
IT WASN'T ONE OF MR. B'S EXPERIMENTS --IT'S A SUPER-VILLAIN!
WHO ARE YOU? WHAT ARE YOU DOING HERE?
YOU ARE SLOW ON THE UPTAKE, AREN'T YOU? I'M THE SOON-TO-BE-NOTORIOUS BENN PARES, BURGLAR EXTRAORDINAIRE--
--AND I'M HERE TO PLUNDER BRAINIAC 5's LAB!
THE CONTENTS OF THIS LITTLE COMPUTER ALONE WILL BRING ME A FORTUNE ON THE INTERPLANETARY BLACK MARKET!

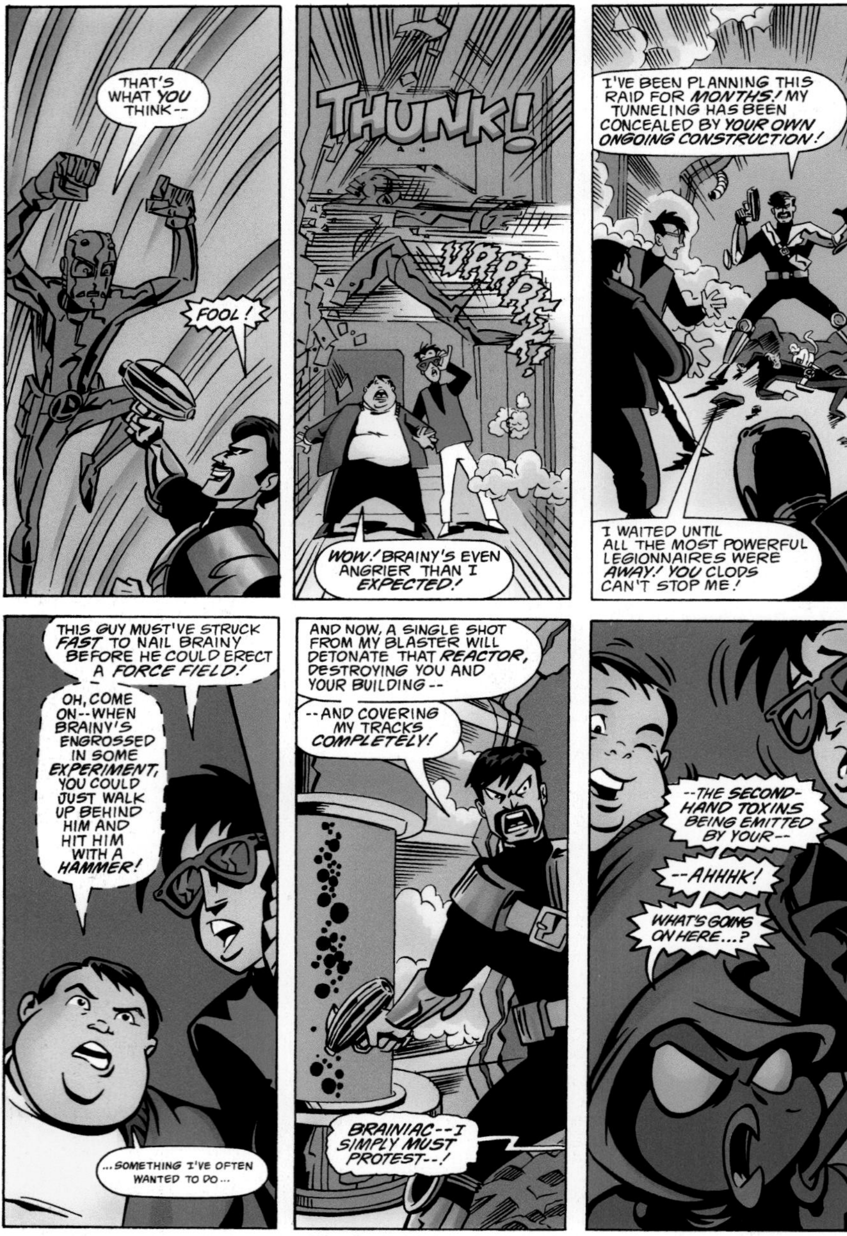

THAT'S WHAT YOU THINK--
FOOL!
THUNK!
URRK!
WOW! BRAINY'S EVEN ANGRIER THAN I EXPECTED!
I'VE BEEN PLANNING THIS RAID FOR MONTHS! MY TUNNELING HAS BEEN CONCEALED BY YOUR OWN ONGOING CONSTRUCTION!
I WAITED UNTIL ALL THE MOST POWERFUL LEGIONNAIRES WERE AWAY! YOU CLODS CAN'T STOP ME!
THIS GUY MUST'VE STRUCK FAST TO NAIL BRAINY BEFORE HE COULD ERECT A FORCE FIELD!
OH, COME ON--WHEN BRAINY'S ENGROSSED IN SOME EXPERIMENT, YOU COULD JUST WALK UP BEHIND HIM AND HIT HIM WITH A HAMMER!
...SOMETHING I'VE OFTEN WANTED TO DO...
AND NOW, A SINGLE SHOT FROM MY BLASTER WILL DETONATE THAT REACTOR, DESTROYING YOU AND YOUR BUILDING--
--AND COVERING MY TRACKS COMPLETELY!
BRAINIAC--I SIMPLY MUST PROTEST--!
--THE SECOND-HAND TOXINS BEING EMITTED BY YOUR--
--AHHHK!
WHAT'S GOING ON HERE...?

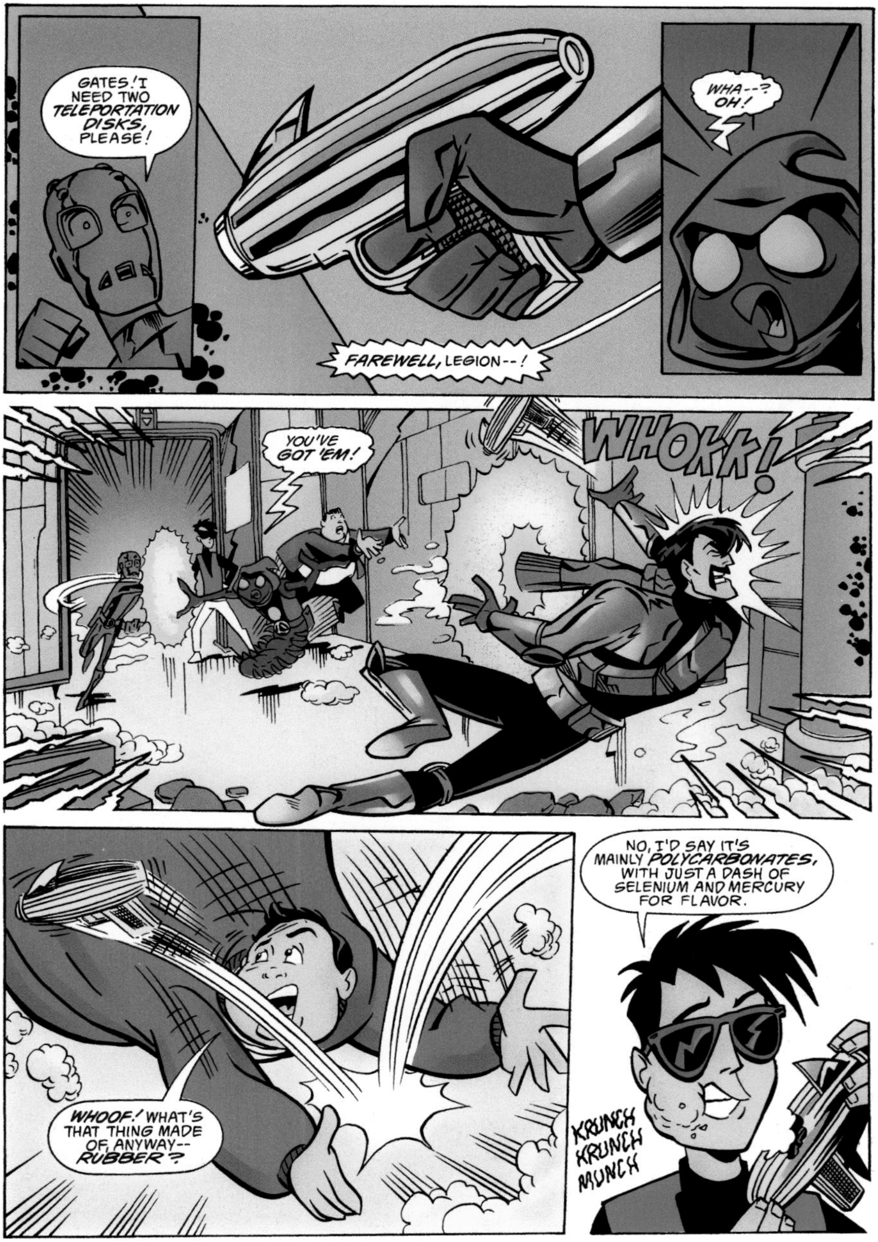
GATES! I NEED TWO TELEPORTATION DISKS, PLEASE!
WHA--? OH!
FAREWELL, LEGION--!
YOU'VE GOT 'EM!
WHOKK!
WHOOF! WHAT'S THAT THING MADE OF, ANYWAY-- RUBBER?
NO, I'D SAY IT'S MAINLY POLYCARBONATES, WITH JUST A DASH OF SELENIUM AND MERCURY FOR FLAVOR.
KRUNCH KRUNCH MUNCH

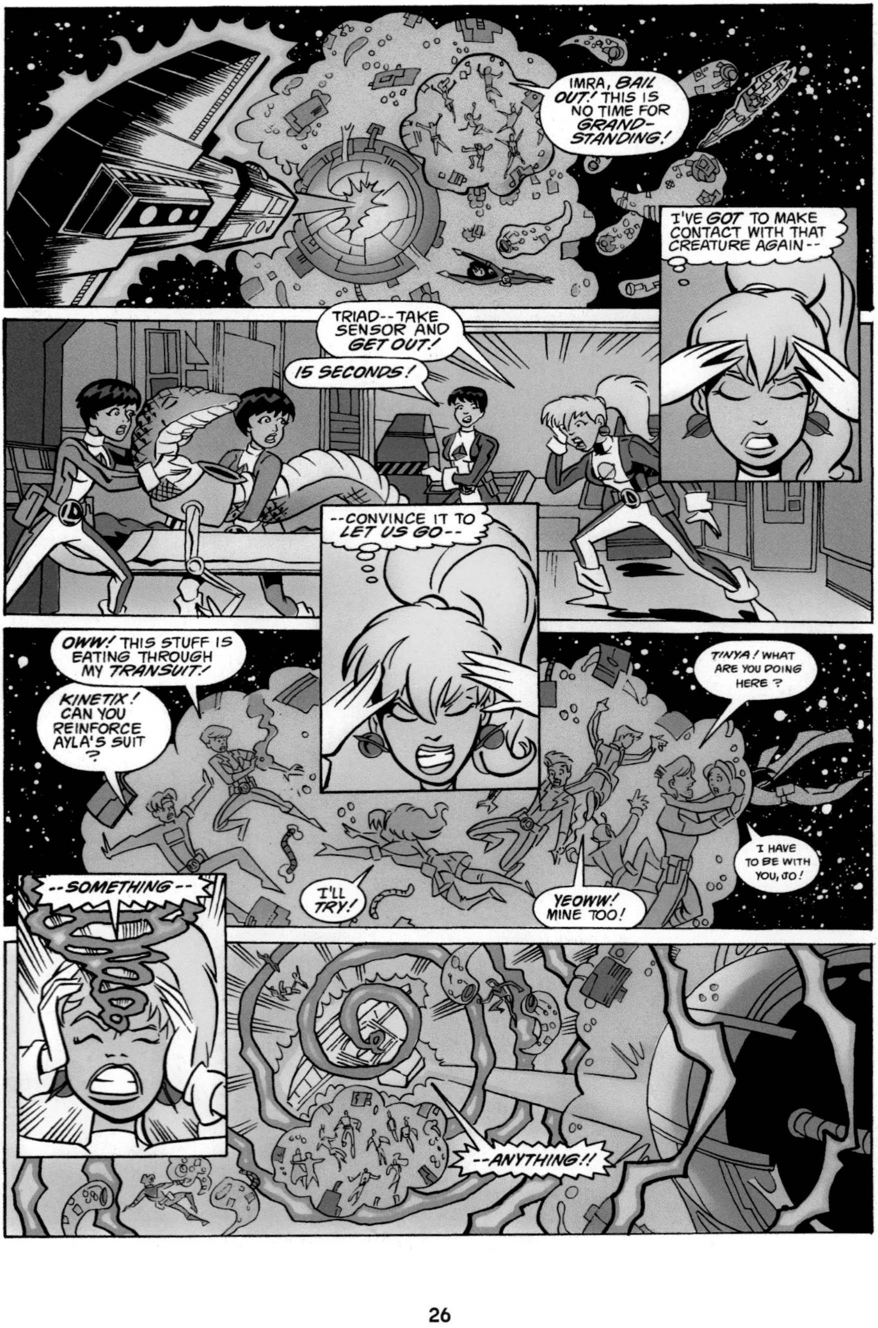
IMRA, BAIL OUT! THIS IS NO TIME FOR GRAND-STANDING!
I'VE GOT TO MAKE CONTACT WITH THAT CREATURE AGAIN--
TRIAD--TAKE SENSOR AND GET OUT!
15 SECONDS!
--CONVINCE IT TO LET US GO--
OWW! THIS STUFF IS EATING THROUGH MY TRANSUIT!
KINETIX! CAN YOU REINFORCE AYLA'S SUIT?
TINYA! WHAT ARE YOU DOING HERE?
I HAVE TO BE WITH YOU, JO!
I'LL TRY!
YEOWW! MINE TOO!
--SOMETHING--
--ANYTHING!!

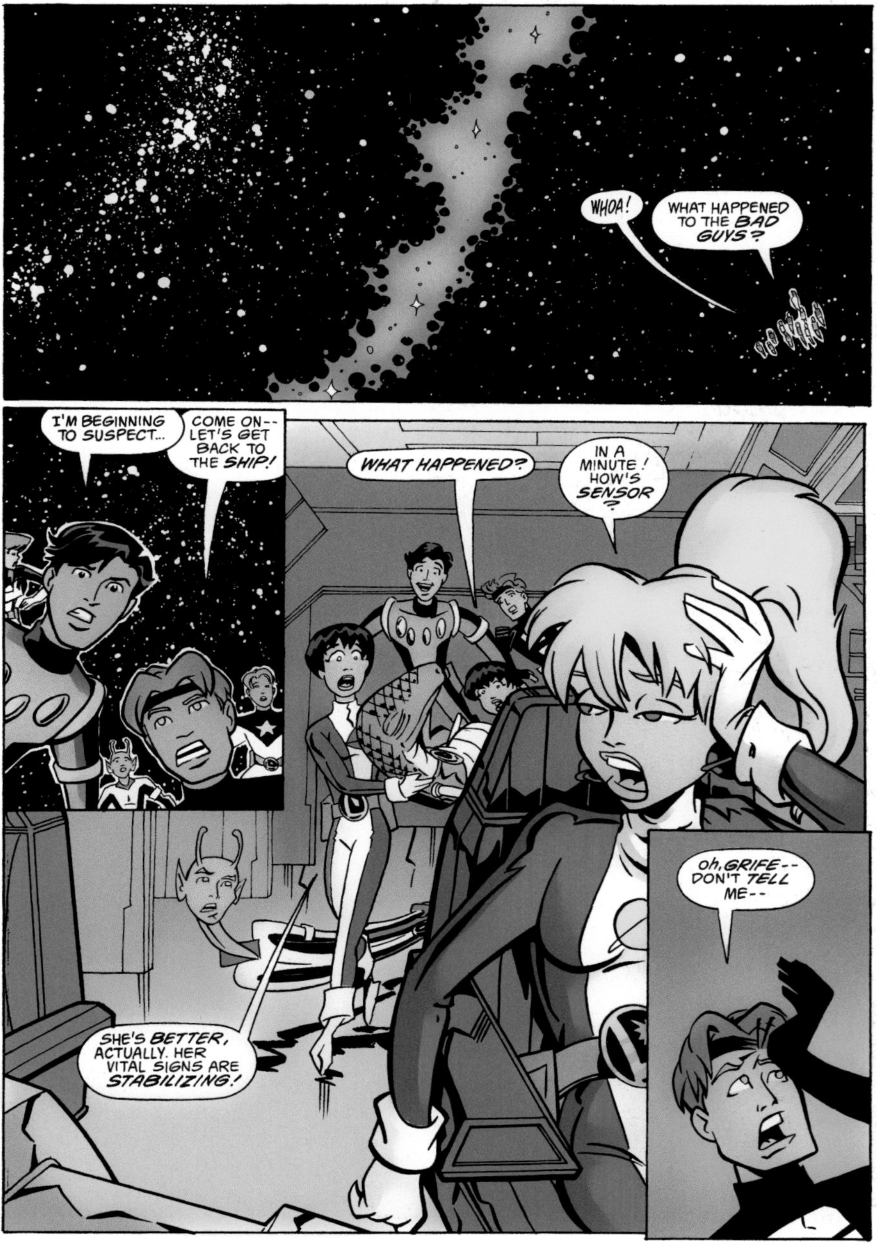
WHOA!
WHAT HAPPENED TO THE BAD GUYS?
I'M BEGINNING TO SUSPECT...
COME ON-- LET'S GET BACK TO THE SHIP!
WHAT HAPPENED?
IN A MINUTE! HOW'S SENSOR?
SHE'S BETTER, ACTUALLY. HER VITAL SIGNS ARE STABILIZING!
oh, GRIFE-- DON'T TELL ME--

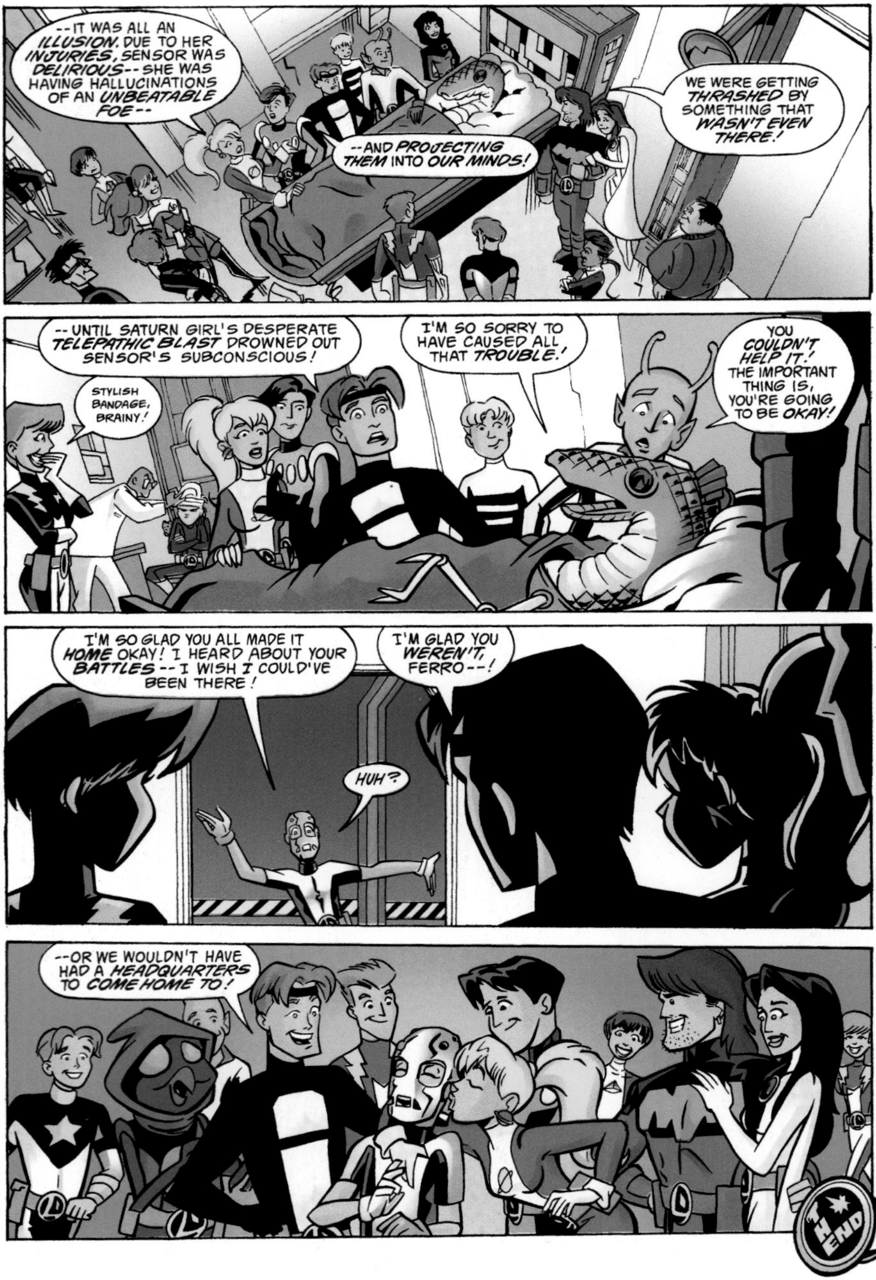
--IT WAS ALL AN ILLUSION. DUE TO HER INJURIES, SENSOR WAS DELIRIOUS--SHE WAS HAVING HALLUCINATIONS OF AN UNBEATABLE FOE--
--AND PROJECTING THEM INTO OUR MINDS!
WE WERE GETTING THRASHED BY SOMETHING THAT WASN'T EVEN THERE!
--UNTIL SATURN GIRL'S DESPERATE TELEPATHIC BLAST DROWNED OUT SENSOR'S SUBCONSCIOUS!
STYLISH BANDAGE, BRAINY!
I'M SO SORRY TO HAVE CAUSED ALL THAT TROUBLE!
YOU COULDN'T HELP IT! THE IMPORTANT THING IS, YOU'RE GOING TO BE OKAY!
I'M SO GLAD YOU ALL MADE IT HOME OKAY! I HEARD ABOUT YOUR BATTLES--I WISH I COULD'VE BEEN THERE!
I'M GLAD YOU WEREN'T, FERRO--!
HUH?
--OR WE WOULDN'T HAVE HAD A HEADQUARTERS TO COME HOME TO!
THE END

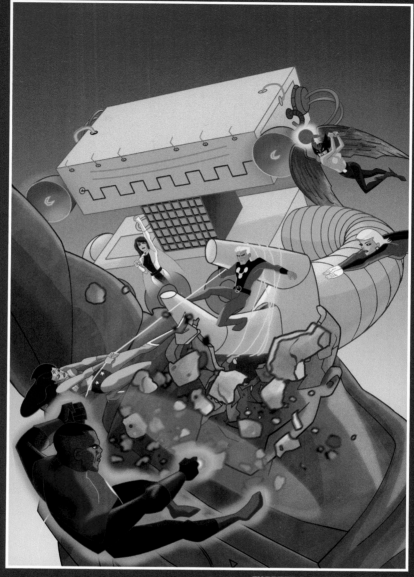

CHAPTER 2: FUTURE IMPERFECT

JUSTICE LEAGUE UNLIMITED

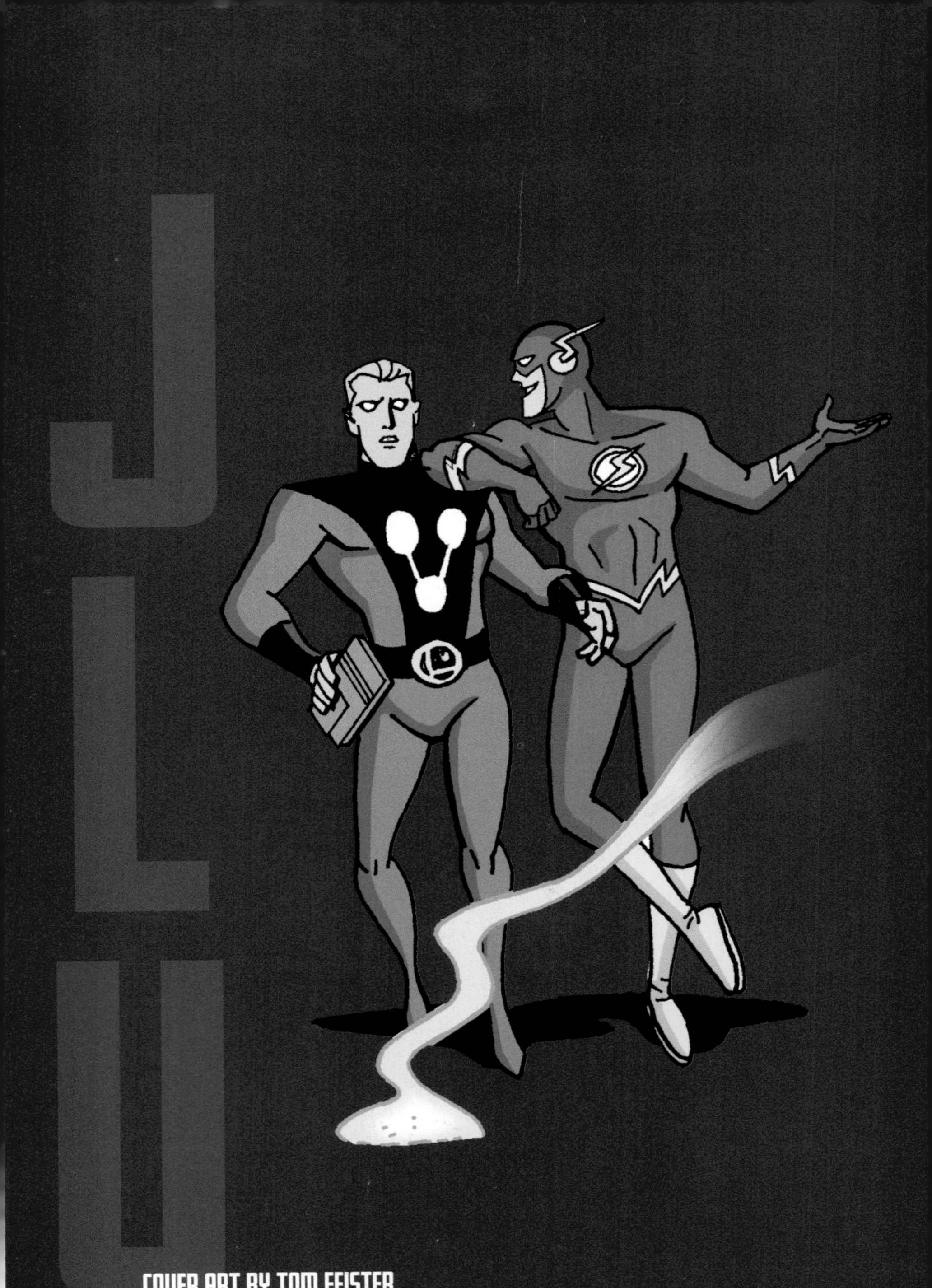
JLU

COVER ART BY TOM FEISTER

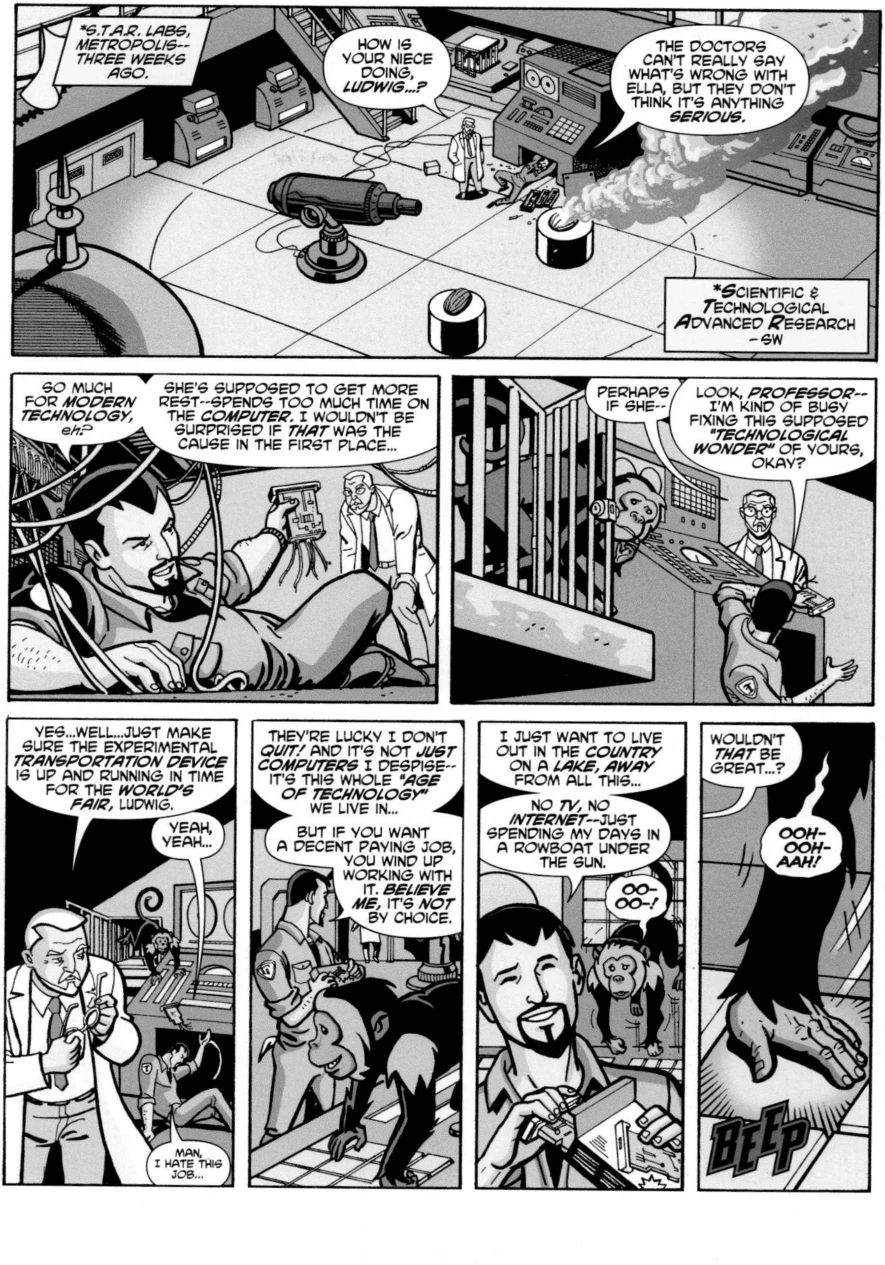
*S.T.A.R. LABS, METROPOLIS-- THREE WEEKS AGO.
HOW IS YOUR NIECE DOING, LUDWIG...?
THE DOCTORS CAN'T REALLY SAY WHAT'S WRONG WITH ELLA, BUT THEY DON'T THINK IT'S ANYTHING SERIOUS.
*SCIENTIFIC & TECHNOLOGICAL ADVANCED RESEARCH -SW
SO MUCH FOR MODERN TECHNOLOGY, eh?
SHE'S SUPPOSED TO GET MORE REST--SPENDS TOO MUCH TIME ON THE COMPUTER. I WOULDN'T BE SURPRISED IF THAT WAS THE CAUSE IN THE FIRST PLACE...
PERHAPS IF SHE--
LOOK, PROFESSOR-- I'M KIND OF BUSY FIXING THIS SUPPOSED "TECHNOLOGICAL WONDER" OF YOURS, OKAY?
YES...WELL...JUST MAKE SURE THE EXPERIMENTAL TRANSPORTATION DEVICE IS UP AND RUNNING IN TIME FOR THE WORLD'S FAIR, LUDWIG.
YEAH, YEAH...
MAN, I HATE THIS JOB...
THEY'RE LUCKY I DON'T QUIT! AND IT'S NOT JUST COMPUTERS I DESPISE-- IT'S THIS WHOLE "AGE OF TECHNOLOGY" WE LIVE IN...
BUT IF YOU WANT A DECENT PAYING JOB, YOU WIND UP WORKING WITH IT. BELIEVE ME, IT'S NOT BY CHOICE.
I JUST WANT TO LIVE OUT IN THE COUNTRY ON A LAKE, AWAY FROM ALL THIS...
NO TV, NO INTERNET--JUST SPENDING MY DAYS IN A ROWBOAT UNDER THE SUN.
OO-OO-!
WOULDN'T THAT BE GREAT...?
OOH-OOH-AAH!
BEEP

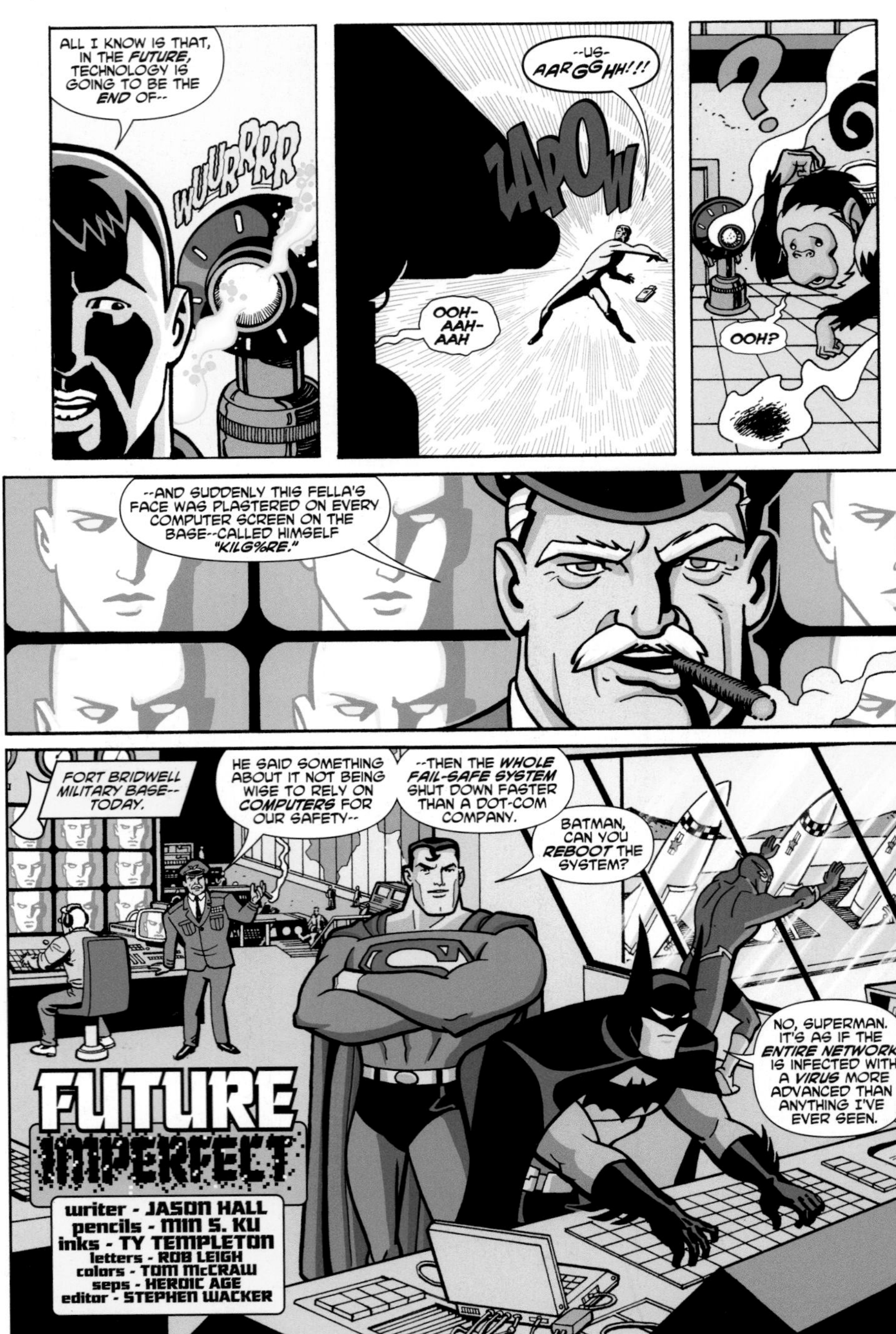
ALL I KNOW IS THAT, IN THE FUTURE, TECHNOLOGY IS GOING TO BE THE END OF--
WUURRRR
--US-- AARGGHH!!!
ZAPOW
OOH-AAH-AAH
OOH?
--AND SUDDENLY THIS FELLA'S FACE WAS PLASTERED ON EVERY COMPUTER SCREEN ON THE BASE--CALLED HIMSELF "KILG%RE."
FORT BRIDWELL MILITARY BASE-- TODAY.
HE SAID SOMETHING ABOUT IT NOT BEING WISE TO RELY ON COMPUTERS FOR OUR SAFETY--
--THEN THE WHOLE FAIL-SAFE SYSTEM SHUT DOWN FASTER THAN A DOT-COM COMPANY.
BATMAN, CAN YOU REBOOT THE SYSTEM?
NO, SUPERMAN. IT'S AS IF THE ENTIRE NETWORK IS INFECTED WITH A VIRUS MORE ADVANCED THAN ANYTHING I'VE EVER SEEN.
FUTURE IMPERFECT
writer - JASON HALL
pencils - MIN S. KU
inks - TY TEMPLETON
letters - ROB LEIGH
colors - TOM McCRAW
seps - HEROIC AGE
editor - STEPHEN WACKER

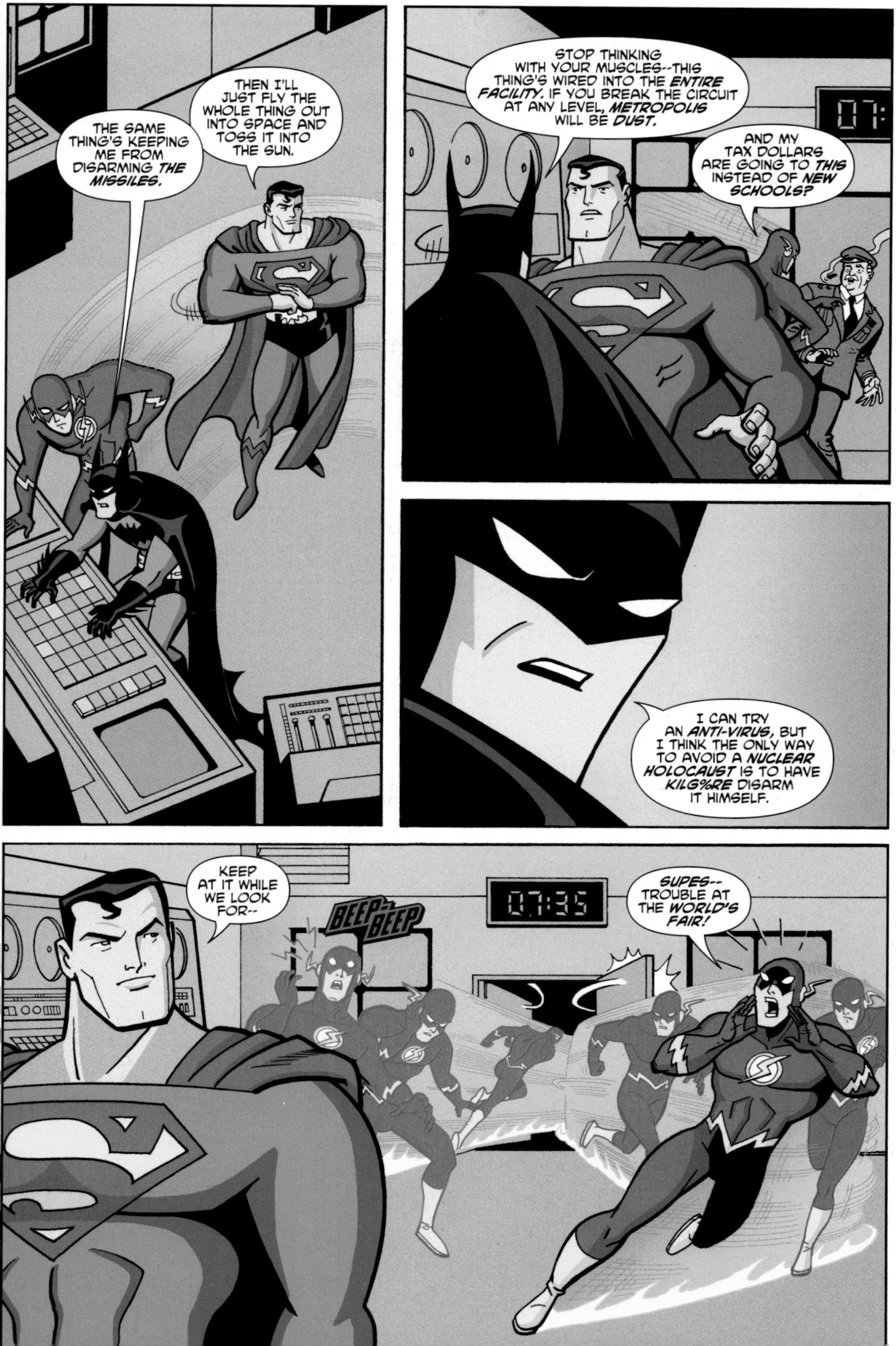
THEN I'LL JUST FLY THE WHOLE THING OUT INTO SPACE AND TOSS IT INTO THE SUN.
THE SAME THING'S KEEPING ME FROM DISARMING THE MISSILES.
STOP THINKING WITH YOUR MUSCLES--THIS THING'S WIRED INTO THE ENTIRE FACILITY. IF YOU BREAK THE CIRCUIT AT ANY LEVEL, METROPOLIS WILL BE DUST.
AND MY TAX DOLLARS ARE GOING TO THIS INSTEAD OF NEW SCHOOLS?
I CAN TRY AN ANTI-VIRUS, BUT I THINK THE ONLY WAY TO AVOID A NUCLEAR HOLOCAUST IS TO HAVE KILG%RE DISARM IT HIMSELF.
KEEP AT IT WHILE WE LOOK FOR--
BEEP-BEEP
07:35
SUPES--TROUBLE AT THE WORLD'S FAIR!

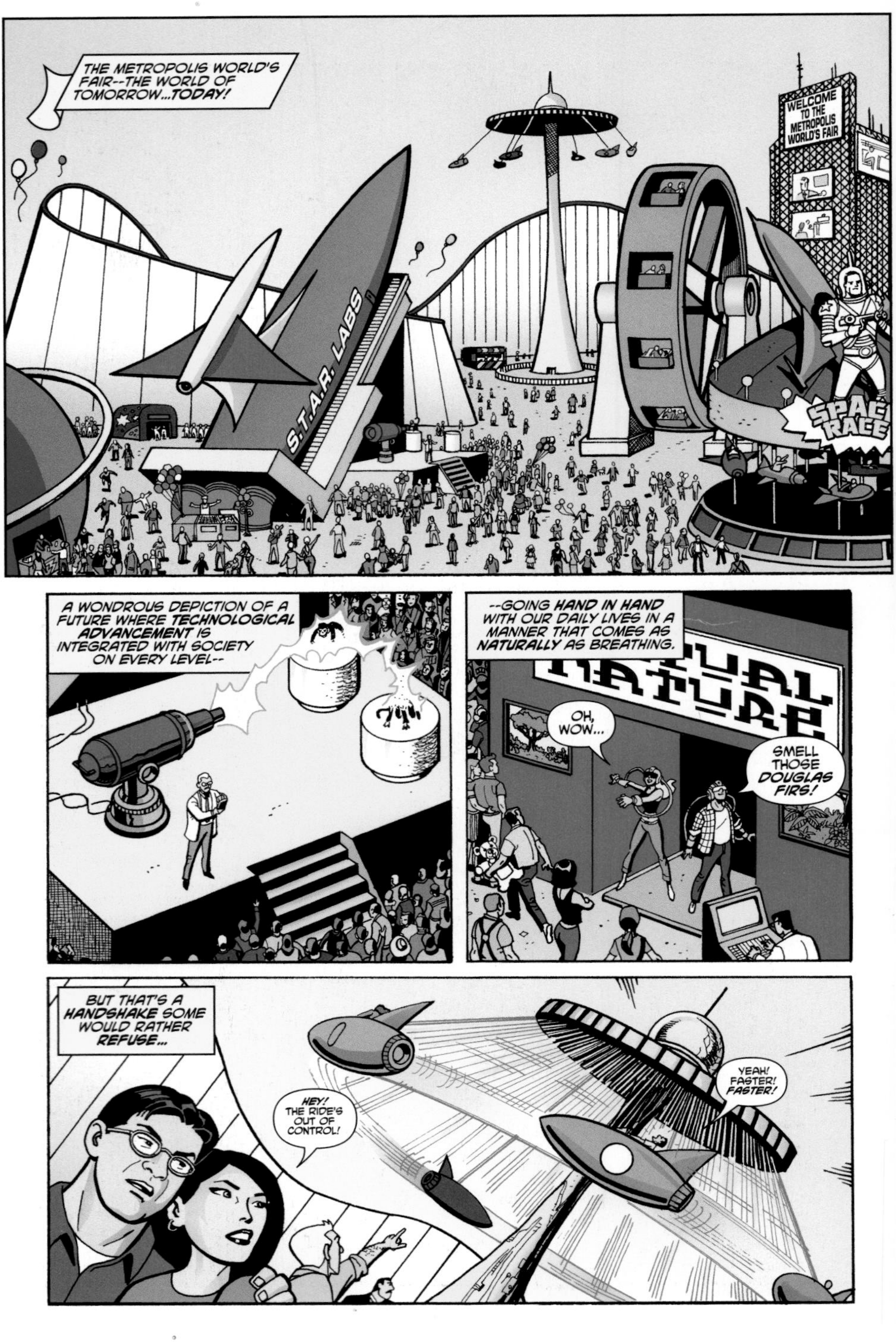
THE METROPOLIS WORLD'S FAIR--THE WORLD OF TOMORROW...TODAY!
WELCOME TO THE METROPOLIS WORLD'S FAIR
S.T.A.R. LABS
A WONDROUS DEPICTION OF A FUTURE WHERE TECHNOLOGICAL ADVANCEMENT IS INTEGRATED WITH SOCIETY ON EVERY LEVEL--
--GOING HAND IN HAND WITH OUR DAILY LIVES IN A MANNER THAT COMES AS NATURALLY AS BREATHING.
OH, WOW...
SMELL THOSE DOUGLAS FIRS!
BUT THAT'S A HANDSHAKE SOME WOULD RATHER REFUSE...
HEY! THE RIDE'S OUT OF CONTROL!
YEAH! FASTER! FASTER!

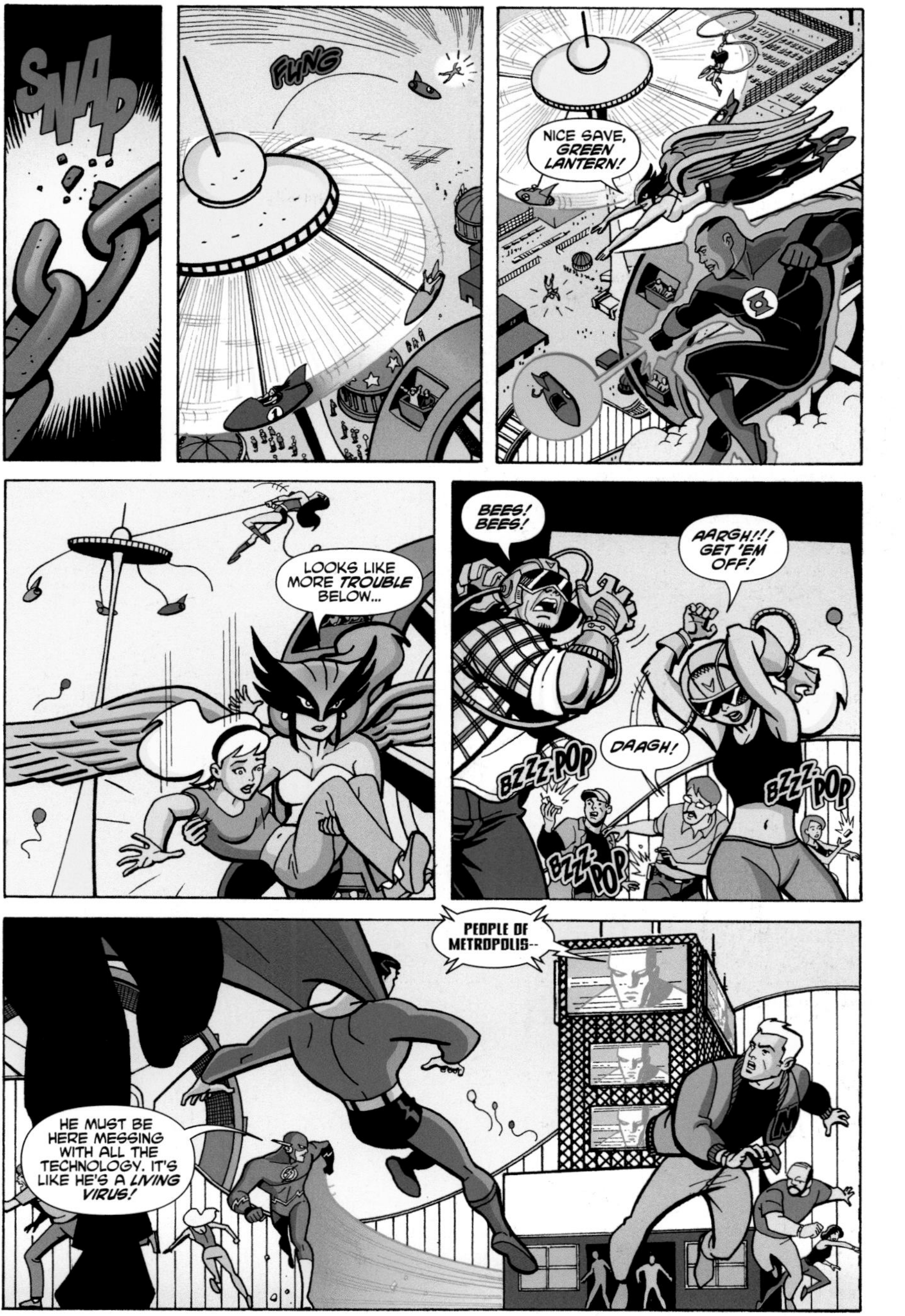
SNAP
FLING
NICE SAVE, GREEN LANTERN!
LOOKS LIKE MORE TROUBLE BELOW...
BEES! BEES!
AARGH!!! GET 'EM OFF!
BZZZ-POP
DAAGH!
BZZZ-POP
BZZZ-POP
PEOPLE OF METROPOLIS--
HE MUST BE HERE MESSING WITH ALL THE TECHNOLOGY. IT'S LIKE HE'S A LIVING VIRUS!

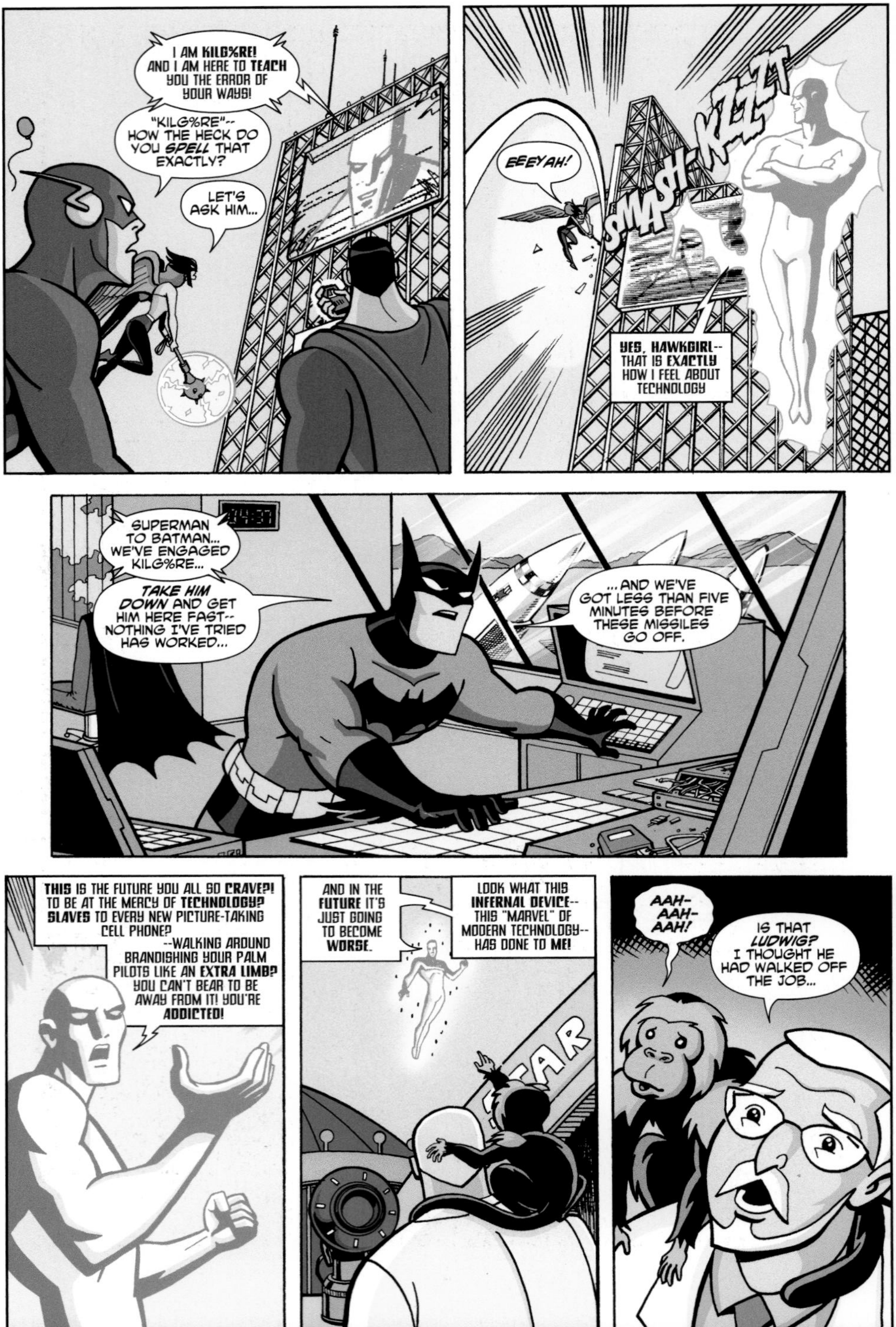
I AM KILG%RE! AND I AM HERE TO TEACH YOU THE ERROR OF YOUR WAYS!
"KILG%RE"-- HOW THE HECK DO YOU SPELL THAT EXACTLY?
LET'S ASK HIM...
EEEYAH!
SMASH-KZZZT
YES, HAWKGIRL-- THAT IS EXACTLY HOW I FEEL ABOUT TECHNOLOGY
SUPERMAN TO BATMAN... WE'VE ENGAGED KILG%RE...
TAKE HIM DOWN AND GET HIM HERE FAST-- NOTHING I'VE TRIED HAS WORKED...
...AND WE'VE GOT LESS THAN FIVE MINUTES BEFORE THESE MISSILES GO OFF.
THIS IS THE FUTURE YOU ALL SO CRAVE?! TO BE AT THE MERCY OF TECHNOLOGY? SLAVES TO EVERY NEW PICTURE-TAKING CELL PHONE?
--WALKING AROUND BRANDISHING YOUR PALM PILOTS LIKE AN EXTRA LIMB? YOU CAN'T BEAR TO BE AWAY FROM IT! YOU'RE ADDICTED!
AND IN THE FUTURE IT'S JUST GOING TO BECOME WORSE.
LOOK WHAT THIS INFERNAL DEVICE-- THIS "MARVEL" OF MODERN TECHNOLOGY-- HAS DONE TO ME!
AAH-AAH-AAH!
IS THAT LUDWIG? I THOUGHT HE HAD WALKED OFF THE JOB...

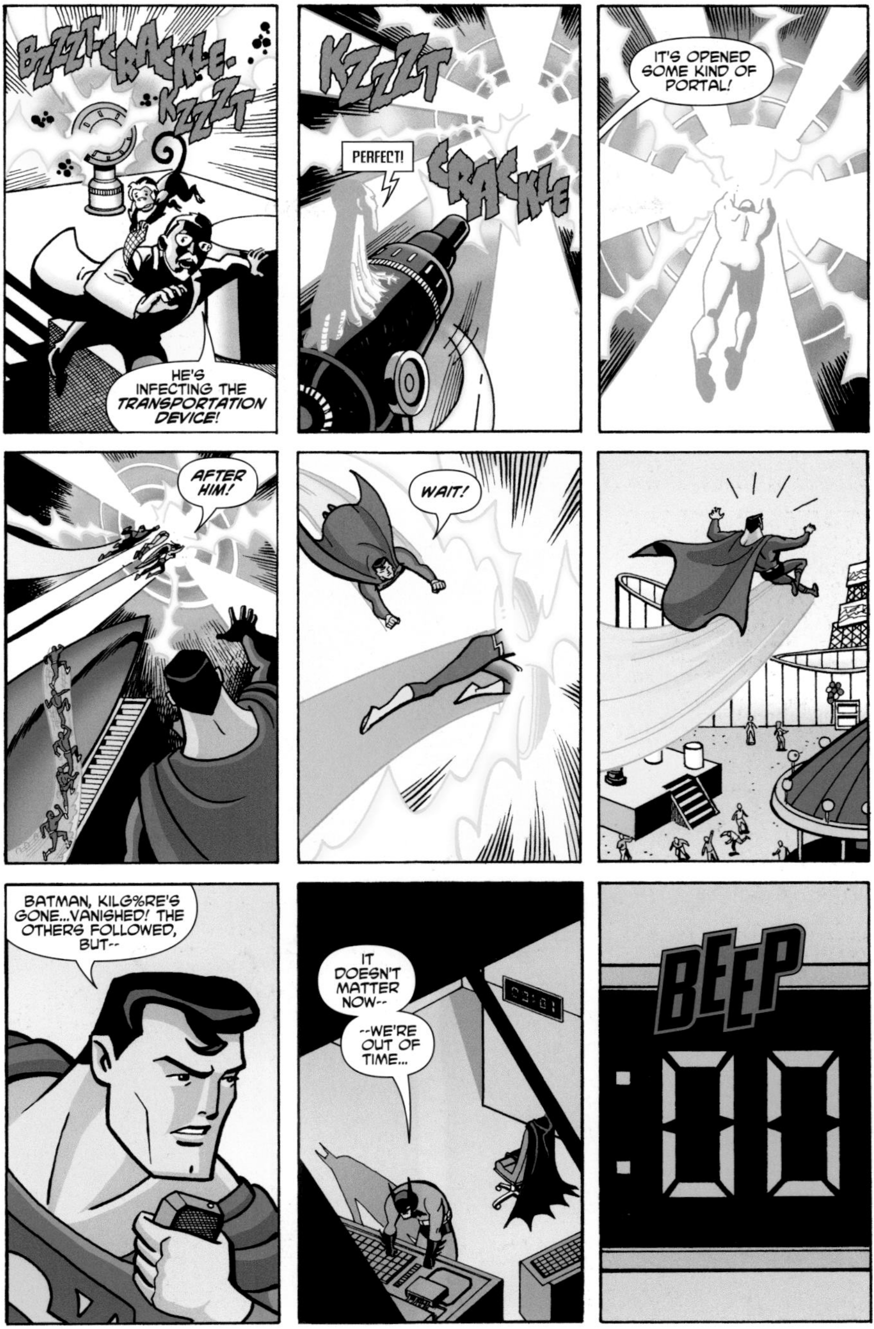
BZZZT-CRACKLE-KZZZZT
HE'S INFECTING THE *TRANSPORTATION DEVICE!*
KZZZZT
PERFECT!
CRACKLE
IT'S OPENED SOME KIND OF PORTAL!
AFTER HIM!
WAIT!
BATMAN, KILG%RE'S GONE...VANISHED! THE OTHERS FOLLOWED, BUT--
IT DOESN'T MATTER NOW--
--WE'RE OUT OF TIME...
BEEP
:00

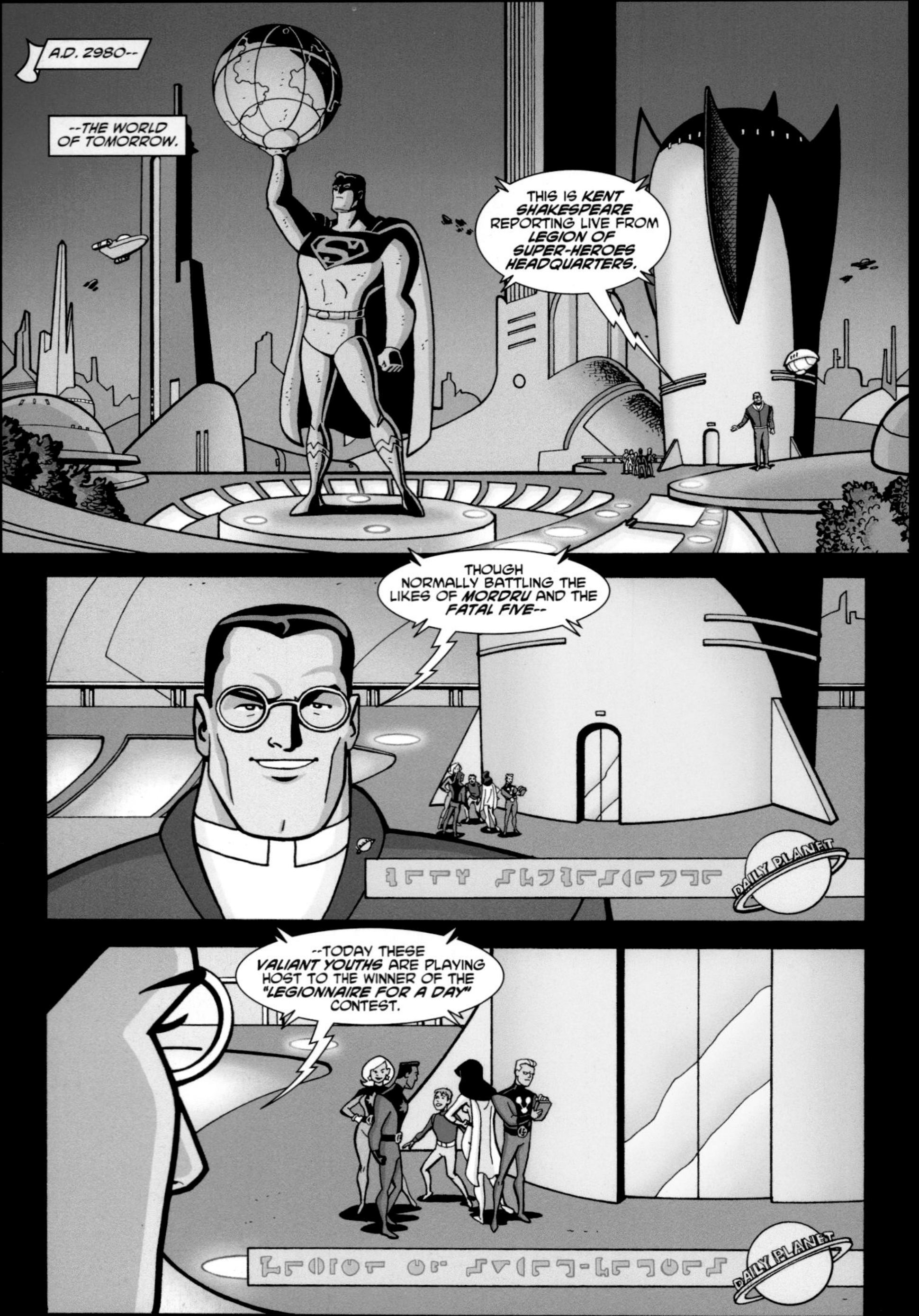
A.D. 2980--
--THE WORLD OF TOMORROW.
THIS IS KENT SHAKESPEARE REPORTING LIVE FROM LEGION OF SUPER-HEROES HEADQUARTERS.
THOUGH NORMALLY BATTLING THE LIKES OF MORDRU AND THE FATAL FIVE--
DAILY PLANET
--TODAY THESE VALIANT YOUTHS ARE PLAYING HOST TO THE WINNER OF THE "LEGIONNAIRE FOR A DAY" CONTEST.
DAILY PLANET

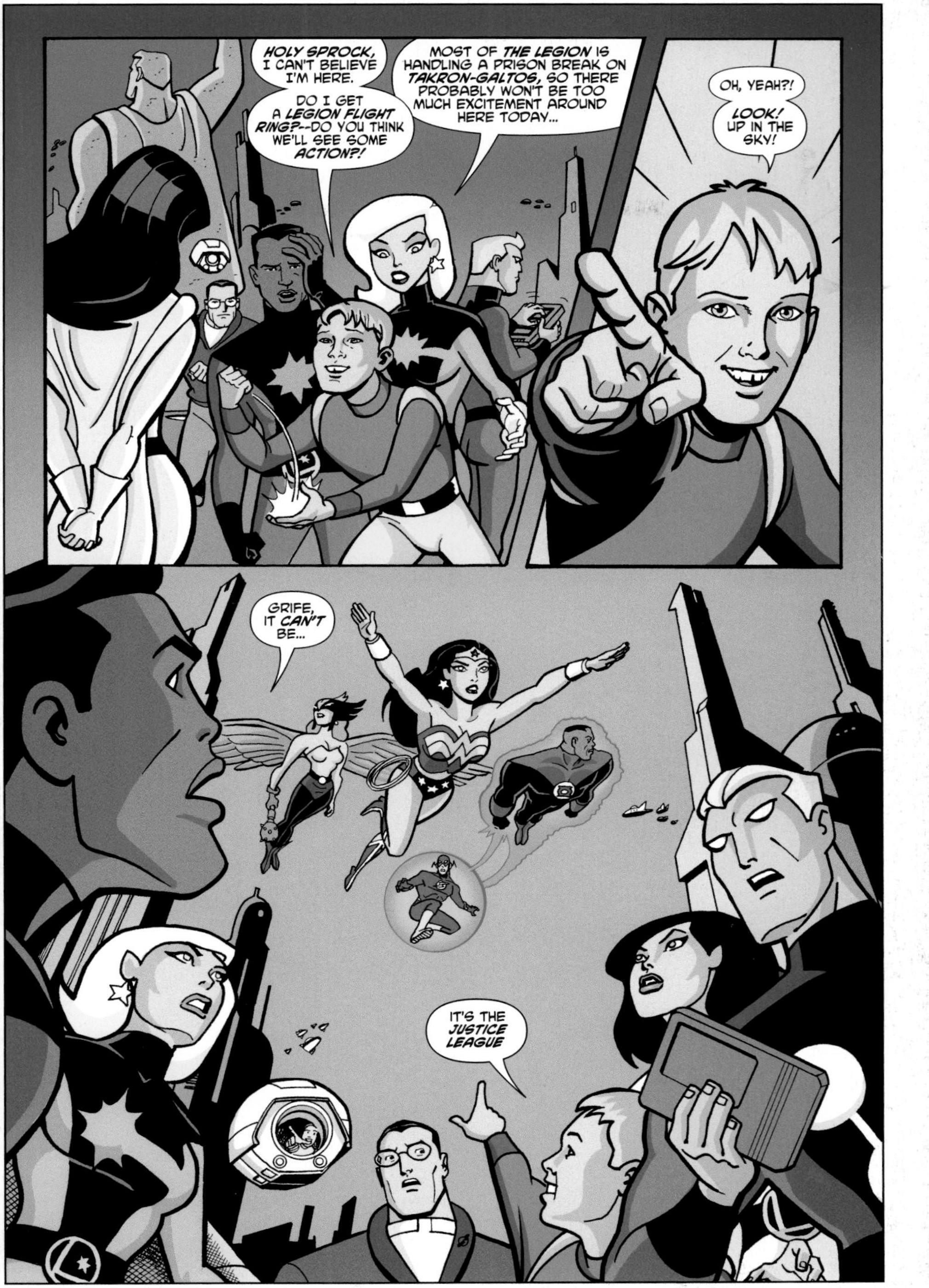
HOLY SPROCK, I CAN'T BELIEVE I'M HERE.
DO I GET A LEGION FLIGHT RING?--DO YOU THINK WE'LL SEE SOME ACTION?!
MOST OF THE LEGION IS HANDLING A PRISON BREAK ON TAKRON-GALTOS, SO THERE PROBABLY WON'T BE TOO MUCH EXCITEMENT AROUND HERE TODAY...
OH, YEAH?!
LOOK! UP IN THE SKY!
GRIFE, IT CAN'T BE...
IT'S THE JUSTICE LEAGUE

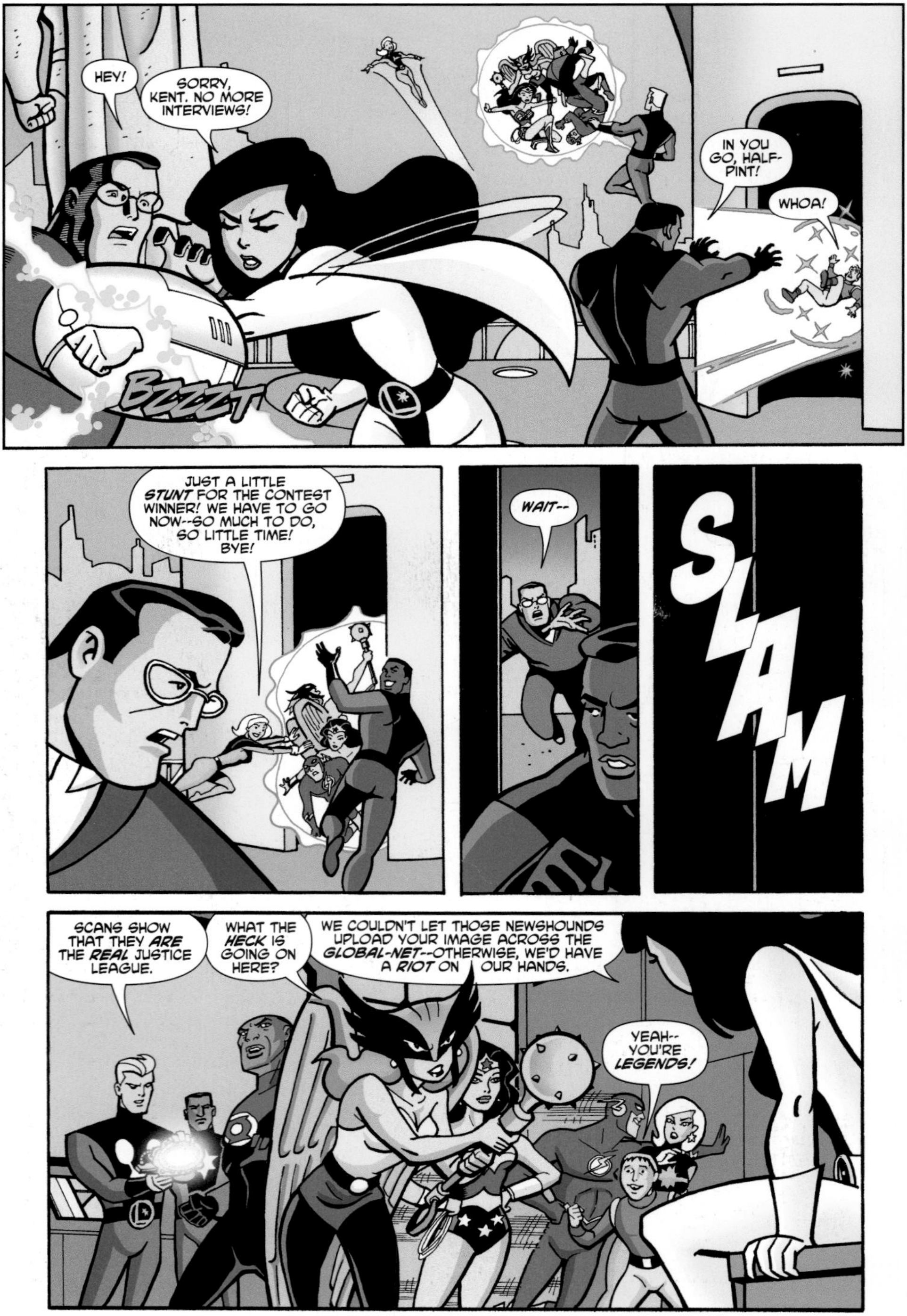
HEY!
SORRY, KENT. NO MORE INTERVIEWS!
IN YOU GO, HALF-PINT!
WHOA!
BZZZZT
JUST A LITTLE STUNT FOR THE CONTEST WINNER! WE HAVE TO GO NOW--SO MUCH TO DO, SO LITTLE TIME! BYE!
WAIT--
SLAM
SCANS SHOW THAT THEY ARE THE REAL JUSTICE LEAGUE.
WHAT THE HECK IS GOING ON HERE?
WE COULDN'T LET THOSE NEWSHOUNDS UPLOAD YOUR IMAGE ACROSS THE GLOBAL-NET--OTHERWISE, WE'D HAVE A RIOT ON OUR HANDS.
YEAH--YOU'RE LEGENDS!

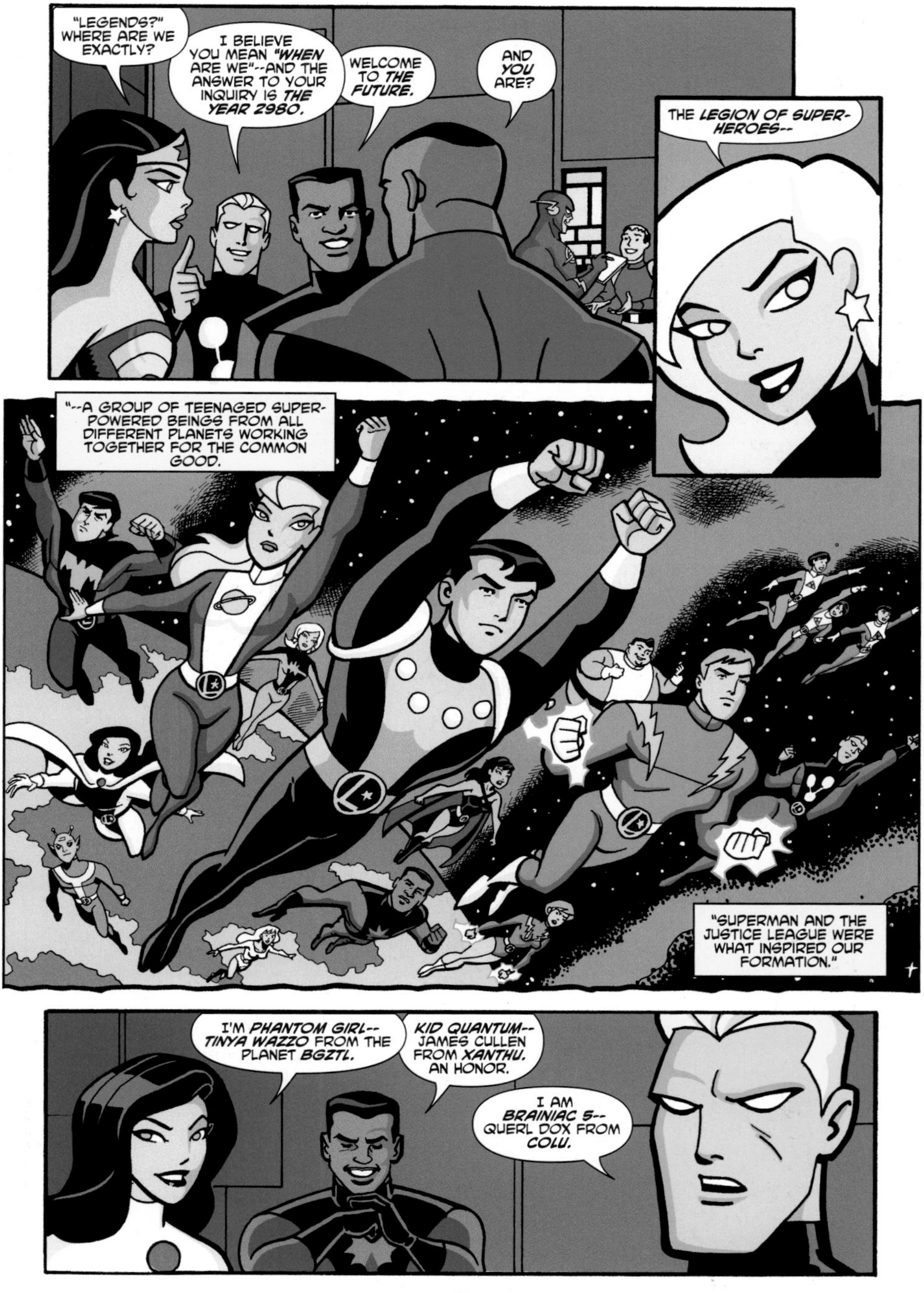
"LEGENDS?" WHERE ARE WE EXACTLY?
I BELIEVE YOU MEAN "WHEN ARE WE"--AND THE ANSWER TO YOUR INQUIRY IS THE YEAR 2980.
WELCOME TO THE FUTURE.
AND YOU ARE?
THE LEGION OF SUPER-HEROES--
"--A GROUP OF TEENAGED SUPER-POWERED BEINGS FROM ALL DIFFERENT PLANETS WORKING TOGETHER FOR THE COMMON GOOD.
"SUPERMAN AND THE JUSTICE LEAGUE WERE WHAT INSPIRED OUR FORMATION."
I'M PHANTOM GIRL--TINYA WAZZO FROM THE PLANET BGZTL.
KID QUANTUM--JAMES CULLEN FROM XANTHU. AN HONOR.
I AM BRAINIAC 5--QUERL DOX FROM COLU.

BRAINIAC?! HE'S ONE OF OUR WORST ENEMIES!

YES-- AND ALSO MY "ANCESTOR" OF SORTS.

AND I'M ANDROMEDA-- LAUREL GAND FROM DAXAM.

DAXAM? WE MET FREEDOM FIGHTERS FROM YOUR PLANET BACK IN THE PAST.

I KNOW--IT'S WELL DOCUMENTED IN MY PLANET'S HISTORY TAPES. THAT MEETING HAD GREAT BEARING ON DAXAM'S FUTURE.

AND WE'RE IN METROPOLIS? SO IT SURVIVED THE EXPLOSION?

WHAT DO I LOOK LIKE, THE ENCYCLOPEDIA GALACTICA?

I'M SORRY, BUT WE CANNOT DIVULGE ANY INFORMATION ABOUT YOUR FUTURE TO YOU. YOUR MERE PRESENCE IS POTENTIALLY DAMAGING TO THE TIMESTREAM.

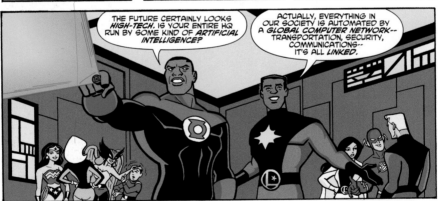

THE FUTURE CERTAINLY LOOKS HIGH-TECH. IS YOUR ENTIRE HQ RUN BY SOME KIND OF ARTIFICIAL INTELLIGENCE?

ACTUALLY, EVERYTHING IN OUR SOCIETY IS AUTOMATED BY A GLOBAL COMPUTER NETWORK-- TRANSPORTATION, SECURITY, COMMUNICATIONS-- IT'S ALL LINKED.

EVERYTHING? PERHAPS KILG%RE WAS RIGHT...

WHO'S "KILG%RE"?

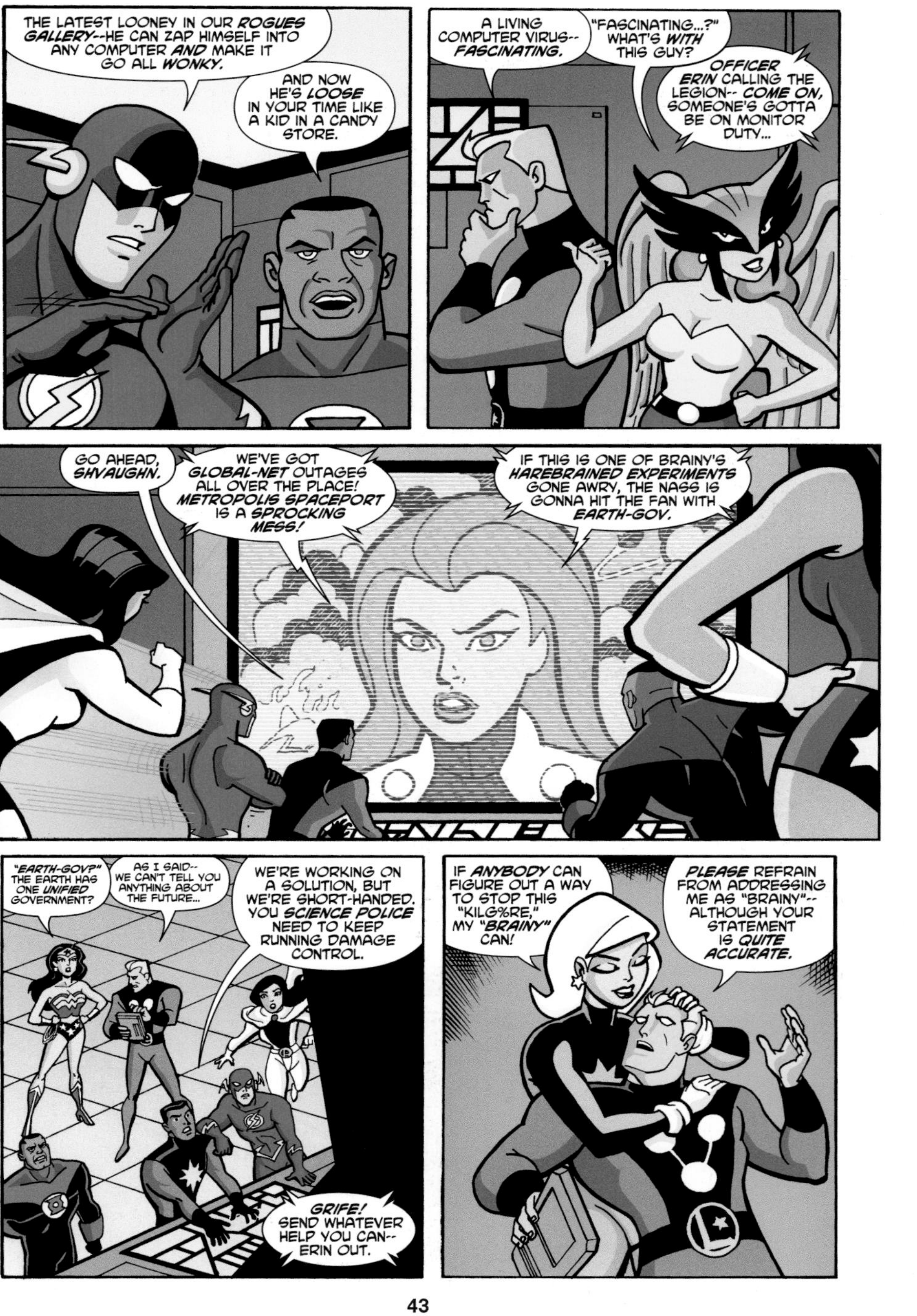
THE LATEST LOONEY IN OUR ROGUES GALLERY--HE CAN ZAP HIMSELF INTO ANY COMPUTER AND MAKE IT GO ALL WONKY.
AND NOW HE'S LOOSE IN YOUR TIME LIKE A KID IN A CANDY STORE.
A LIVING COMPUTER VIRUS-- FASCINATING.
"FASCINATING...?" WHAT'S WITH THIS GUY?
OFFICER ERIN CALLING THE LEGION-- COME ON, SOMEONE'S GOTTA BE ON MONITOR DUTY...
GO AHEAD, SHVAUGHN.
WE'VE GOT GLOBAL-NET OUTAGES ALL OVER THE PLACE! METROPOLIS SPACEPORT IS A SPROCKING MESS!
IF THIS IS ONE OF BRAINY'S HAREBRAINED EXPERIMENTS GONE AWRY, THE NASS IS GONNA HIT THE FAN WITH EARTH-GOV.
"EARTH-GOV?" THE EARTH HAS ONE UNIFIED GOVERNMENT?
AS I SAID-- WE CAN'T TELL YOU ANYTHING ABOUT THE FUTURE...
WE'RE WORKING ON A SOLUTION, BUT WE'RE SHORT-HANDED. YOU SCIENCE POLICE NEED TO KEEP RUNNING DAMAGE CONTROL.
GRIFE! SEND WHATEVER HELP YOU CAN-- ERIN OUT.
IF ANYBODY CAN FIGURE OUT A WAY TO STOP THIS "KILG%RE," MY "BRAINY" CAN!
PLEASE REFRAIN FROM ADDRESSING ME AS "BRAINY"-- ALTHOUGH YOUR STATEMENT IS QUITE ACCURATE.

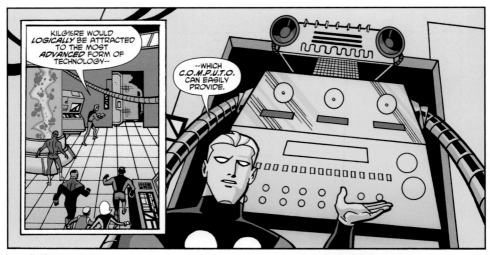

KILG%RE WOULD *LOGICALLY* BE ATTRACTED TO THE MOST *ADVANCED* FORM OF TECHNOLOGY--

--WHICH *C.O.M.P.U.T.O.* CAN EASILY PROVIDE.

BRAINY! HOW CAN YOU PUT THAT...*THING* BACK ON-LINE? IT ALMOST *KILLED* ONE OF OUR TEAMMATES!

TECHNICALLY, ONLY *ONE-THIRD* OF A TEAMMATE, SINCE *TRIPLICATE GIRL* IS A *CARGGITE* AND CAN SPLIT INTO THREE.

BUT I HAVE SINCE REVISED ITS PROGRAMMING, SO THERE *SHOULD* BE NO SIMILAR INCIDENTS.

Ooh, BRAINY-- SOMETIMES I WANT TO DROP-KICK YOU TO *TITAN!*

SORRY TO INTERRUPT YOUR *LOVERS' SPAT--*

--BUT SINCE WE CAN'T HAVE THE *JUSTICE LEAGUE* RUNNING AROUND IN THE *30TH CENTURY--*

--I THOUGHT A COUPLE OF NEW *"LEGION RESERVES"* WOULD BE JUST THE THING TO GIVE THE SCIENCE POLICE A HAND!

HEY, CHECK OUT THE JUSTICE LEAGUE BABES!

NICE DUDS, GALS!

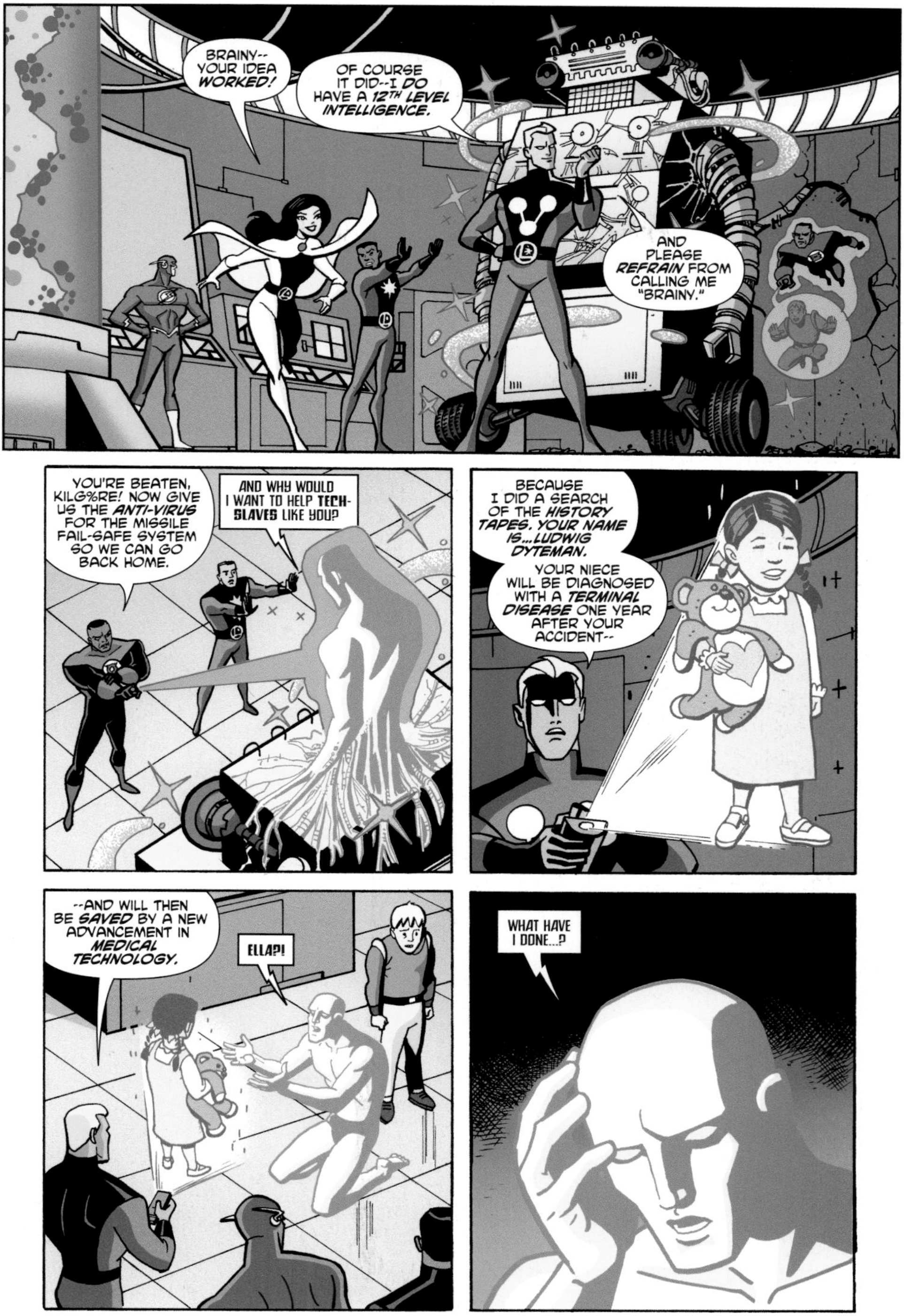

BRAINY-- YOUR IDEA WORKED!
OF COURSE IT DID--I DO HAVE A 12TH LEVEL INTELLIGENCE.
AND PLEASE REFRAIN FROM CALLING ME "BRAINY."
YOU'RE BEATEN, KILG%RE! NOW GIVE US THE ANTI-VIRUS FOR THE MISSILE FAIL-SAFE SYSTEM SO WE CAN GO BACK HOME.
AND WHY WOULD I WANT TO HELP TECH-SLAVES LIKE YOU?
BECAUSE I DID A SEARCH OF THE HISTORY TAPES. YOUR NAME IS...LUDWIG DYTEMAN.
YOUR NIECE WILL BE DIAGNOSED WITH A TERMINAL DISEASE ONE YEAR AFTER YOUR ACCIDENT--
--AND WILL THEN BE SAVED BY A NEW ADVANCEMENT IN MEDICAL TECHNOLOGY.
ELLA?!
WHAT HAVE I DONE...?

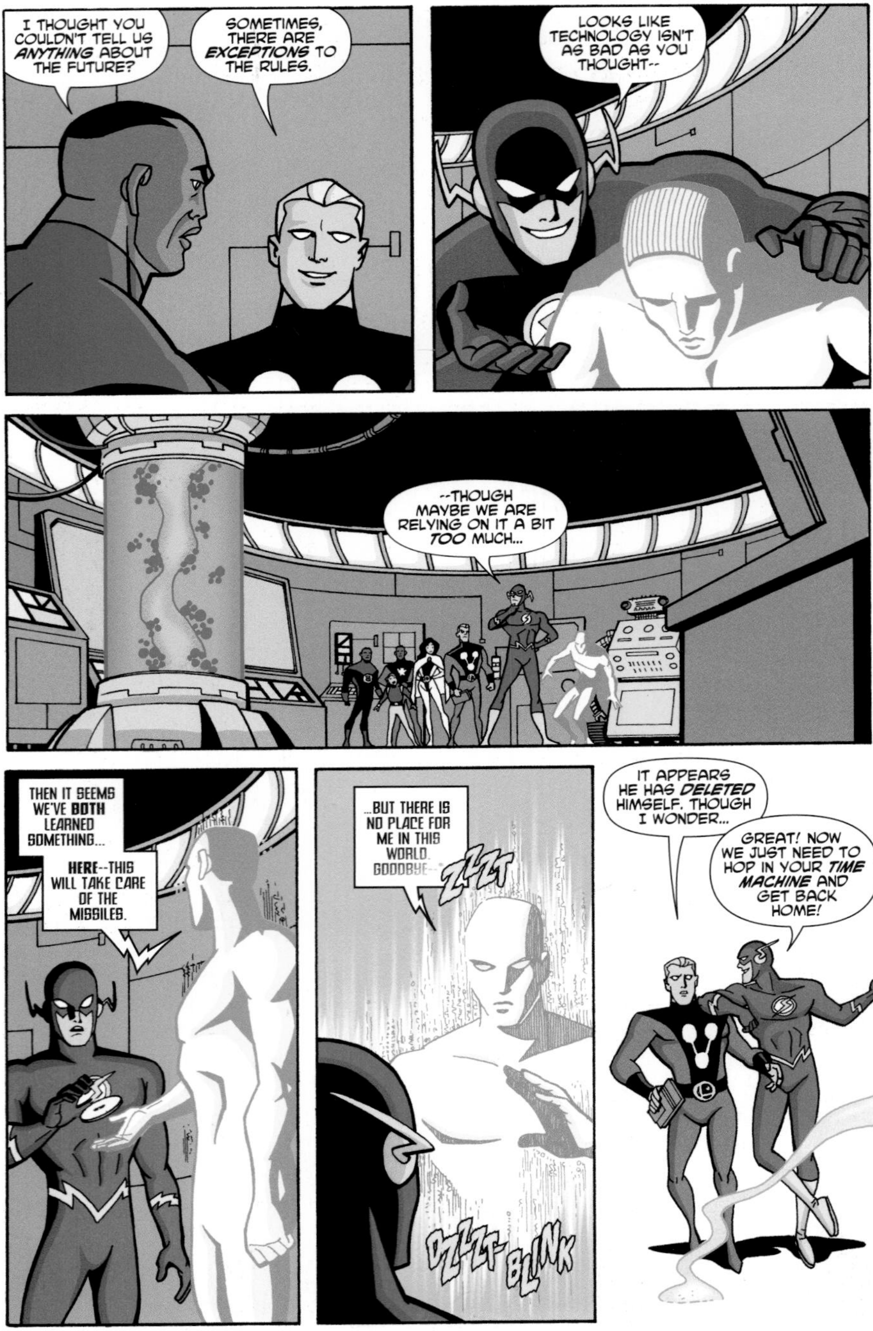
I THOUGHT YOU COULDN'T TELL US ANYTHING ABOUT THE FUTURE?
SOMETIMES, THERE ARE EXCEPTIONS TO THE RULES.
LOOKS LIKE TECHNOLOGY ISN'T AS BAD AS YOU THOUGHT--
--THOUGH MAYBE WE ARE RELYING ON IT A BIT TOO MUCH...
THEN IT SEEMS WE'VE BOTH LEARNED SOMETHING...
HERE--THIS WILL TAKE CARE OF THE MISSILES.
...BUT THERE IS NO PLACE FOR ME IN THIS WORLD. GOODBYE--
ZZZT
DZZZT-BLINK
IT APPEARS HE HAS DELETED HIMSELF. THOUGH I WONDER...
GREAT! NOW WE JUST NEED TO HOP IN YOUR TIME MACHINE AND GET BACK HOME!

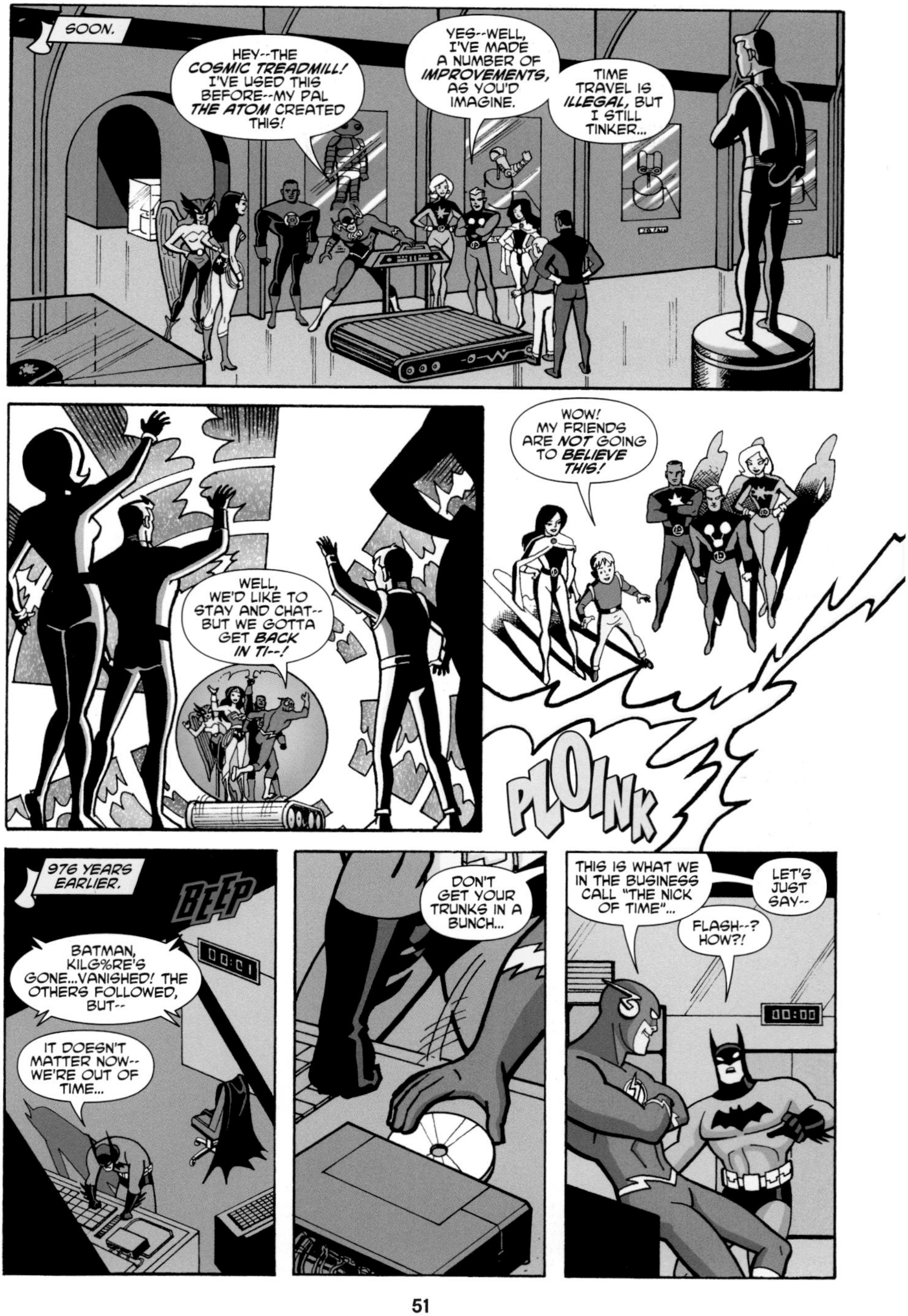
SOON.
HEY--THE *COSMIC TREADMILL!* I'VE USED THIS BEFORE--MY PAL *THE ATOM* CREATED THIS!
YES--WELL, I'VE MADE A NUMBER OF *IMPROVEMENTS,* AS YOU'D IMAGINE.
TIME TRAVEL IS *ILLEGAL,* BUT I STILL TINKER...
WOW! MY FRIENDS ARE *NOT* GOING TO *BELIEVE THIS!*
WELL, WE'D LIKE TO STAY AND CHAT--BUT WE GOTTA GET *BACK IN TI--!*
PLOINK
976 YEARS EARLIER.
BEEP
BATMAN, KILG%RE'S GONE...VANISHED! THE OTHERS FOLLOWED, BUT--
IT DOESN'T MATTER NOW--WE'RE OUT OF TIME...
00:01
DON'T GET YOUR TRUNKS IN A BUNCH...
THIS IS WHAT WE IN THE BUSINESS CALL "THE NICK OF TIME"...
LET'S JUST SAY--
FLASH--? HOW?!
00:00

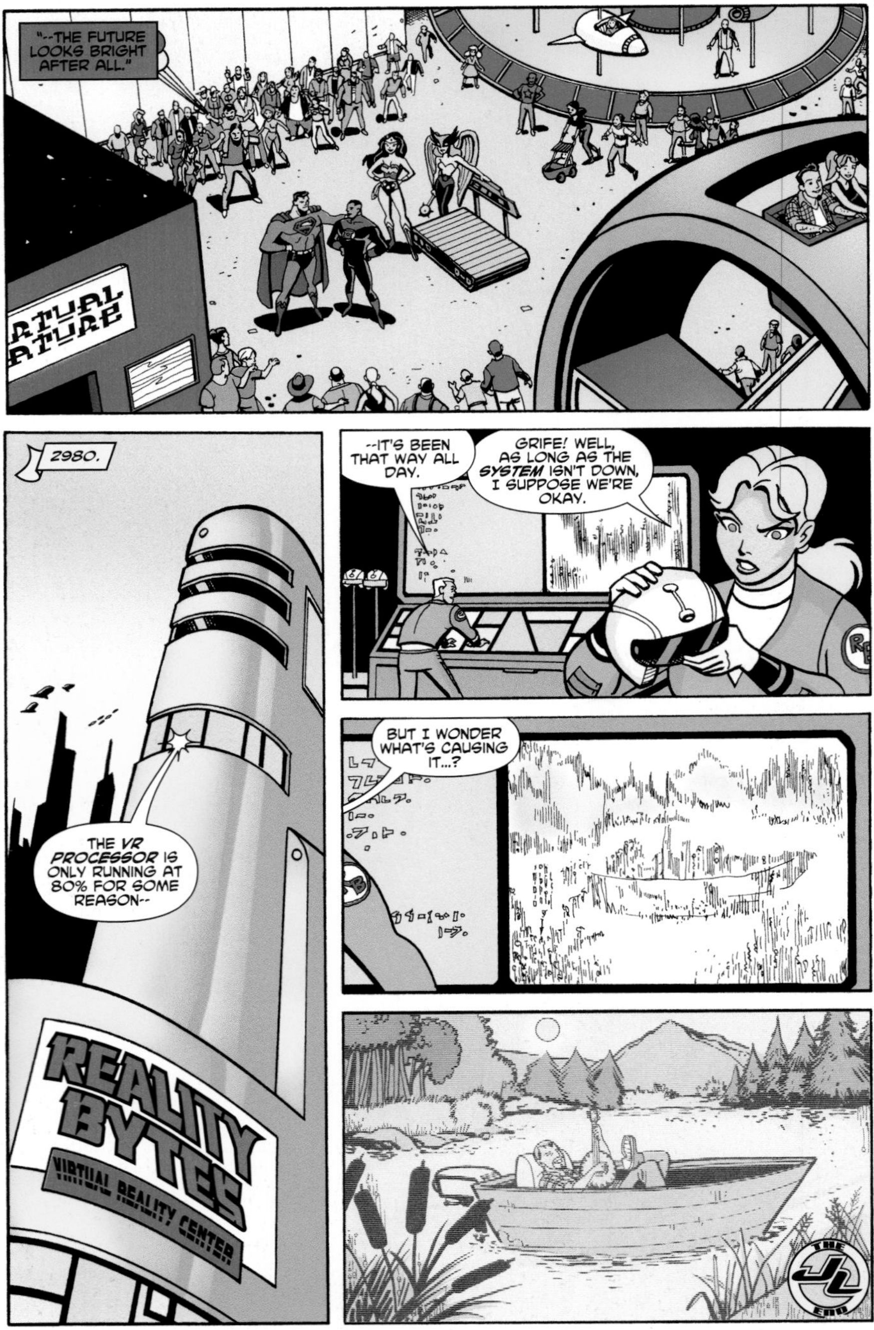
"--THE FUTURE LOOKS BRIGHT AFTER ALL."
2980.
THE VR PROCESSOR IS ONLY RUNNING AT 80% FOR SOME REASON--
--IT'S BEEN THAT WAY ALL DAY.
GRIFE! WELL, AS LONG AS THE SYSTEM ISN'T DOWN, I SUPPOSE WE'RE OKAY.
BUT I WONDER WHAT'S CAUSING IT...?
REALITY BYTES
VIRTUAL REALITY CENTER
THE END

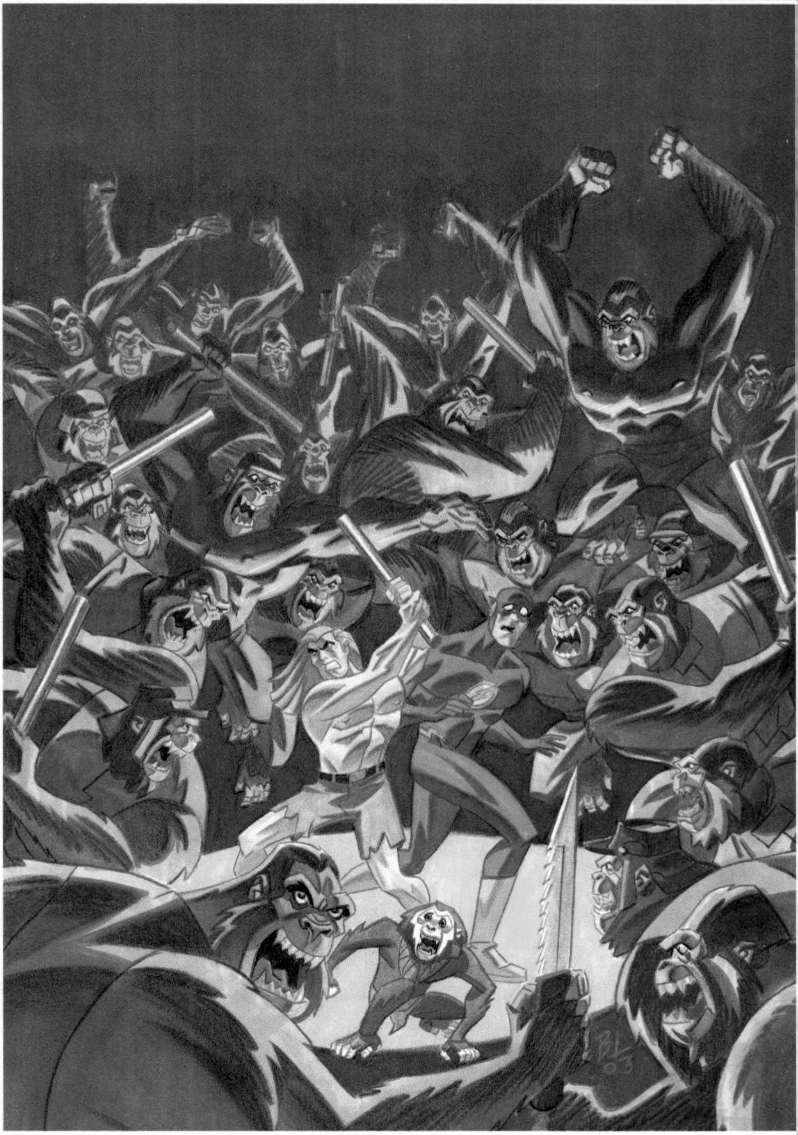

CHAPTER 3: THIS BETTER WORLD

JUSTICE LEAGUE UNLIMITED

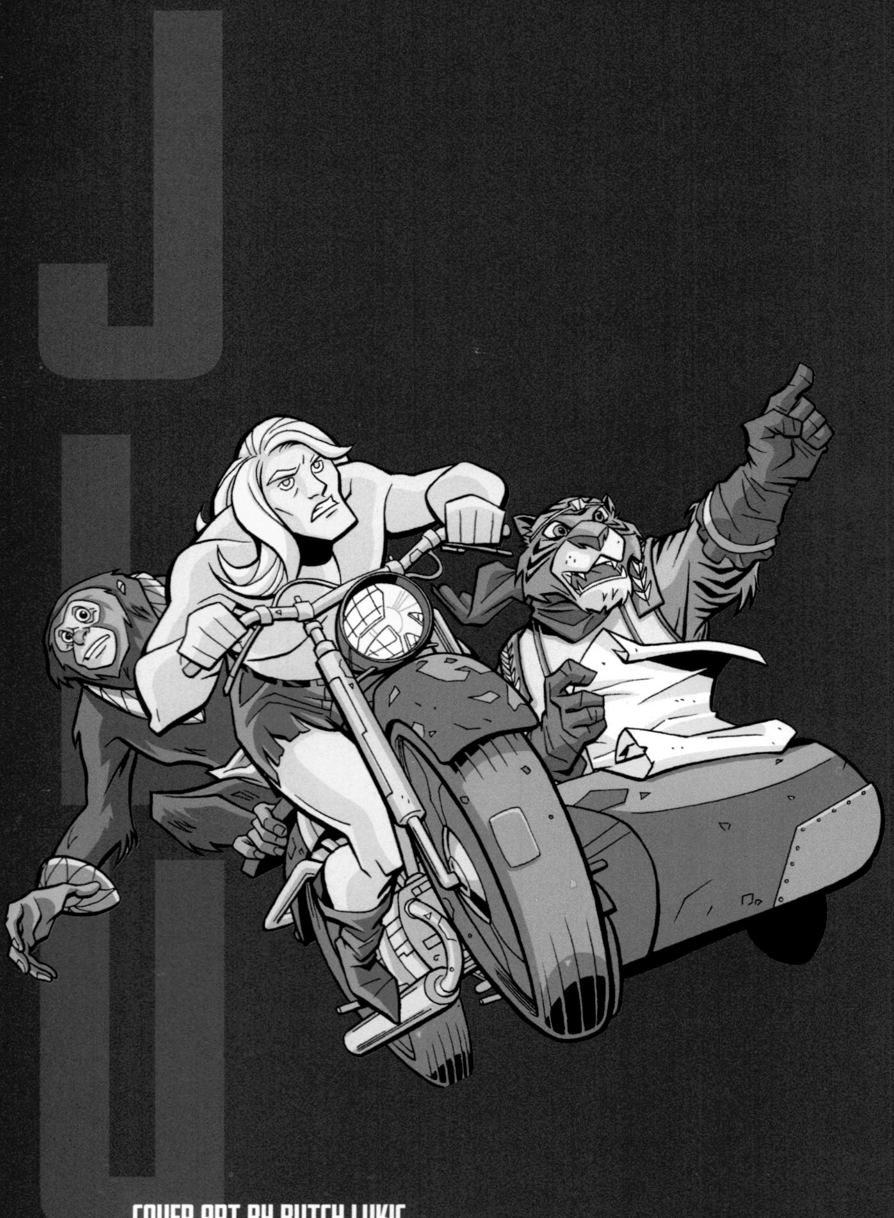

COVER ART BY BUTCH LUKIC

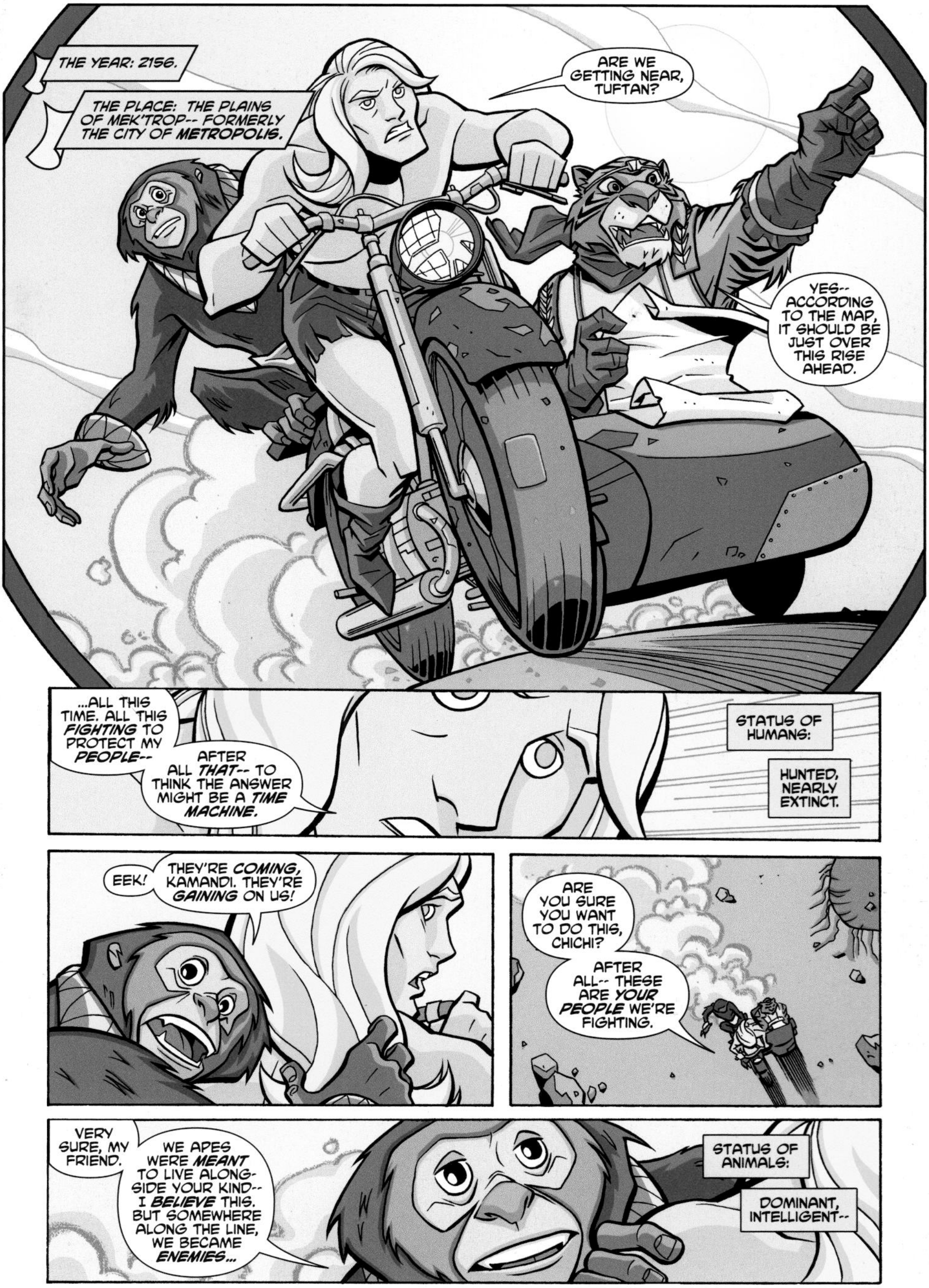
THE YEAR: 2156.
THE PLACE: THE PLAINS OF MEK'TROP-- FORMERLY THE CITY OF METROPOLIS.
ARE WE GETTING NEAR, TUFTAN?
YES-- ACCORDING TO THE MAP, IT SHOULD BE JUST OVER THIS RISE AHEAD.
...ALL THIS TIME. ALL THIS FIGHTING TO PROTECT MY PEOPLE--
AFTER ALL THAT-- TO THINK THE ANSWER MIGHT BE A TIME MACHINE.
STATUS OF HUMANS:
HUNTED, NEARLY EXTINCT.
EEK!
THEY'RE COMING, KAMANDI. THEY'RE GAINING ON US!
ARE YOU SURE YOU WANT TO DO THIS, CHICHI?
AFTER ALL-- THESE ARE YOUR PEOPLE WE'RE FIGHTING.
VERY SURE, MY FRIEND.
WE APES WERE MEANT TO LIVE ALONGSIDE YOUR KIND-- I BELIEVE THIS. BUT SOMEWHERE ALONG THE LINE, WE BECAME ENEMIES...
STATUS OF ANIMALS:
DOMINANT, INTELLIGENT--

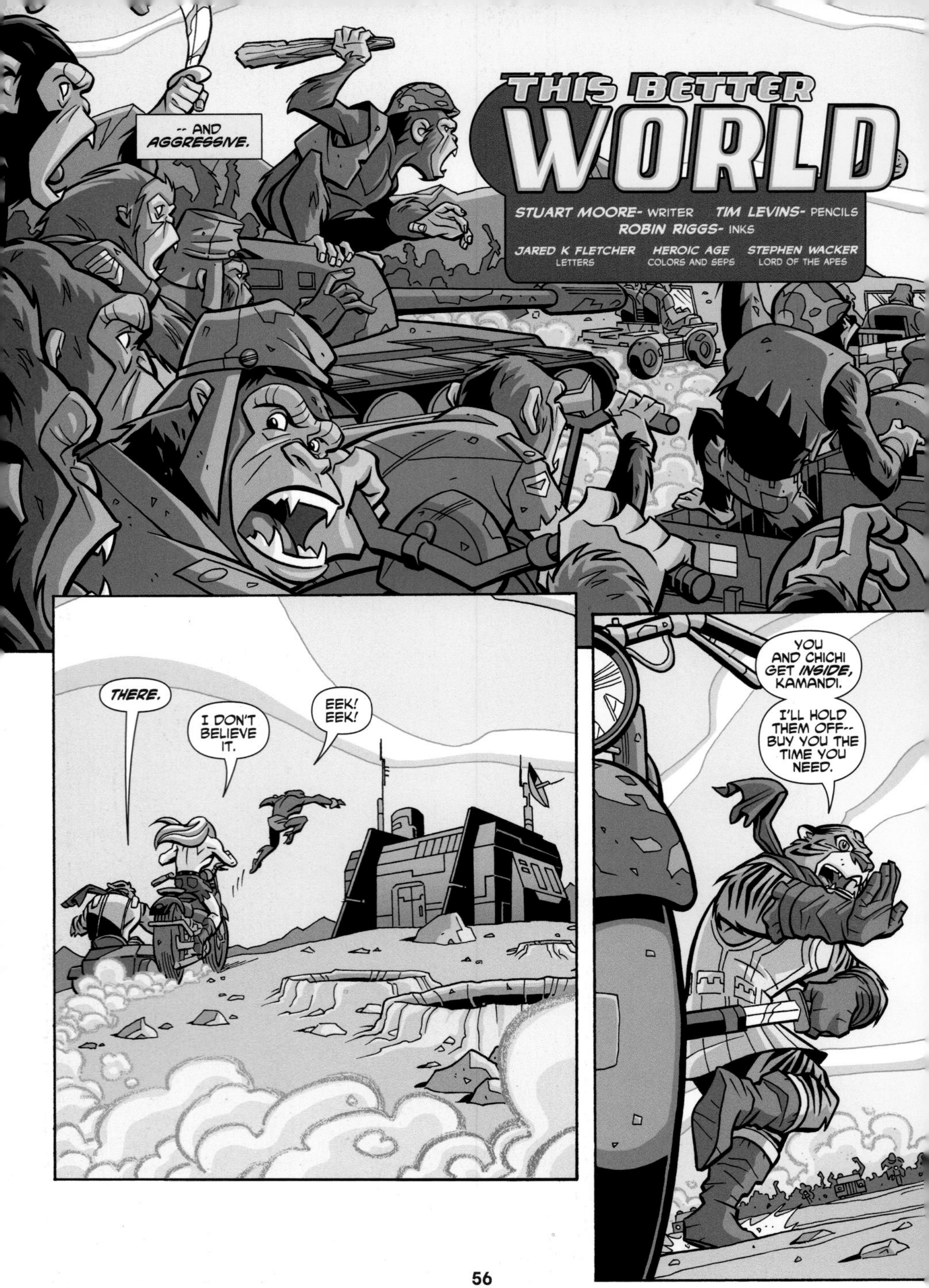
-- AND AGGRESSIVE.
THIS BETTER WORLD
STUART MOORE- WRITER
TIM LEVINS- PENCILS
ROBIN RIGGS- INKS
JARED K FLETCHER LETTERS
HEROIC AGE COLORS AND SEPS
STEPHEN WACKER LORD OF THE APES
THERE.
I DON'T BELIEVE IT.
EEK! EEK!
YOU AND CHICHI GET INSIDE, KAMANDI.
I'LL HOLD THEM OFF-- BUY YOU THE TIME YOU NEED.

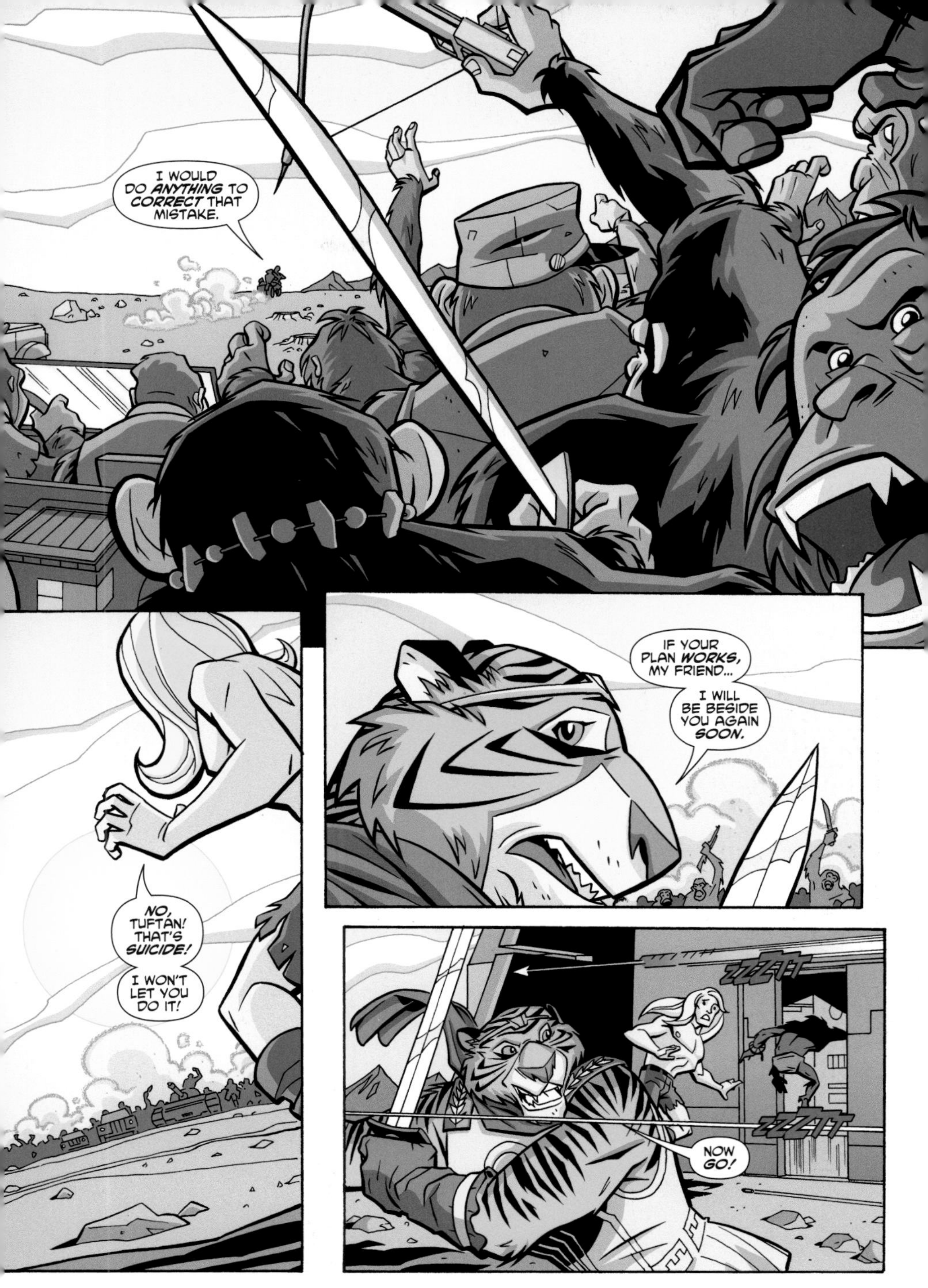
I WOULD DO *ANYTHING* TO *CORRECT* THAT MISTAKE.
IF YOUR PLAN *WORKS*, MY FRIEND...
I WILL BE BESIDE YOU AGAIN *SOON.*
NO, TUFTAN! THAT'S *SUICIDE!*
I WON'T LET YOU DO IT!
ZZZZTT
ZZZZTT
NOW *GO!*

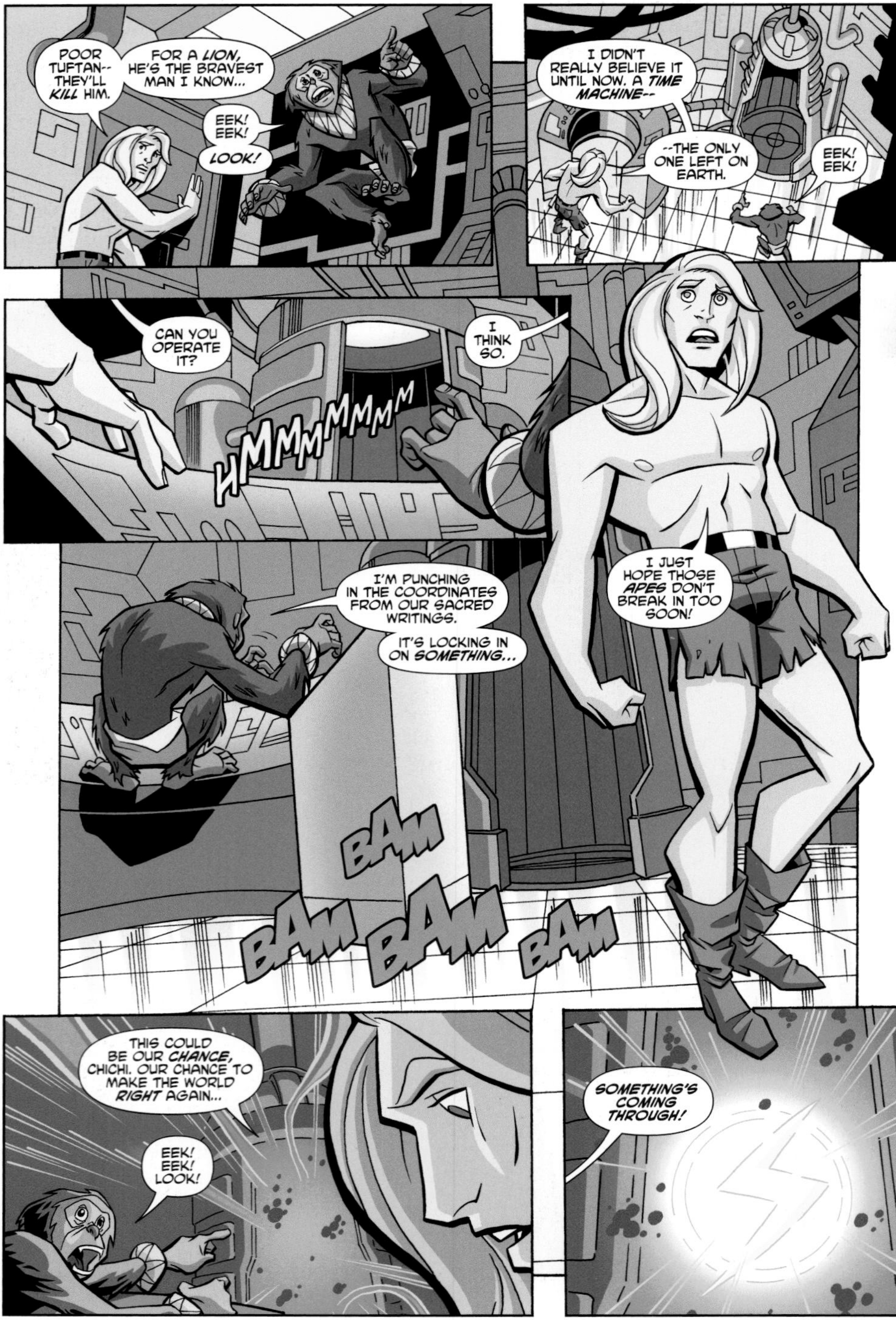
POOR TUFTAN-- THEY'LL KILL HIM.
FOR A LION, HE'S THE BRAVEST MAN I KNOW...
EEK! EEK!
LOOK!
I DIDN'T REALLY BELIEVE IT UNTIL NOW. A TIME MACHINE--
--THE ONLY ONE LEFT ON EARTH.
EEK! EEK!
CAN YOU OPERATE IT?
I THINK SO.
HMMMMMMMM
I'M PUNCHING IN THE COORDINATES FROM OUR SACRED WRITINGS.
IT'S LOCKING IN ON SOMETHING...
I JUST HOPE THOSE APES DON'T BREAK IN TOO SOON!
BAM
BAM
BAM
BAM
THIS COULD BE OUR CHANCE, CHICHI. OUR CHANCE TO MAKE THE WORLD RIGHT AGAIN...
EEK! EEK! LOOK!
SOMETHING'S COMING THROUGH!

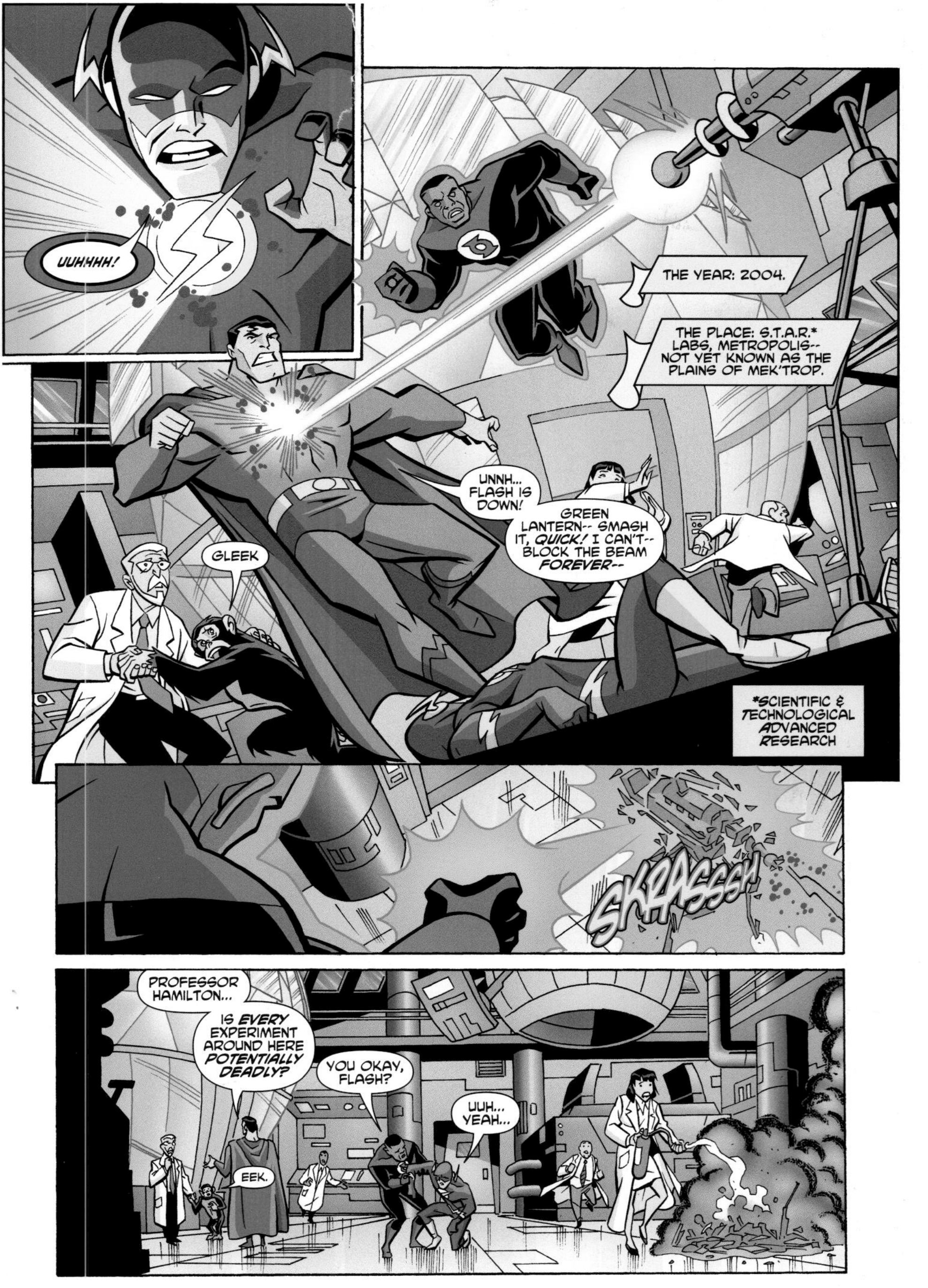
UUHHHH!
THE YEAR: 2004.
THE PLACE: S.T.A.R.* LABS, METROPOLIS-- NOT YET KNOWN AS THE PLAINS OF MEK'TROP.
UNNH... FLASH IS DOWN!
GREEN LANTERN-- SMASH IT, QUICK! I CAN'T-- BLOCK THE BEAM FOREVER--
GLEEK
*SCIENTIFIC & TECHNOLOGICAL ADVANCED RESEARCH
SKRASSSH
PROFESSOR HAMILTON...
IS EVERY EXPERIMENT AROUND HERE POTENTIALLY DEADLY?
YOU OKAY, FLASH?
UUH... YEAH...
EEK.

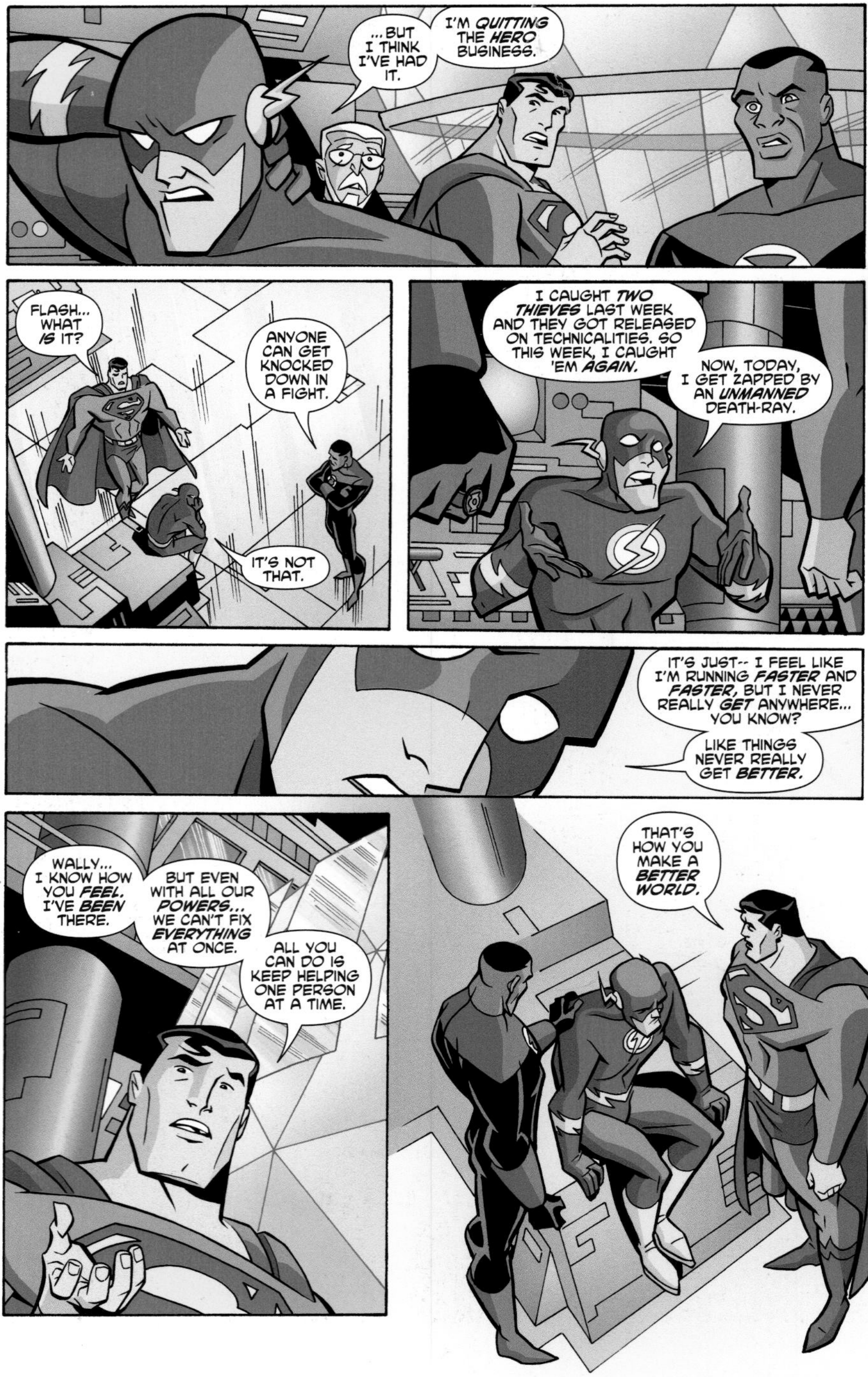
...BUT I THINK I'VE HAD IT.
I'M QUITTING THE HERO BUSINESS.
FLASH... WHAT IS IT?
ANYONE CAN GET KNOCKED DOWN IN A FIGHT.
IT'S NOT THAT.
I CAUGHT TWO THIEVES LAST WEEK AND THEY GOT RELEASED ON TECHNICALITIES. SO THIS WEEK, I CAUGHT 'EM AGAIN.
NOW, TODAY, I GET ZAPPED BY AN UNMANNED DEATH-RAY.
IT'S JUST-- I FEEL LIKE I'M RUNNING FASTER AND FASTER, BUT I NEVER REALLY GET ANYWHERE... YOU KNOW?
LIKE THINGS NEVER REALLY GET BETTER.
WALLY... I KNOW HOW YOU FEEL. I'VE BEEN THERE.
BUT EVEN WITH ALL OUR POWERS... WE CAN'T FIX EVERYTHING AT ONCE.
ALL YOU CAN DO IS KEEP HELPING ONE PERSON AT A TIME.
THAT'S HOW YOU MAKE A BETTER WORLD.

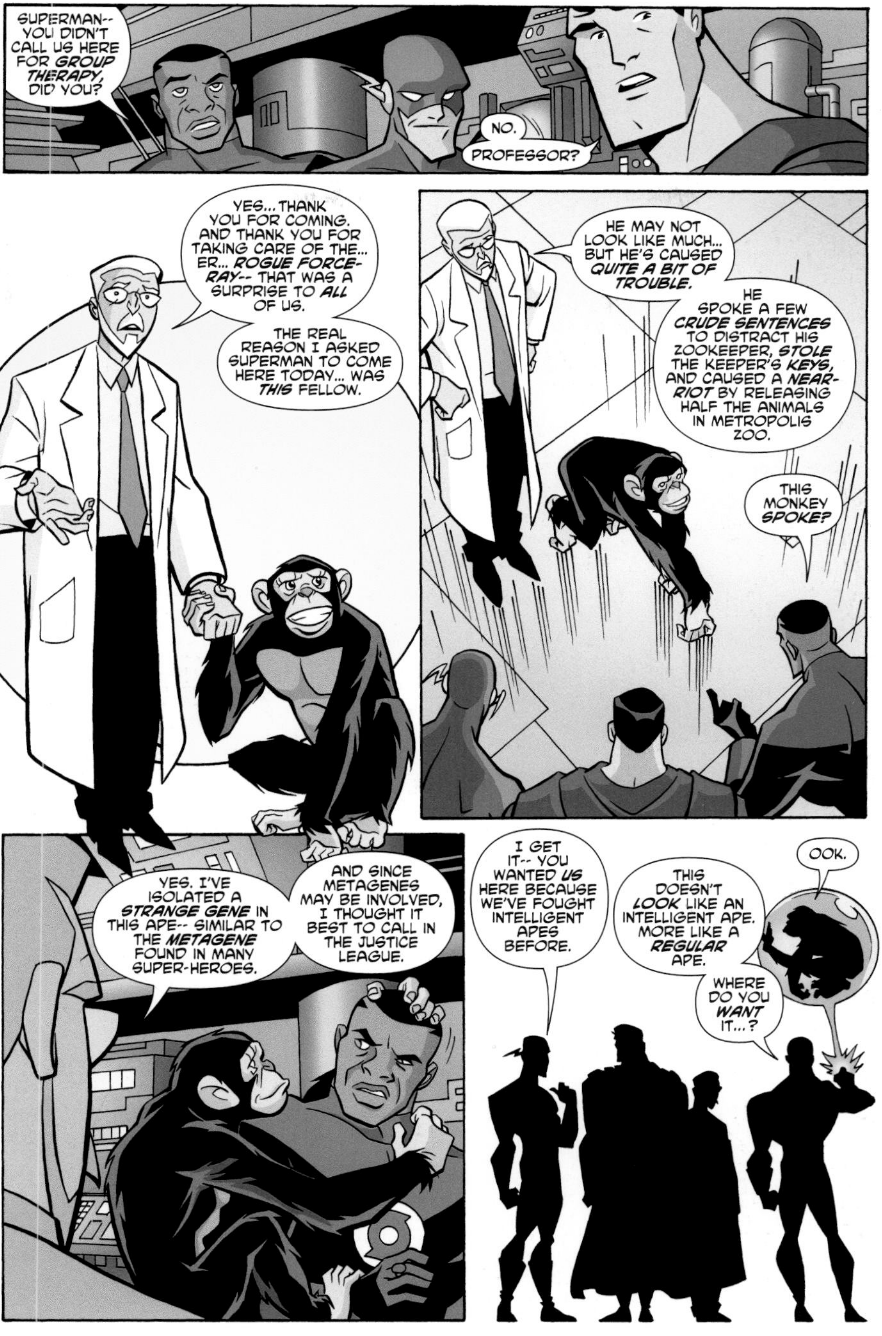
SUPERMAN-- YOU DIDN'T CALL US HERE FOR GROUP THERAPY, DID YOU?
NO.
PROFESSOR?
YES... THANK YOU FOR COMING. AND THANK YOU FOR TAKING CARE OF THE... ER... ROGUE FORCE-RAY-- THAT WAS A SURPRISE TO ALL OF US.
THE REAL REASON I ASKED SUPERMAN TO COME HERE TODAY... WAS THIS FELLOW.
HE MAY NOT LOOK LIKE MUCH... BUT HE'S CAUSED QUITE A BIT OF TROUBLE.
HE SPOKE A FEW CRUDE SENTENCES TO DISTRACT HIS ZOOKEEPER, STOLE THE KEEPER'S KEYS, AND CAUSED A NEAR-RIOT BY RELEASING HALF THE ANIMALS IN METROPOLIS ZOO.
THIS MONKEY SPOKE?
YES. I'VE ISOLATED A STRANGE GENE IN THIS APE-- SIMILAR TO THE METAGENE FOUND IN MANY SUPER-HEROES.
AND SINCE METAGENES MAY BE INVOLVED, I THOUGHT IT BEST TO CALL IN THE JUSTICE LEAGUE.
I GET IT-- YOU WANTED US HERE BECAUSE WE'VE FOUGHT INTELLIGENT APES BEFORE.
THIS DOESN'T LOOK LIKE AN INTELLIGENT APE. MORE LIKE A REGULAR APE.
OOK.
WHERE DO YOU WANT IT...?

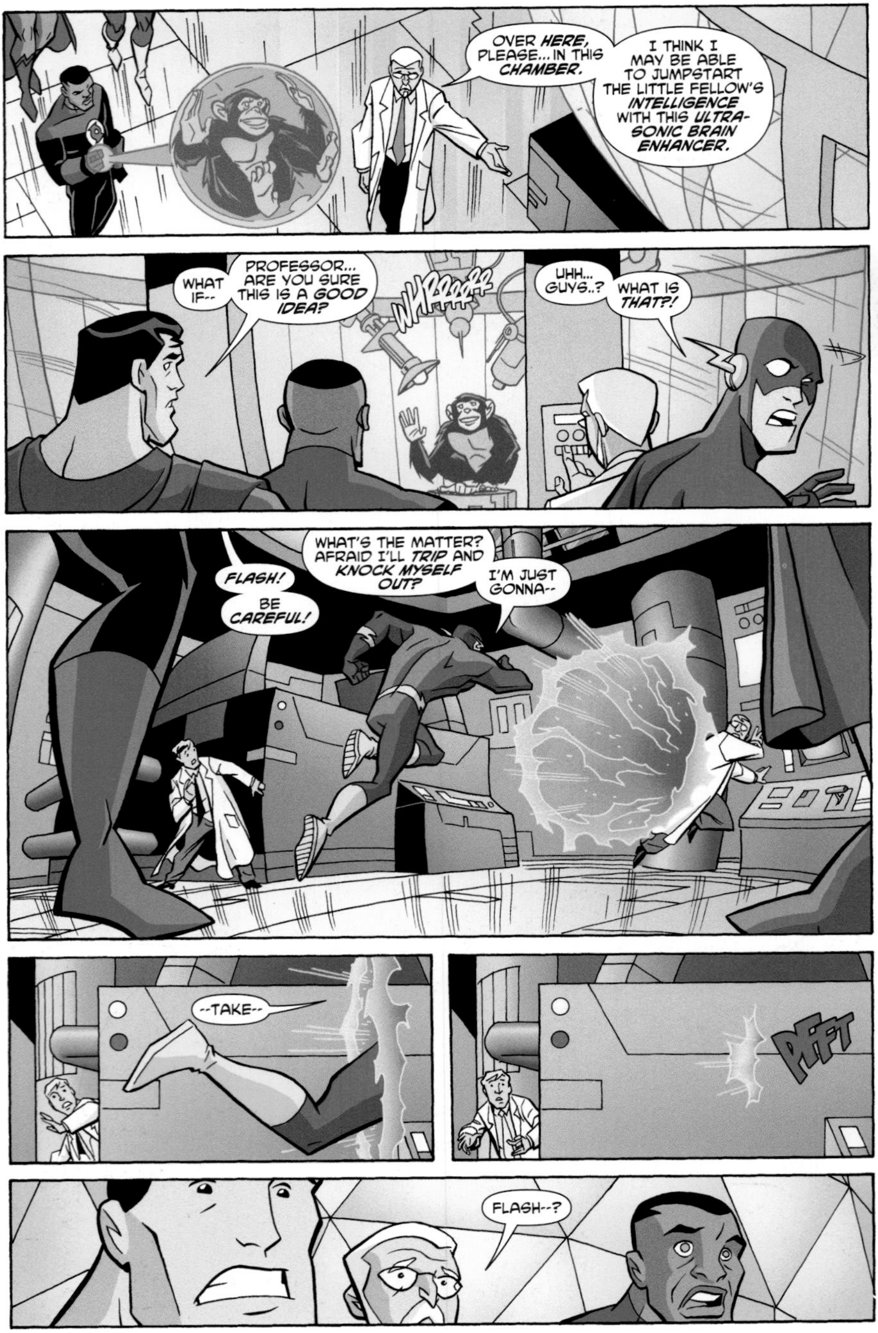
OVER HERE, PLEASE... IN THIS CHAMBER.
I THINK I MAY BE ABLE TO JUMPSTART THE LITTLE FELLOW'S INTELLIGENCE WITH THIS ULTRA-SONIC BRAIN ENHANCER.
WHAT IF--
PROFESSOR... ARE YOU SURE THIS IS A GOOD IDEA?
WHRRRRRR
UHH... GUYS..?
WHAT IS THAT?!
FLASH!
BE CAREFUL!
WHAT'S THE MATTER? AFRAID I'LL TRIP AND KNOCK MYSELF OUT?
I'M JUST GONNA--
--TAKE--
PFFT
FLASH--?

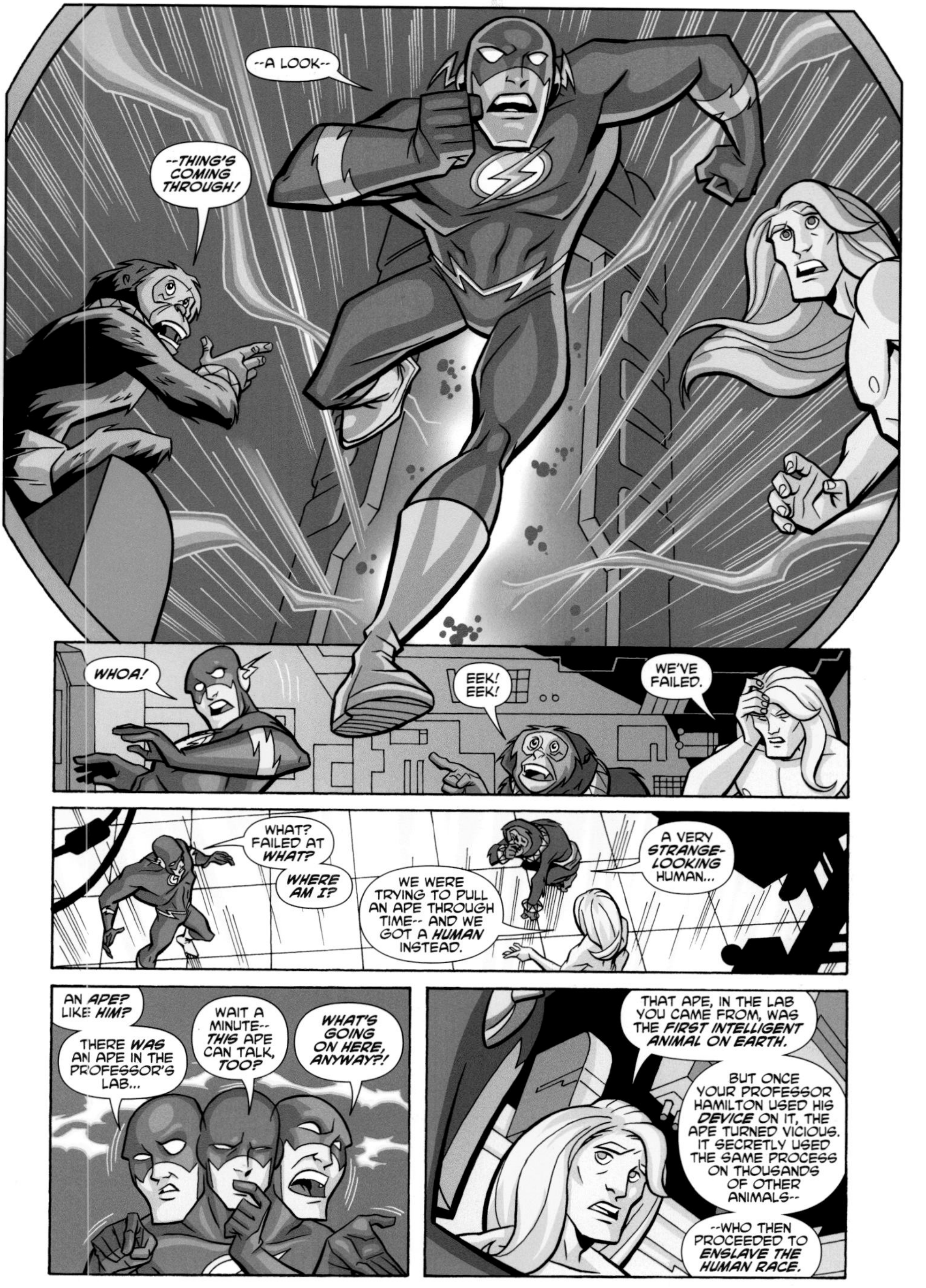

--A LOOK--
--THING'S COMING THROUGH!
WHOA!
EEK! EEK!
WE'VE FAILED.
WHAT? FAILED AT WHAT?
WHERE AM I?
WE WERE TRYING TO PULL AN APE THROUGH TIME-- AND WE GOT A HUMAN INSTEAD.
A VERY STRANGE-LOOKING HUMAN...
AN APE? LIKE HIM?
THERE WAS AN APE IN THE PROFESSOR'S LAB...
WAIT A MINUTE-- THIS APE CAN TALK, TOO?
WHAT'S GOING ON HERE, ANYWAY?!
THAT APE, IN THE LAB YOU CAME FROM, WAS THE FIRST INTELLIGENT ANIMAL ON EARTH.
BUT ONCE YOUR PROFESSOR HAMILTON USED HIS DEVICE ON IT, THE APE TURNED VICIOUS. IT SECRETLY USED THE SAME PROCESS ON THOUSANDS OF OTHER ANIMALS--
--WHO THEN PROCEEDED TO ENSLAVE THE HUMAN RACE.

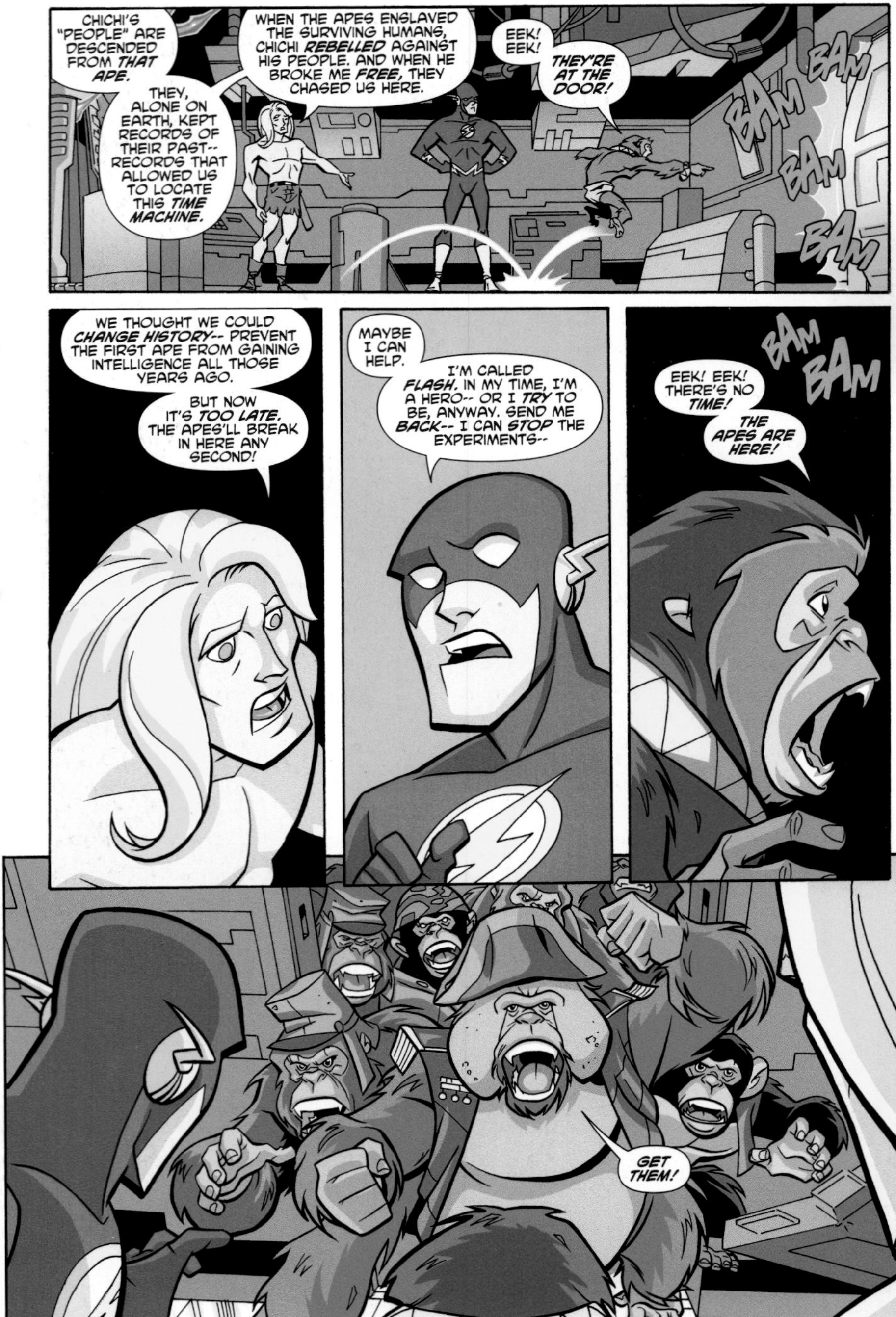
CHICHI'S "PEOPLE" ARE DESCENDED FROM THAT APE.
THEY, ALONE ON EARTH, KEPT RECORDS OF THEIR PAST-- RECORDS THAT ALLOWED US TO LOCATE THIS TIME MACHINE.
WHEN THE APES ENSLAVED THE SURVIVING HUMANS, CHICHI REBELLED AGAINST HIS PEOPLE. AND WHEN HE BROKE ME FREE, THEY CHASED US HERE.
EEK! EEK!
THEY'RE AT THE DOOR!
BAM BAM
BAM
BAM
BAM
WE THOUGHT WE COULD CHANGE HISTORY-- PREVENT THE FIRST APE FROM GAINING INTELLIGENCE ALL THOSE YEARS AGO.
BUT NOW IT'S TOO LATE. THE APES'LL BREAK IN HERE ANY SECOND!
MAYBE I CAN HELP.
I'M CALLED FLASH. IN MY TIME, I'M A HERO-- OR I TRY TO BE, ANYWAY. SEND ME BACK-- I CAN STOP THE EXPERIMENTS--
BAM
BAM
EEK! EEK! THERE'S NO TIME!
THE APES ARE HERE!
GET THEM!

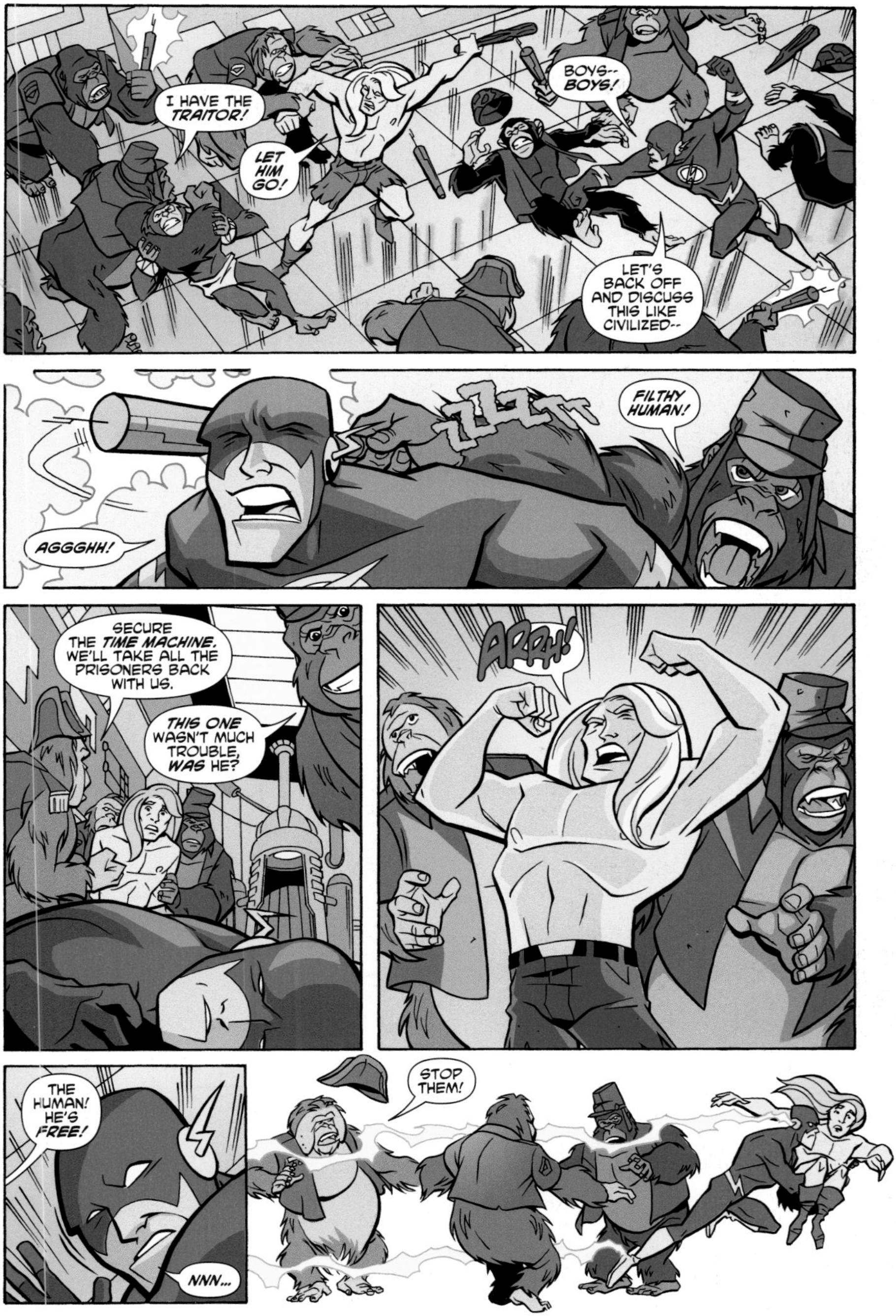
I HAVE THE *TRAITOR!*
LET HIM GO!
BOYS-- *BOYS!*
LET'S BACK OFF AND DISCUSS THIS LIKE CIVILIZED--
FILTHY HUMAN!
AGGGHH!
SECURE THE *TIME MACHINE.* WE'LL TAKE ALL THE PRISONERS BACK WITH US.
THIS ONE WASN'T MUCH TROUBLE, *WAS* HE?
ARRH!
THE HUMAN! HE'S *FREE!*
NNN...
STOP THEM!

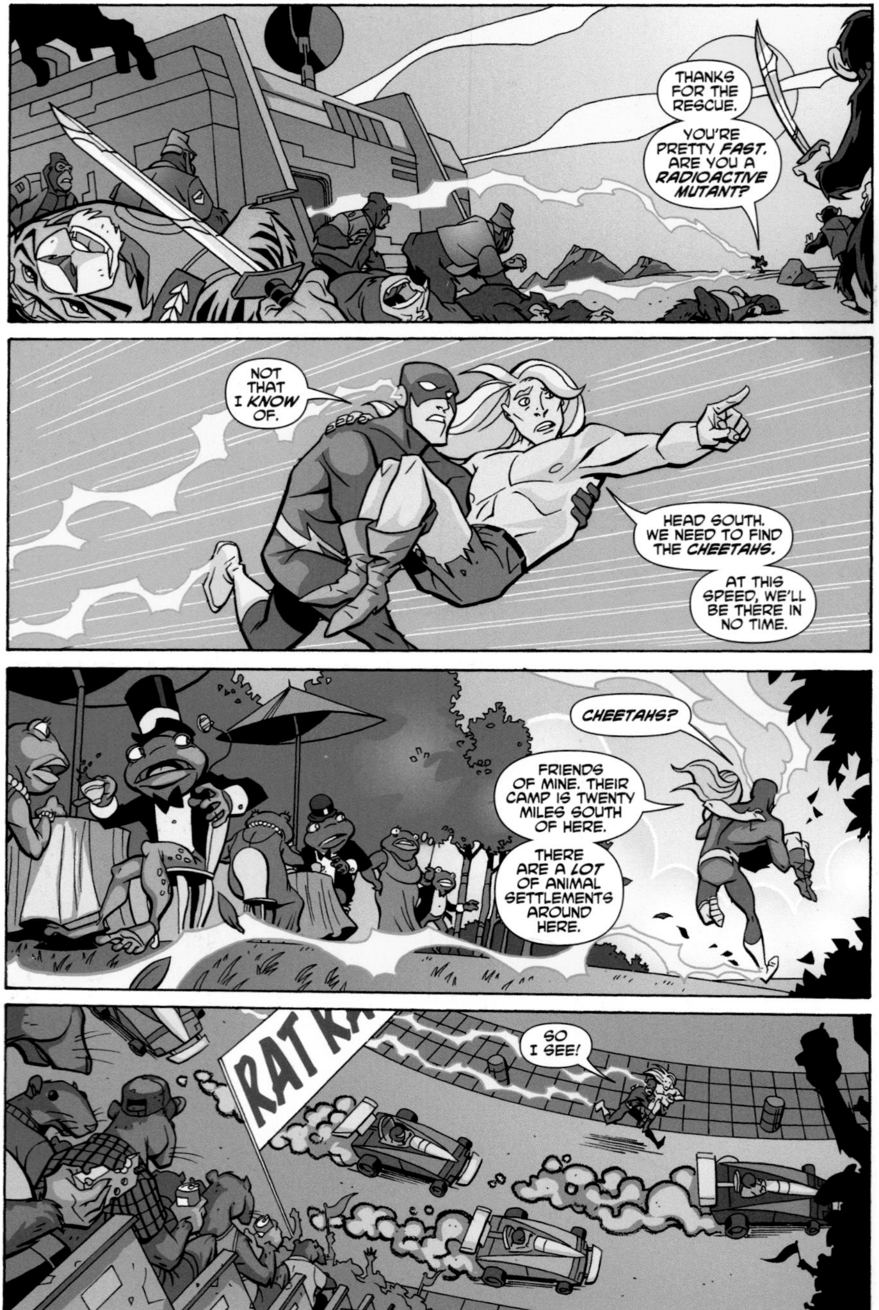

THANKS FOR THE RESCUE.
YOU'RE PRETTY *FAST.* ARE YOU A *RADIOACTIVE MUTANT?*
NOT THAT I *KNOW* OF.
HEAD SOUTH. WE NEED TO FIND THE *CHEETAHS.*
AT THIS SPEED, WE'LL BE THERE IN NO TIME.
CHEETAHS?
FRIENDS OF MINE. THEIR CAMP IS TWENTY MILES SOUTH OF HERE.
THERE ARE A *LOT* OF ANIMAL SETTLEMENTS AROUND HERE.
SO I SEE!
RAT RA

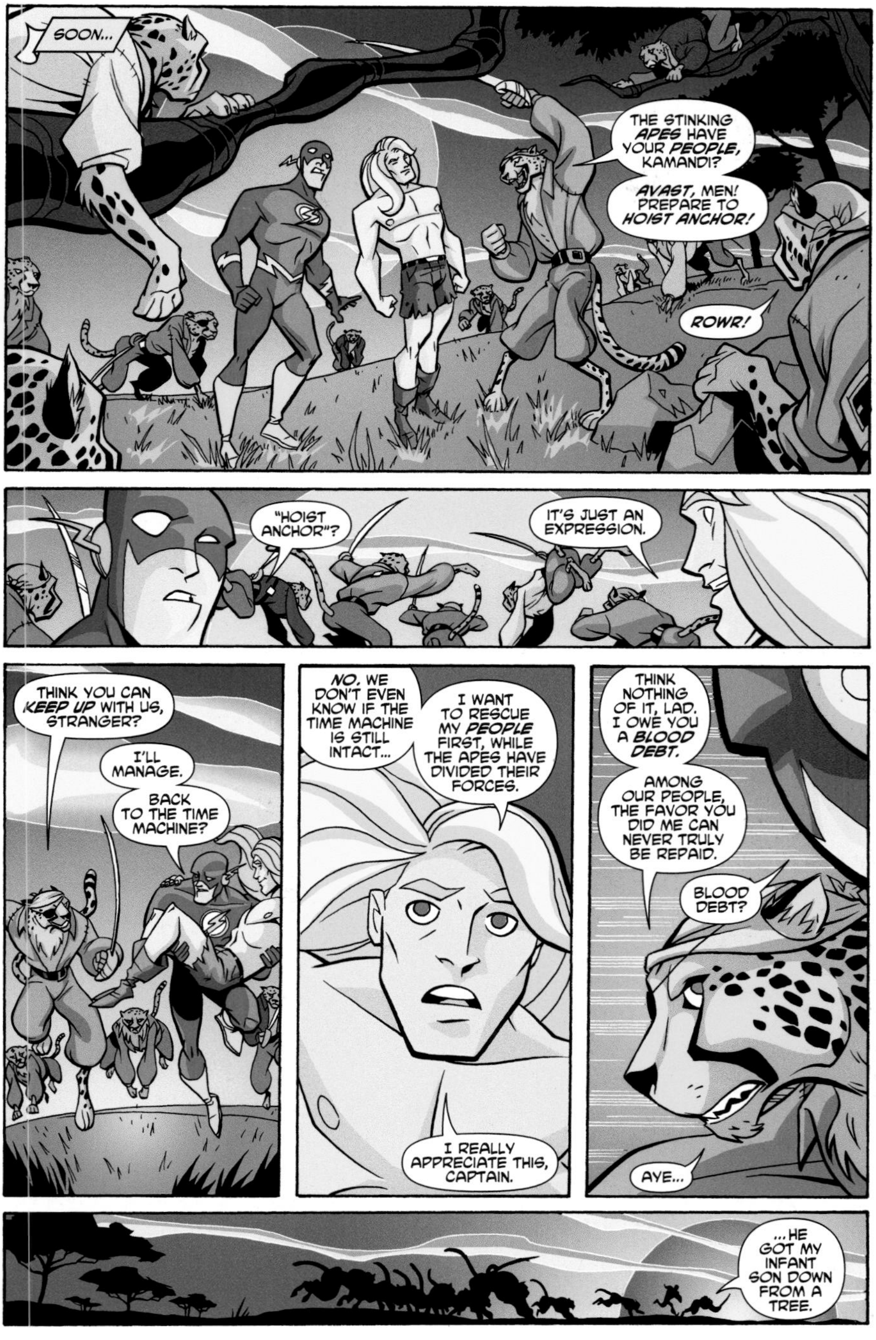
SOON...
THE STINKING APES HAVE YOUR PEOPLE, KAMANDI?
AVAST, MEN! PREPARE TO HOIST ANCHOR!
ROWR!
"HOIST ANCHOR"?
IT'S JUST AN EXPRESSION.
THINK YOU CAN KEEP UP WITH US, STRANGER?
I'LL MANAGE.
BACK TO THE TIME MACHINE?
NO. WE DON'T EVEN KNOW IF THE TIME MACHINE IS STILL INTACT...
I WANT TO RESCUE MY PEOPLE FIRST, WHILE THE APES HAVE DIVIDED THEIR FORCES.
I REALLY APPRECIATE THIS, CAPTAIN.
THINK NOTHING OF IT, LAD. I OWE YOU A BLOOD DEBT.
AMONG OUR PEOPLE, THE FAVOR YOU DID ME CAN NEVER TRULY BE REPAID.
BLOOD DEBT?
AYE...
...HE GOT MY INFANT SON DOWN FROM A TREE.

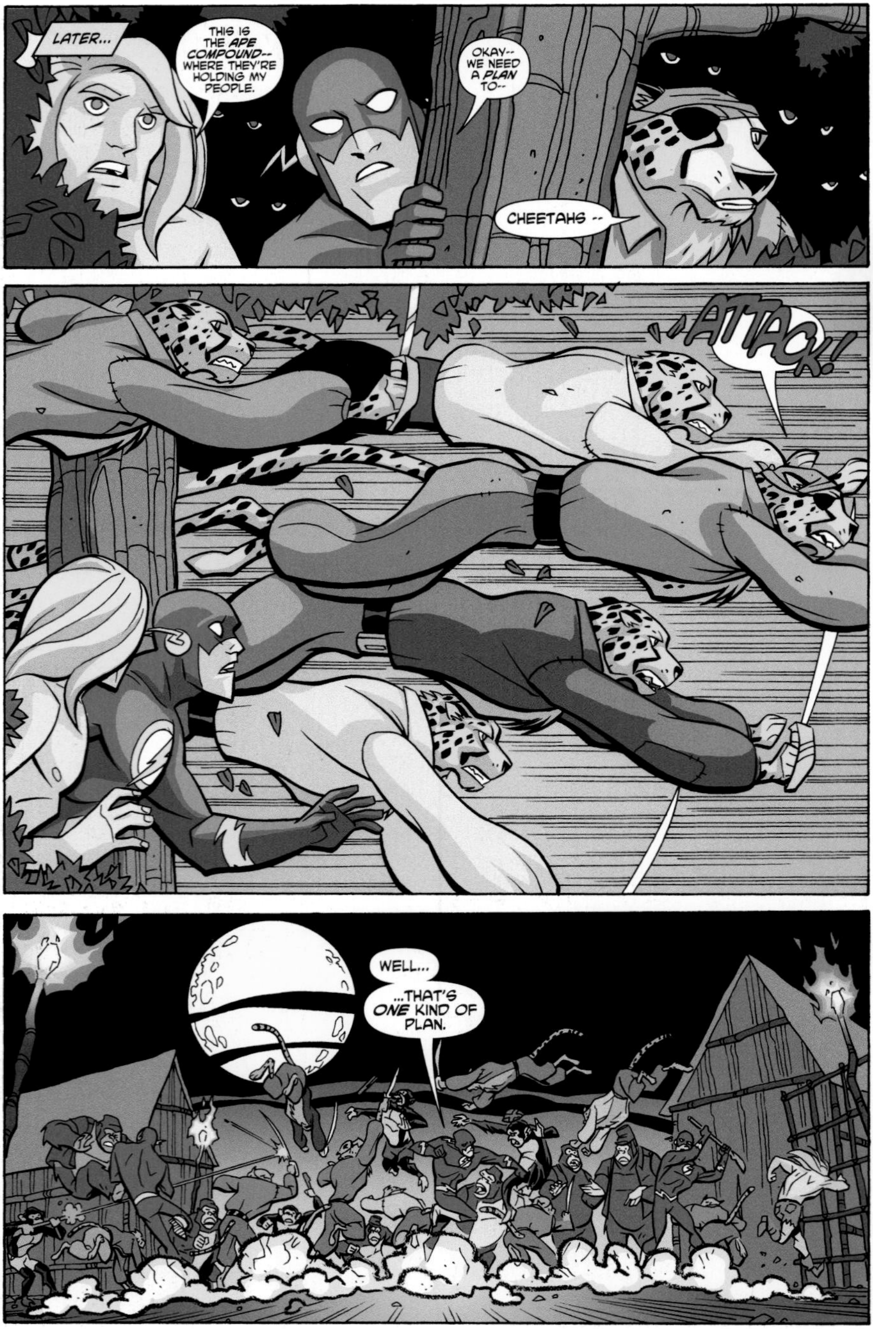
LATER...
THIS IS THE APE COMPOUND-- WHERE THEY'RE HOLDING MY PEOPLE.
OKAY-- WE NEED A PLAN TO--
CHEETAHS --
ATTACK!
WELL...
...THAT'S ONE KIND OF PLAN.

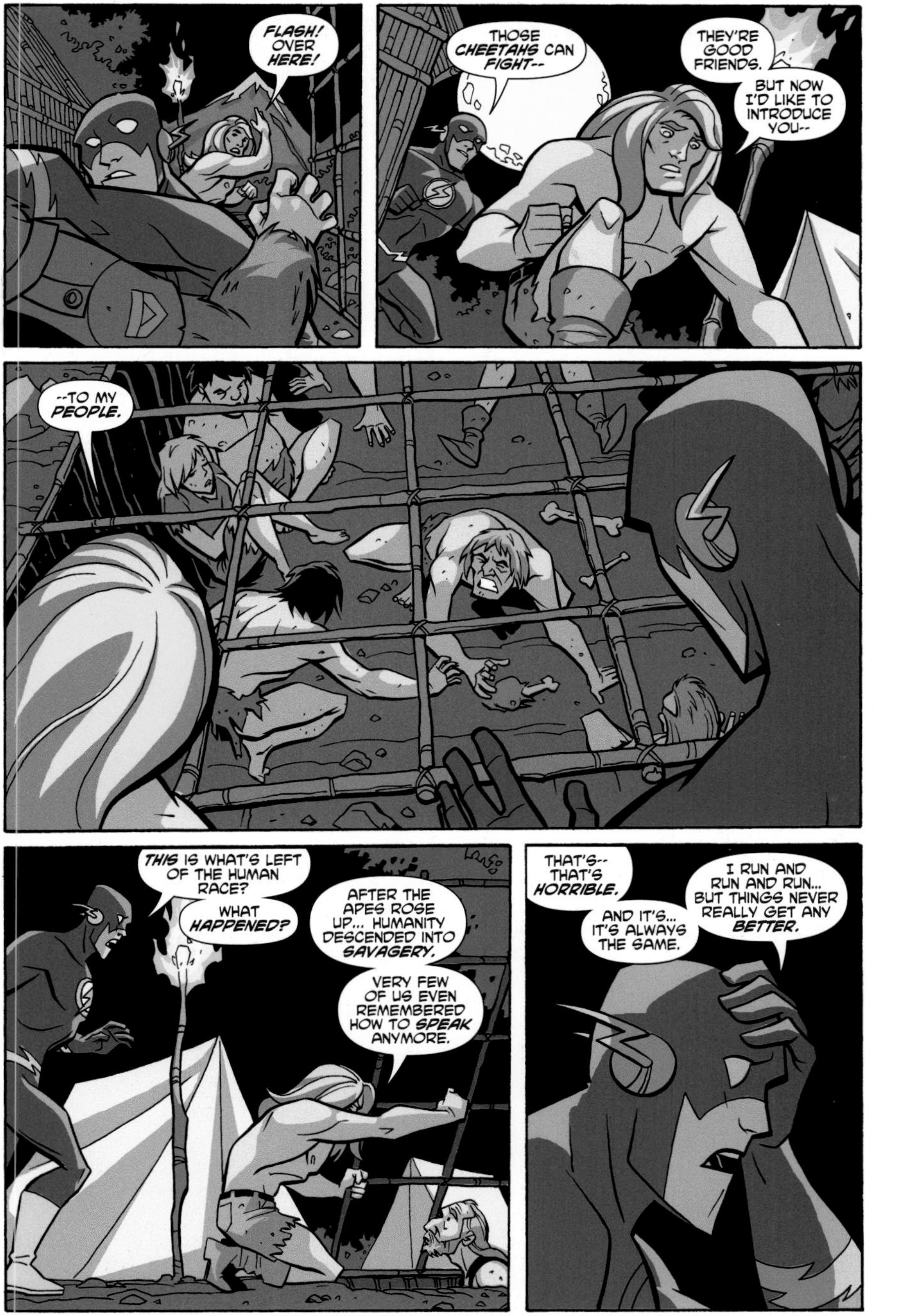
FLASH! OVER HERE!
THOSE CHEETAHS CAN FIGHT--
THEY'RE GOOD FRIENDS.
BUT NOW I'D LIKE TO INTRODUCE YOU--
--TO MY PEOPLE.
THIS IS WHAT'S LEFT OF THE HUMAN RACE?
WHAT HAPPENED?
AFTER THE APES ROSE UP... HUMANITY DESCENDED INTO SAVAGERY.
VERY FEW OF US EVEN REMEMBERED HOW TO SPEAK ANYMORE.
THAT'S-- THAT'S HORRIBLE.
AND IT'S... IT'S ALWAYS THE SAME.
I RUN AND RUN AND RUN... BUT THINGS NEVER REALLY GET ANY BETTER.

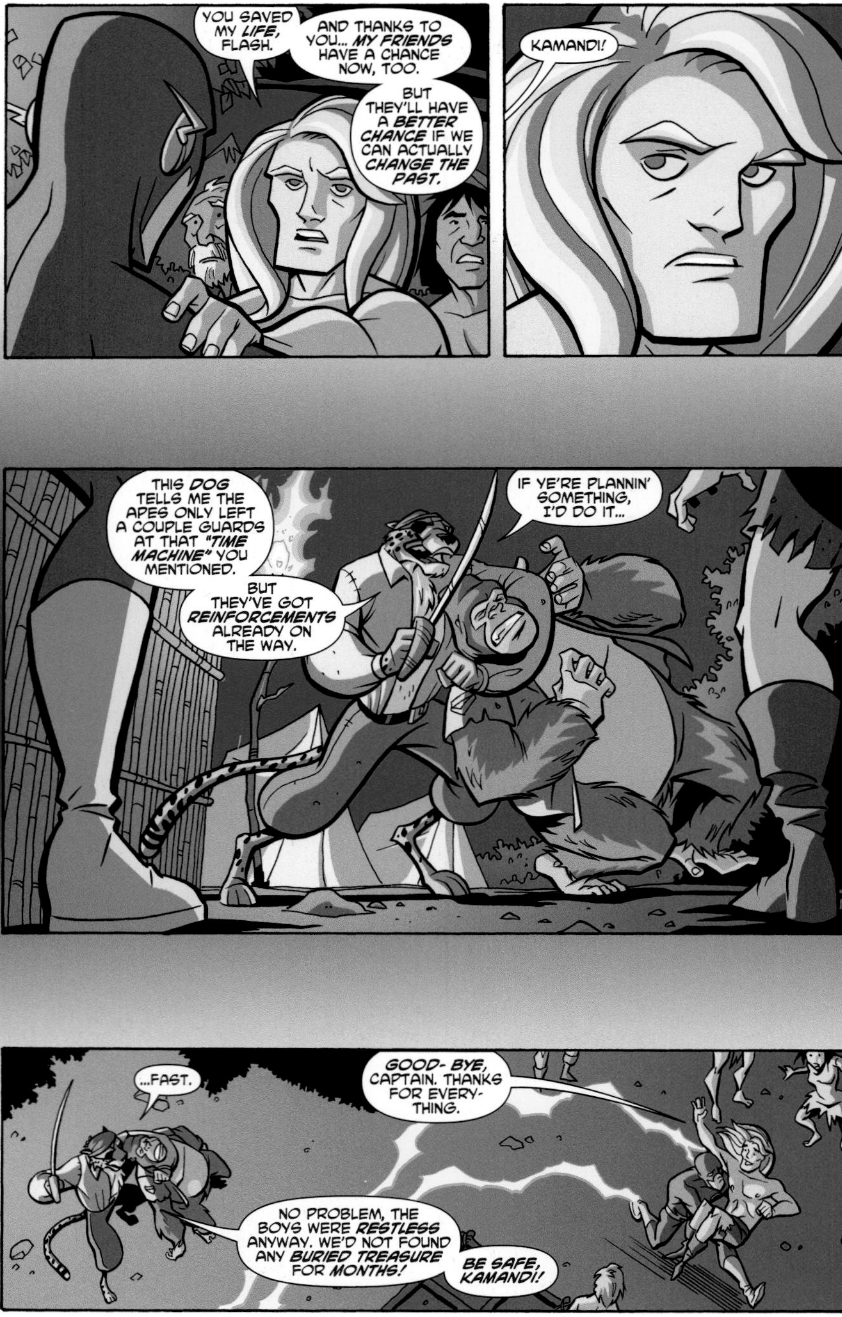
YOU SAVED MY *LIFE*, FLASH.
AND THANKS TO YOU... *MY FRIENDS* HAVE A CHANCE NOW, TOO.
BUT THEY'LL HAVE A *BETTER CHANCE* IF WE CAN ACTUALLY *CHANGE THE PAST*.
KAMANDI!
THIS *DOG* TELLS ME THE APES ONLY LEFT A COUPLE GUARDS AT THAT *"TIME MACHINE"* YOU MENTIONED.
BUT THEY'VE GOT *REINFORCEMENTS* ALREADY ON THE WAY.
IF YE'RE PLANNIN' SOMETHING, I'D DO IT...
...FAST.
GOOD- BYE, CAPTAIN. THANKS FOR EVERY-THING.
NO PROBLEM, THE BOYS WERE *RESTLESS* ANYWAY. WE'D NOT FOUND ANY *BURIED TREASURE* FOR *MONTHS!*
BE SAFE, KAMANDI!

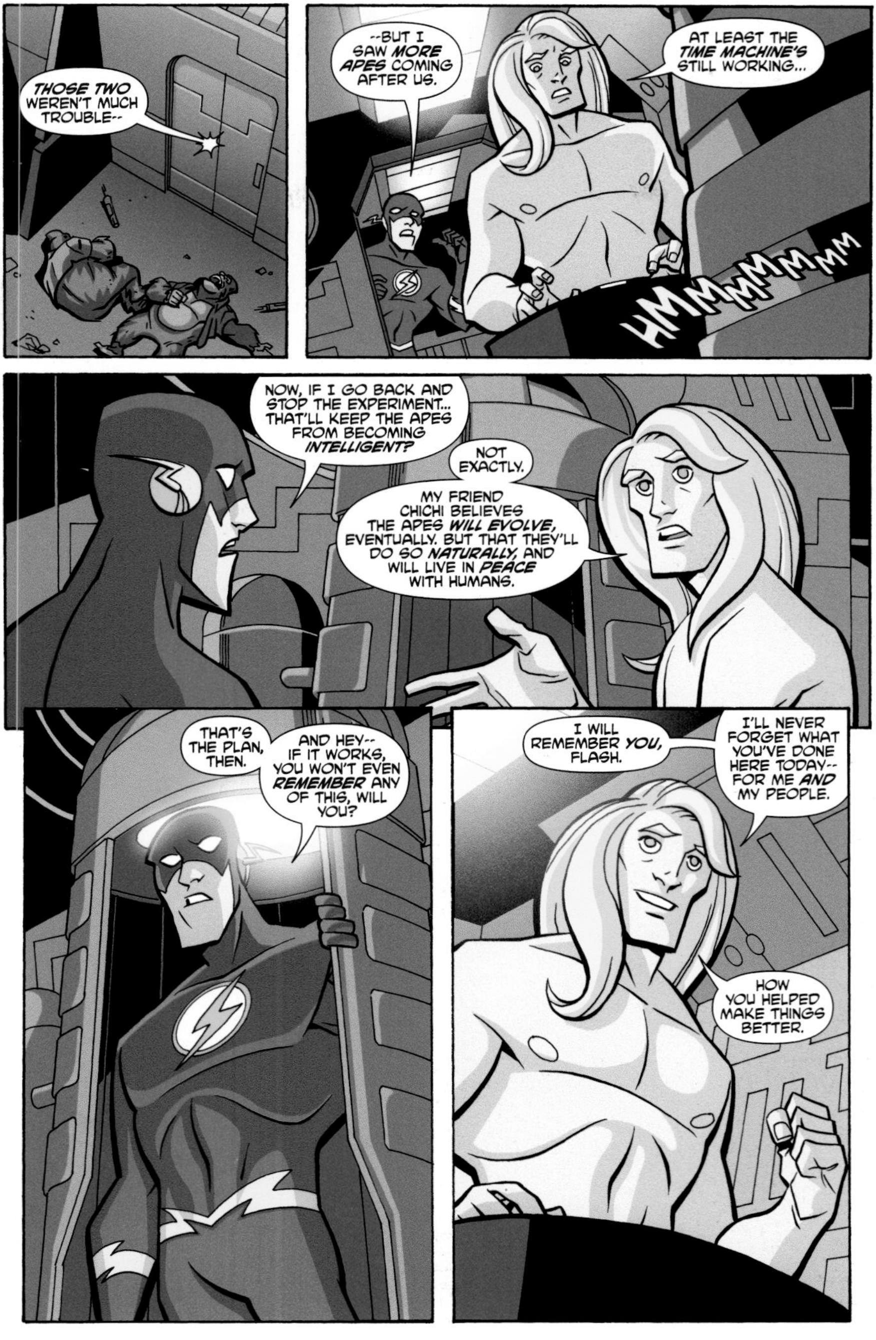
THOSE TWO WEREN'T MUCH TROUBLE--
--BUT I SAW MORE APES COMING AFTER US.
AT LEAST THE TIME MACHINE'S STILL WORKING...
HMMMMMMMMM
NOW, IF I GO BACK AND STOP THE EXPERIMENT... THAT'LL KEEP THE APES FROM BECOMING INTELLIGENT?
NOT EXACTLY.
MY FRIEND CHICHI BELIEVES THE APES WILL EVOLVE, EVENTUALLY. BUT THAT THEY'LL DO SO NATURALLY, AND WILL LIVE IN PEACE WITH HUMANS.
THAT'S THE PLAN, THEN.
AND HEY-- IF IT WORKS, YOU WON'T EVEN REMEMBER ANY OF THIS, WILL YOU?
I WILL REMEMBER YOU, FLASH.
I'LL NEVER FORGET WHAT YOU'VE DONE HERE TODAY-- FOR ME AND MY PEOPLE.
HOW YOU HELPED MAKE THINGS BETTER.

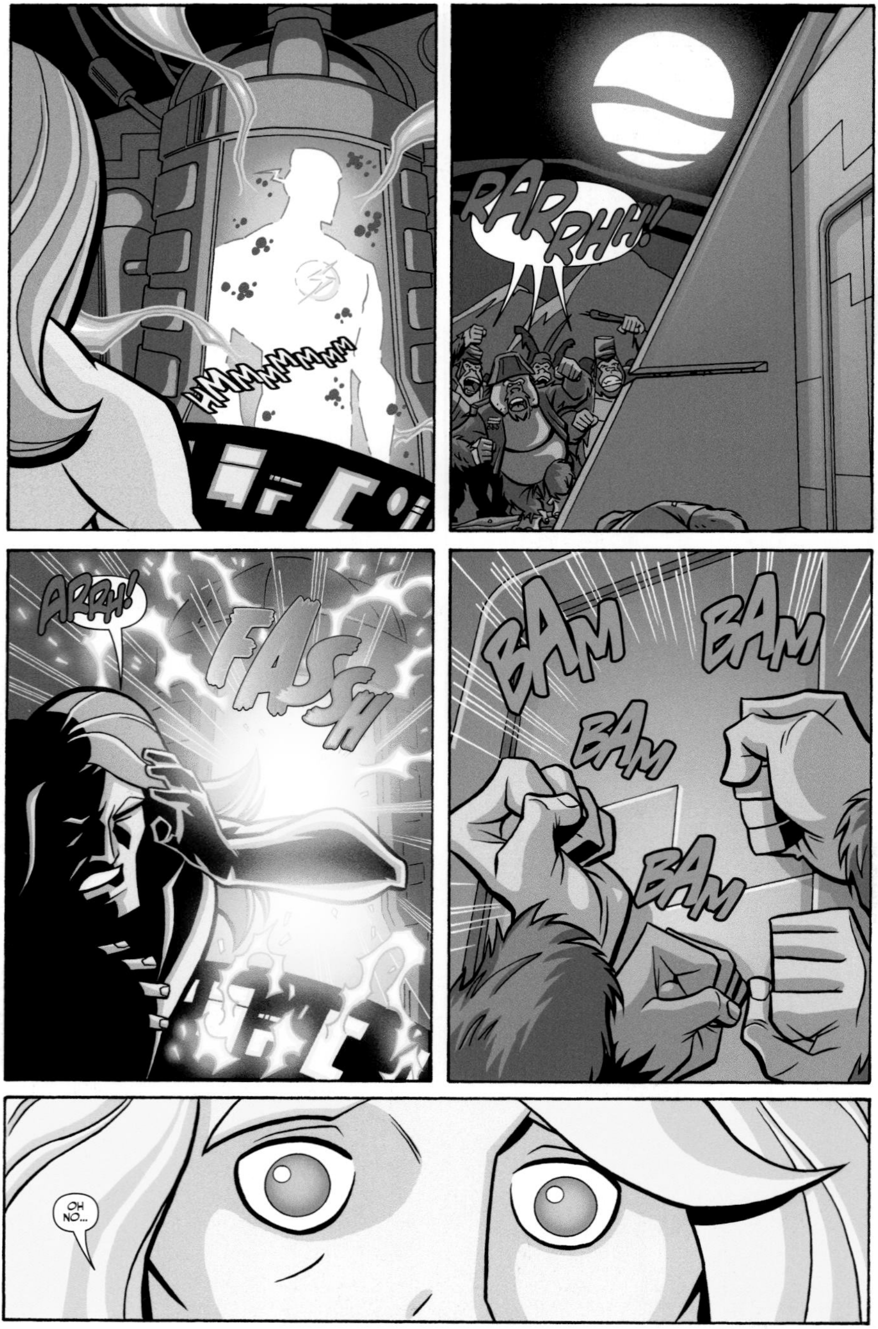
HMMMMMMMM
RARRHH!
ARRH!
FASSH
BAM
BAM
BAM
BAM
OH NO...

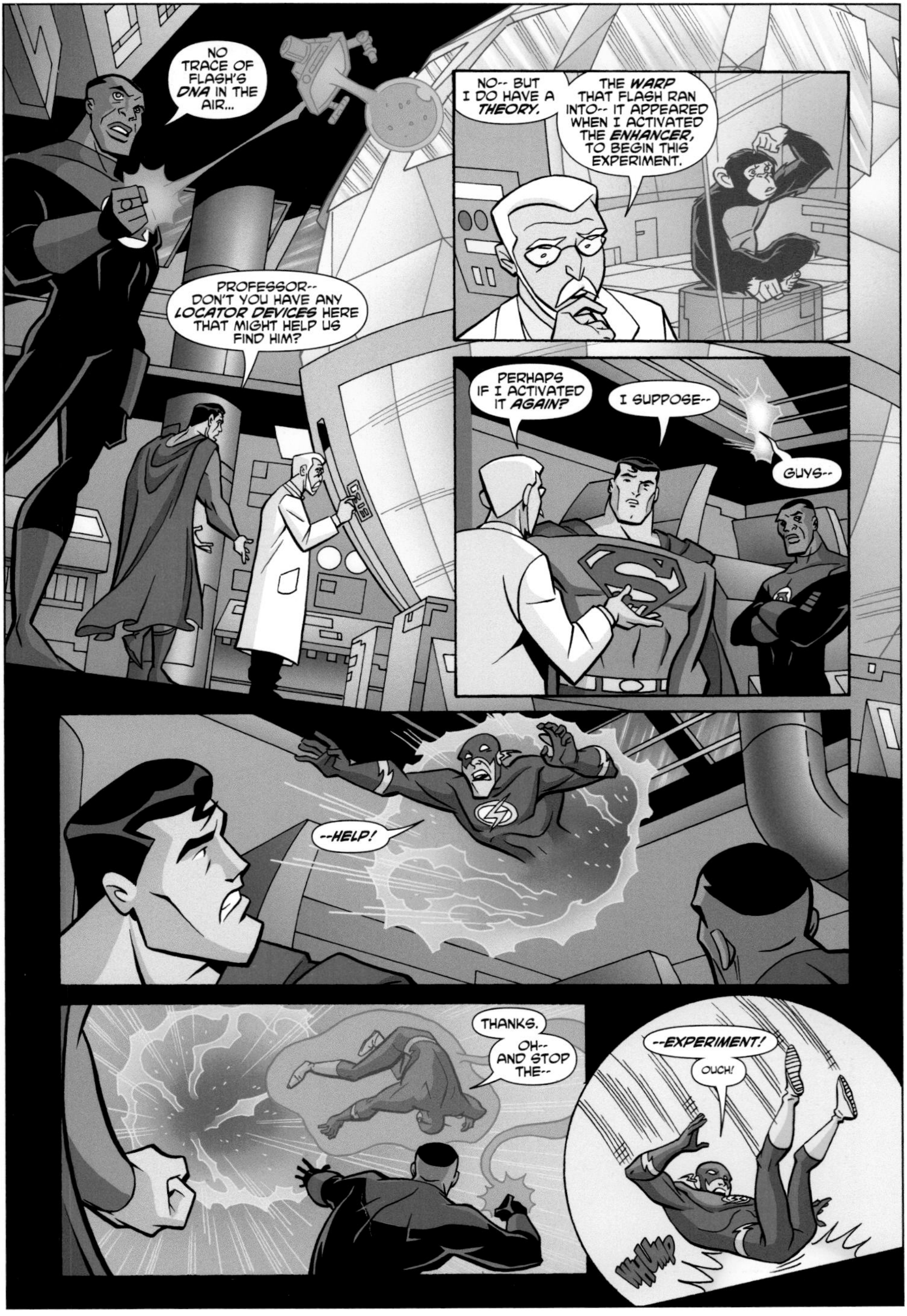

NO TRACE OF FLASH'S *DNA* IN THE AIR...
PROFESSOR-- DON'T YOU HAVE ANY *LOCATOR DEVICES* HERE THAT MIGHT HELP US FIND HIM?
NO-- BUT I DO HAVE A *THEORY.*
THE *WARP* THAT FLASH RAN INTO-- IT APPEARED WHEN I ACTIVATED THE *ENHANCER,* TO BEGIN THIS EXPERIMENT.
PERHAPS IF I ACTIVATED IT *AGAIN?*
I SUPPOSE--
GUYS--
--HELP!
THANKS.
OH-- AND STOP THE--
--EXPERIMENT!
OUCH!
WHUMP

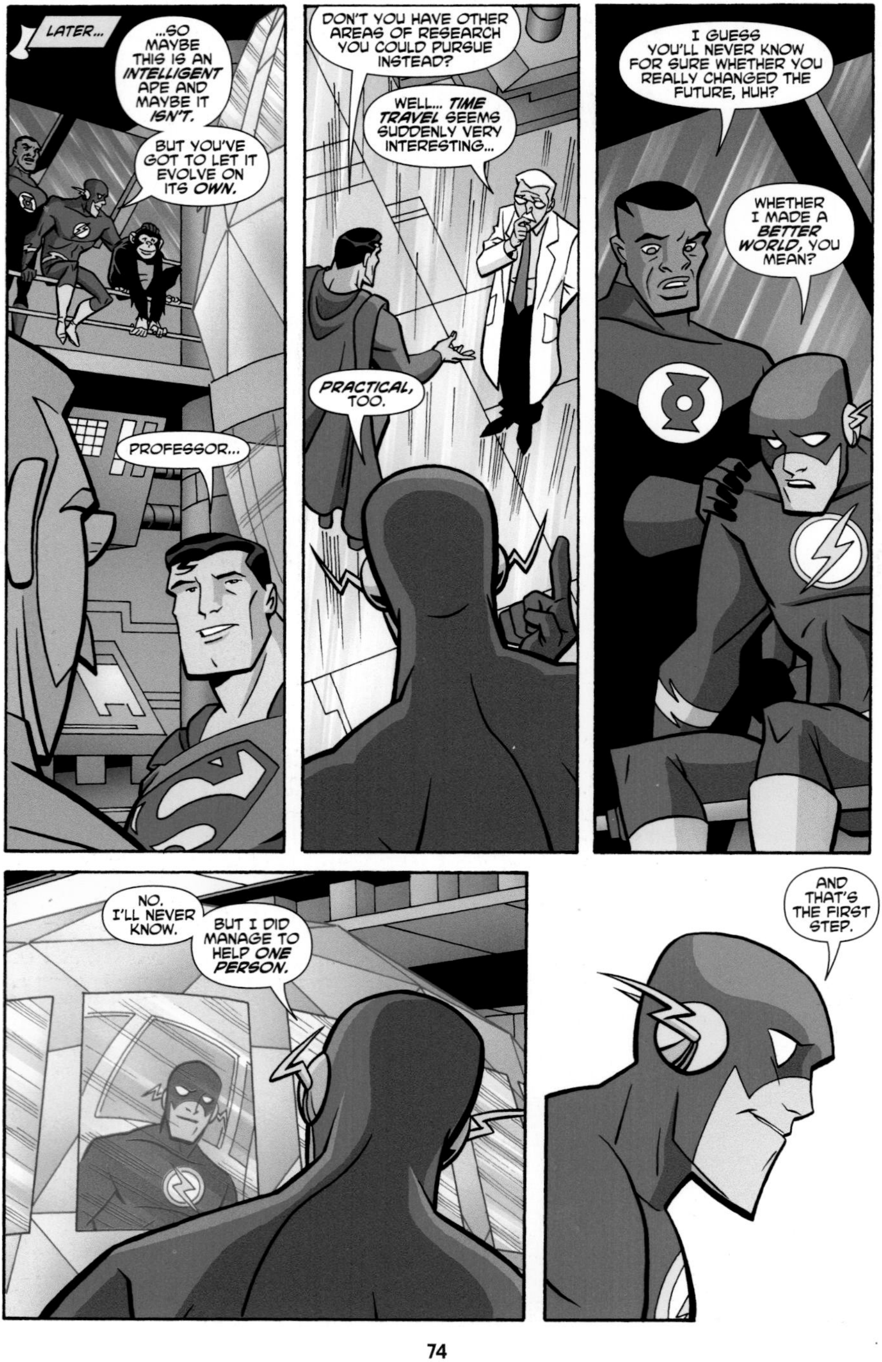
LATER...
...SO MAYBE THIS IS AN INTELLIGENT APE AND MAYBE IT ISN'T.
BUT YOU'VE GOT TO LET IT EVOLVE ON ITS OWN.
PROFESSOR...
DON'T YOU HAVE OTHER AREAS OF RESEARCH YOU COULD PURSUE INSTEAD?
WELL... TIME TRAVEL SEEMS SUDDENLY VERY INTERESTING...
PRACTICAL, TOO.
I GUESS YOU'LL NEVER KNOW FOR SURE WHETHER YOU REALLY CHANGED THE FUTURE, HUH?
WHETHER I MADE A BETTER WORLD, YOU MEAN?
NO. I'LL NEVER KNOW.
BUT I DID MANAGE TO HELP ONE PERSON.
AND THAT'S THE FIRST STEP.

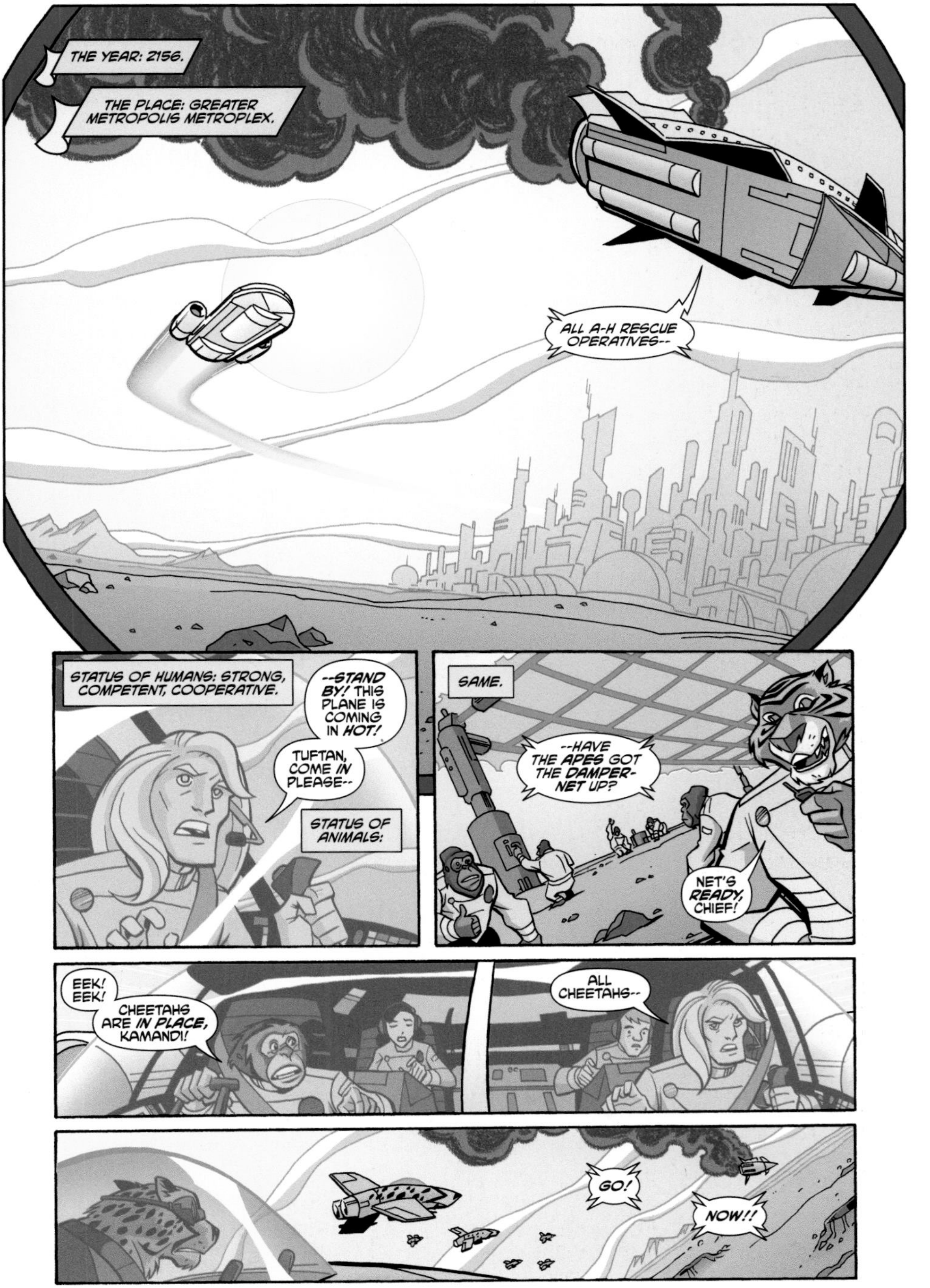
THE YEAR: 2156.
THE PLACE: GREATER METROPOLIS METROPLEX.
ALL A-H RESCUE OPERATIVES--
STATUS OF HUMANS: STRONG, COMPETENT, COOPERATIVE.
--STAND BY! THIS PLANE IS COMING IN HOT!
TUFTAN, COME IN PLEASE--
STATUS OF ANIMALS:
SAME.
--HAVE THE APES GOT THE DAMPER-NET UP?
NET'S READY, CHIEF!
EEK! EEK!
CHEETAHS ARE IN PLACE, KAMANDI!
ALL CHEETAHS--
GO!
NOW!!

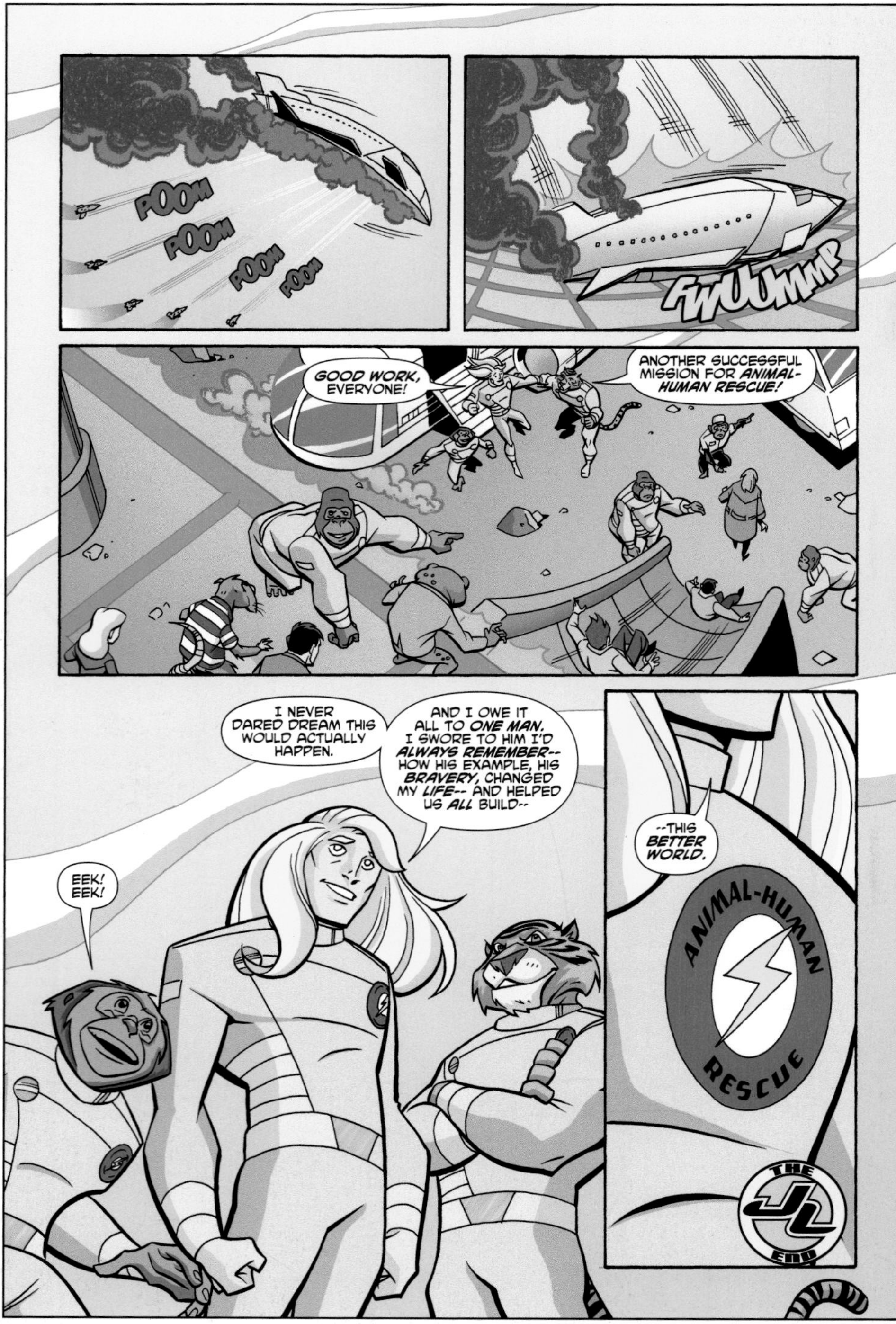
POOM
POOM
POOM
POOM
FWUUMMP
GOOD WORK, EVERYONE!
ANOTHER SUCCESSFUL MISSION FOR ANIMAL-HUMAN RESCUE!
I NEVER DARED DREAM THIS WOULD ACTUALLY HAPPEN.
AND I OWE IT ALL TO ONE MAN. I SWORE TO HIM I'D ALWAYS REMEMBER-- HOW HIS EXAMPLE, HIS BRAVERY, CHANGED MY LIFE-- AND HELPED US ALL BUILD--
EEK! EEK!
--THIS BETTER WORLD.
ANIMAL-HUMAN RESCUE
THE END

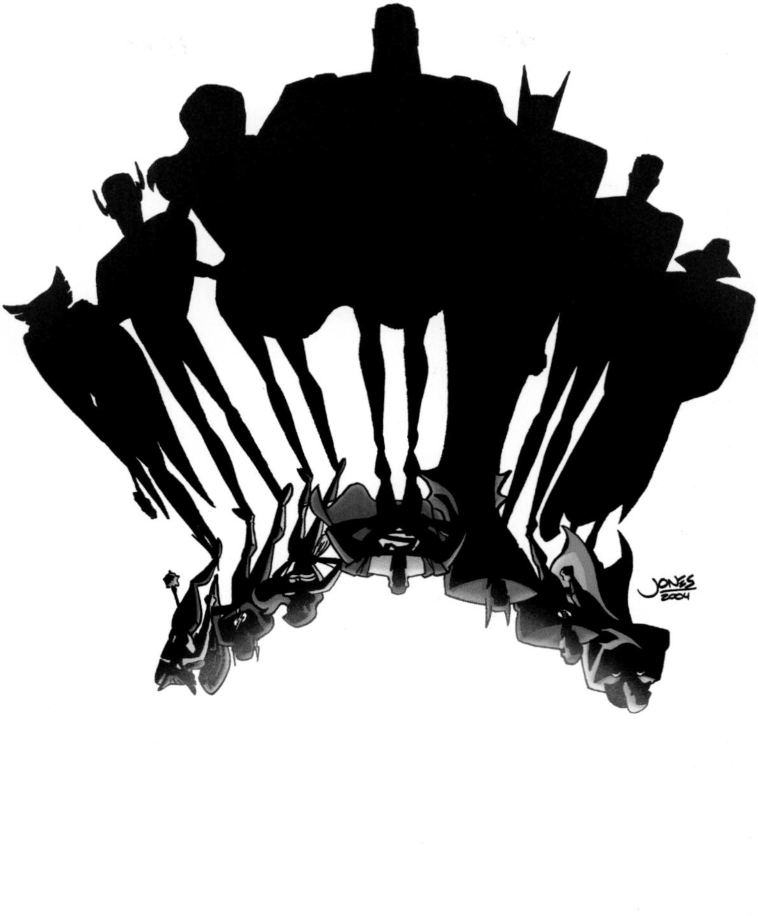
JONES
2004

CHAPTER 4: PAST TENSE

JUSTICE LEAGUE UNLIMITED

COVER ART BY CHRIS JONES

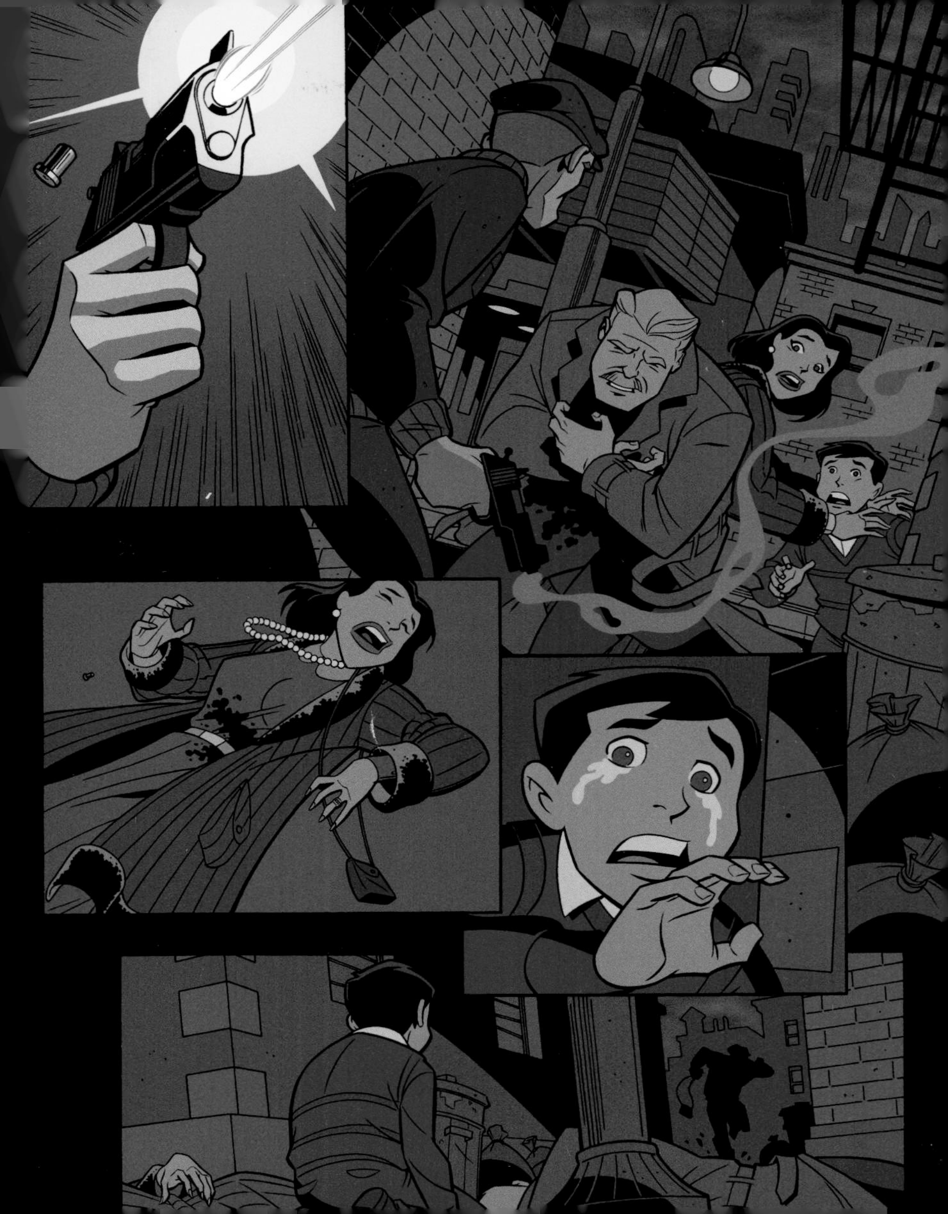

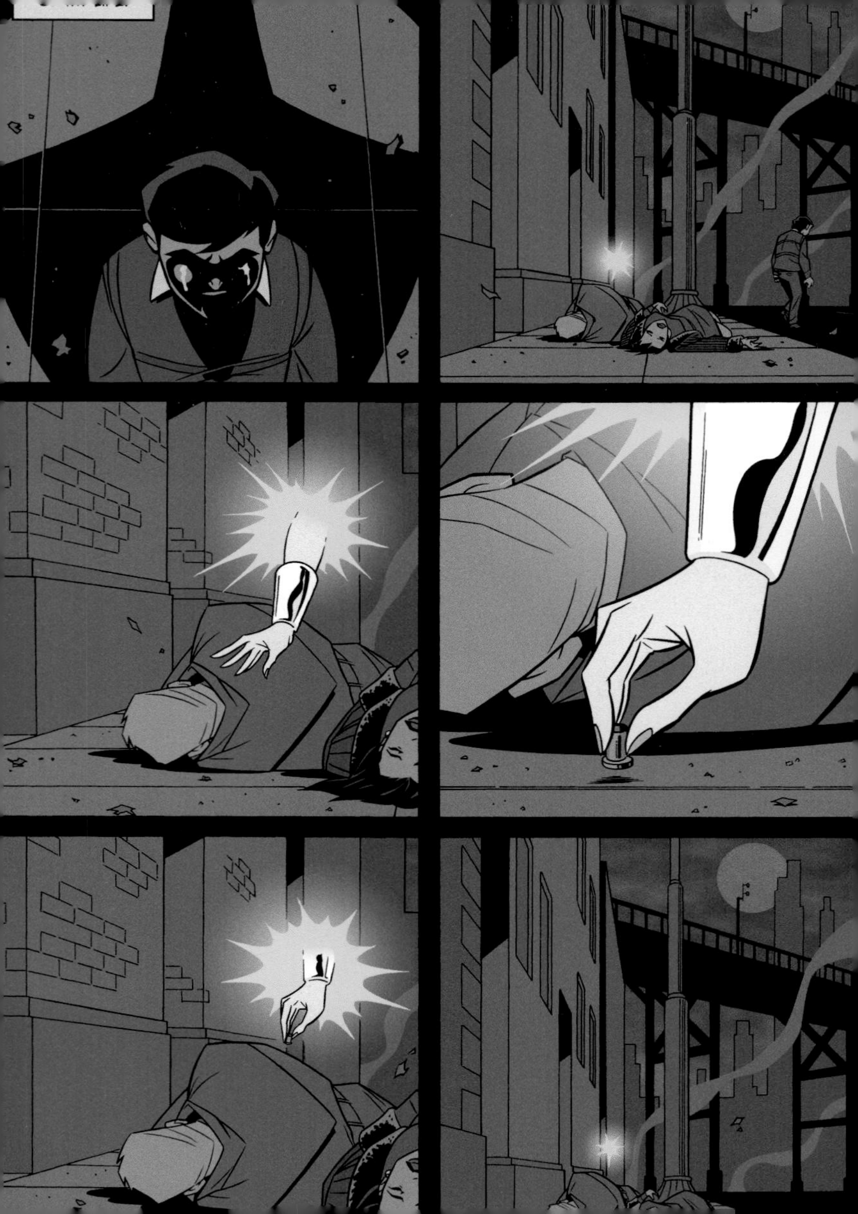

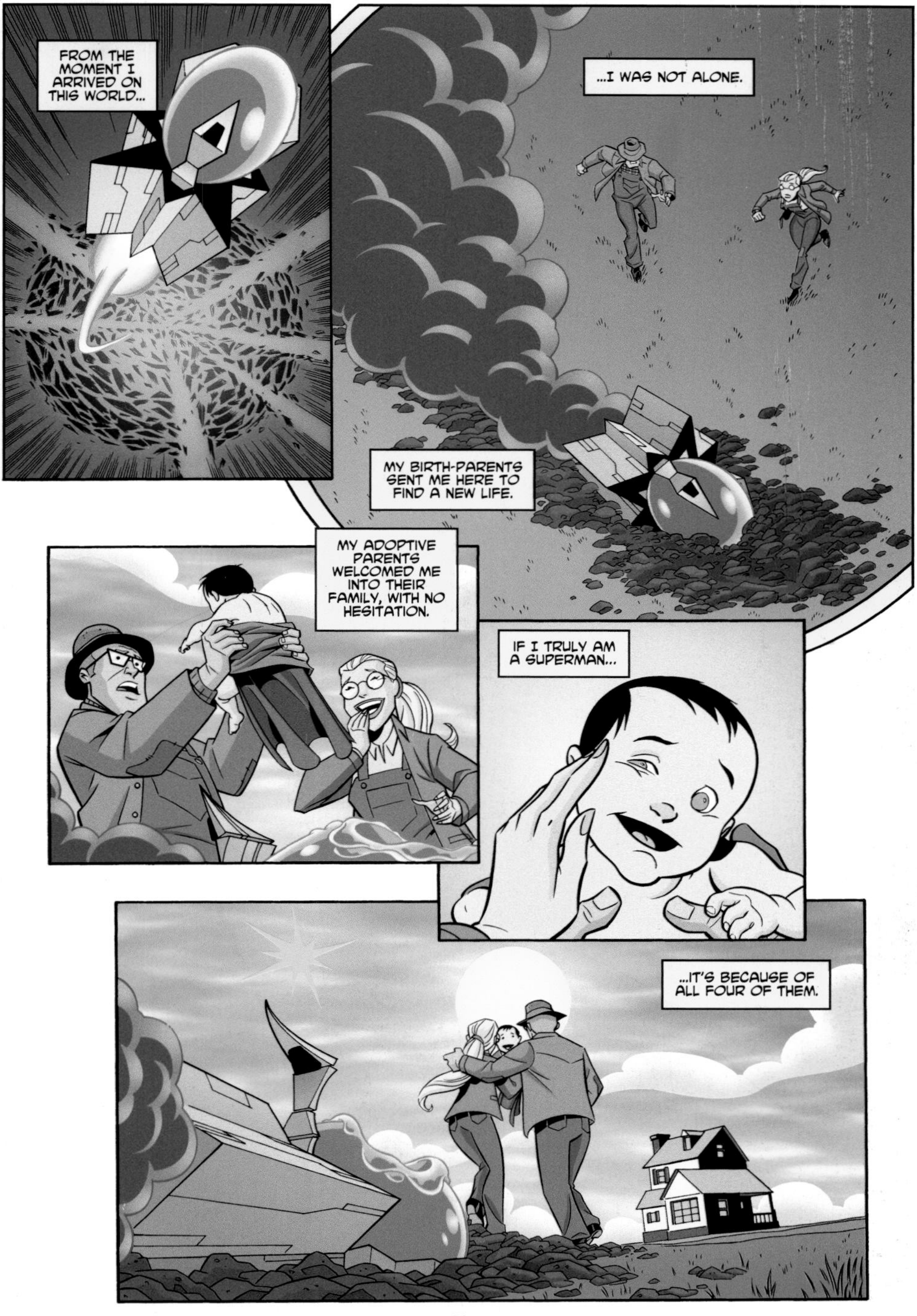
FROM THE MOMENT I ARRIVED ON THIS WORLD...
...I WAS NOT ALONE.
MY BIRTH-PARENTS SENT ME HERE TO FIND A NEW LIFE.
MY ADOPTIVE PARENTS WELCOMED ME INTO THEIR FAMILY, WITH NO HESITATION.
IF I TRULY AM A SUPERMAN...
...IT'S BECAUSE OF ALL FOUR OF THEM.

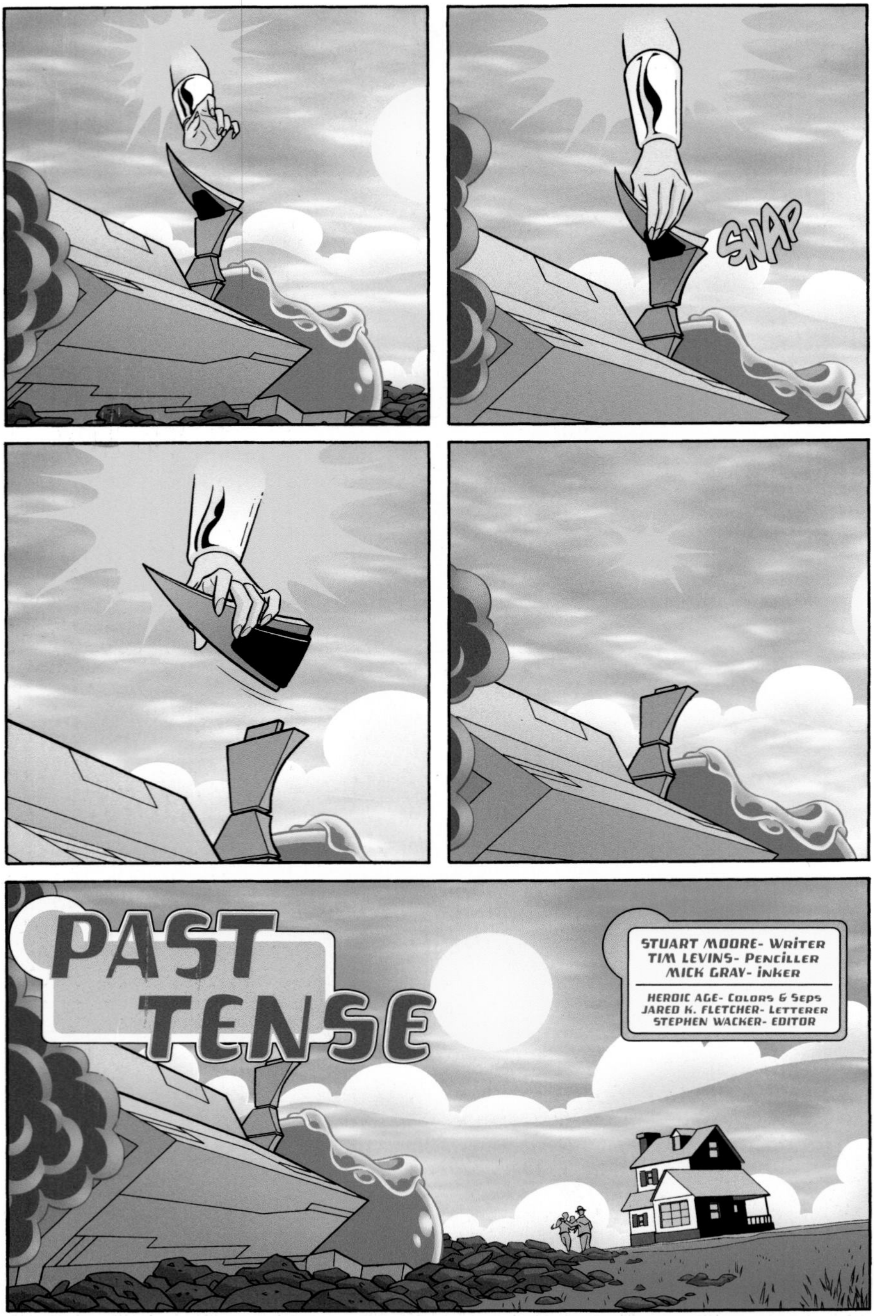
SNAP
PAST TENSE
STUART MOORE- Writer
TIM LEVINS- Penciller
MICK GRAY- inker
HEROIC AGE- Colors & Seps
JARED K. FLETCHER- Letterer
STEPHEN WACKER- EDITOR

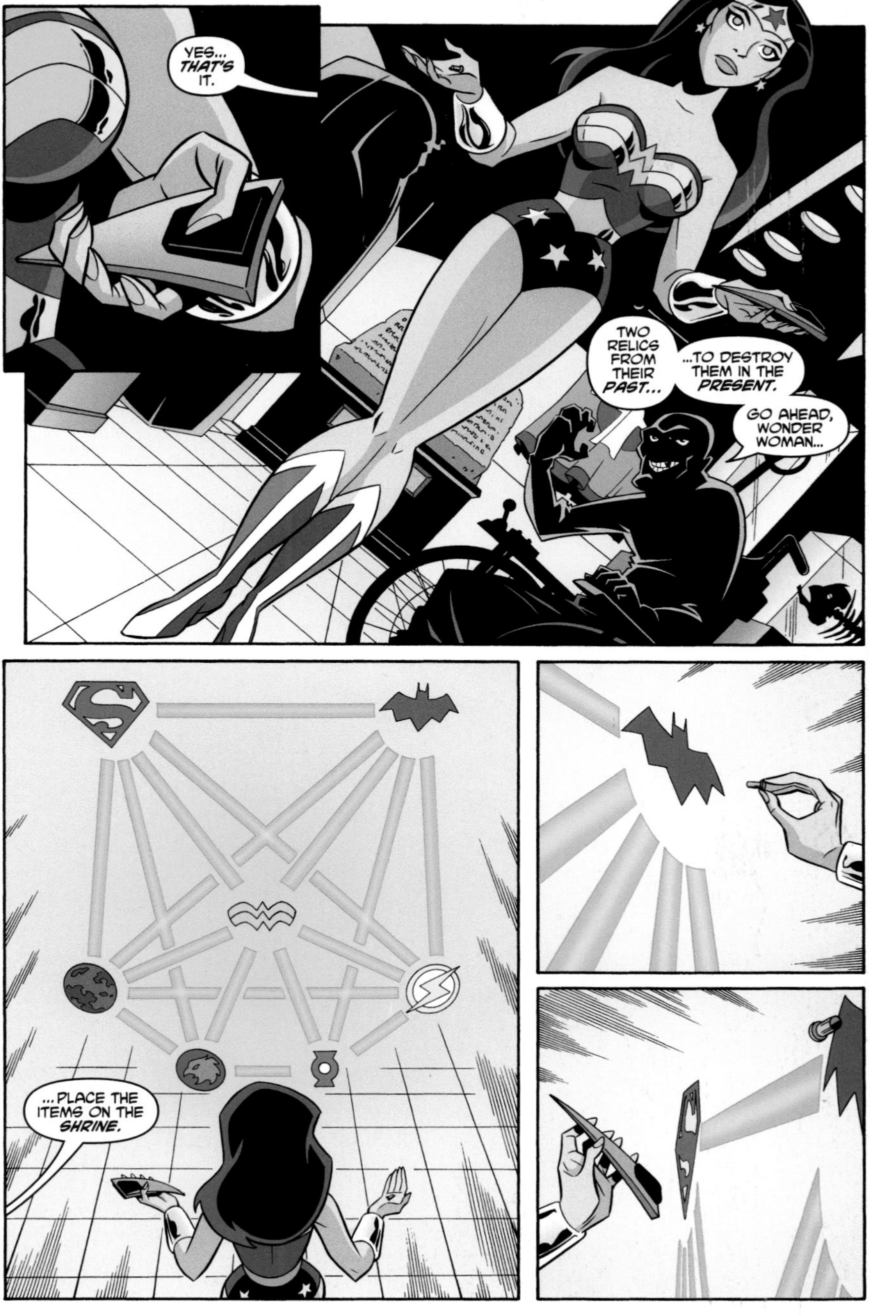
YES... THAT'S IT.
TWO RELICS FROM THEIR PAST...
...TO DESTROY THEM IN THE PRESENT.
GO AHEAD, WONDER WOMAN...
...PLACE THE ITEMS ON THE SHRINE.

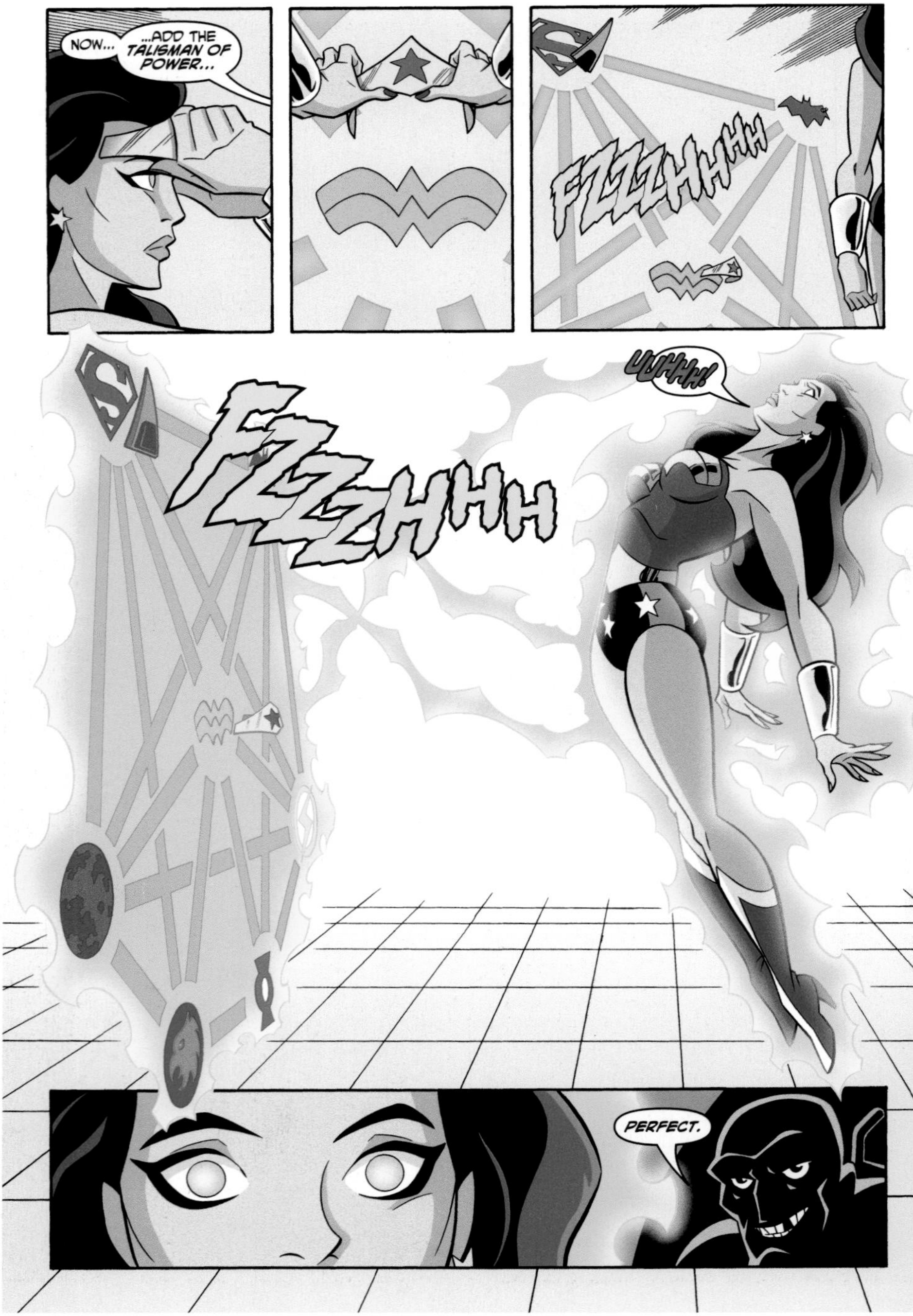
NOW...
...ADD THE TALISMAN OF POWER...
FZZZHHHH
FZZZHHHH
UUHHH!
PERFECT.

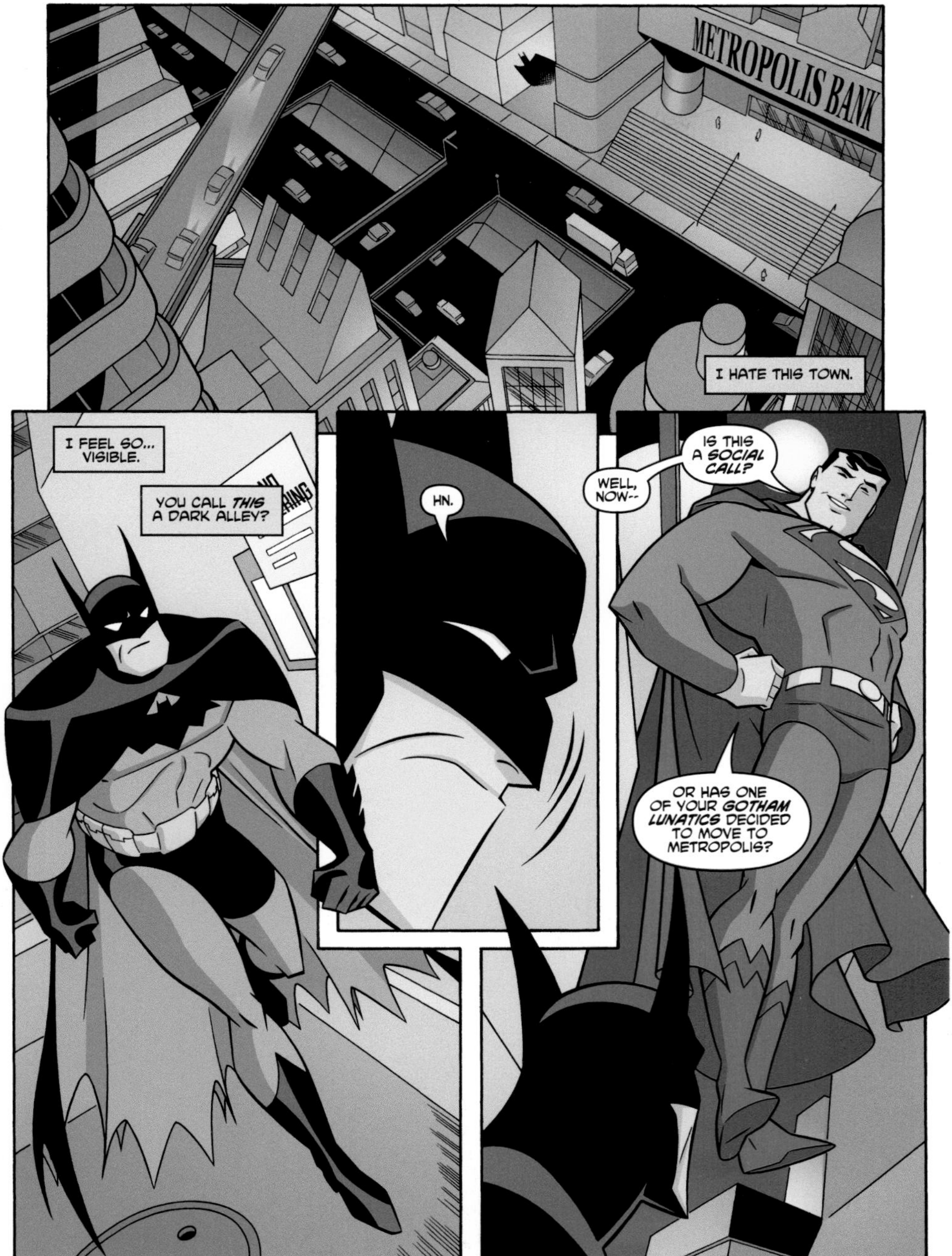
METROPOLIS BANK
I HATE THIS TOWN.
I FEEL SO... VISIBLE.
YOU CALL *THIS* A DARK ALLEY?
HN.
WELL, NOW--
IS THIS A *SOCIAL CALL?*
OR HAS ONE OF YOUR *GOTHAM LUNATICS* DECIDED TO MOVE TO METROPOLIS?

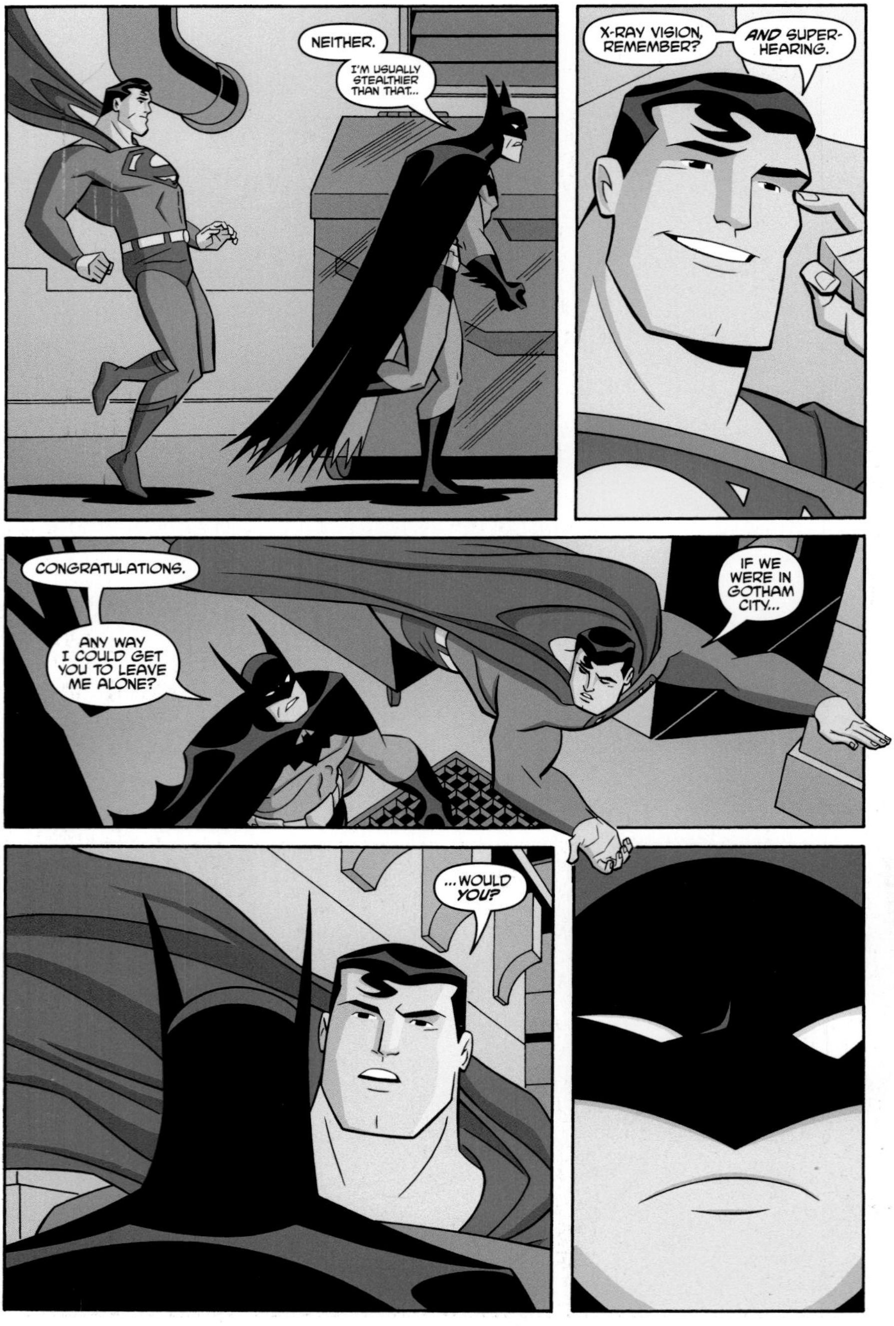
NEITHER.
I'M USUALLY STEALTHIER THAN THAT...
X-RAY VISION, REMEMBER?
AND SUPER-HEARING.
CONGRATULATIONS.
ANY WAY I COULD GET YOU TO LEAVE ME ALONE?
IF WE WERE IN GOTHAM CITY...
...WOULD *YOU*?

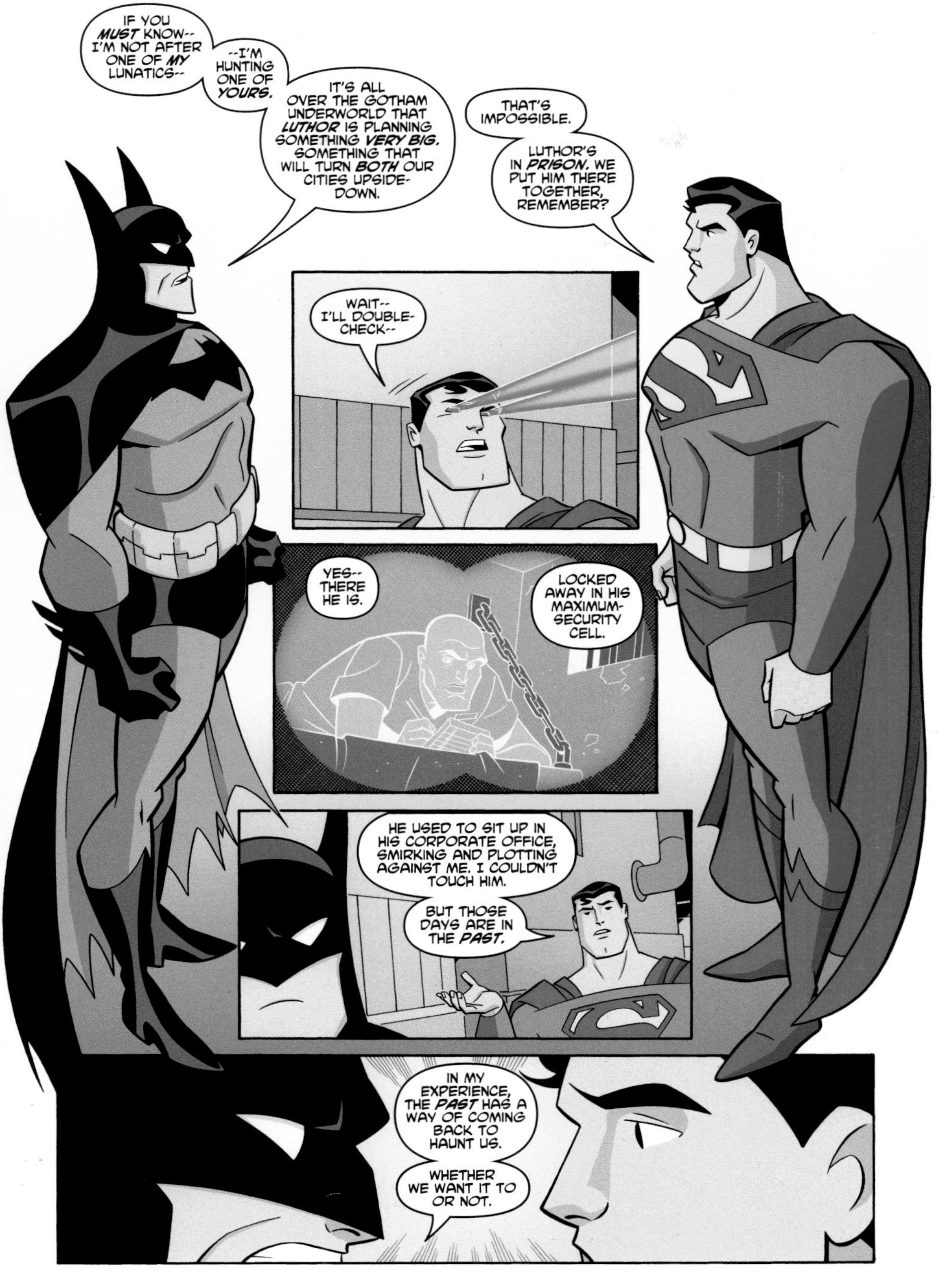
IF YOU MUST KNOW-- I'M NOT AFTER ONE OF MY LUNATICS--
--I'M HUNTING ONE OF YOURS.
IT'S ALL OVER THE GOTHAM UNDERWORLD THAT LUTHOR IS PLANNING SOMETHING VERY BIG. SOMETHING THAT WILL TURN BOTH OUR CITIES UPSIDE-DOWN.
THAT'S IMPOSSIBLE.
LUTHOR'S IN PRISON. WE PUT HIM THERE TOGETHER, REMEMBER?
WAIT-- I'LL DOUBLE-CHECK--
YES-- THERE HE IS.
LOCKED AWAY IN HIS MAXIMUM-SECURITY CELL.
HE USED TO SIT UP IN HIS CORPORATE OFFICE, SMIRKING AND PLOTTING AGAINST ME. I COULDN'T TOUCH HIM.
BUT THOSE DAYS ARE IN THE PAST.
IN MY EXPERIENCE, THE PAST HAS A WAY OF COMING BACK TO HAUNT US.
WHETHER WE WANT IT TO OR NOT.

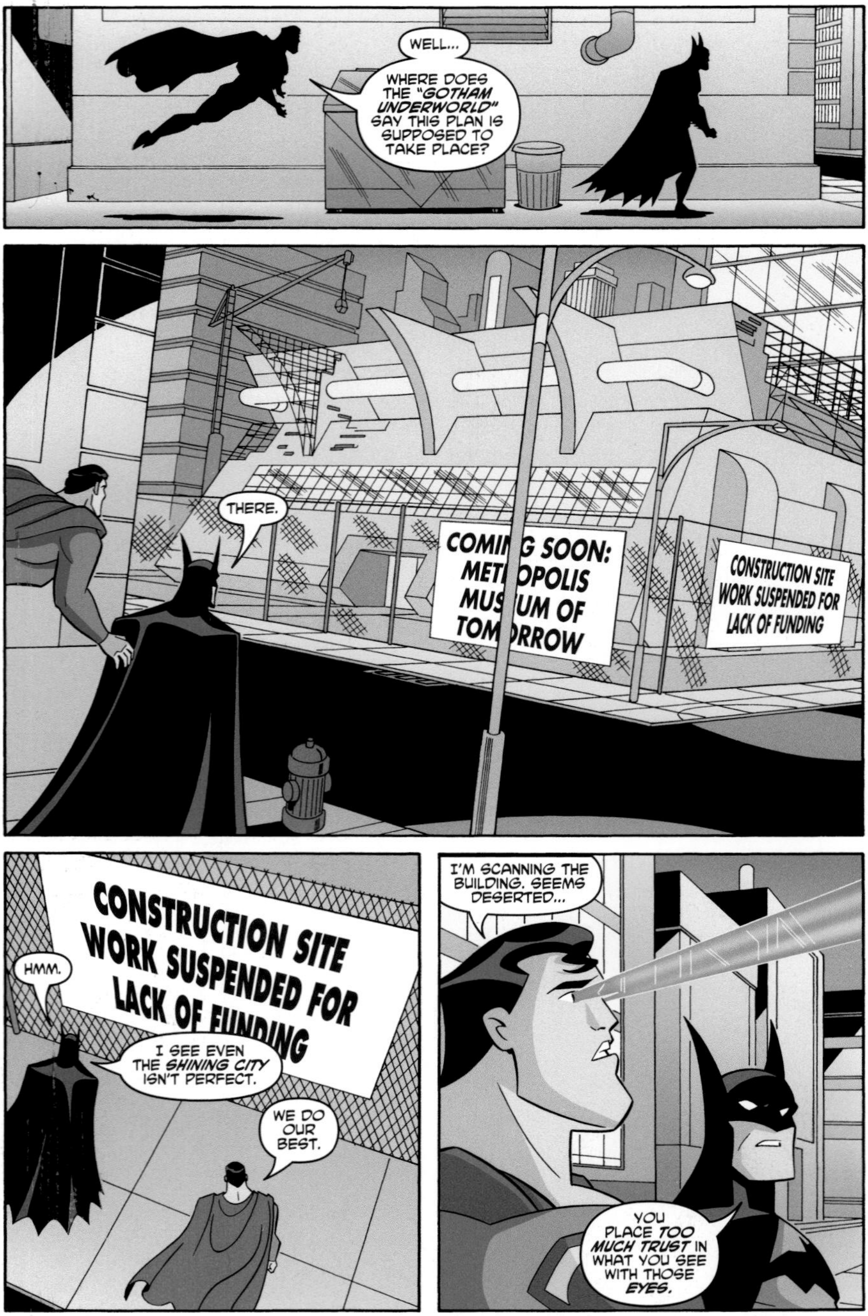
WELL...
WHERE DOES THE "GOTHAM UNDERWORLD" SAY THIS PLAN IS SUPPOSED TO TAKE PLACE?
THERE.
COMING SOON: METROPOLIS MUSEUM OF TOMORROW
CONSTRUCTION SITE WORK SUSPENDED FOR LACK OF FUNDING
CONSTRUCTION SITE WORK SUSPENDED FOR LACK OF FUNDING
HMM.
I SEE EVEN THE SHINING CITY ISN'T PERFECT.
WE DO OUR BEST.
I'M SCANNING THE BUILDING. SEEMS DESERTED...
YOU PLACE TOO MUCH TRUST IN WHAT YOU SEE WITH THOSE EYES.

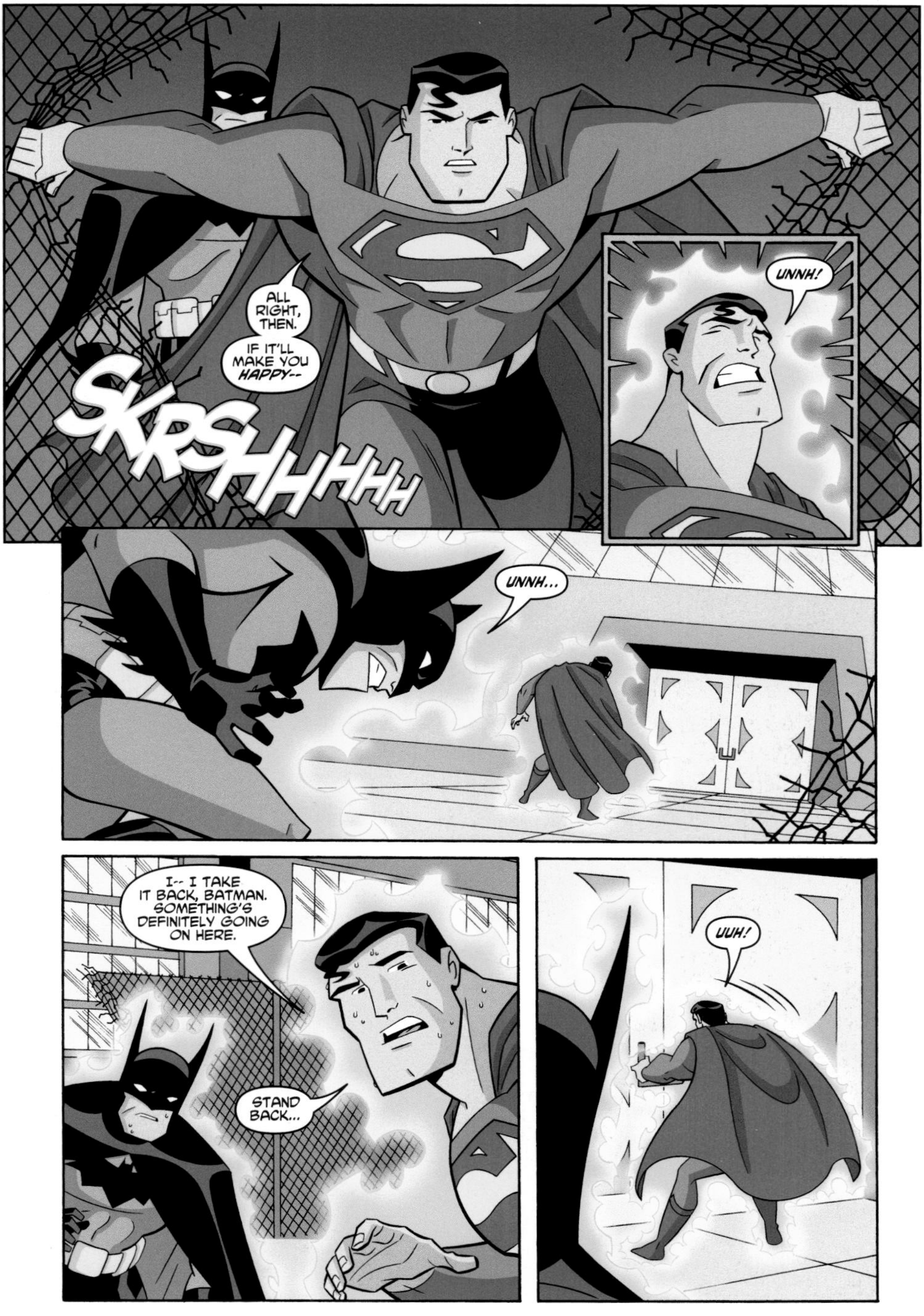
ALL RIGHT, THEN.
IF IT'LL MAKE YOU HAPPY--
SKRSHHHHH
UNNH!
UNNH...
I-- I TAKE IT BACK, BATMAN. SOMETHING'S DEFINITELY GOING ON HERE.
STAND BACK...
UUH!

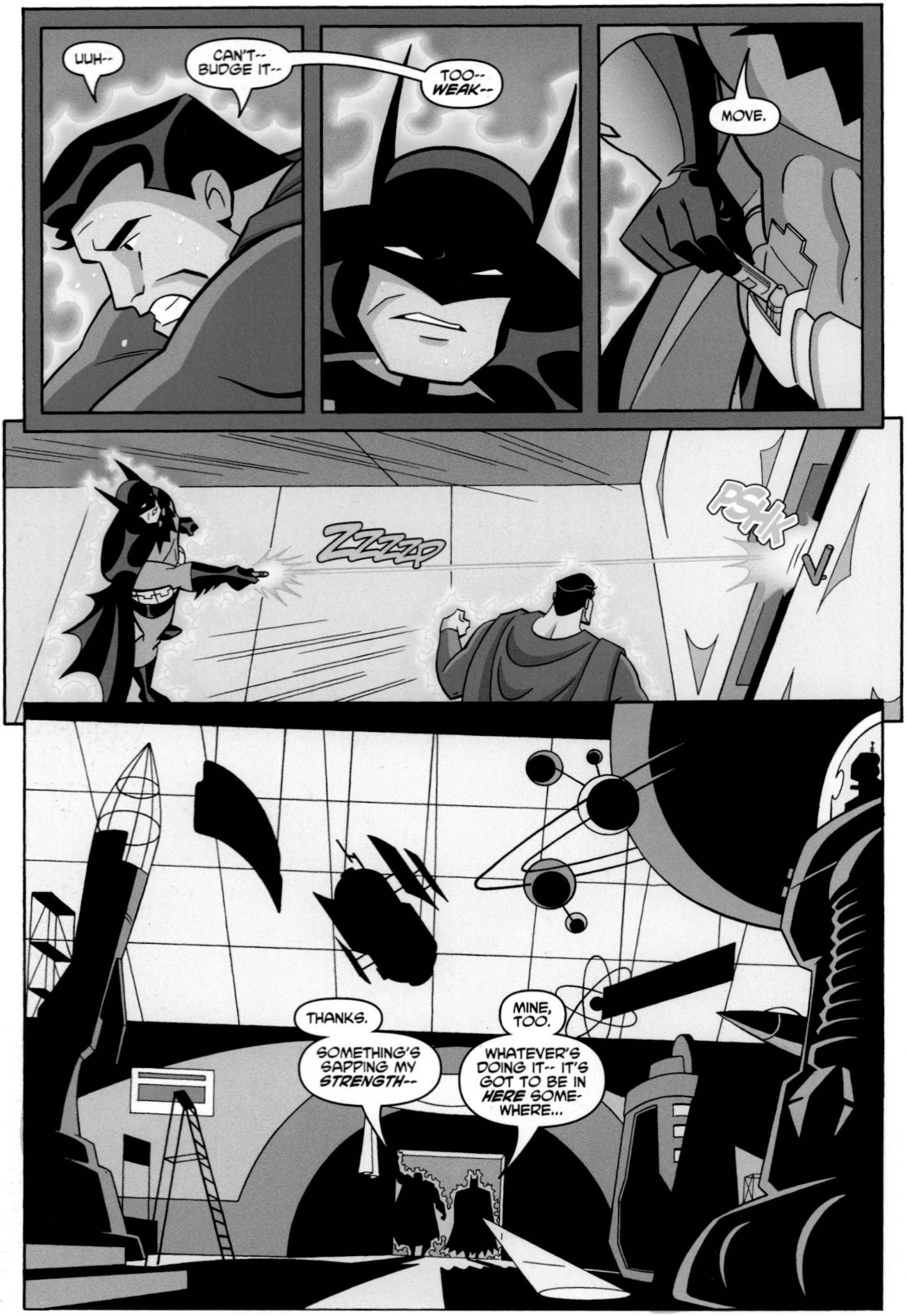
UUH--
CAN'T-- BUDGE IT--
TOO-- WEAK--
MOVE.
ZZZZAP
PSHK
THANKS.
SOMETHING'S SAPPING MY STRENGTH--
MINE, TOO.
WHATEVER'S DOING IT-- IT'S GOT TO BE IN HERE SOME-WHERE...

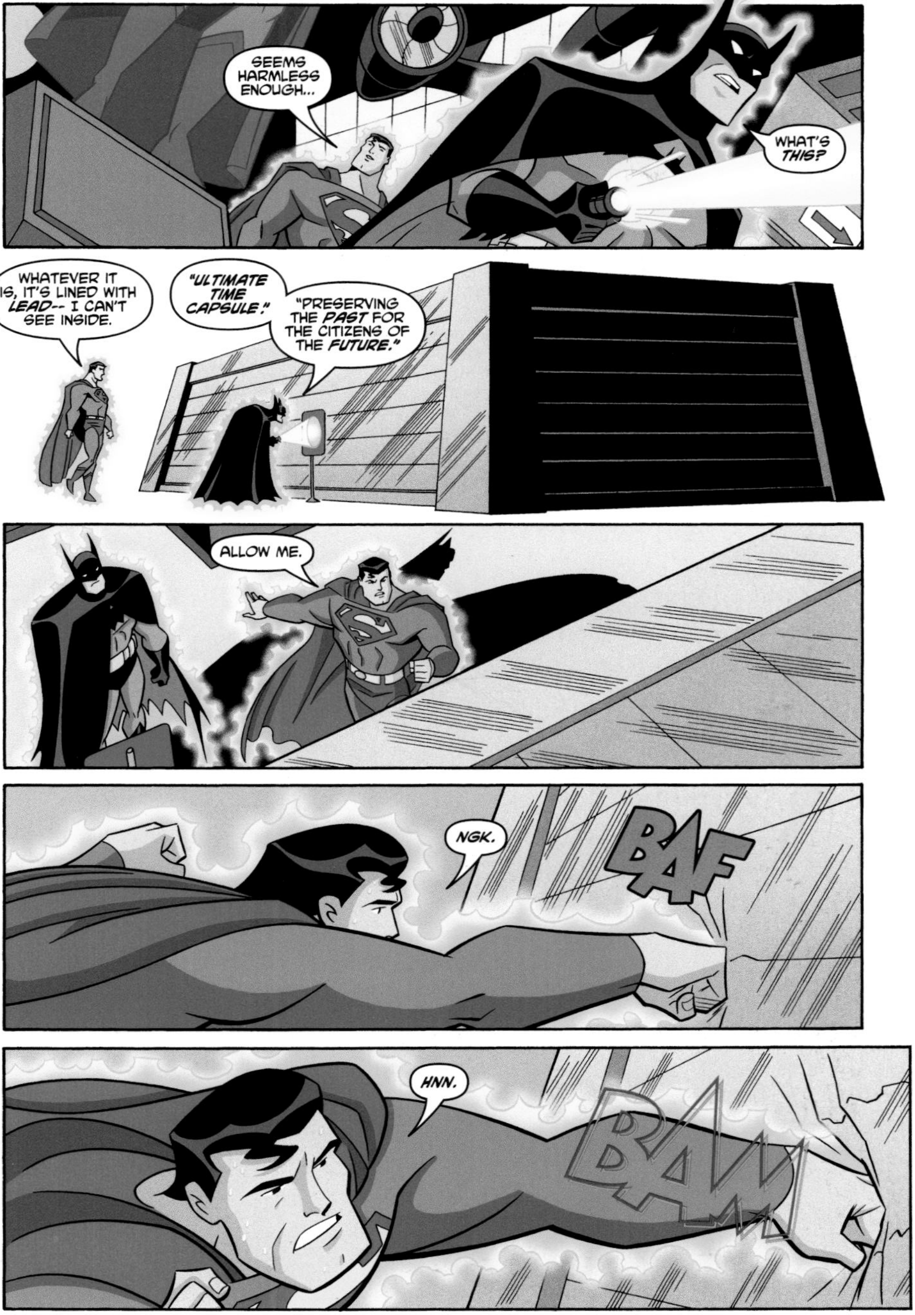
SEEMS HARMLESS ENOUGH...
WHAT'S *THIS?*
WHATEVER IT IS, IT'S LINED WITH *LEAD*-- I CAN'T SEE INSIDE.
"ULTIMATE TIME CAPSULE."
"PRESERVING THE *PAST* FOR THE CITIZENS OF THE *FUTURE.*"
ALLOW ME.
NGK.
BAF
HNN.
BAM

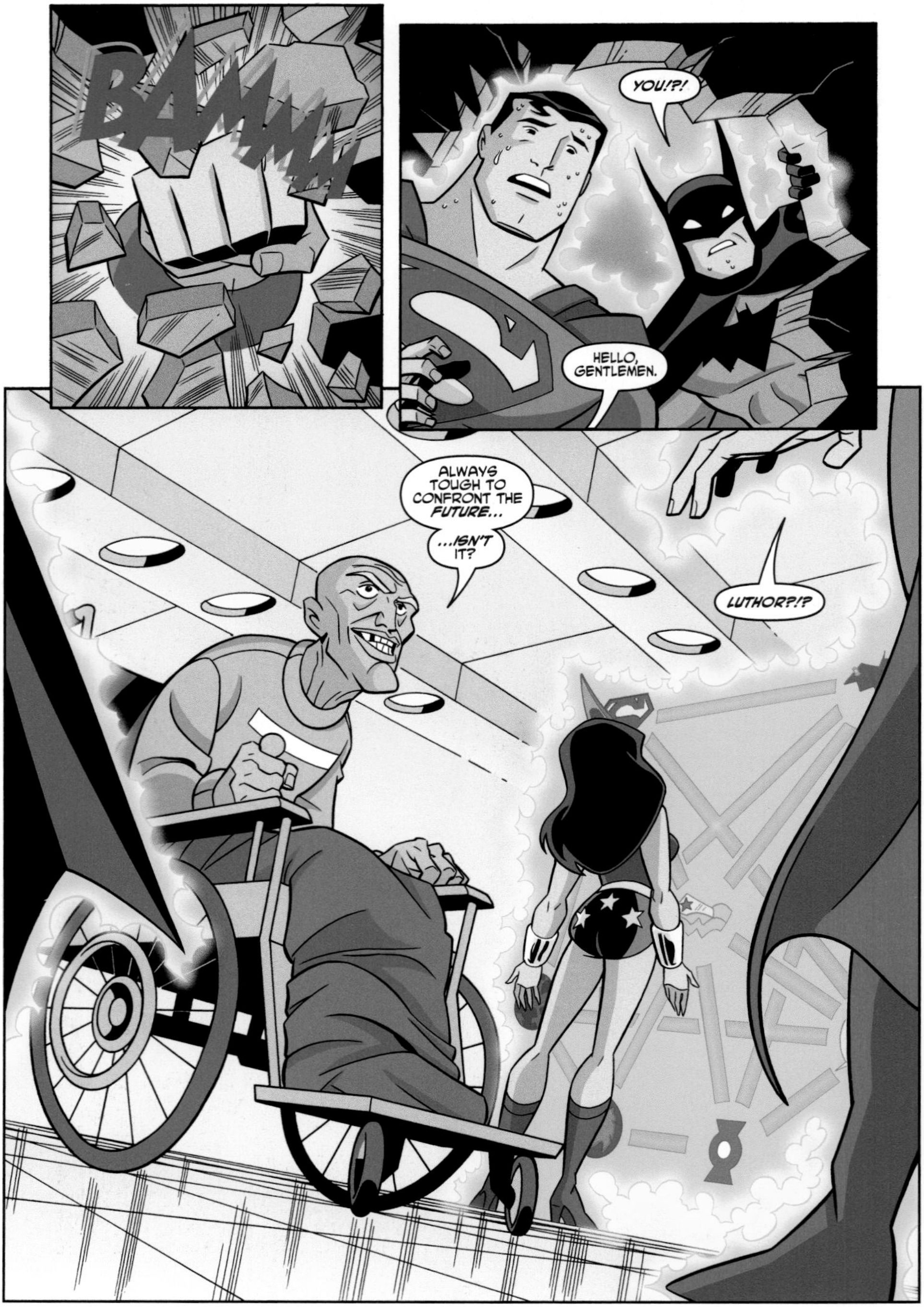
BAMMM
YOU!?!
HELLO, GENTLEMEN.
ALWAYS TOUGH TO CONFRONT THE FUTURE...
...ISN'T IT?
LUTHOR?!?

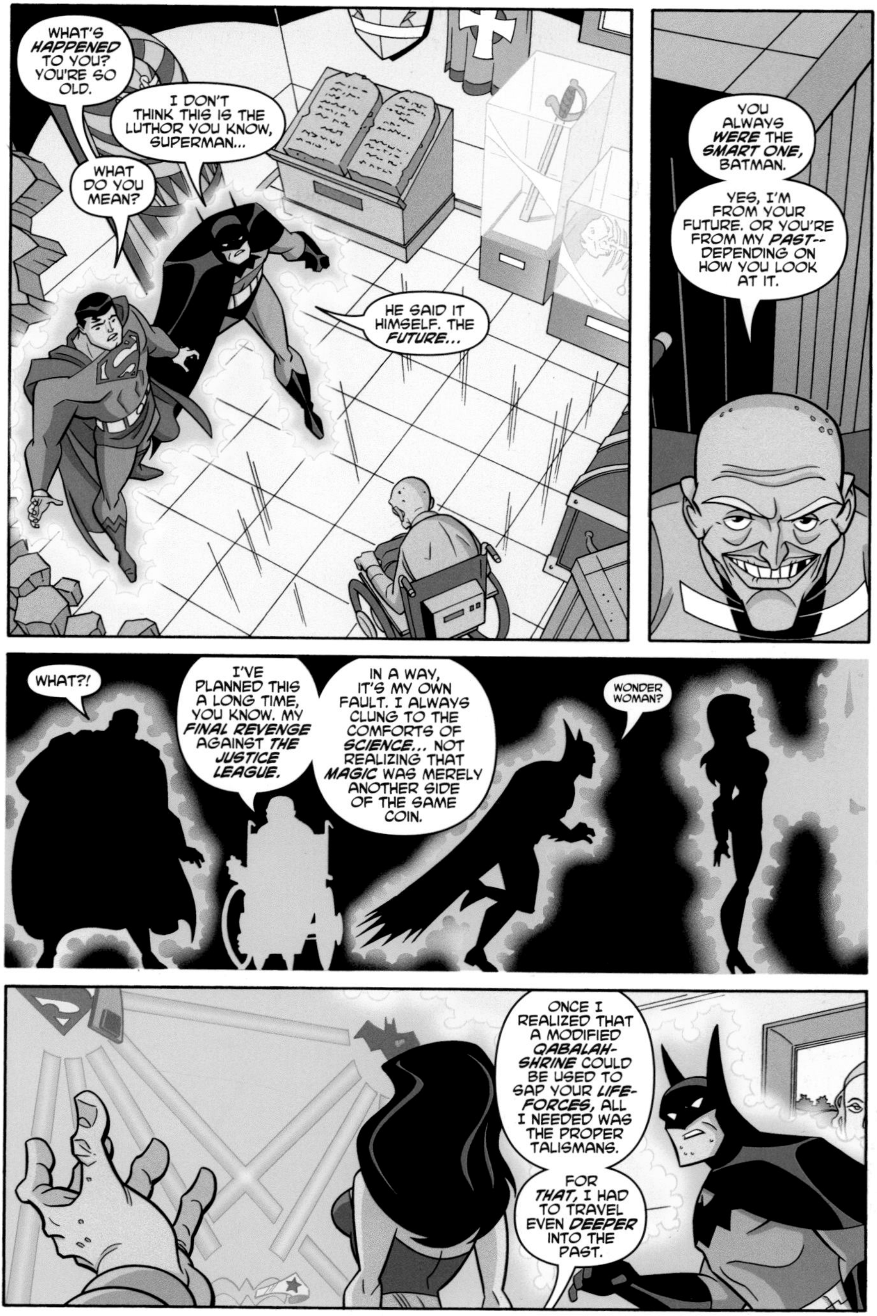
WHAT'S HAPPENED TO YOU? YOU'RE SO OLD.
I DON'T THINK THIS IS THE LUTHOR YOU KNOW, SUPERMAN...
WHAT DO YOU MEAN?
HE SAID IT HIMSELF. THE FUTURE...
YOU ALWAYS WERE THE SMART ONE, BATMAN.
YES, I'M FROM YOUR FUTURE. OR YOU'RE FROM MY PAST-- DEPENDING ON HOW YOU LOOK AT IT.
WHAT?!
I'VE PLANNED THIS A LONG TIME, YOU KNOW. MY FINAL REVENGE AGAINST THE JUSTICE LEAGUE.
IN A WAY, IT'S MY OWN FAULT. I ALWAYS CLUNG TO THE COMFORTS OF SCIENCE... NOT REALIZING THAT MAGIC WAS MERELY ANOTHER SIDE OF THE SAME COIN.
WONDER WOMAN?
ONCE I REALIZED THAT A MODIFIED QABALAH-SHRINE COULD BE USED TO SAP YOUR LIFE-FORCES, ALL I NEEDED WAS THE PROPER TALISMANS.
FOR THAT, I HAD TO TRAVEL EVEN DEEPER INTO THE PAST.

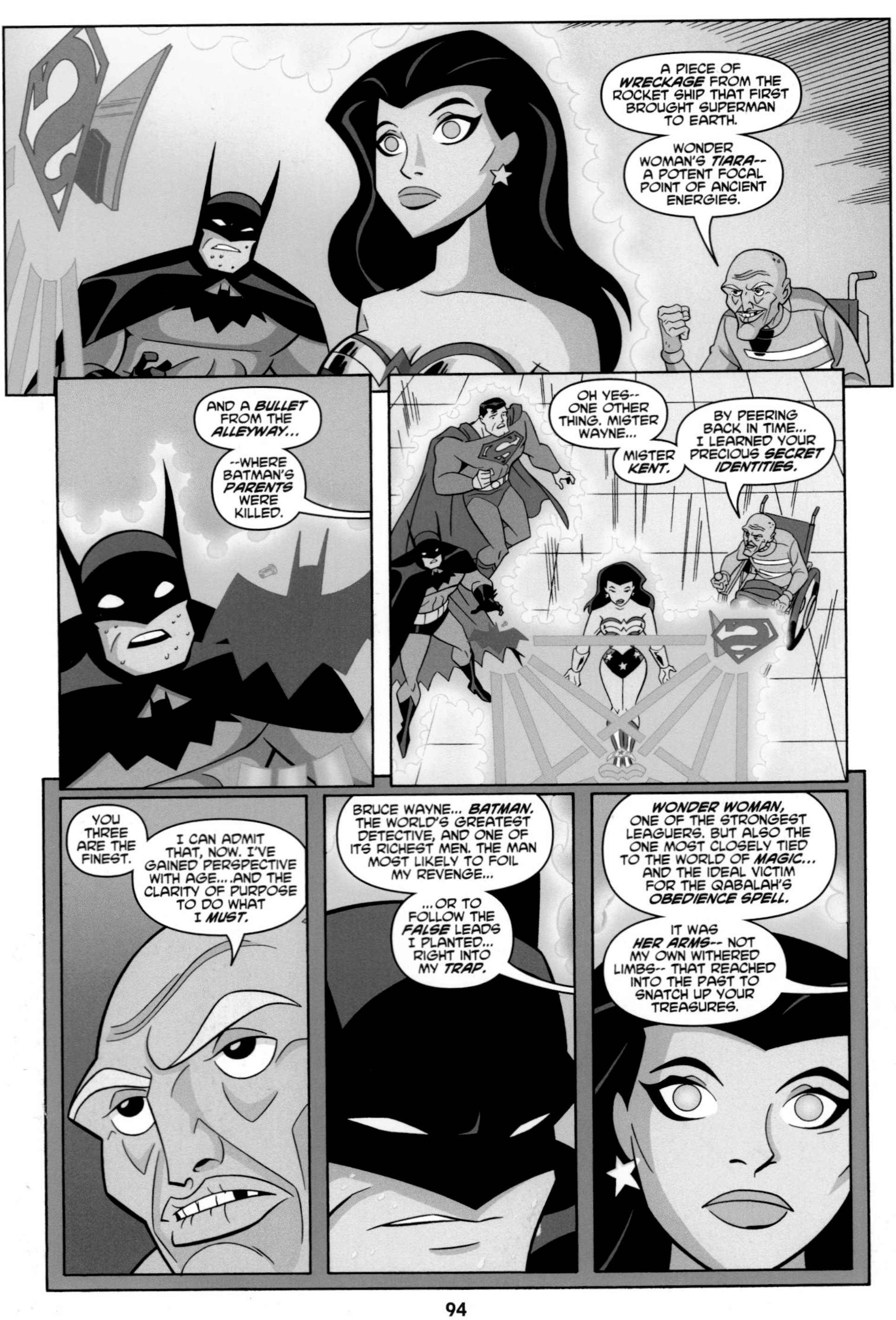
A PIECE OF WRECKAGE FROM THE ROCKET SHIP THAT FIRST BROUGHT SUPERMAN TO EARTH.
WONDER WOMAN'S TIARA-- A POTENT FOCAL POINT OF ANCIENT ENERGIES.
AND A BULLET FROM THE ALLEYWAY...
--WHERE BATMAN'S PARENTS WERE KILLED.
OH YES-- ONE OTHER THING. MISTER WAYNE...
MISTER KENT.
BY PEERING BACK IN TIME... I LEARNED YOUR PRECIOUS SECRET IDENTITIES.
YOU THREE ARE THE FINEST.
I CAN ADMIT THAT, NOW. I'VE GAINED PERSPECTIVE WITH AGE....AND THE CLARITY OF PURPOSE TO DO WHAT I MUST.
BRUCE WAYNE... BATMAN. THE WORLD'S GREATEST DETECTIVE, AND ONE OF ITS RICHEST MEN. THE MAN MOST LIKELY TO FOIL MY REVENGE...
...OR TO FOLLOW THE FALSE LEADS I PLANTED... RIGHT INTO MY TRAP.
WONDER WOMAN, ONE OF THE STRONGEST LEAGUERS. BUT ALSO THE ONE MOST CLOSELY TIED TO THE WORLD OF MAGIC... AND THE IDEAL VICTIM FOR THE QABALAH'S OBEDIENCE SPELL.
IT WAS HER ARMS-- NOT MY OWN WITHERED LIMBS-- THAT REACHED INTO THE PAST TO SNATCH UP YOUR TREASURES.

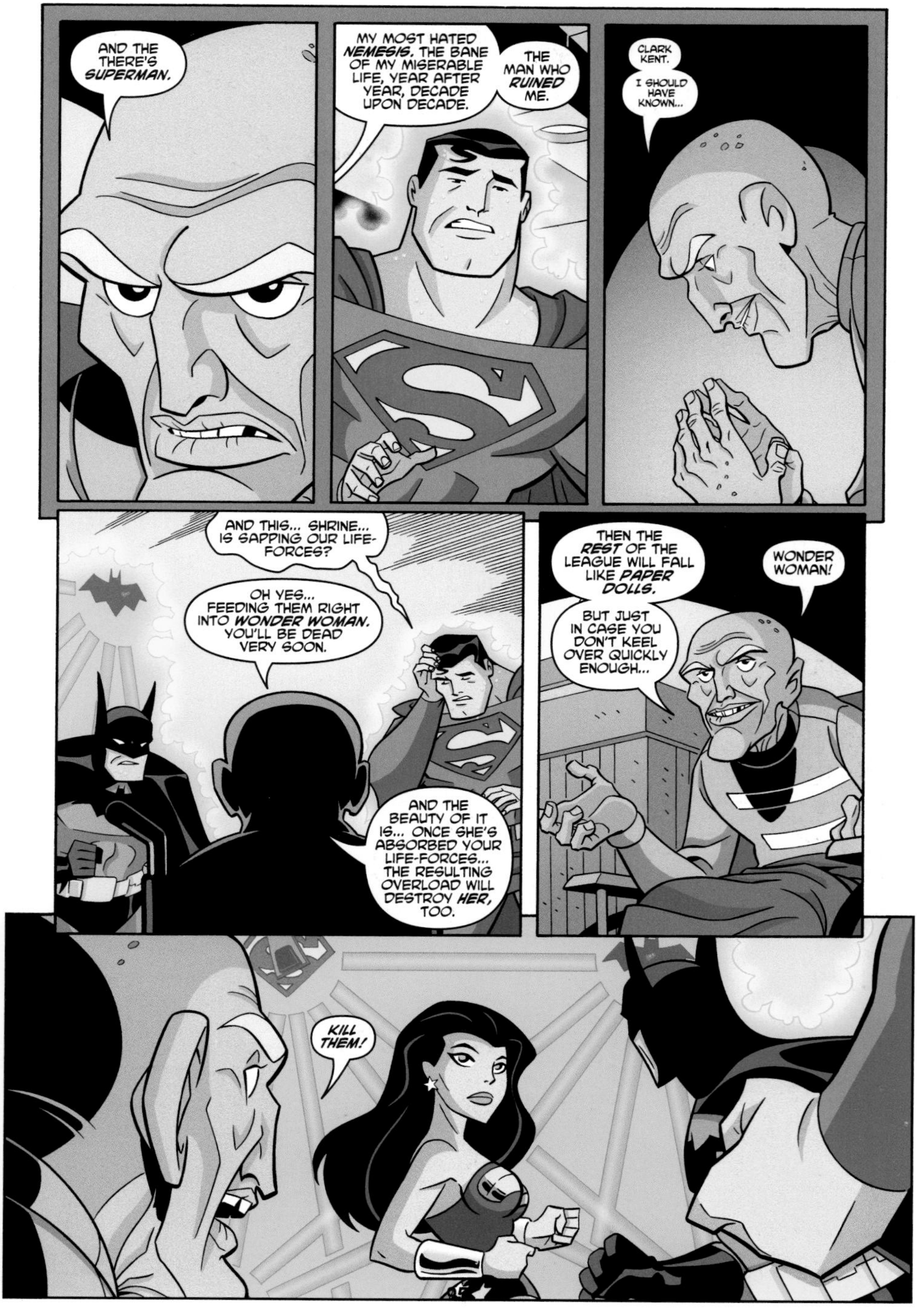

AND THE THERE'S SUPERMAN.
MY MOST HATED NEMESIS. THE BANE OF MY MISERABLE LIFE, YEAR AFTER YEAR, DECADE UPON DECADE.
THE MAN WHO RUINED ME.
CLARK KENT.
I SHOULD HAVE KNOWN...
AND THIS... SHRINE... IS SAPPING OUR LIFE-FORCES?
OH YES... FEEDING THEM RIGHT INTO WONDER WOMAN. YOU'LL BE DEAD VERY SOON.
AND THE BEAUTY OF IT IS... ONCE SHE'S ABSORBED YOUR LIFE-FORCES... THE RESULTING OVERLOAD WILL DESTROY HER, TOO.
THEN THE REST OF THE LEAGUE WILL FALL LIKE PAPER DOLLS.
BUT JUST IN CASE YOU DON'T KEEL OVER QUICKLY ENOUGH...
WONDER WOMAN!
KILL THEM!

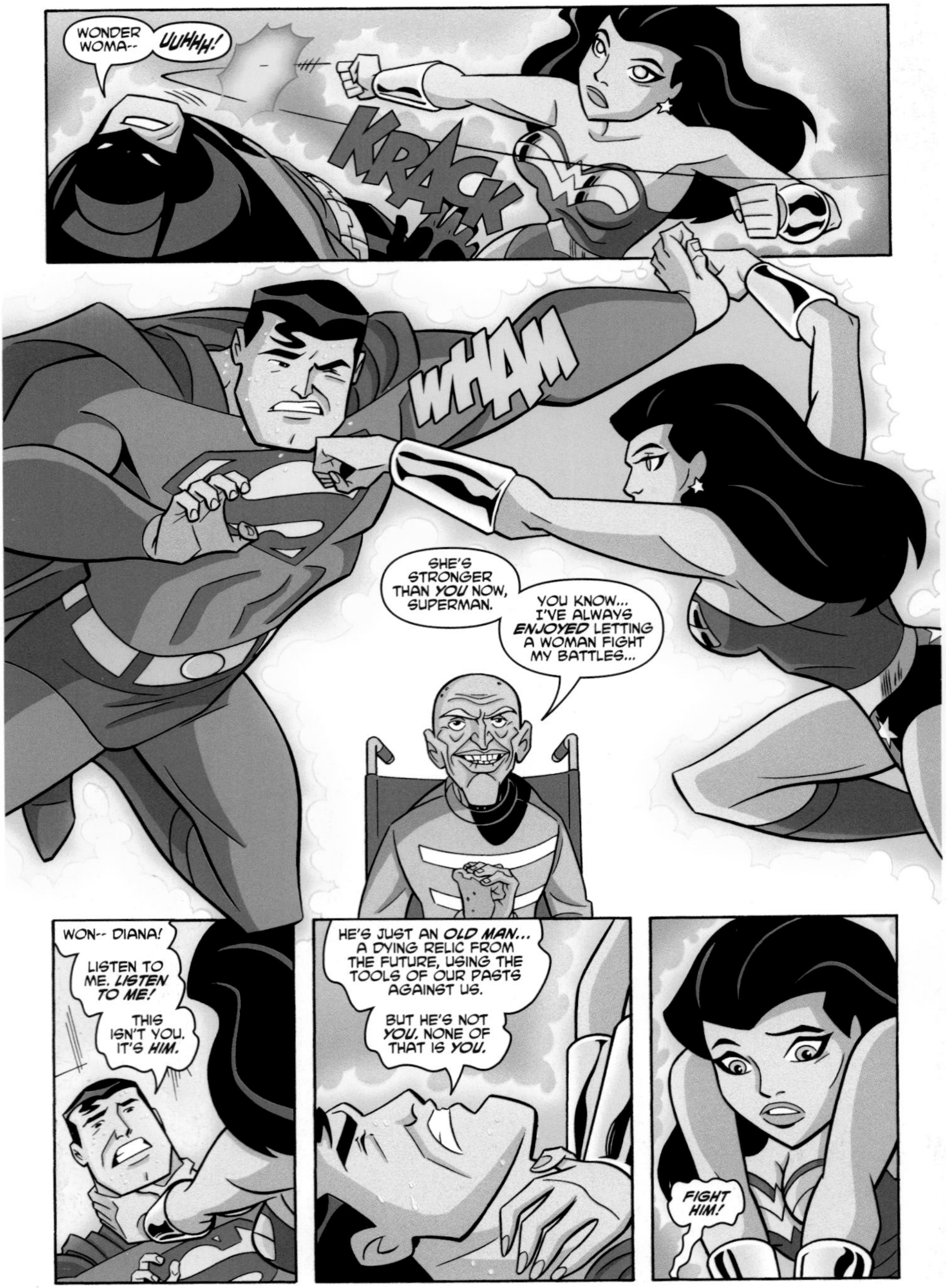
WONDER WOMA--
UUHHH!
KRACK
WHAM
SHE'S STRONGER THAN YOU NOW, SUPERMAN.
YOU KNOW... I'VE ALWAYS ENJOYED LETTING A WOMAN FIGHT MY BATTLES...
WON-- DIANA!
LISTEN TO ME. LISTEN TO ME!
THIS ISN'T YOU. IT'S HIM.
HE'S JUST AN OLD MAN... A DYING RELIC FROM THE FUTURE, USING THE TOOLS OF OUR PASTS AGAINST US.
BUT HE'S NOT YOU. NONE OF THAT IS YOU.
FIGHT HIM!

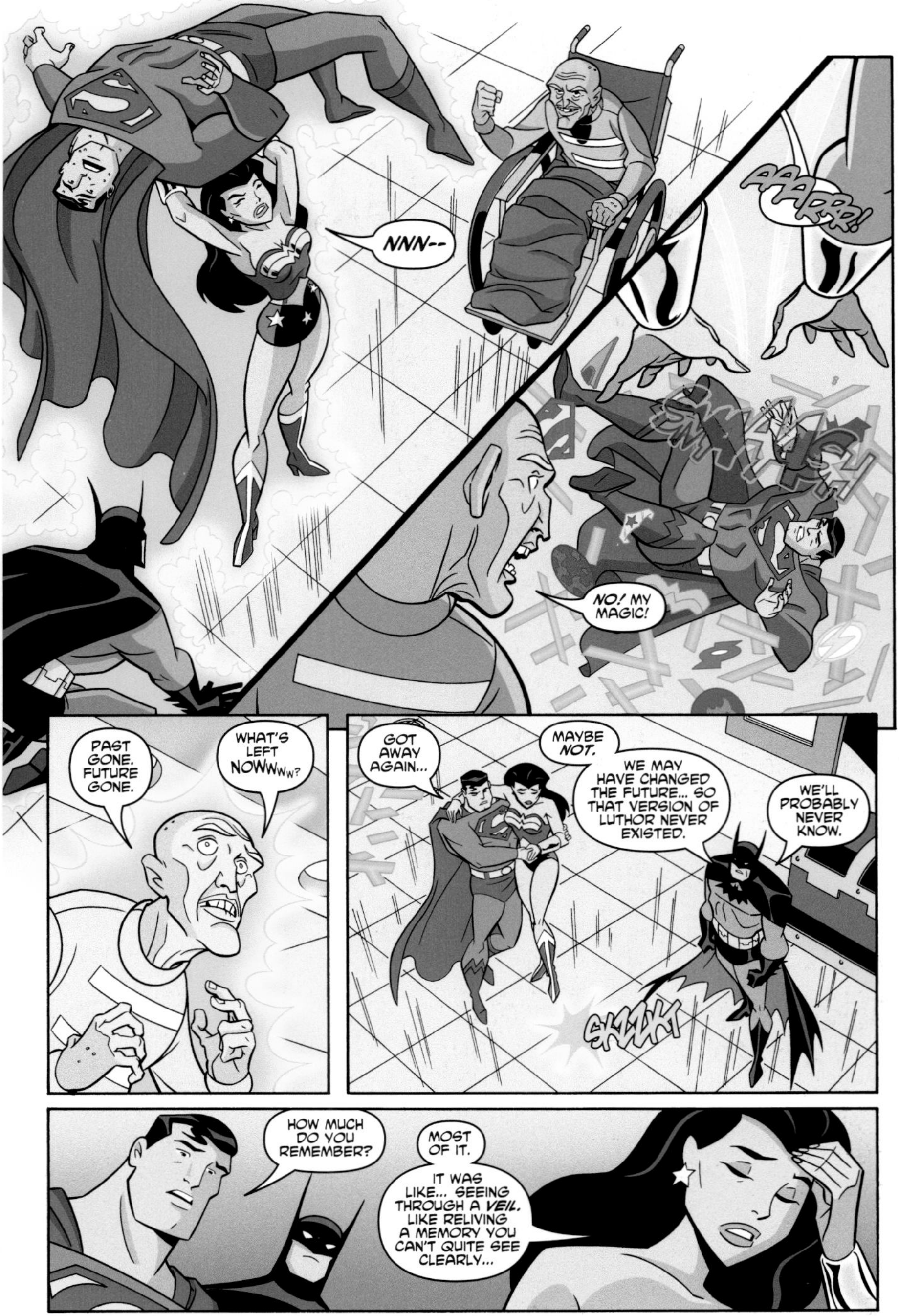
NNN--
AAARRR!
SMAAAACK!
NO! MY MAGIC!
PAST GONE. FUTURE GONE.
WHAT'S LEFT NOWWwww?
GOT AWAY AGAIN...
MAYBE NOT.
WE MAY HAVE CHANGED THE FUTURE... SO THAT VERSION OF LUTHOR NEVER EXISTED.
WE'LL PROBABLY NEVER KNOW.
SKLLK!
HOW MUCH DO YOU REMEMBER?
MOST OF IT.
IT WAS LIKE... SEEING THROUGH A VEIL. LIKE RELIVING A MEMORY YOU CAN'T QUITE SEE CLEARLY...

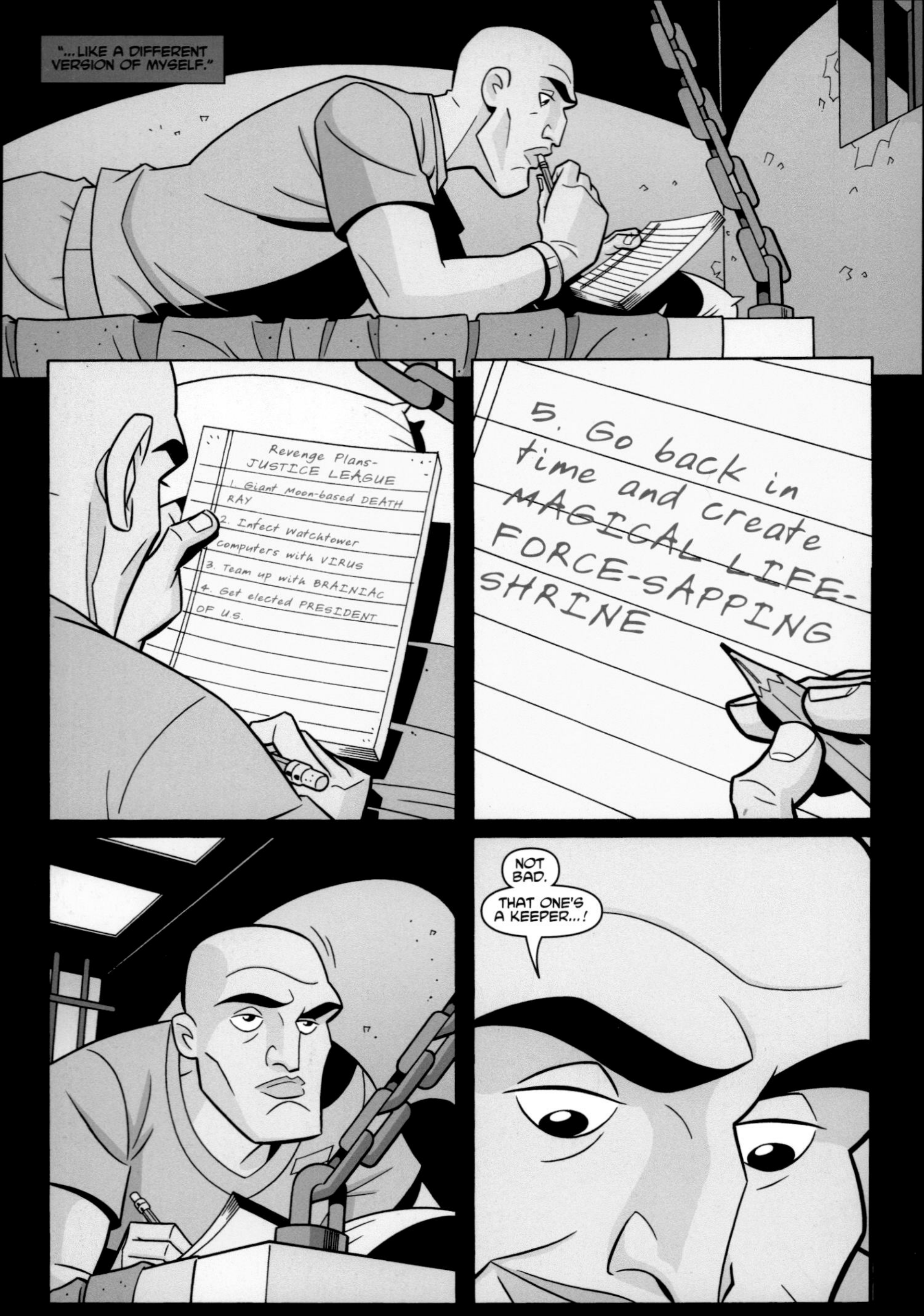
"...LIKE A DIFFERENT VERSION OF MYSELF."
Revenge Plans- JUSTICE LEAGUE
1. Giant Moon-based DEATH RAY
2. Infect Watchtower Computers with VIRUS
3. Team up with BRAINIAC
4. Get elected PRESIDENT OF U.S.
5. Go back in time and create MAGICAL LIFE- FORCE-SAPPING SHRINE
NOT BAD.
THAT ONE'S A KEEPER...!

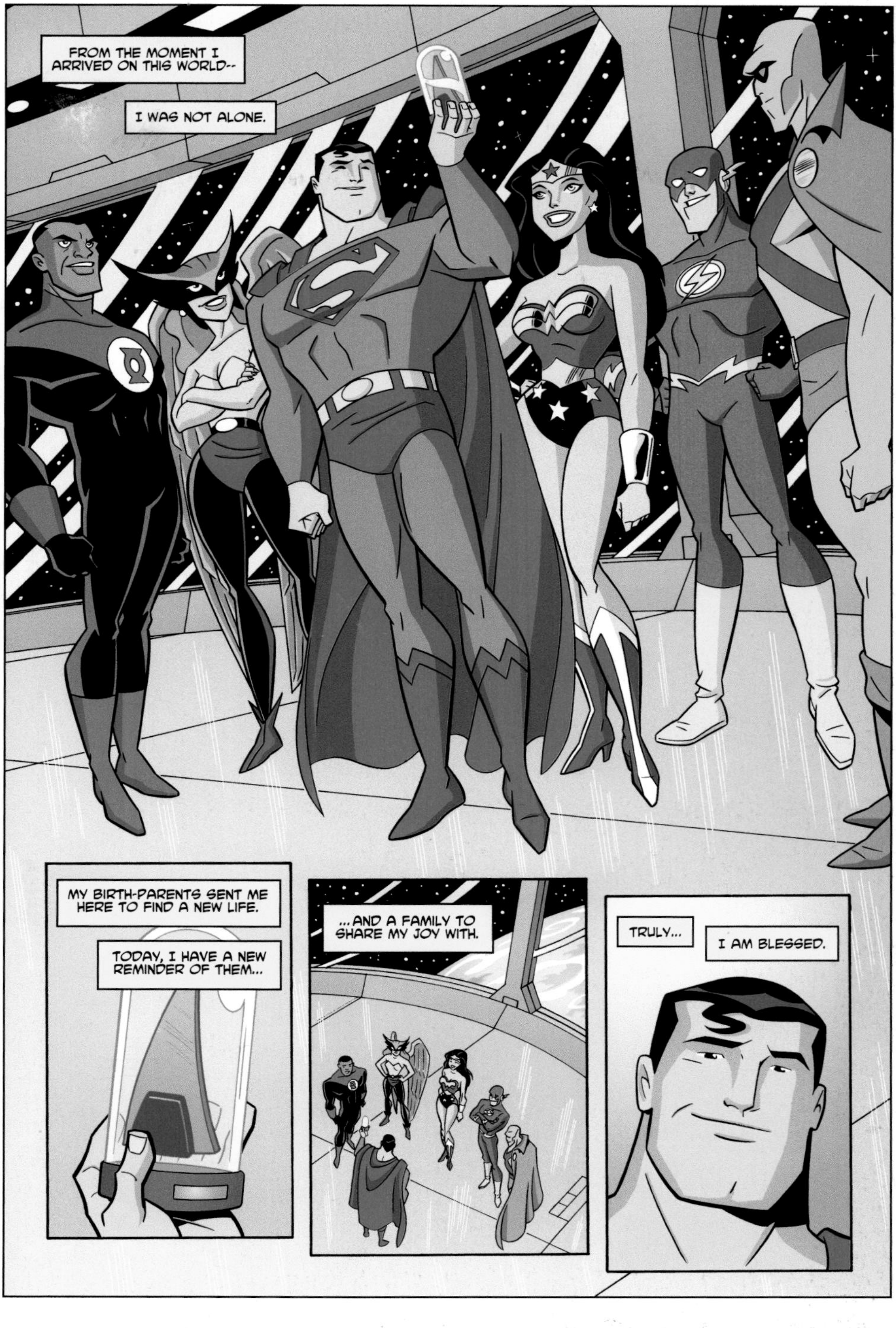
FROM THE MOMENT I ARRIVED ON THIS WORLD--
I WAS NOT ALONE.
MY BIRTH-PARENTS SENT ME HERE TO FIND A NEW LIFE.
TODAY, I HAVE A NEW REMINDER OF THEM...
...AND A FAMILY TO SHARE MY JOY WITH.
TRULY...
I AM BLESSED.

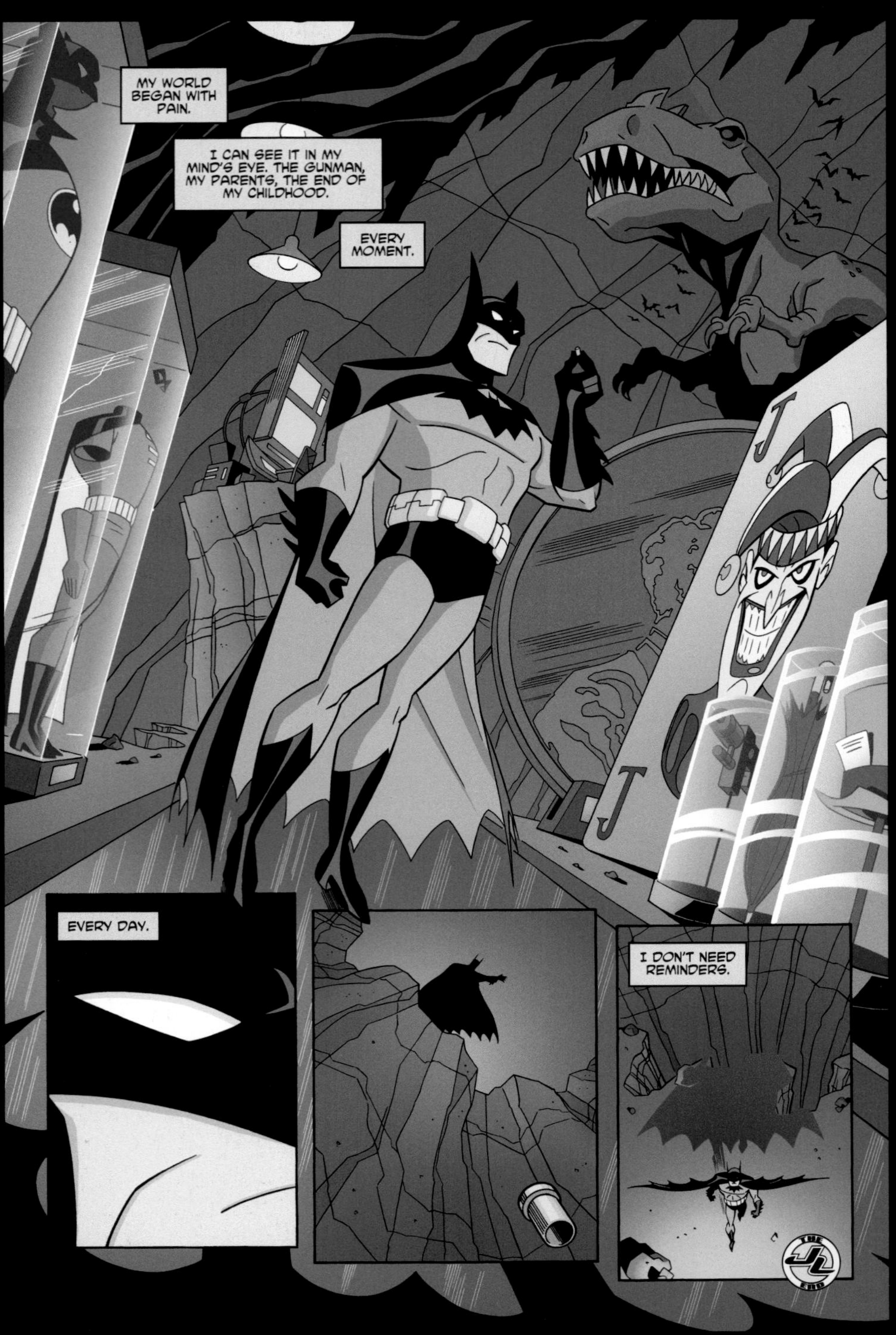
MY WORLD BEGAN WITH PAIN.
I CAN SEE IT IN MY MIND'S EYE. THE GUNMAN, MY PARENTS, THE END OF MY CHILDHOOD.
EVERY MOMENT.
EVERY DAY.
I DON'T NEED REMINDERS.
THE END

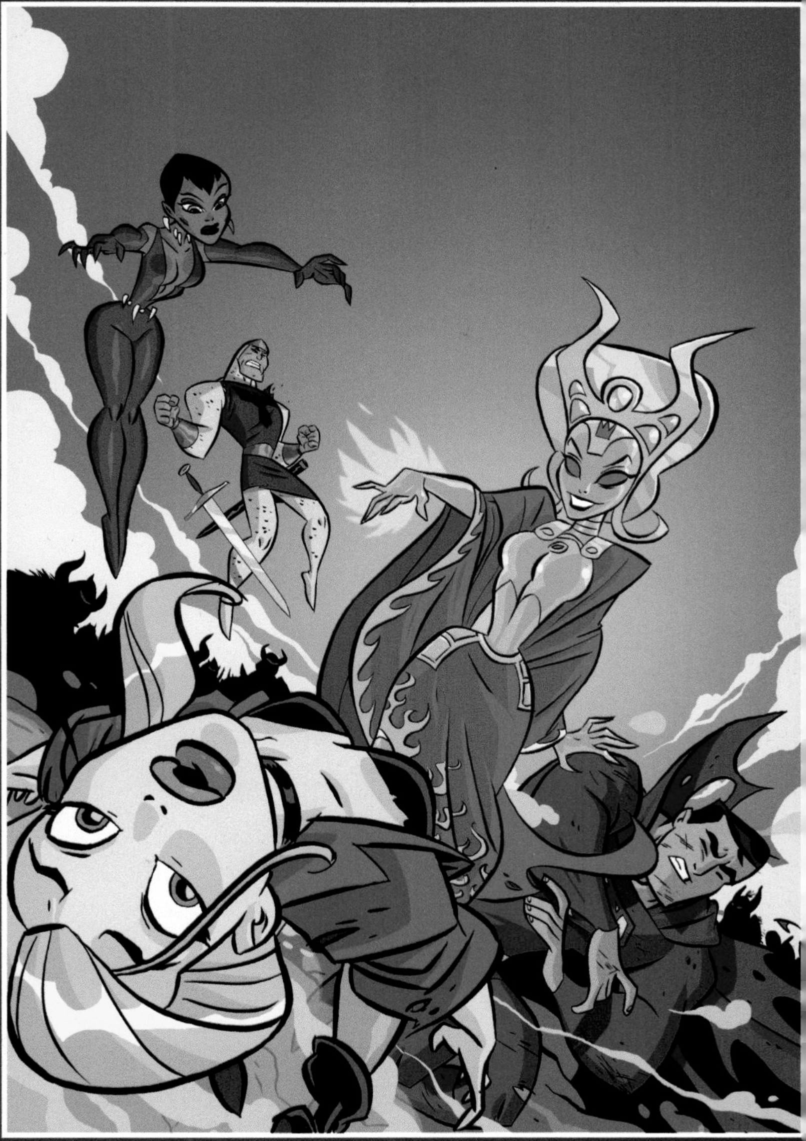

CHAPTER 5: CASTLE PERILOUS

JUSTICE LEAGUE UNLIMITED

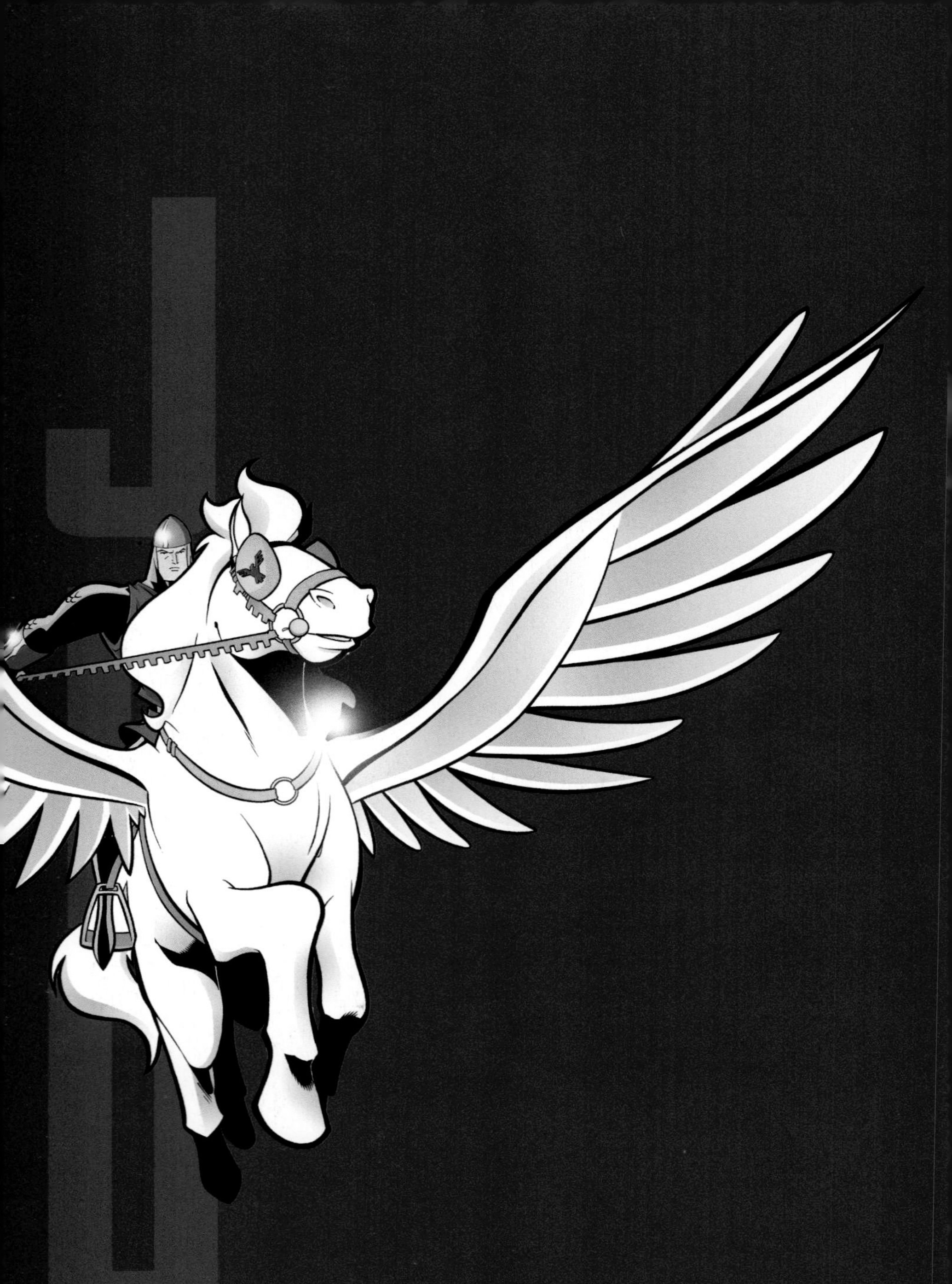

COVER ART BY BEN CALDWELL

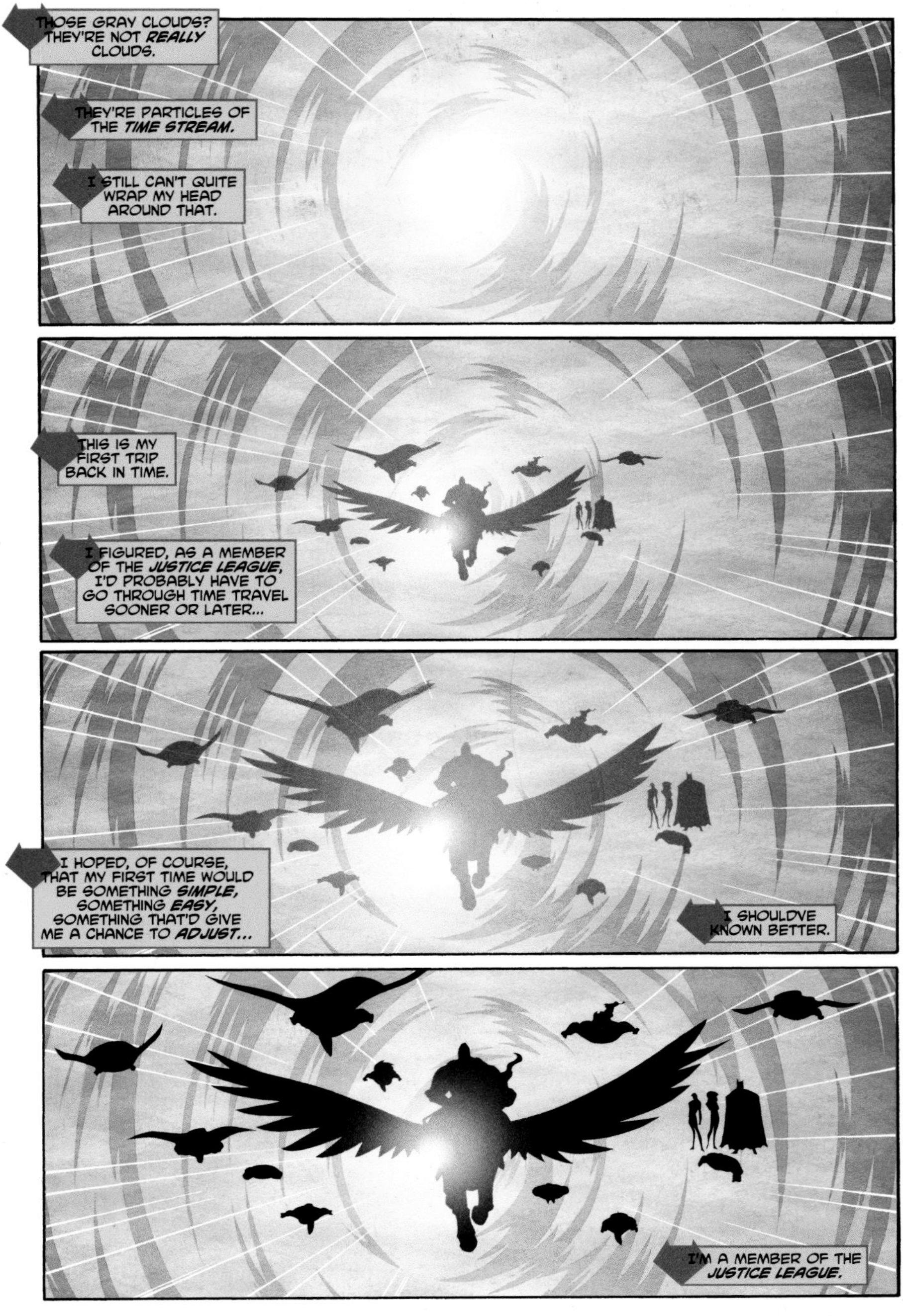

THOSE GRAY CLOUDS? THEY'RE NOT *REALLY* CLOUDS.
THEY'RE PARTICLES OF THE *TIME STREAM.*
I STILL CAN'T QUITE WRAP MY HEAD AROUND THAT.
THIS IS MY FIRST TRIP BACK IN TIME.
I FIGURED, AS A MEMBER OF THE *JUSTICE LEAGUE,* I'D PROBABLY HAVE TO GO THROUGH TIME TRAVEL SOONER OR LATER...
I HOPED, OF COURSE, THAT MY FIRST TIME WOULD BE SOMETHING *SIMPLE,* SOMETHING *EASY,* SOMETHING THAT'D GIVE ME A CHANCE TO *ADJUST...*
I SHOULDVE KNOWN BETTER.
I'M A MEMBER OF THE *JUSTICE LEAGUE.*

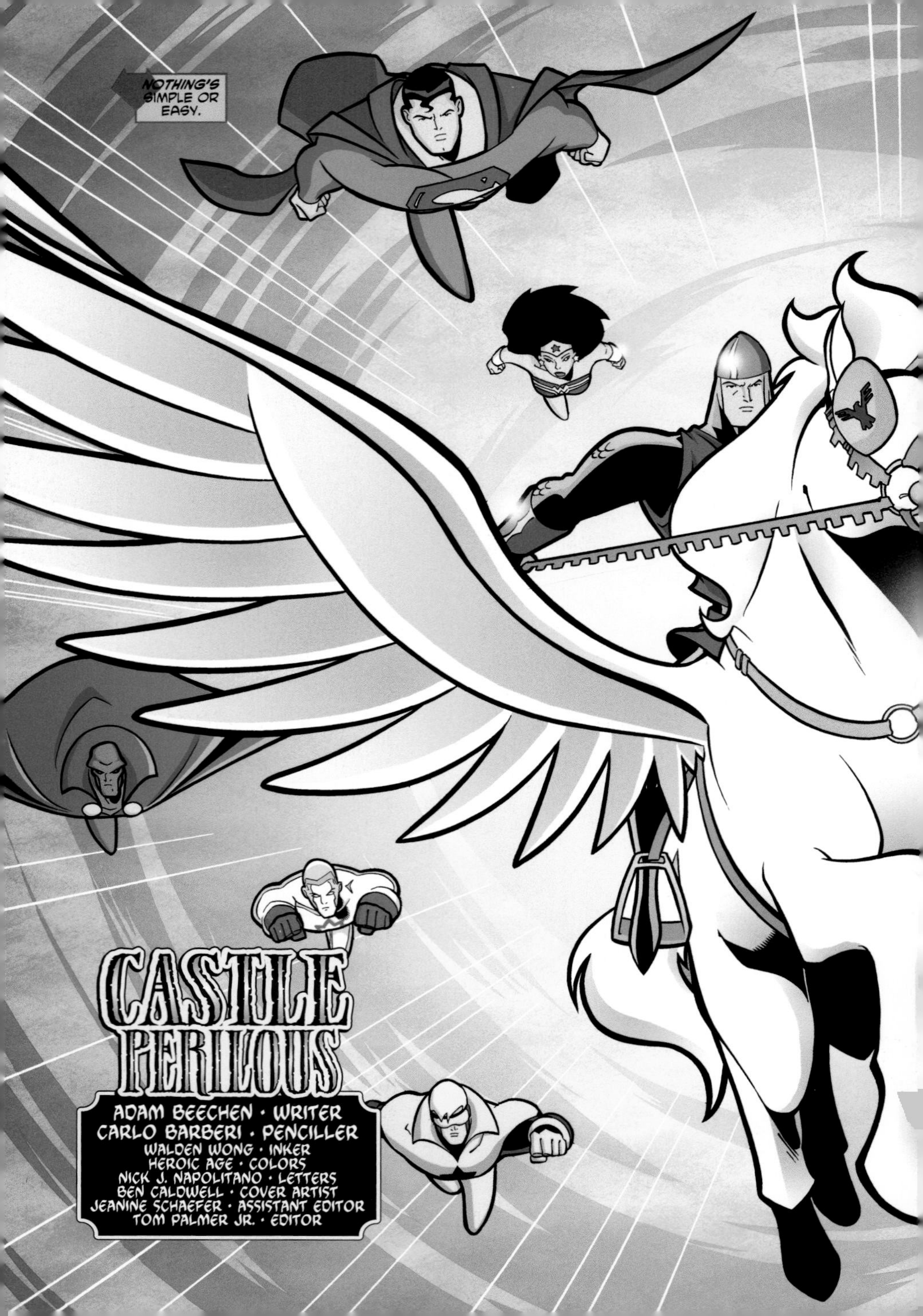
NOTHING'S SIMPLE OR EASY.
CASTLE PERILOUS
ADAM BEECHEN · WRITER
CARLO BARBERI · PENCILLER
WALDEN WONG · INKER
HEROIC AGE · COLORS
NICK J. NAPOLITANO · LETTERS
BEN CALDWELL · COVER ARTIST
JEANINE SCHAEFER · ASSISTANT EDITOR
TOM PALMER JR. · EDITOR

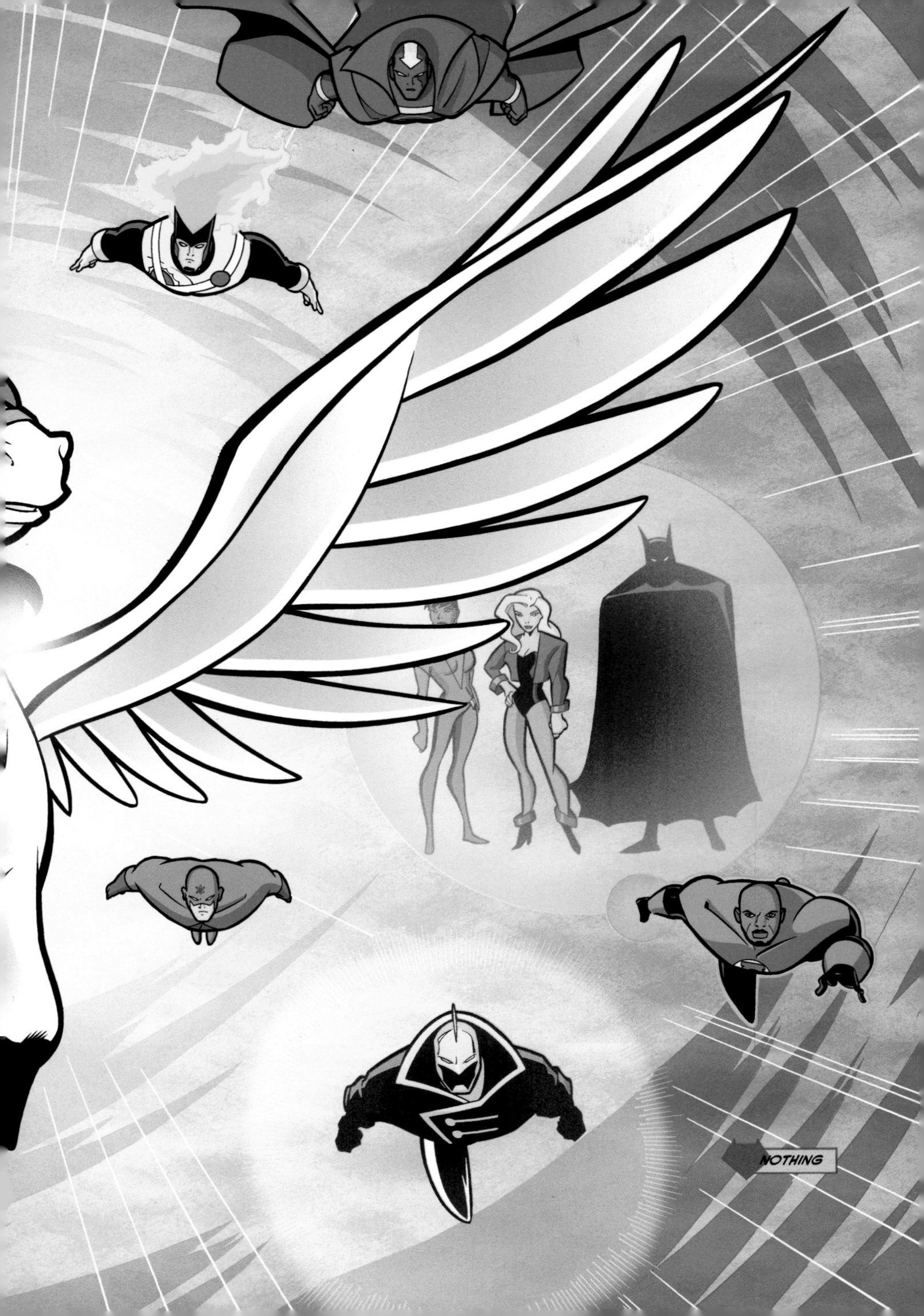
NOTHING

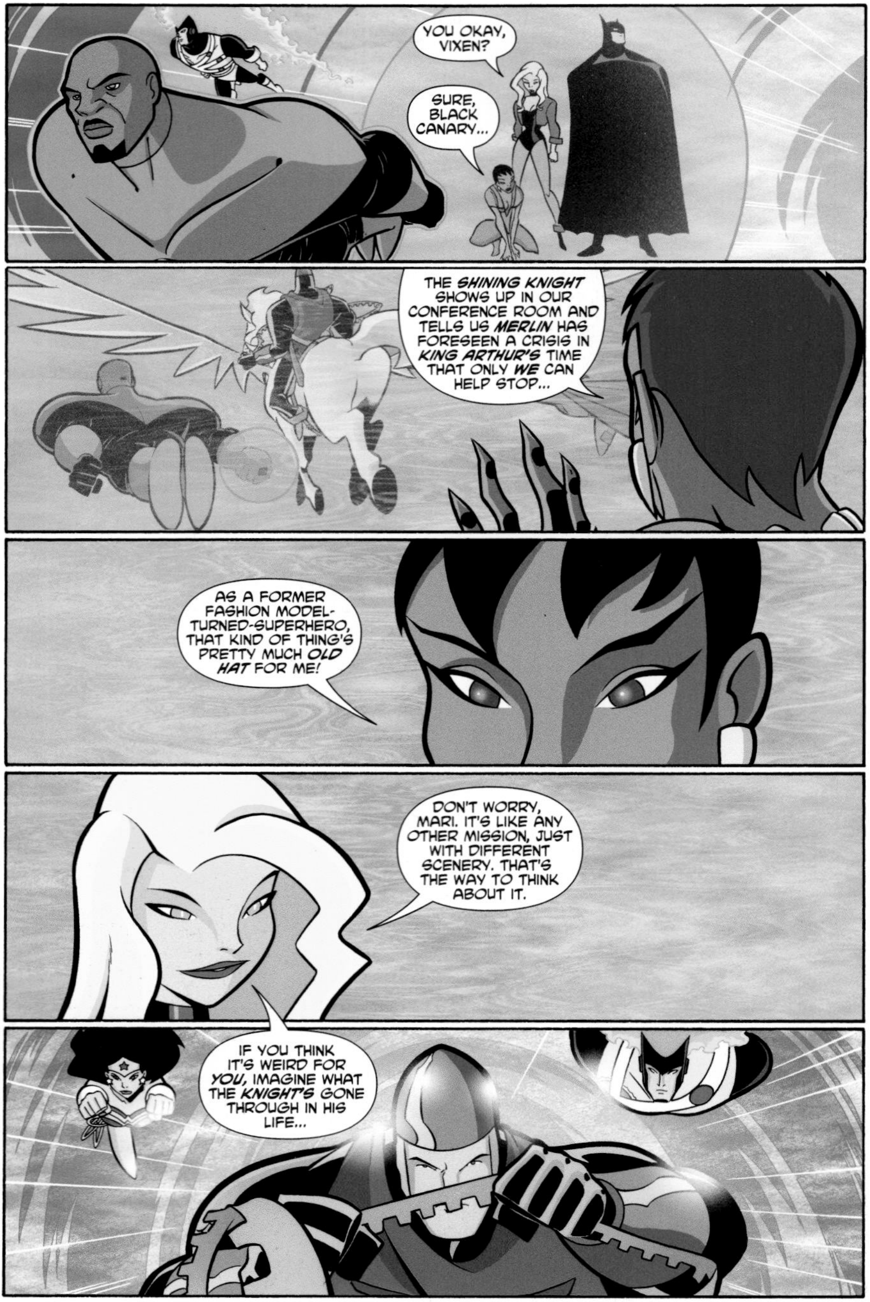
YOU OKAY, VIXEN?
SURE, BLACK CANARY...
THE SHINING KNIGHT SHOWS UP IN OUR CONFERENCE ROOM AND TELLS US MERLIN HAS FORESEEN A CRISIS IN KING ARTHUR'S TIME THAT ONLY WE CAN HELP STOP...
AS A FORMER FASHION MODEL-TURNED-SUPERHERO, THAT KIND OF THING'S PRETTY MUCH OLD HAT FOR ME!
DON'T WORRY, MARI. IT'S LIKE ANY OTHER MISSION, JUST WITH DIFFERENT SCENERY. THAT'S THE WAY TO THINK ABOUT IT.
IF YOU THINK IT'S WEIRD FOR YOU, IMAGINE WHAT THE KNIGHT'S GONE THROUGH IN HIS LIFE...

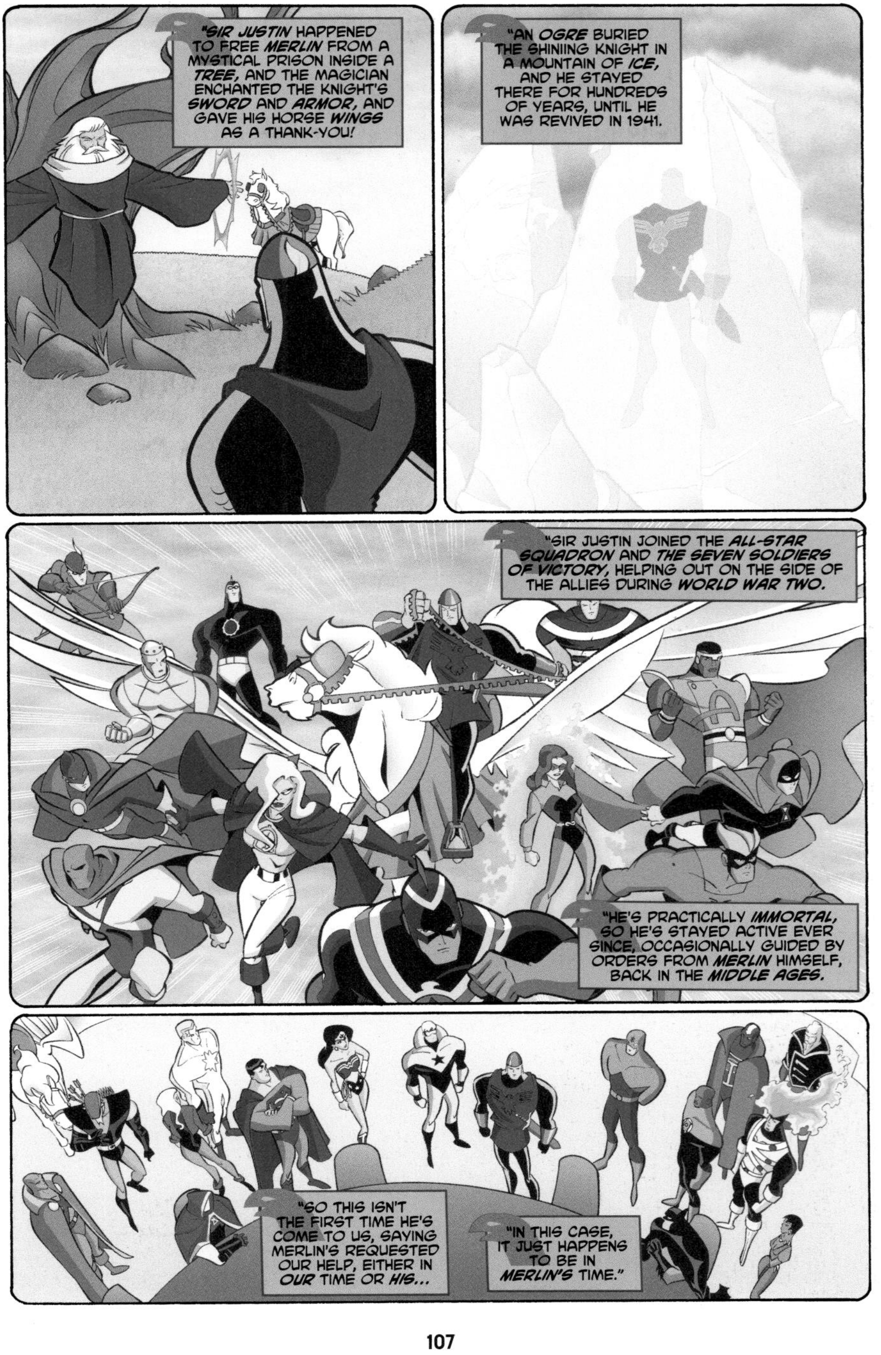
"SIR JUSTIN HAPPENED TO FREE MERLIN FROM A MYSTICAL PRISON INSIDE A TREE, AND THE MAGICIAN ENCHANTED THE KNIGHT'S SWORD AND ARMOR, AND GAVE HIS HORSE WINGS AS A THANK-YOU!
"AN OGRE BURIED THE SHINIING KNIGHT IN A MOUNTAIN OF ICE, AND HE STAYED THERE FOR HUNDREDS OF YEARS, UNTIL HE WAS REVIVED IN 1941.
"SIR JUSTIN JOINED THE ALL-STAR SQUADRON AND THE SEVEN SOLDIERS OF VICTORY, HELPING OUT ON THE SIDE OF THE ALLIES DURING WORLD WAR TWO.
"HE'S PRACTICALLY IMMORTAL, SO HE'S STAYED ACTIVE EVER SINCE, OCCASIONALLY GUIDED BY ORDERS FROM MERLIN HIMSELF, BACK IN THE MIDDLE AGES.
"SO THIS ISN'T THE FIRST TIME HE'S COME TO US, SAYING MERLIN'S REQUESTED OUR HELP, EITHER IN OUR TIME OR HIS...
"IN THIS CASE, IT JUST HAPPENS TO BE IN MERLIN'S TIME."

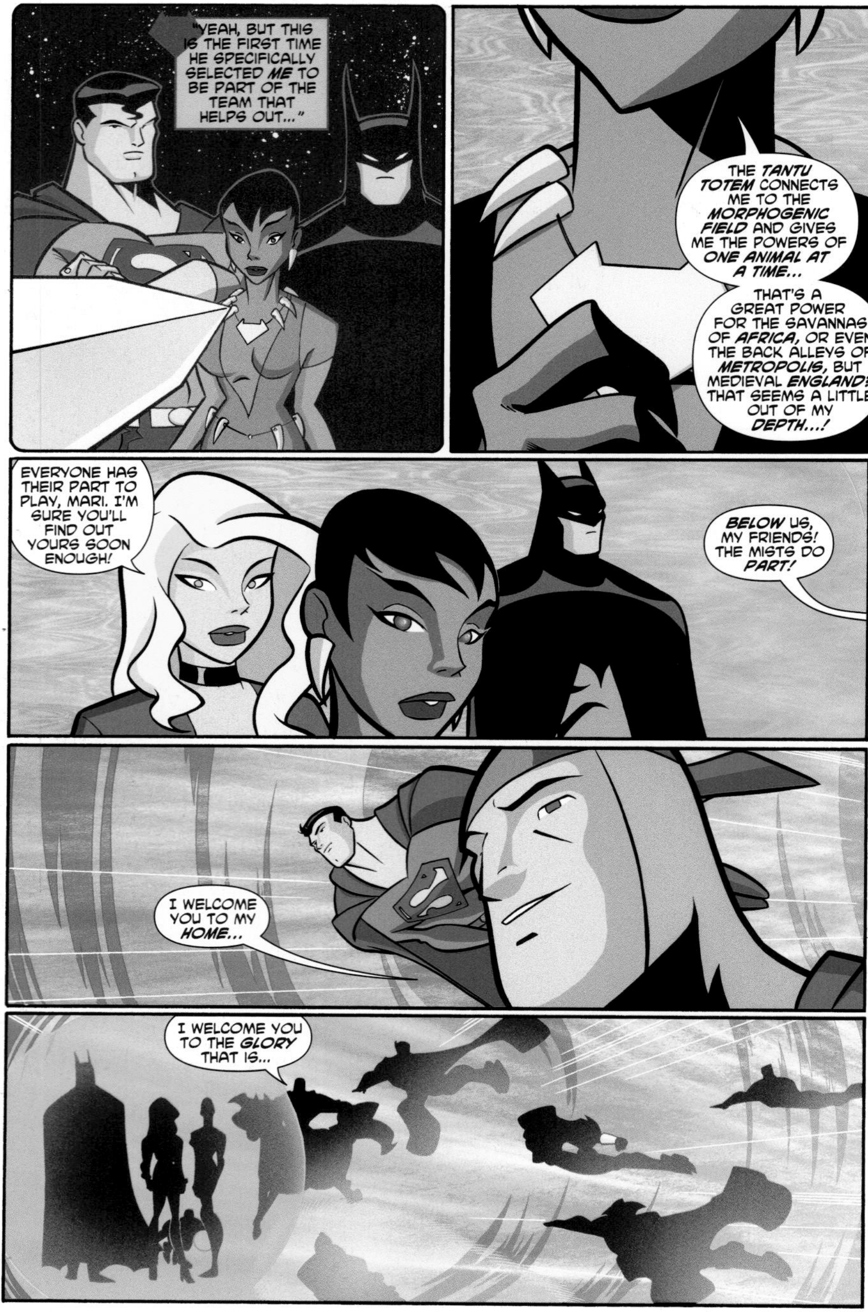
"YEAH, BUT THIS IS THE FIRST TIME HE SPECIFICALLY SELECTED ME TO BE PART OF THE TEAM THAT HELPS OUT..."
THE TANTU TOTEM CONNECTS ME TO THE MORPHOGENIC FIELD AND GIVES ME THE POWERS OF ONE ANIMAL AT A TIME...
THAT'S A GREAT POWER FOR THE SAVANNAS OF AFRICA, OR EVEN THE BACK ALLEYS OF METROPOLIS, BUT MEDIEVAL ENGLAND? THAT SEEMS A LITTLE OUT OF MY DEPTH...!
EVERYONE HAS THEIR PART TO PLAY, MARI. I'M SURE YOU'LL FIND OUT YOURS SOON ENOUGH!
BELOW US, MY FRIENDS! THE MISTS DO PART!
I WELCOME YOU TO MY HOME...
I WELCOME YOU TO THE GLORY THAT IS...

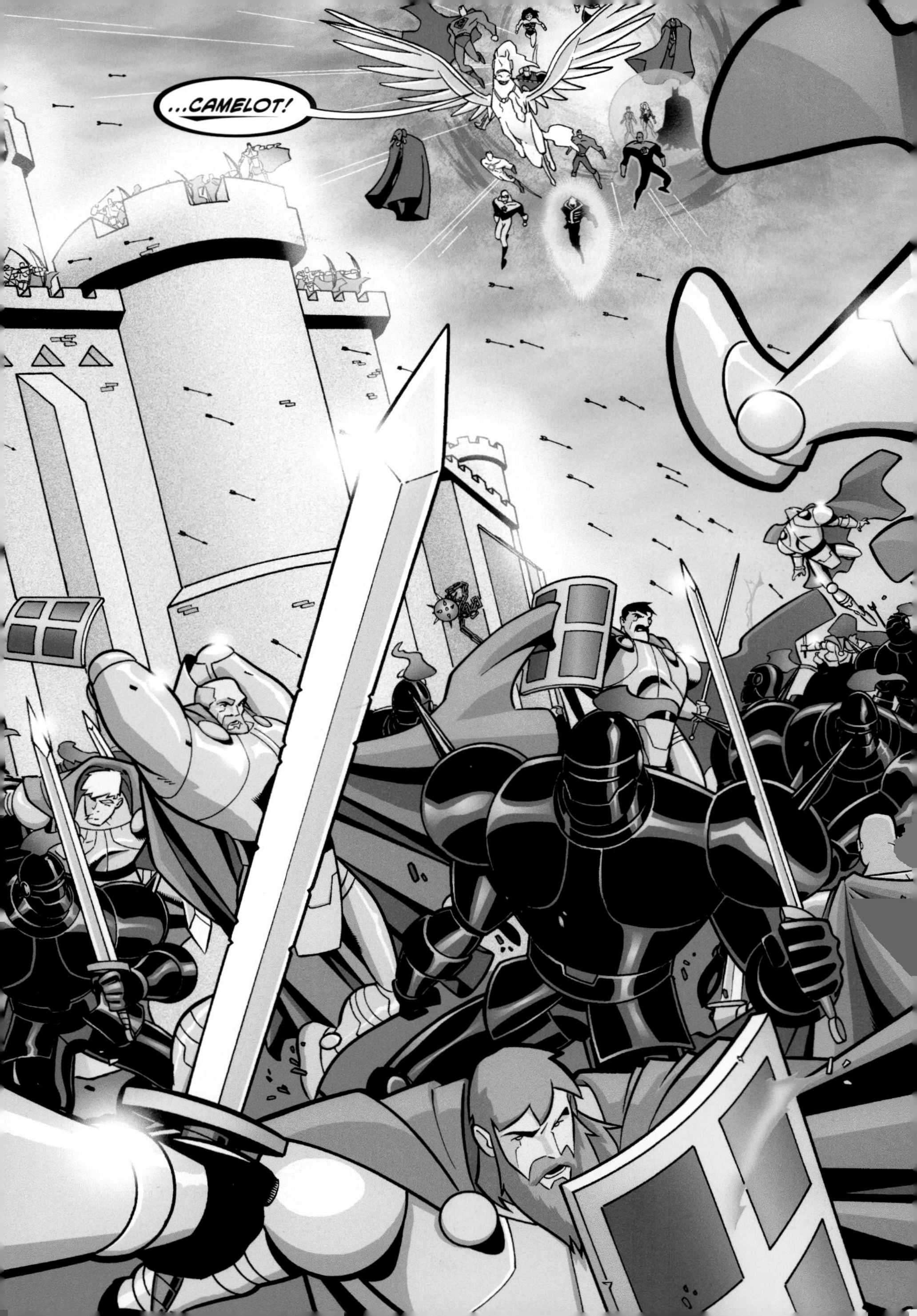
...CAMELOT!

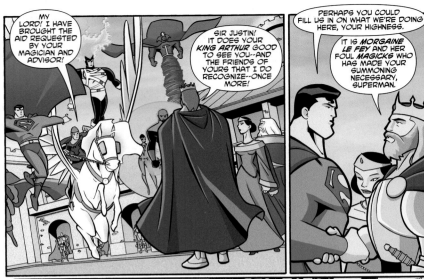

MY LORD! I HAVE BROUGHT THE AID REQUESTED BY YOUR MAGICIAN AND ADVISOR!

SIR JUSTIN! IT DOES YOUR *KING ARTHUR* GOOD TO SEE YOU--AND THE FRIENDS OF YOURS THAT I DO RECOGNIZE--ONCE MORE!

PERHAPS YOU COULD FILL US IN ON WHAT WE'RE DOING HERE, YOUR HIGHNESS.

IT IS *MORGAINE LE FEY* AND HER FOUL *MAGICKS* WHO HAS MADE YOUR SUMMONING NECESSARY, SUPERMAN.

KNOWING THE VILLAINY THE *BLACK KNIGHT* HAS PERPETRATED ON HIS OWN, SHE HAS SUMMONED VERSIONS OF THE EVIL ONE FROM THE *NEAR PAST* AND *NEAR FUTURE*...

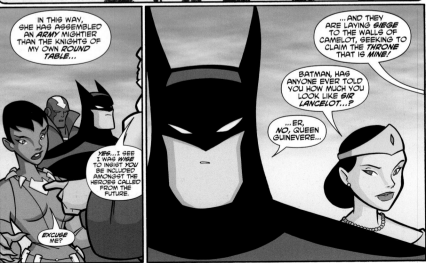

IN THIS WAY, SHE HAS ASSEMBLED AN *ARMY* MIGHTIER THAN THE KNIGHTS OF MY OWN *ROUND TABLE*...

...AND THEY ARE LAYING *SIEGE* TO THE WALLS OF CAMELOT, SEEKING TO CLAIM THE *THRONE* THAT IS *MINE!*

BATMAN, HAS ANYONE EVER TOLD YOU HOW MUCH YOU LOOK LIKE *SIR LANCELOT*...?

...ER, *NO,* QUEEN GUINEVERE...

YES...I SEE I WAS *WISE* TO INSIST *YOU* BE INCLUDED AMONGST THE HEROES CALLED FROM THE FUTURE.

EXCUSE ME?

110

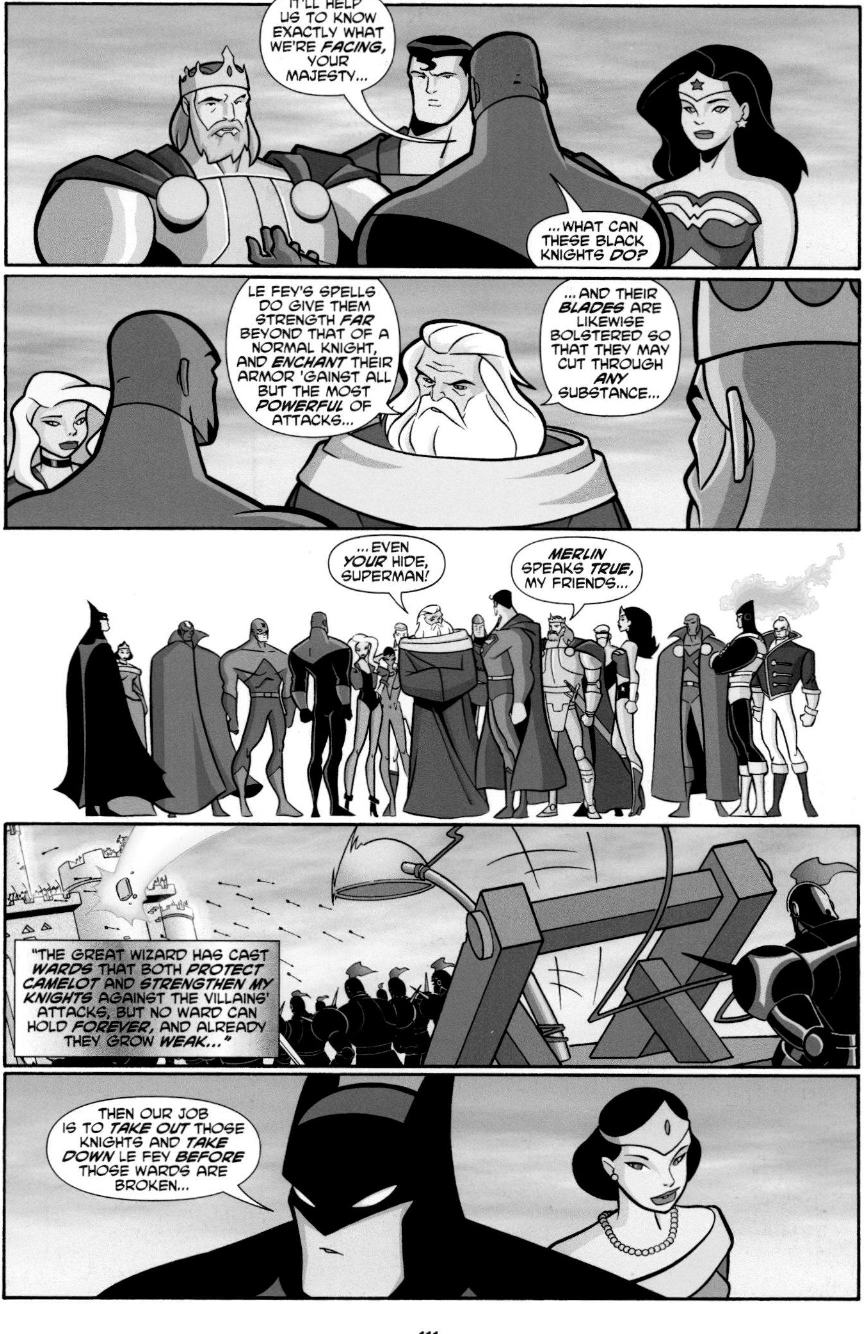
IT'LL HELP US TO KNOW EXACTLY WHAT WE'RE *FACING,* YOUR MAJESTY...
...WHAT CAN THESE BLACK KNIGHTS *DO?*
LE FEY'S SPELLS DO GIVE THEM STRENGTH *FAR* BEYOND THAT OF A NORMAL KNIGHT, AND *ENCHANT* THEIR ARMOR 'GAINST ALL BUT THE MOST *POWERFUL* OF ATTACKS...
...AND THEIR *BLADES* ARE LIKEWISE BOLSTERED SO THAT THEY MAY CUT THROUGH *ANY* SUBSTANCE...
...EVEN *YOUR* HIDE, SUPERMAN!
MERLIN SPEAKS *TRUE,* MY FRIENDS...
"THE GREAT WIZARD HAS CAST *WARDS* THAT BOTH *PROTECT CAMELOT* AND *STRENGTHEN MY KNIGHTS* AGAINST THE VILLAINS' ATTACKS, BUT NO WARD CAN HOLD *FOREVER,* AND ALREADY THEY GROW *WEAK...*"
THEN OUR JOB IS TO *TAKE OUT* THOSE KNIGHTS AND *TAKE DOWN* LE FEY *BEFORE* THOSE WARDS ARE BROKEN...

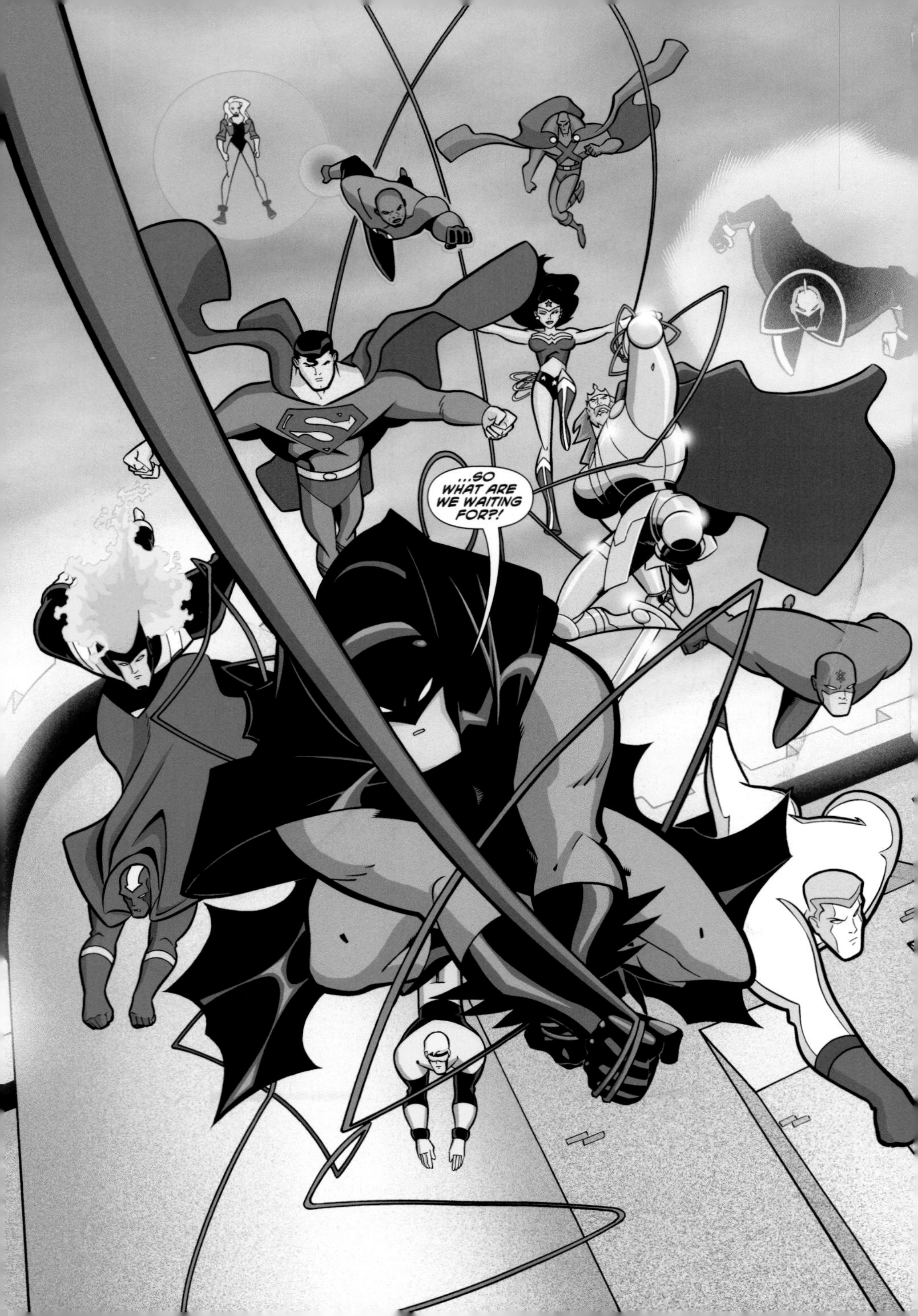
...SO WHAT ARE WE WAITING FOR?!

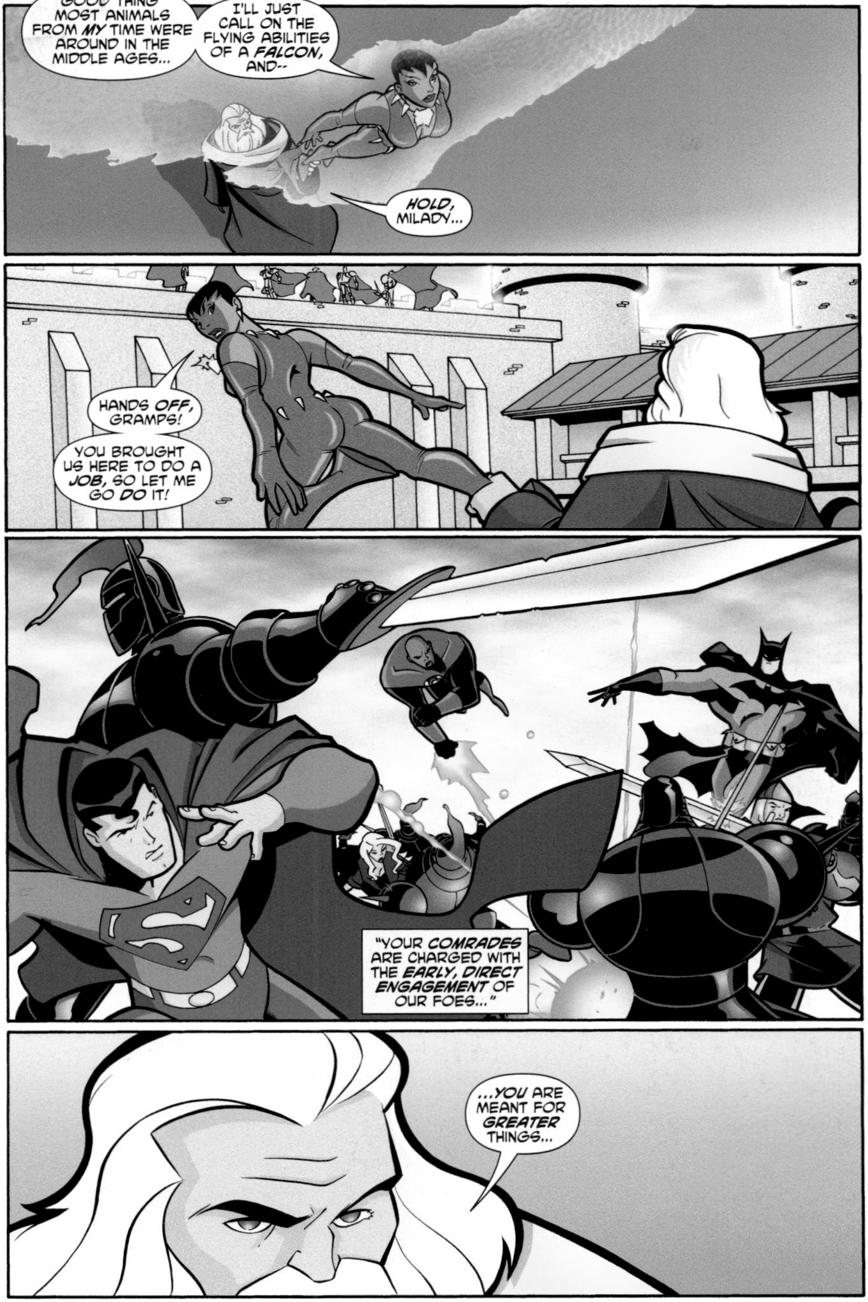
GOOD THING MOST ANIMALS FROM MY TIME WERE AROUND IN THE MIDDLE AGES...
I'LL JUST CALL ON THE FLYING ABILITIES OF A FALCON, AND--
HOLD, MILADY...
HANDS OFF, GRAMPS!
YOU BROUGHT US HERE TO DO A JOB, SO LET ME GO DO IT!
"YOUR COMRADES ARE CHARGED WITH THE EARLY, DIRECT ENGAGEMENT OF OUR FOES..."
...YOU ARE MEANT FOR GREATER THINGS...

COME, *VARLETS!* TASTE THE STEEL OF *EXCALIBUR* AND KNOW THAT CAMELOT SHALL *NOT* BE YOURS TODAY...OR ANY *OTHER* DAY!

SURE *TALKS* LIKE A KING, DOESN'T HE?

IF ANY MAN *SHOULD,* GREEN LANTERN...

...IT'S *HIM.*

SSSHHHHHSSSSPHHHHH

SPLENDID SHOWING, GOOD SIR! I, *SIR LANCELOT,* COULD HAVE DONE NO BETTER!

I SAY, RATHER A *RESEMBLANCE* BETWEEN US, WHAT?

SAME CHIN, I DO BELIEVE.

I HADN'T NOTICED.

THIS ISN'T SO *BAD,* ACTUALLY...

...ONCE YOU GET IN THE *SWING* OF IT!

KA-CANNG

SHHSSANNG

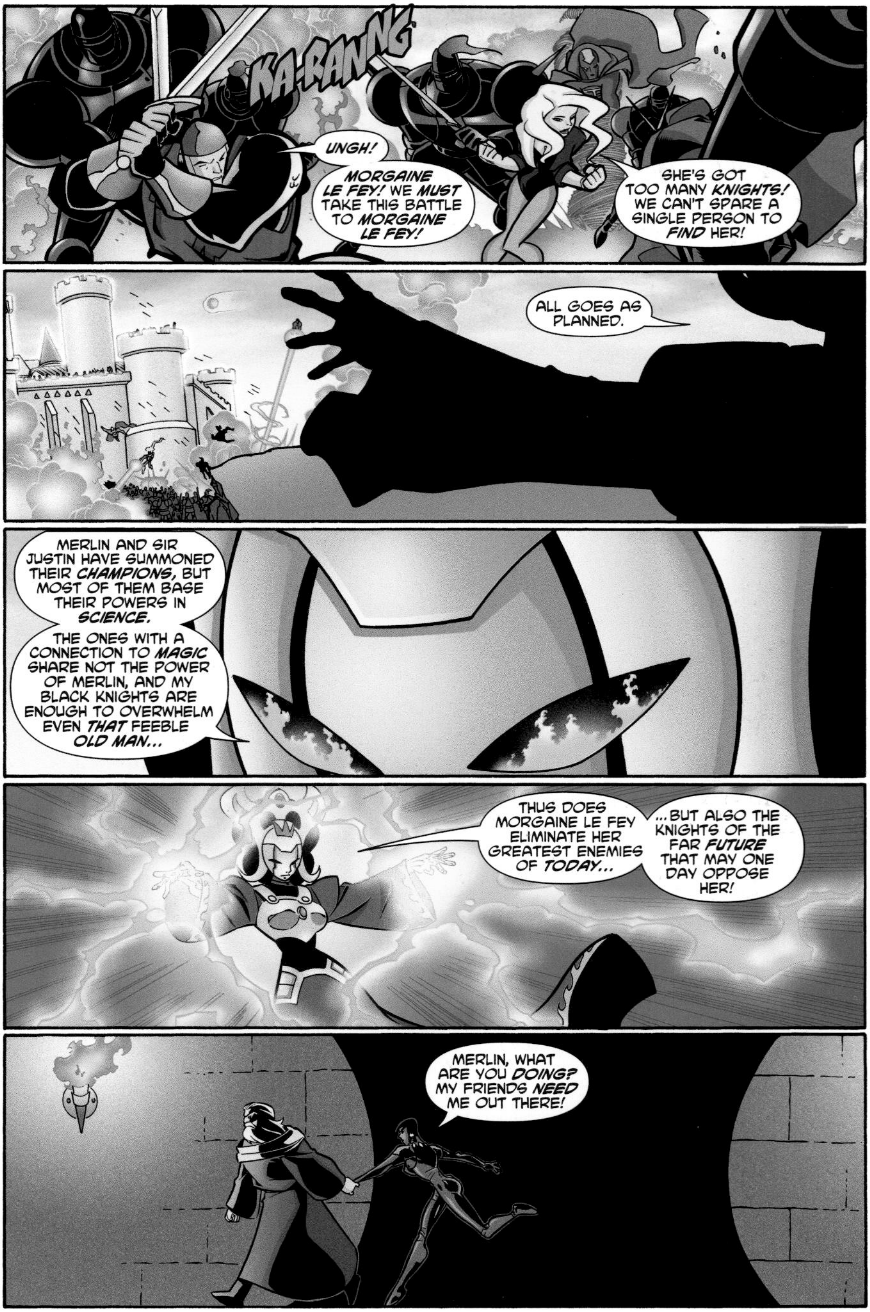
KA-RANNG
UNGH!
MORGAINE LE FEY! WE MUST TAKE THIS BATTLE TO MORGAINE LE FEY!
SHE'S GOT TOO MANY KNIGHTS! WE CAN'T SPARE A SINGLE PERSON TO FIND HER!
ALL GOES AS PLANNED.
MERLIN AND SIR JUSTIN HAVE SUMMONED THEIR CHAMPIONS, BUT MOST OF THEM BASE THEIR POWERS IN SCIENCE.
THE ONES WITH A CONNECTION TO MAGIC SHARE NOT THE POWER OF MERLIN, AND MY BLACK KNIGHTS ARE ENOUGH TO OVERWHELM EVEN THAT FEEBLE OLD MAN...
THUS DOES MORGAINE LE FEY ELIMINATE HER GREATEST ENEMIES OF TODAY...
...BUT ALSO THE KNIGHTS OF THE FAR FUTURE THAT MAY ONE DAY OPPOSE HER!
MERLIN, WHAT ARE YOU DOING? MY FRIENDS NEED ME OUT THERE!

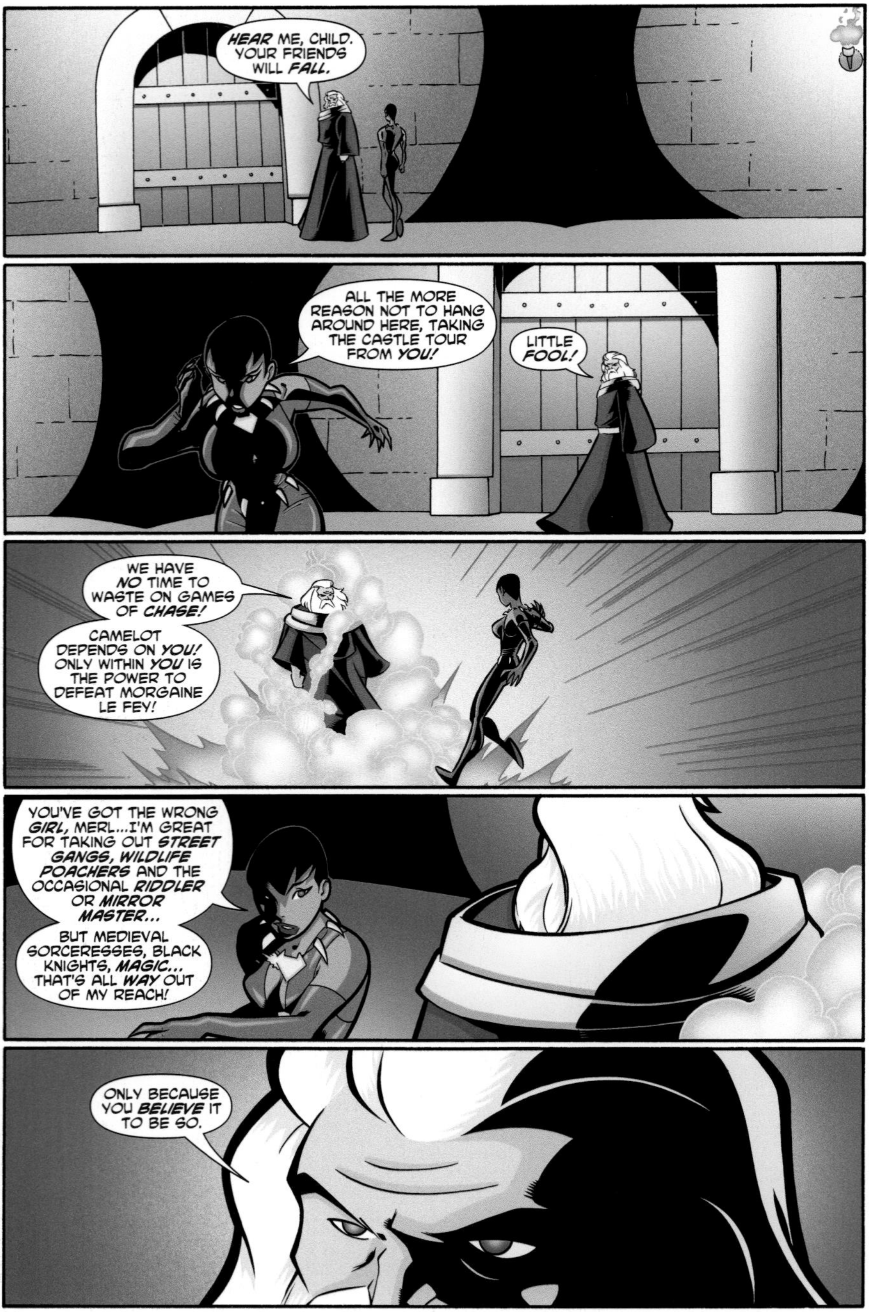
HEAR ME, CHILD. YOUR FRIENDS WILL FALL.
ALL THE MORE REASON NOT TO HANG AROUND HERE, TAKING THE CASTLE TOUR FROM YOU!
LITTLE FOOL!
WE HAVE NO TIME TO WASTE ON GAMES OF CHASE!
CAMELOT DEPENDS ON YOU! ONLY WITHIN YOU IS THE POWER TO DEFEAT MORGAINE LE FEY!
YOU'VE GOT THE WRONG GIRL, MERL...I'M GREAT FOR TAKING OUT STREET GANGS, WILDLIFE POACHERS AND THE OCCASIONAL RIDDLER OR MIRROR MASTER...
BUT MEDIEVAL SORCERESSES, BLACK KNIGHTS, MAGIC... THAT'S ALL WAY OUT OF MY REACH!
ONLY BECAUSE YOU BELIEVE IT TO BE SO.

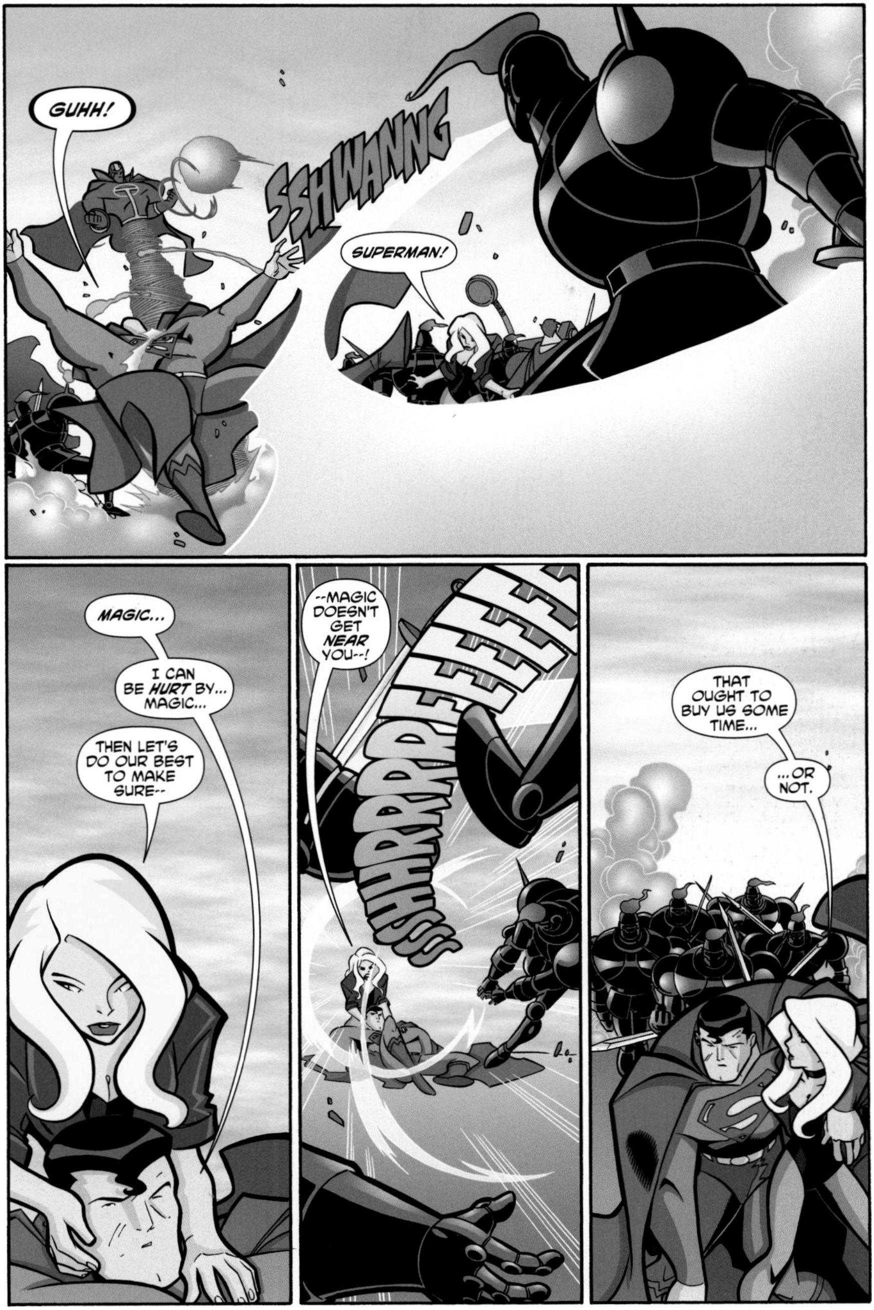
GUHH!
SSHWANNG
SUPERMAN!
MAGIC...
I CAN BE *HURT* BY... MAGIC...
THEN LET'S DO OUR BEST TO MAKE SURE--
--MAGIC DOESN'T GET *NEAR* YOU--!
SSHRRREEEEE
THAT OUGHT TO BUY US SOME TIME...
...OR NOT.

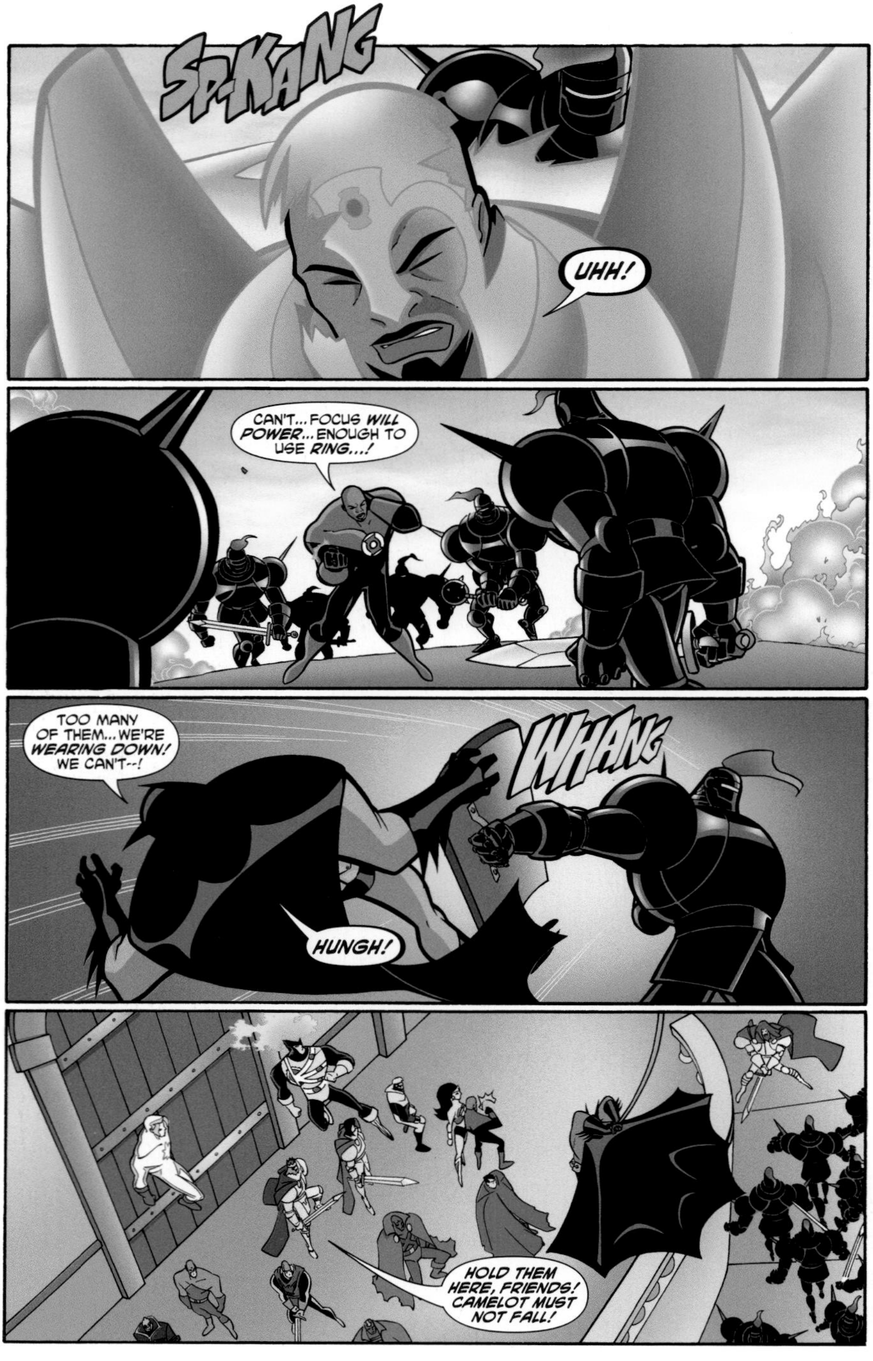
SP-KANG
UHH!
CAN'T... FOCUS WILL POWER... ENOUGH TO USE RING...!
TOO MANY OF THEM... WE'RE WEARING DOWN! WE CAN'T--!
WHANG
HUNGH!
HOLD THEM HERE, FRIENDS! CAMELOT MUST NOT FALL!

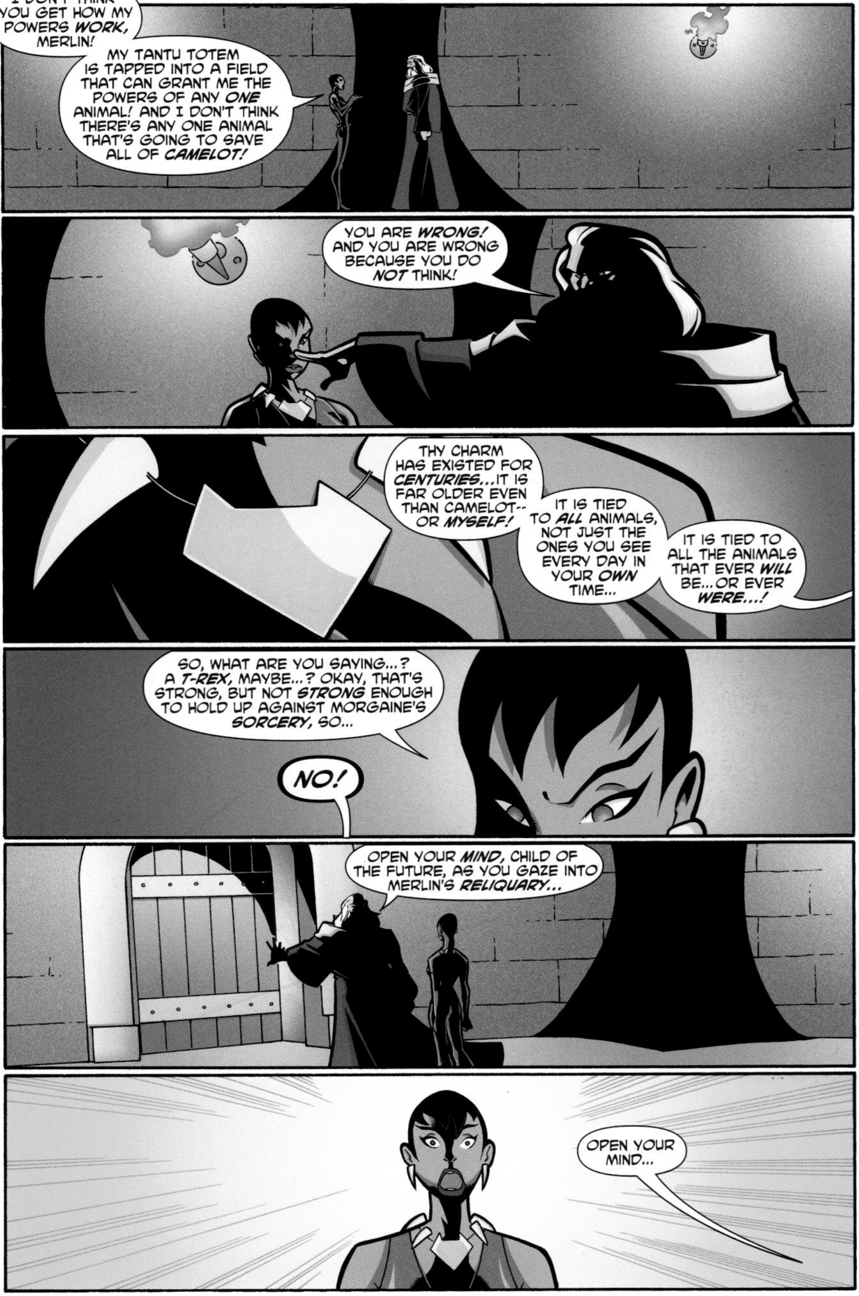
I DON'T THINK YOU GET HOW MY POWERS WORK, MERLIN!
MY TANTU TOTEM IS TAPPED INTO A FIELD THAT CAN GRANT ME THE POWERS OF ANY ONE ANIMAL! AND I DON'T THINK THERE'S ANY ONE ANIMAL THAT'S GOING TO SAVE ALL OF CAMELOT!
YOU ARE WRONG! AND YOU ARE WRONG BECAUSE YOU DO NOT THINK!
THY CHARM HAS EXISTED FOR CENTURIES... IT IS FAR OLDER EVEN THAN CAMELOT-- OR MYSELF!
IT IS TIED TO ALL ANIMALS, NOT JUST THE ONES YOU SEE EVERY DAY IN YOUR OWN TIME...
IT IS TIED TO ALL THE ANIMALS THAT EVER WILL BE... OR EVER WERE...!
SO, WHAT ARE YOU SAYING...? A T-REX, MAYBE...? OKAY, THAT'S STRONG, BUT NOT STRONG ENOUGH TO HOLD UP AGAINST MORGAINE'S SORCERY, SO...
NO!
OPEN YOUR MIND, CHILD OF THE FUTURE, AS YOU GAZE INTO MERLIN'S RELIQUARY...
OPEN YOUR MIND...

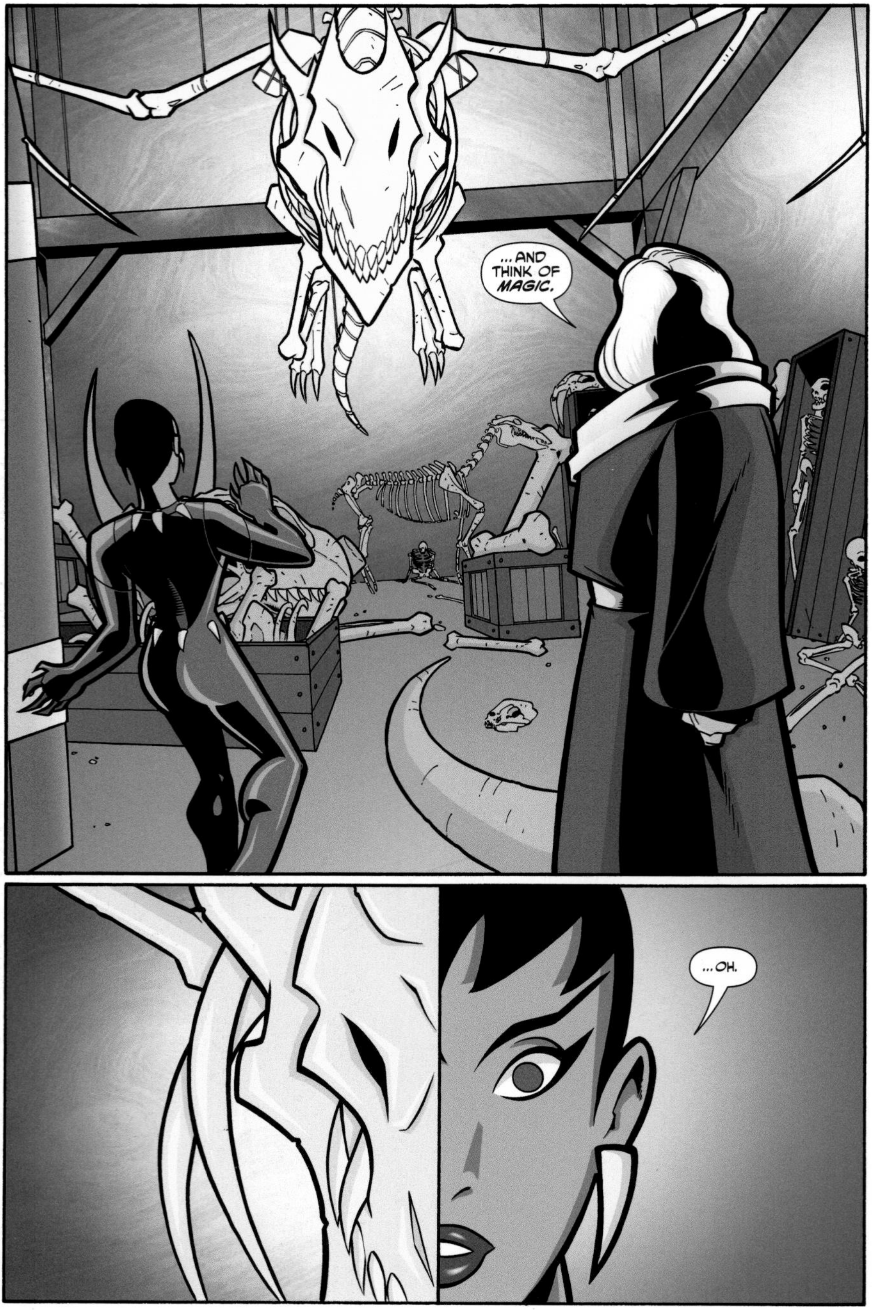
...AND THINK OF MAGIC.
...OH.

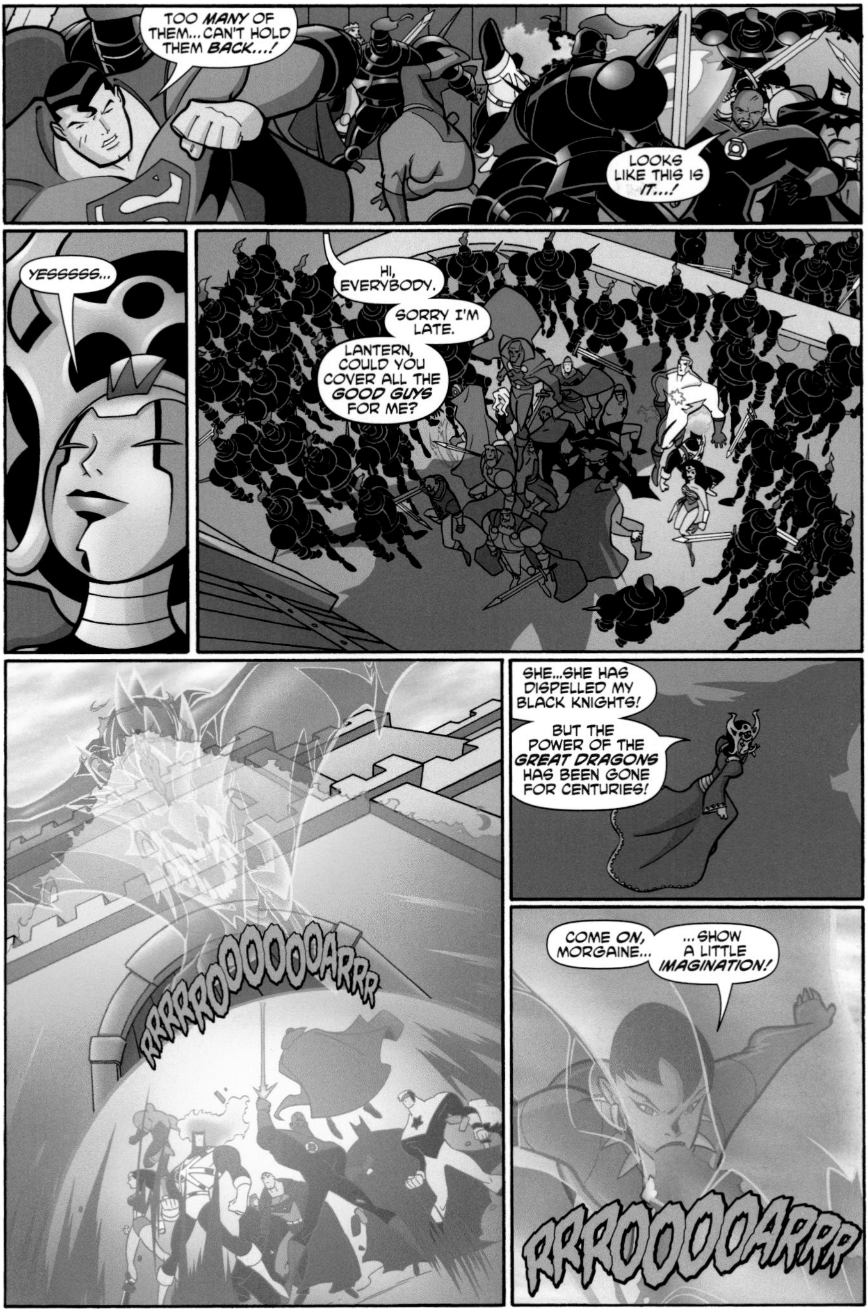
TOO MANY OF THEM...CAN'T HOLD THEM BACK...!
LOOKS LIKE THIS IS IT...!
YESSSSS...
HI, EVERYBODY.
SORRY I'M LATE.
LANTERN, COULD YOU COVER ALL THE GOOD GUYS FOR ME?
RRRRROOOOOOARRR
SHE...SHE HAS DISPELLED MY BLACK KNIGHTS!
BUT THE POWER OF THE GREAT DRAGONS HAS BEEN GONE FOR CENTURIES!
COME ON, MORGAINE...
...SHOW A LITTLE IMAGINATION!
RRROOOOOARRR

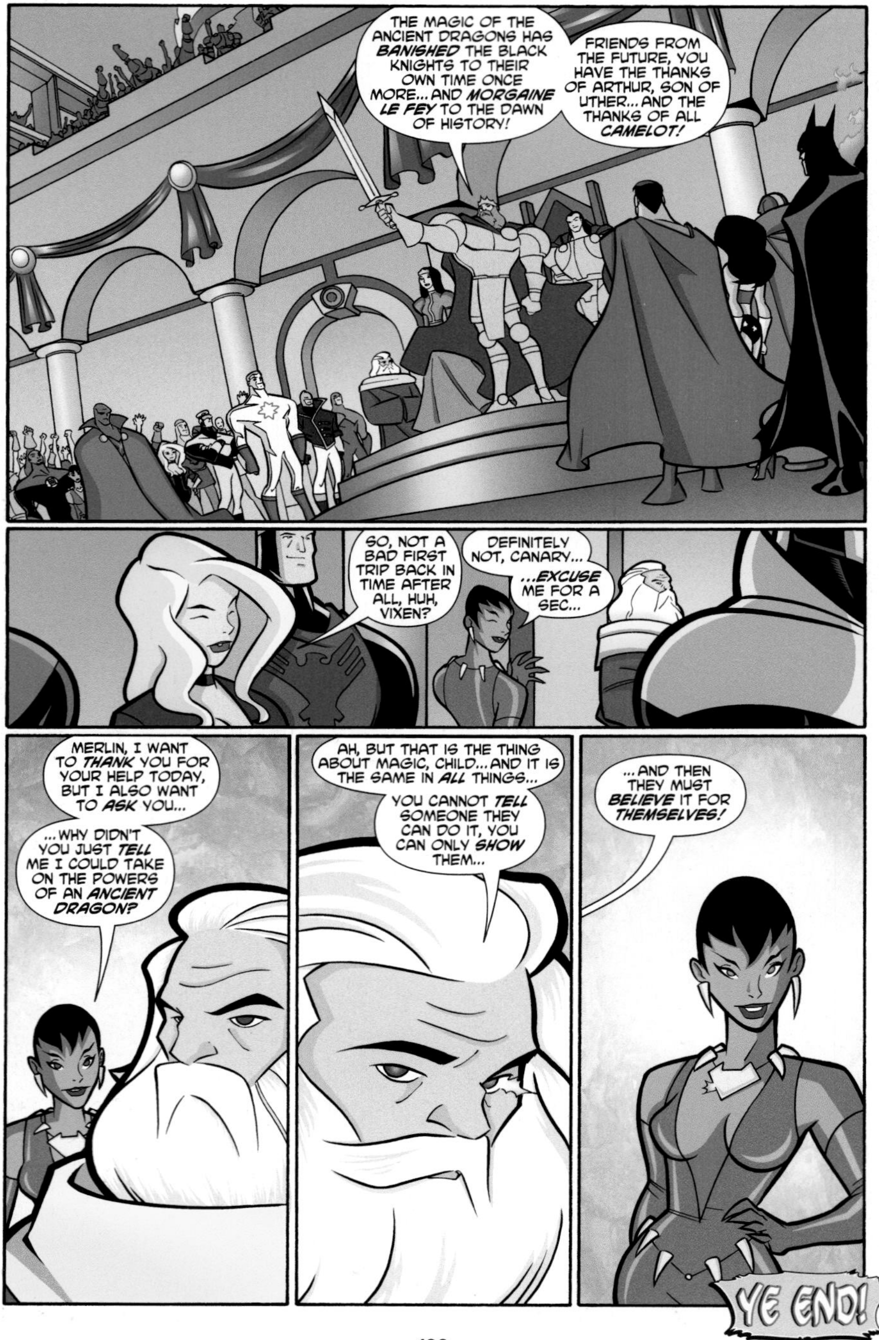

THE MAGIC OF THE ANCIENT DRAGONS HAS BANISHED THE BLACK KNIGHTS TO THEIR OWN TIME ONCE MORE... AND MORGAINE LE FEY TO THE DAWN OF HISTORY!
FRIENDS FROM THE FUTURE, YOU HAVE THE THANKS OF ARTHUR, SON OF UTHER... AND THE THANKS OF ALL CAMELOT!
SO, NOT A BAD FIRST TRIP BACK IN TIME AFTER ALL, HUH, VIXEN?
DEFINITELY NOT, CANARY...
...EXCUSE ME FOR A SEC...
MERLIN, I WANT TO THANK YOU FOR YOUR HELP TODAY, BUT I ALSO WANT TO ASK YOU...
...WHY DIDN'T YOU JUST TELL ME I COULD TAKE ON THE POWERS OF AN ANCIENT DRAGON?
AH, BUT THAT IS THE THING ABOUT MAGIC, CHILD... AND IT IS THE SAME IN ALL THINGS...
YOU CANNOT TELL SOMEONE THEY CAN DO IT, YOU CAN ONLY SHOW THEM...
...AND THEN THEY MUST BELIEVE IT FOR THEMSELVES!
YE END!

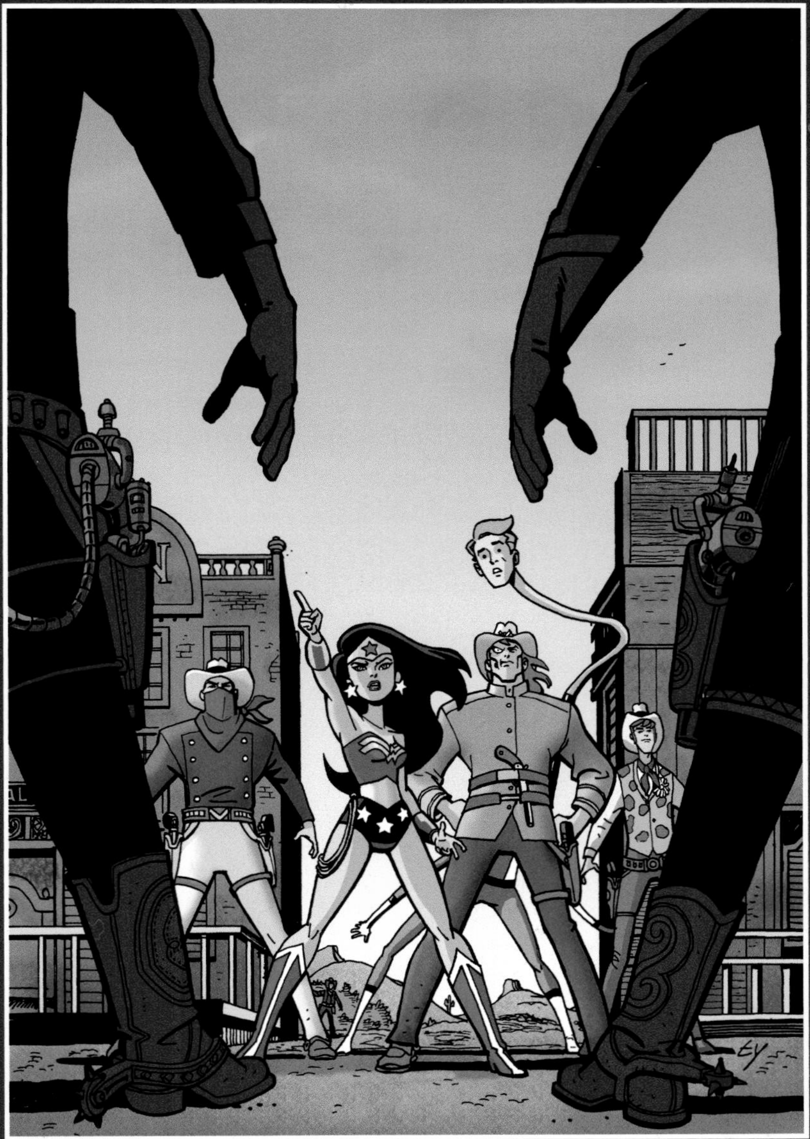

CHAPTER 6: THE JUSTICE RANGERS RIDE AGAIN!

JUSTICE LEAGUE UNLIMITED

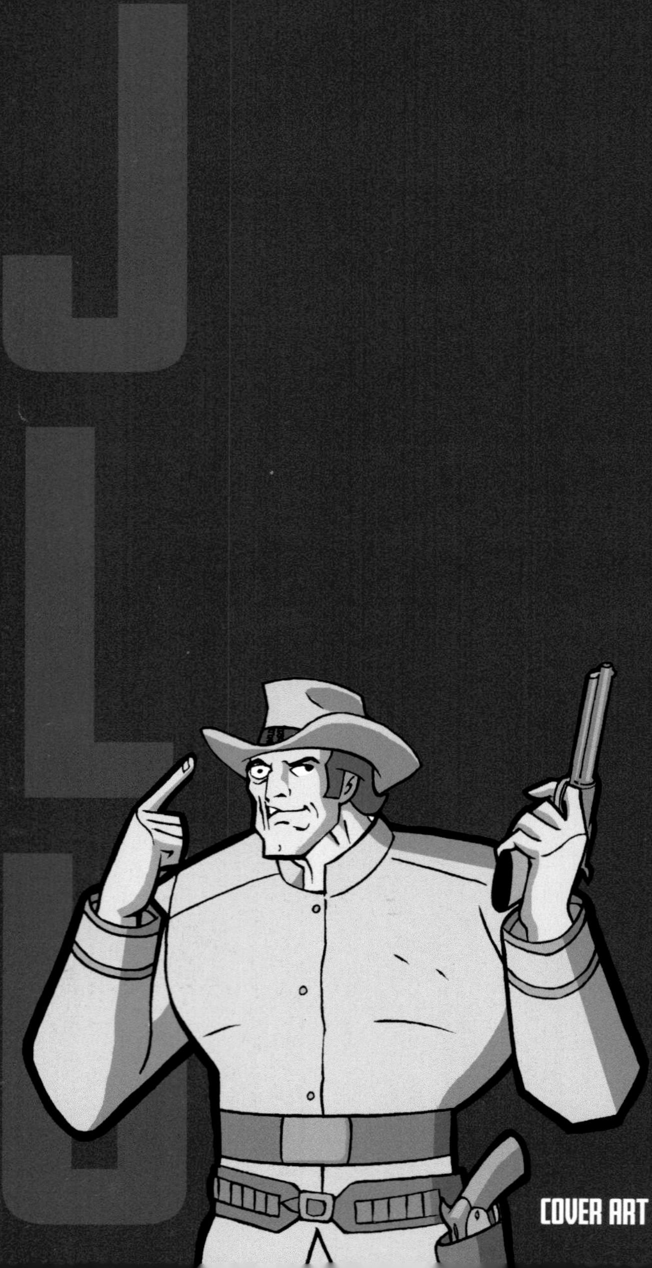

COVER ART BY TY TEMPLETON

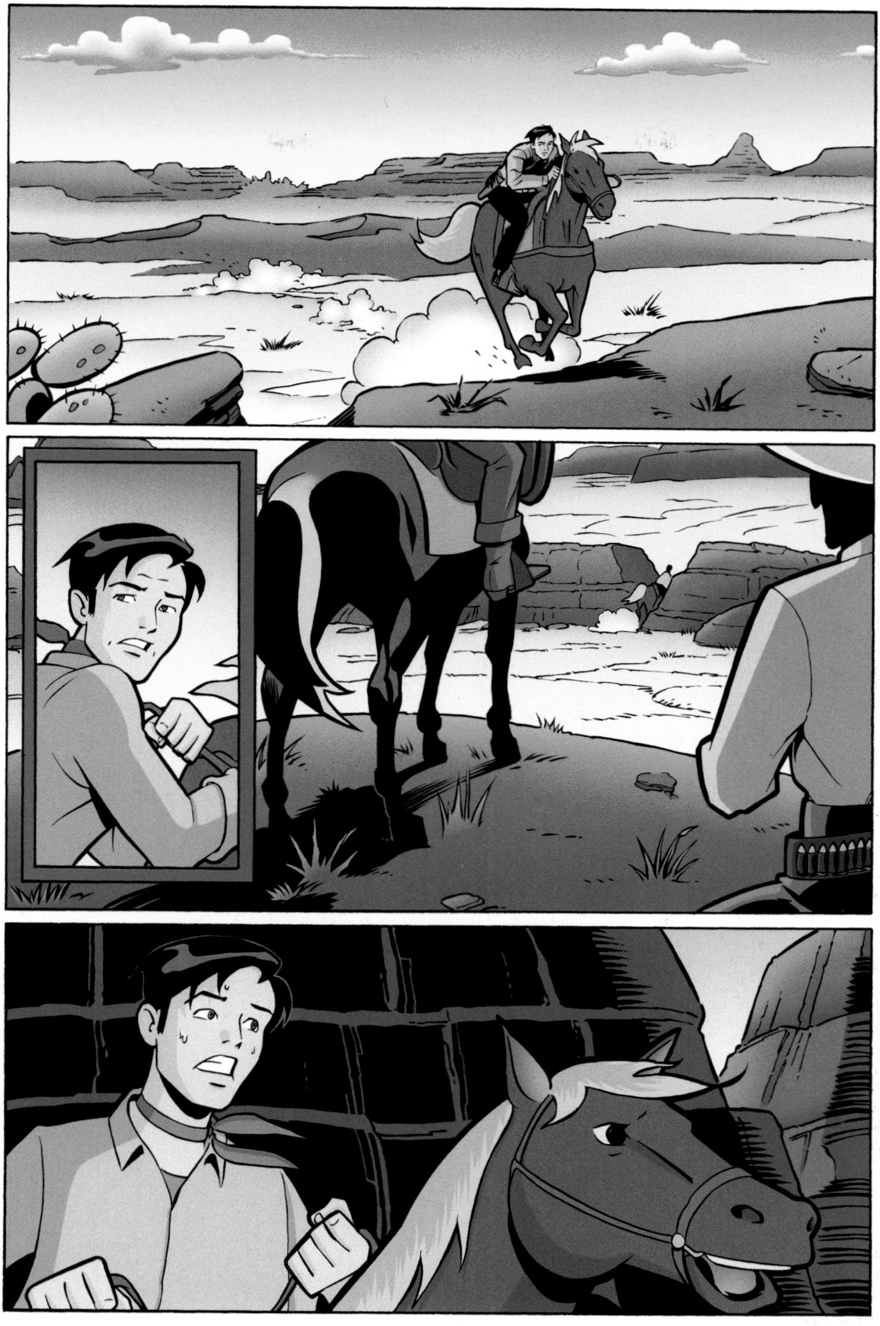

THE JUSTICE RANGERS RIDE AGAIN!

Adam Beechen - Script   Gordon Purcell - Pencils   Bob Petrecca - Inks
Heroic Age - Colors   Travis Lanham - Letters   Michael Wright - Ridin' Shotgun

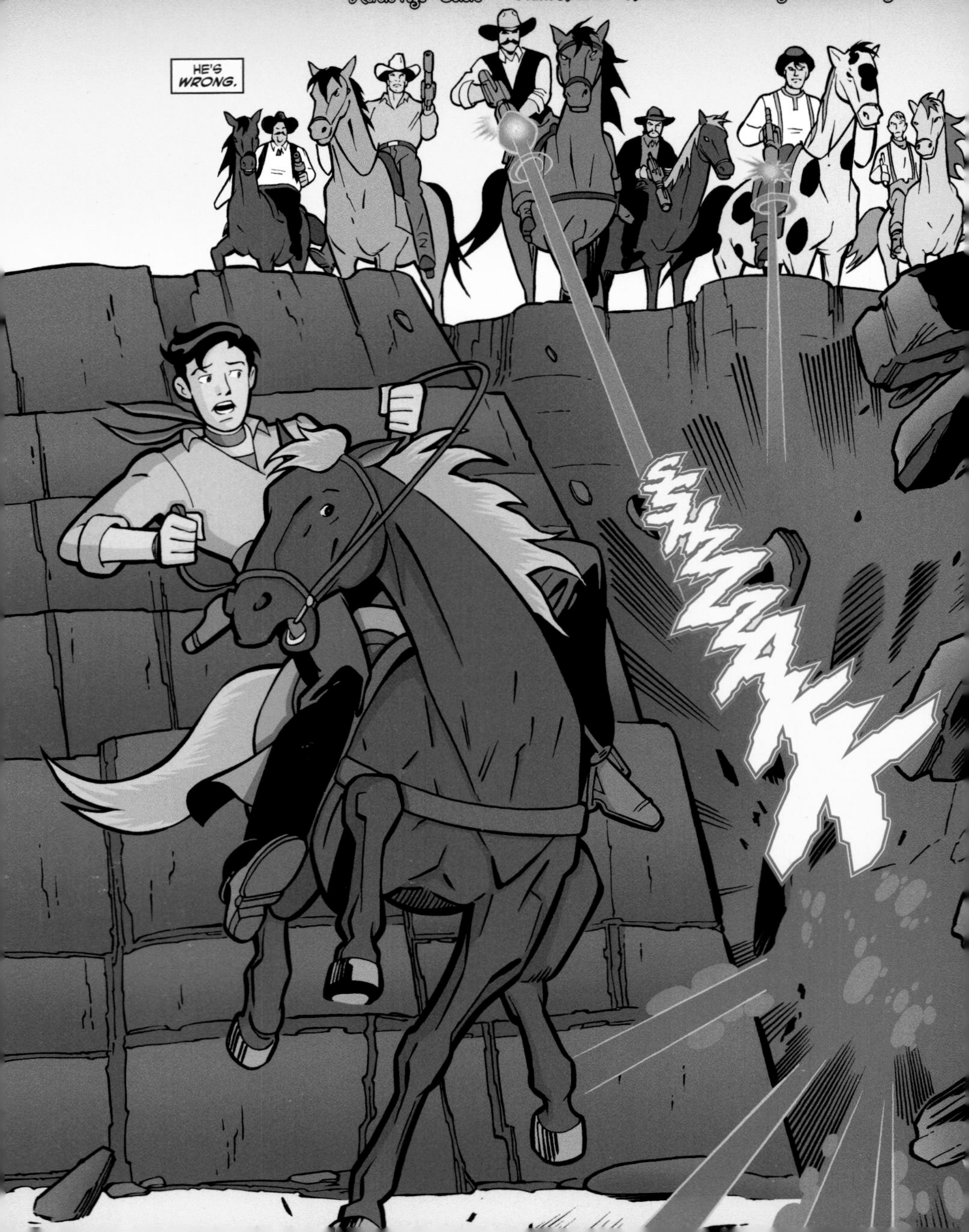
HE'S WRONG.
SHHZZAKK

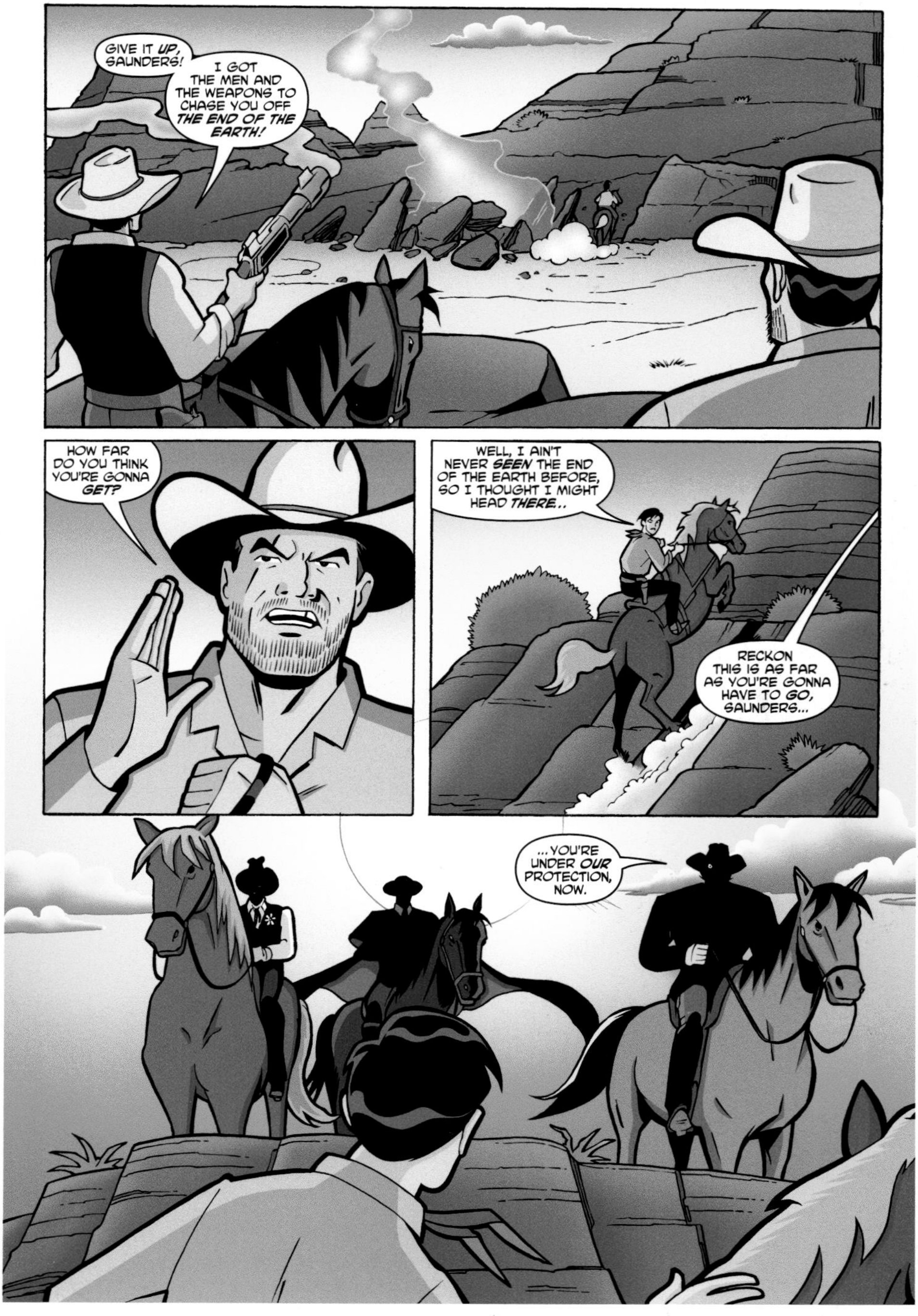
GIVE IT UP, SAUNDERS!
I GOT THE MEN AND THE WEAPONS TO CHASE YOU OFF THE END OF THE EARTH!
HOW FAR DO YOU THINK YOU'RE GONNA GET?
WELL, I AIN'T NEVER SEEN THE END OF THE EARTH BEFORE, SO I THOUGHT I MIGHT HEAD THERE...
RECKON THIS IS AS FAR AS YOU'RE GONNA HAVE TO GO, SAUNDERS...
...YOU'RE UNDER OUR PROTECTION, NOW.

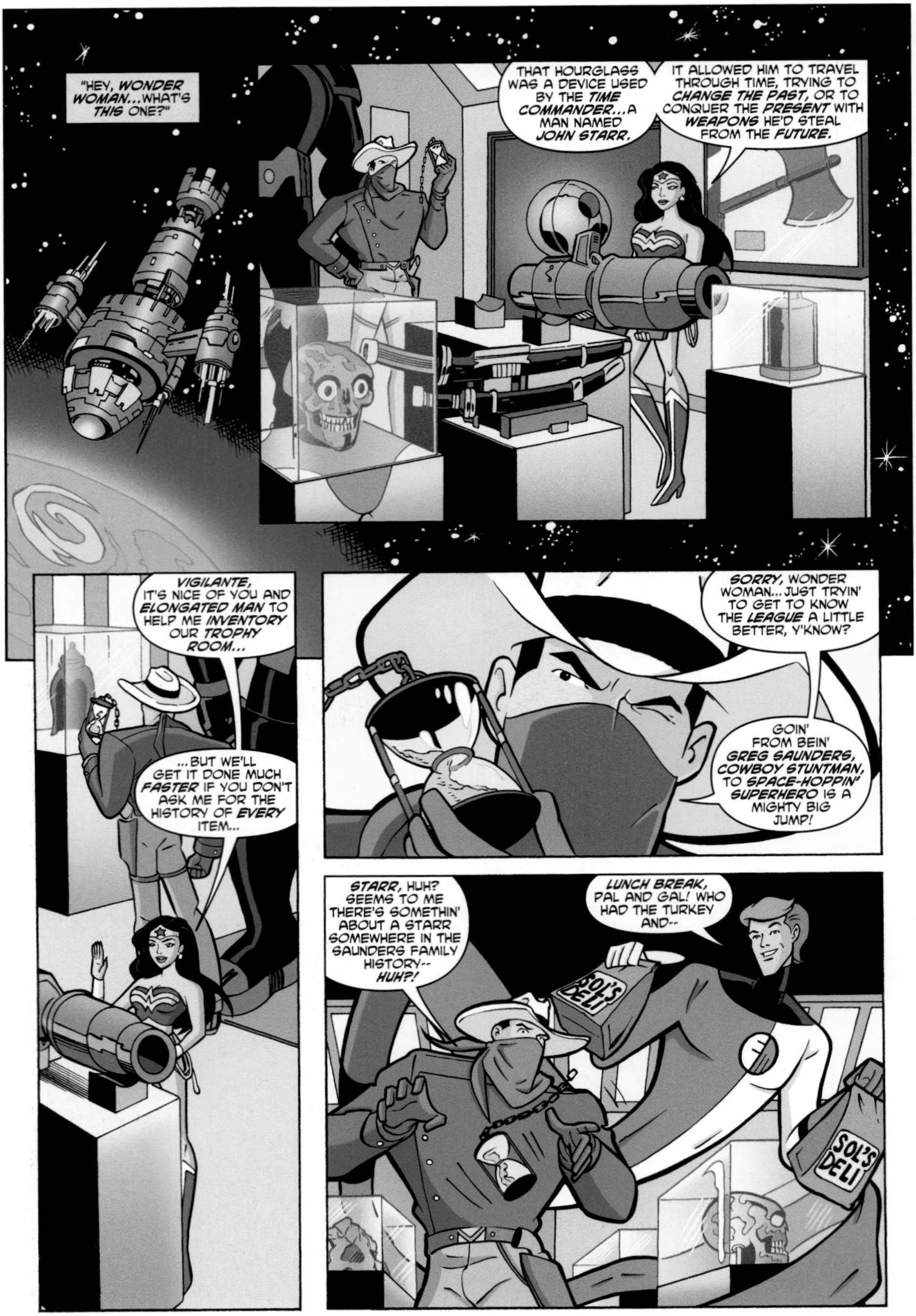
"HEY, WONDER WOMAN... WHAT'S THIS ONE?"
THAT HOURGLASS WAS A DEVICE USED BY THE TIME COMMANDER... A MAN NAMED JOHN STARR.
IT ALLOWED HIM TO TRAVEL THROUGH TIME, TRYING TO CHANGE THE PAST, OR TO CONQUER THE PRESENT WITH WEAPONS HE'D STEAL FROM THE FUTURE.
VIGILANTE, IT'S NICE OF YOU AND ELONGATED MAN TO HELP ME INVENTORY OUR TROPHY ROOM...
...BUT WE'LL GET IT DONE MUCH FASTER IF YOU DON'T ASK ME FOR THE HISTORY OF EVERY ITEM...
SORRY, WONDER WOMAN... JUST TRYIN' TO GET TO KNOW THE LEAGUE A LITTLE BETTER, Y'KNOW?
GOIN' FROM BEIN' GREG SAUNDERS, COWBOY STUNTMAN, TO SPACE-HOPPIN' SUPERHERO IS A MIGHTY BIG JUMP!
STARR, HUH? SEEMS TO ME THERE'S SOMETHIN' ABOUT A STARR SOMEWHERE IN THE SAUNDERS FAMILY HISTORY-- HUH?!
LUNCH BREAK, PAL AND GAL! WHO HAD THE TURKEY AND--
SOL'S DELI
SOL'S DELI

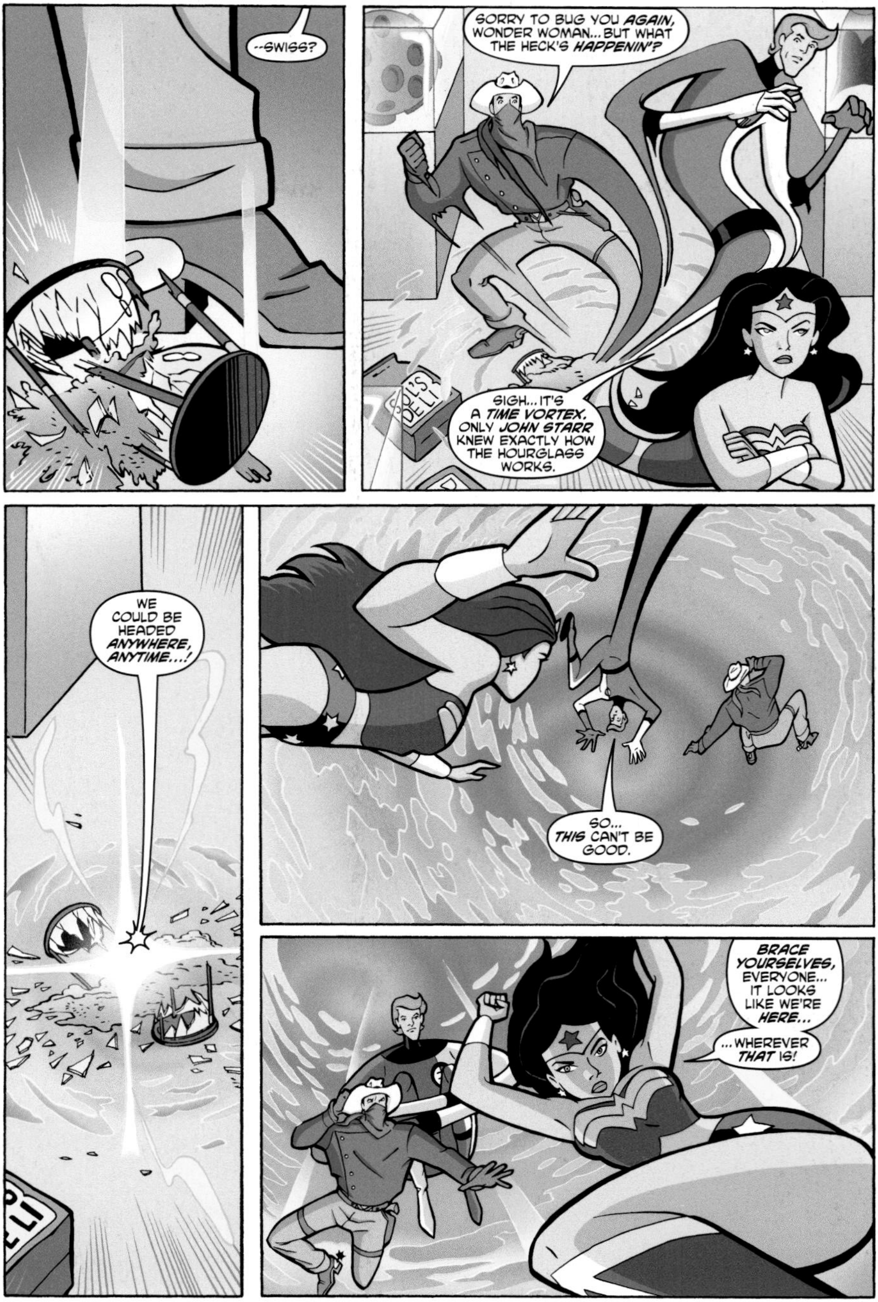
--SWISS?
SORRY TO BUG YOU AGAIN, WONDER WOMAN... BUT WHAT THE HECK'S HAPPENIN'?
SIGH... IT'S A TIME VORTEX. ONLY JOHN STARR KNEW EXACTLY HOW THE HOURGLASS WORKS.
WE COULD BE HEADED ANYWHERE, ANYTIME...!
SO... THIS CAN'T BE GOOD.
BRACE YOURSELVES, EVERYONE... IT LOOKS LIKE WE'RE HERE...
...WHEREVER THAT IS!

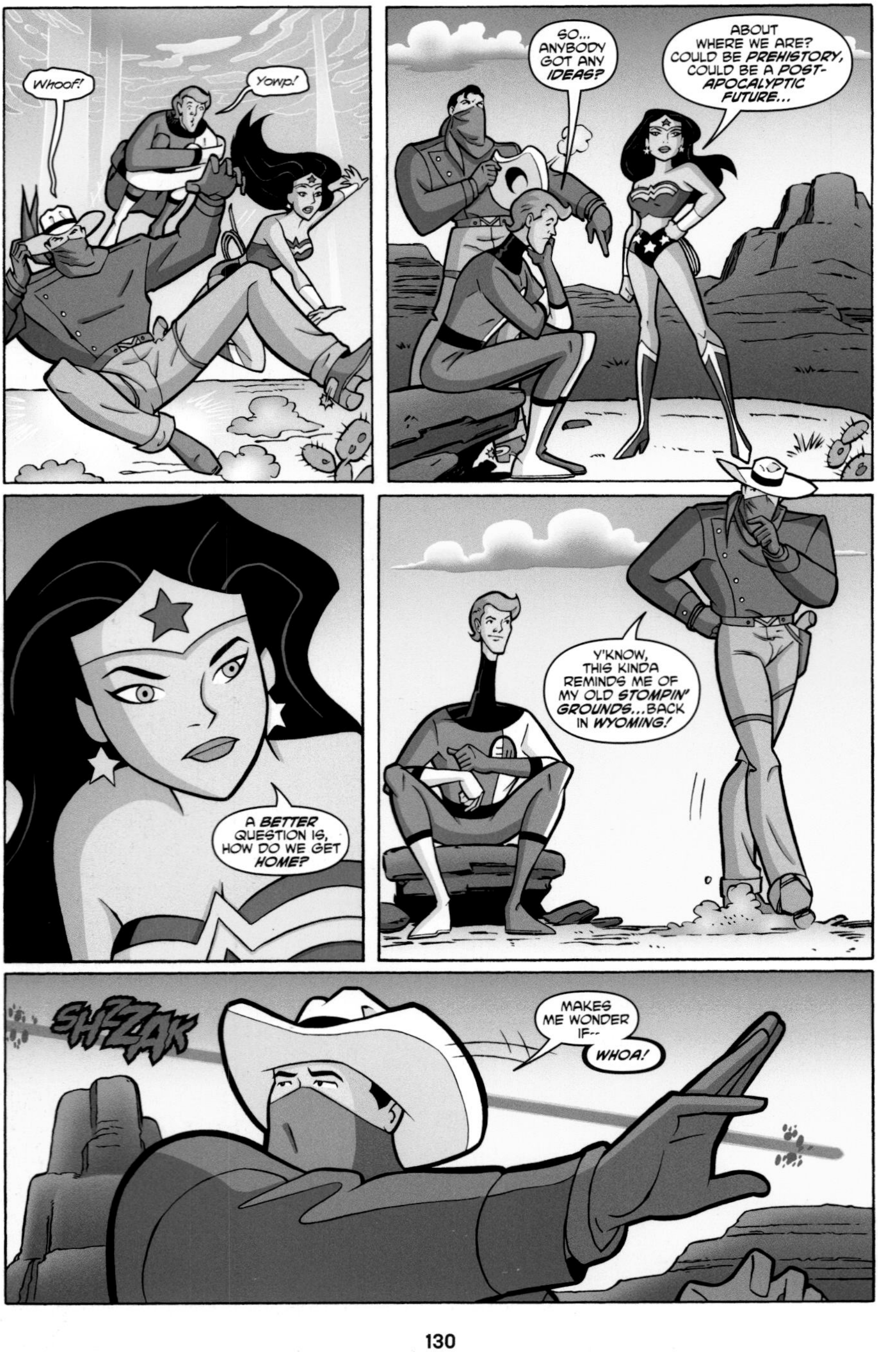
Whoof!
Yowp!
SO... ANYBODY GOT ANY IDEAS?
ABOUT WHERE WE ARE? COULD BE PREHISTORY, COULD BE A POST-APOCALYPTIC FUTURE...
A BETTER QUESTION IS, HOW DO WE GET HOME?
Y'KNOW, THIS KINDA REMINDS ME OF MY OLD STOMPIN' GROUNDS...BACK IN WYOMING!
SHZZAK
MAKES ME WONDER IF--
WHOA!

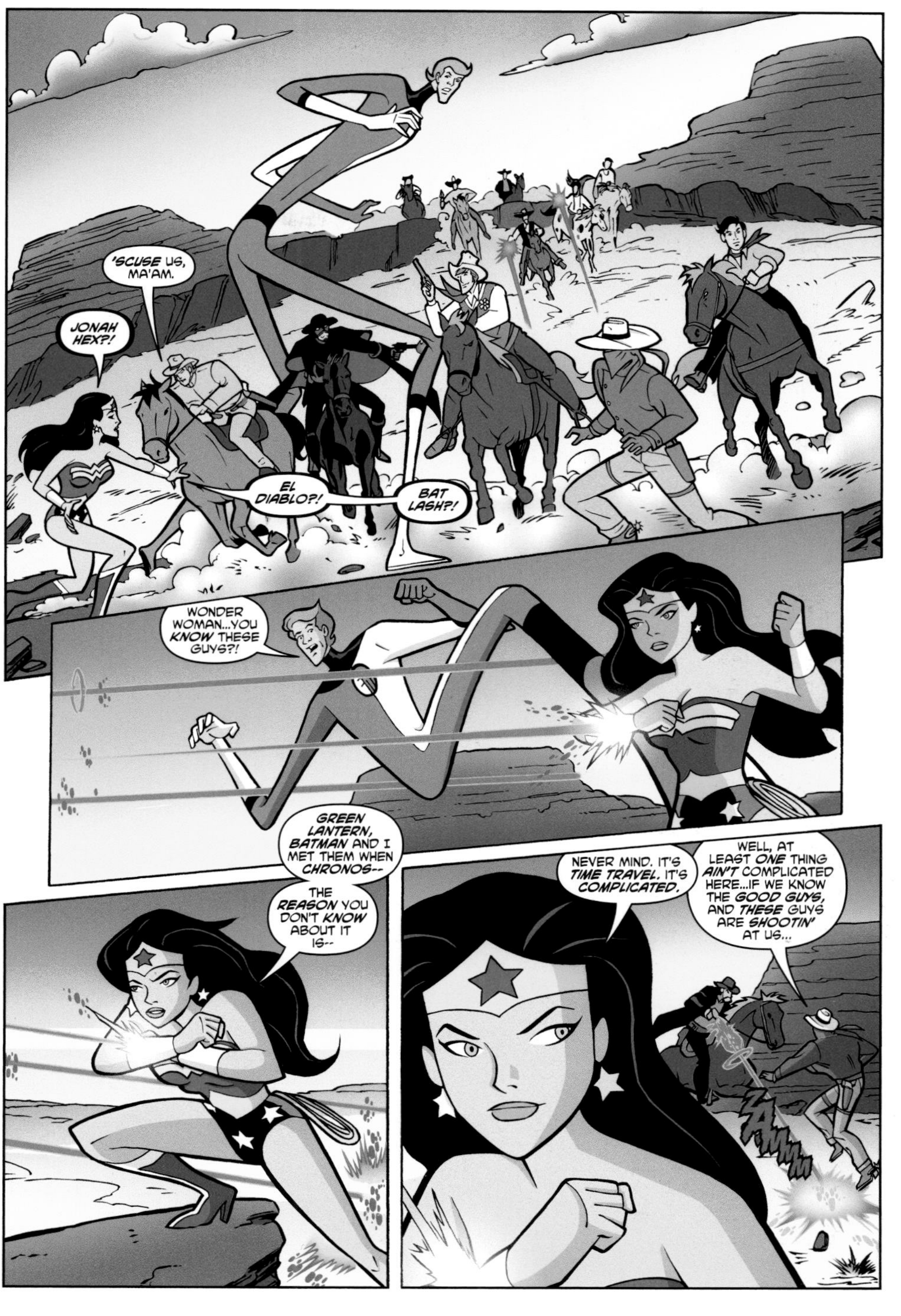

JONAH HEX?!
'SCUSE US, MA'AM.
EL DIABLO?!
BAT LASH?!
WONDER WOMAN...YOU KNOW THESE GUYS?!
GREEN LANTERN, BATMAN AND I MET THEM WHEN CHRONOS--
THE REASON YOU DON'T KNOW ABOUT IT IS--
NEVER MIND. IT'S TIME TRAVEL. IT'S COMPLICATED.
WELL, AT LEAST ONE THING AIN'T COMPLICATED HERE...IF WE KNOW THE GOOD GUYS, AND THESE GUYS ARE SHOOTIN' AT US...

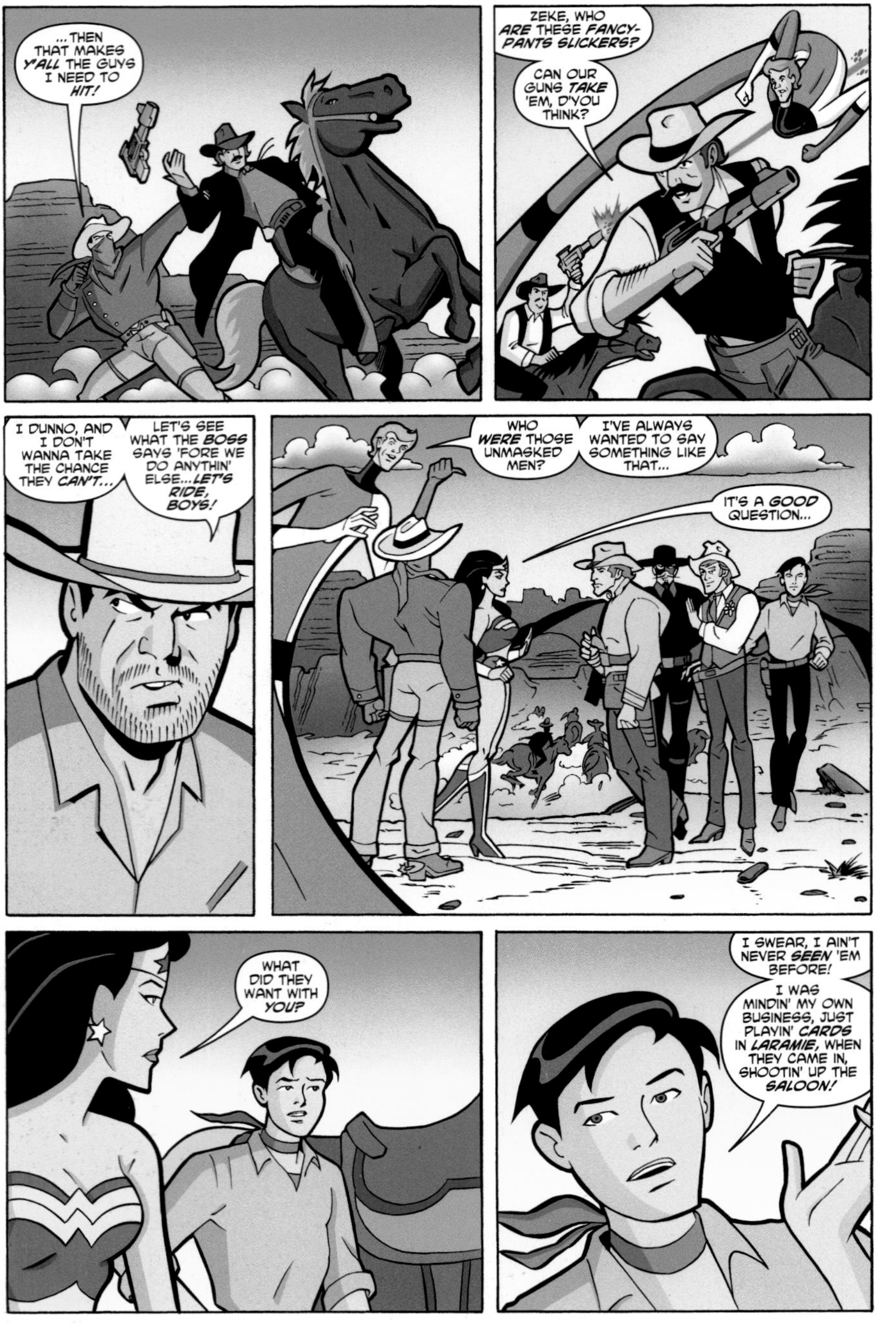
...THEN THAT MAKES Y'ALL THE GUYS I NEED TO HIT!
ZEKE, WHO ARE THESE FANCY-PANTS SLICKERS?
CAN OUR GUNS TAKE 'EM, D'YOU THINK?
I DUNNO, AND I DON'T WANNA TAKE THE CHANCE THEY CAN'T...
LET'S SEE WHAT THE BOSS SAYS 'FORE WE DO ANYTHIN' ELSE...LET'S RIDE, BOYS!
WHO WERE THOSE UNMASKED MEN?
I'VE ALWAYS WANTED TO SAY SOMETHING LIKE THAT...
IT'S A GOOD QUESTION...
WHAT DID THEY WANT WITH YOU?
I SWEAR, I AIN'T NEVER SEEN 'EM BEFORE!
I WAS MINDIN' MY OWN BUSINESS, JUST PLAYIN' CARDS IN LARAMIE, WHEN THEY CAME IN, SHOOTIN' UP THE SALOON!

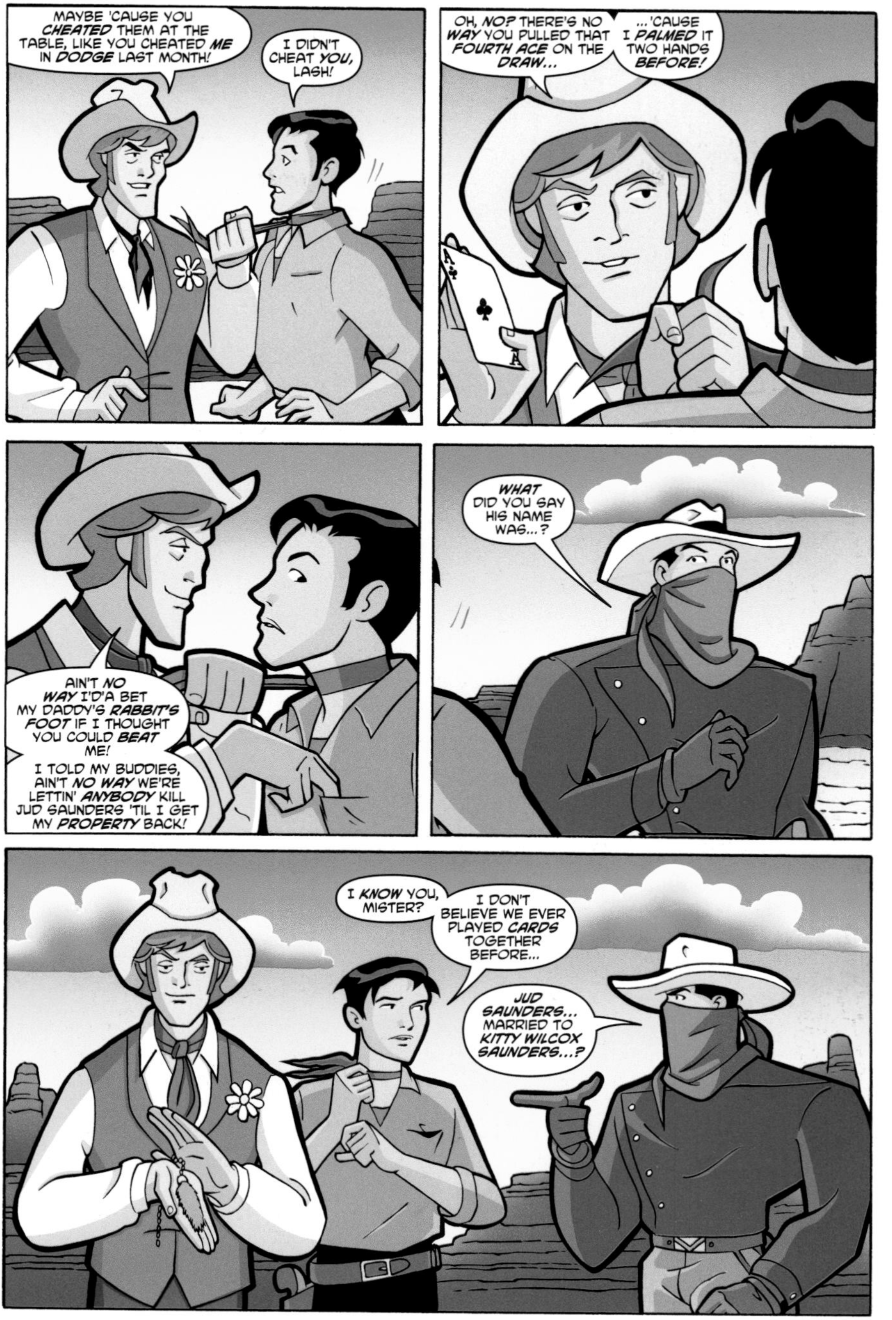
MAYBE 'CAUSE YOU CHEATED THEM AT THE TABLE, LIKE YOU CHEATED ME IN DODGE LAST MONTH!
I DIDN'T CHEAT YOU, LASH!
OH, NO? THERE'S NO WAY YOU PULLED THAT FOURTH ACE ON THE DRAW...
...'CAUSE I PALMED IT TWO HANDS BEFORE!
AIN'T NO WAY I'D'A BET MY DADDY'S RABBIT'S FOOT IF I THOUGHT YOU COULD BEAT ME!
I TOLD MY BUDDIES, AIN'T NO WAY WE'RE LETTIN' ANYBODY KILL JUD SAUNDERS 'TIL I GET MY PROPERTY BACK!
WHAT DID YOU SAY HIS NAME WAS...?
I KNOW YOU, MISTER?
I DON'T BELIEVE WE EVER PLAYED CARDS TOGETHER BEFORE...
JUD SAUNDERS... MARRIED TO KITTY WILCOX SAUNDERS...?

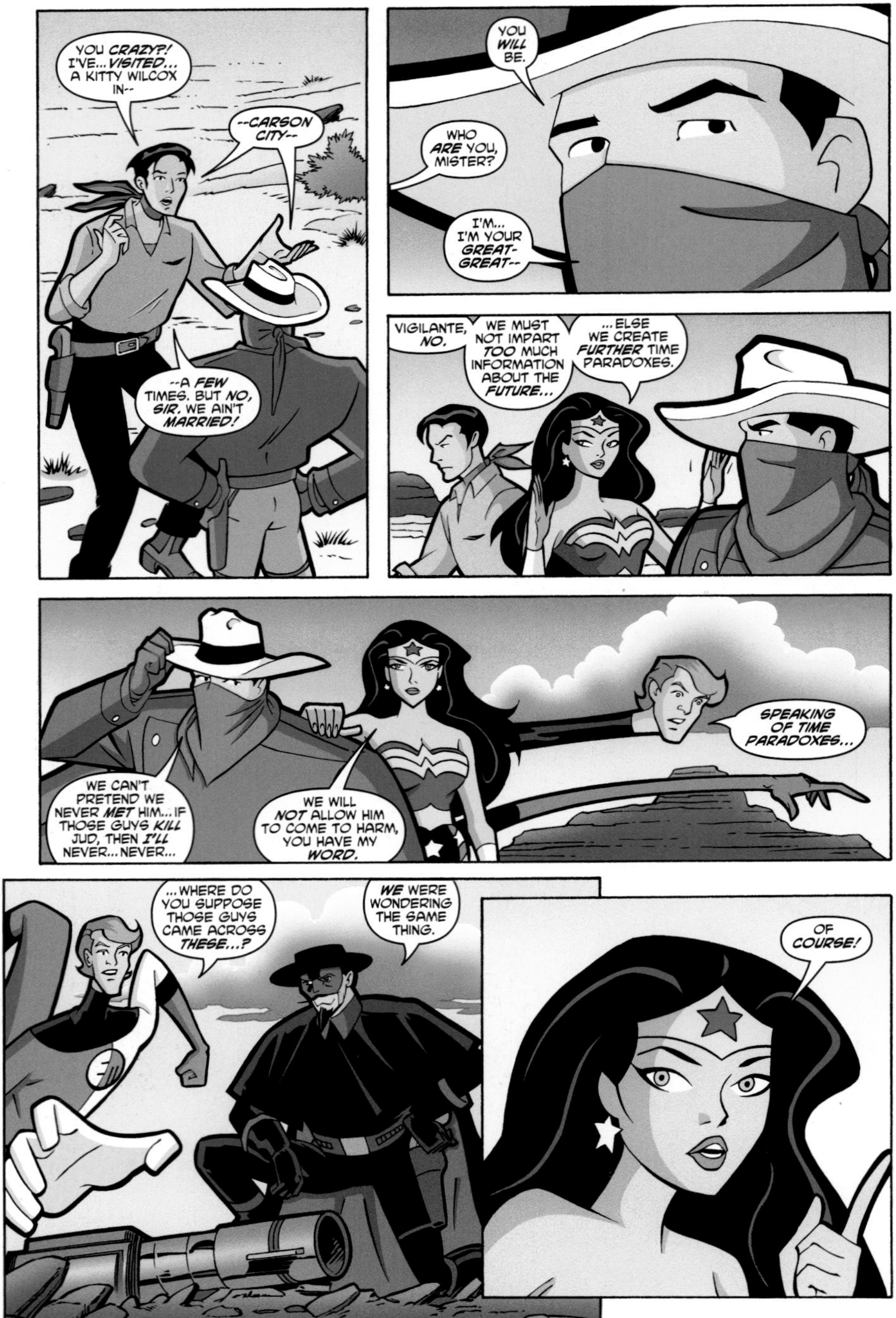
YOU CRAZY?! I'VE... VISITED... A KITTY WILCOX IN--
--CARSON CITY--
--A FEW TIMES. BUT NO, SIR. WE AIN'T MARRIED!
YOU WILL BE.
WHO ARE YOU, MISTER?
I'M... I'M YOUR GREAT-GREAT--
VIGILANTE, NO.
WE MUST NOT IMPART TOO MUCH INFORMATION ABOUT THE FUTURE...
...ELSE WE CREATE FURTHER TIME PARADOXES.
WE CAN'T PRETEND WE NEVER MET HIM... IF THOSE GUYS KILL JUD, THEN I'LL NEVER... NEVER...
WE WILL NOT ALLOW HIM TO COME TO HARM, YOU HAVE MY WORD.
SPEAKING OF TIME PARADOXES...
...WHERE DO YOU SUPPOSE THOSE GUYS CAME ACROSS THESE...?
WE WERE WONDERING THE SAME THING.
OF COURSE!

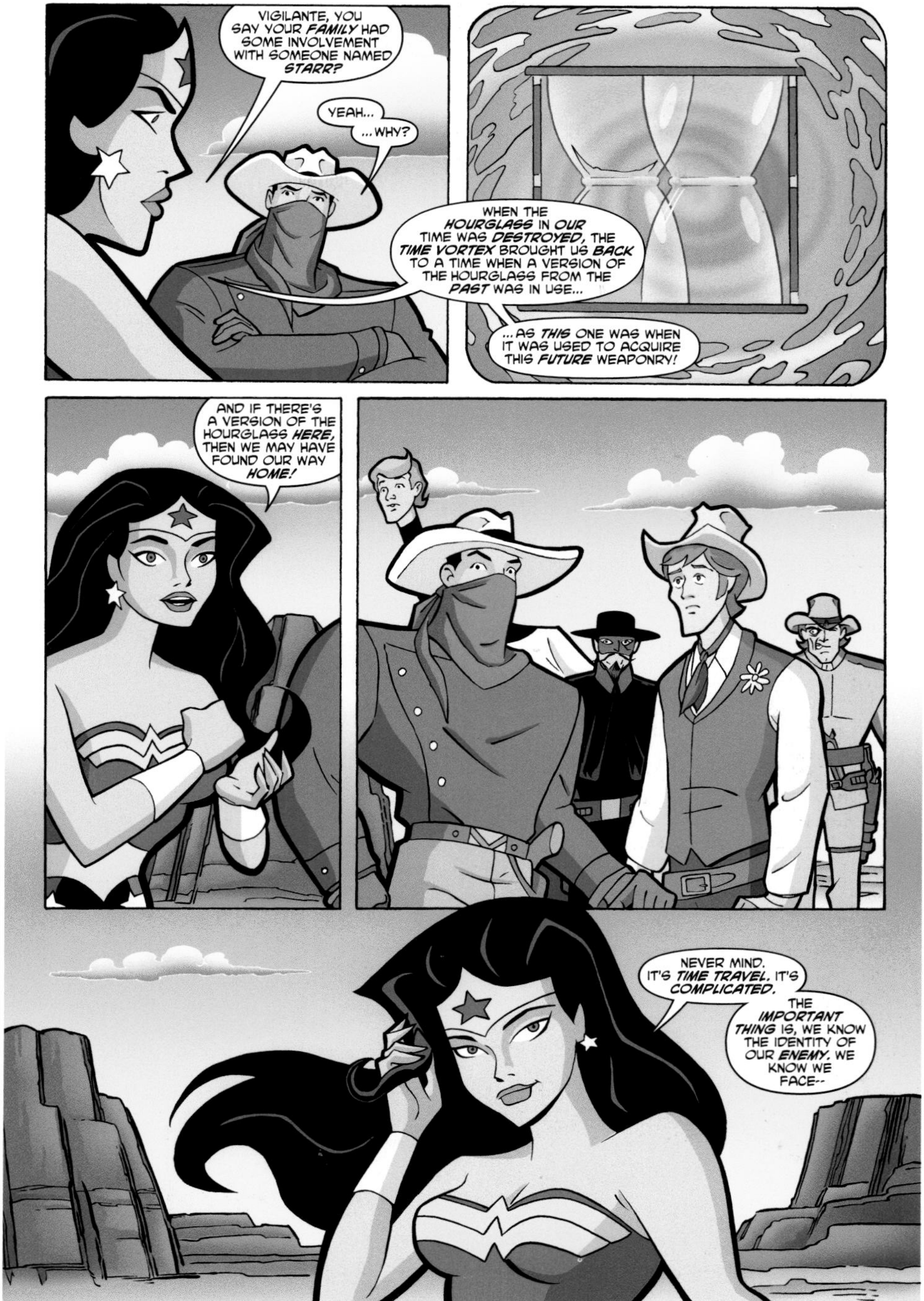
VIGILANTE, YOU SAY YOUR FAMILY HAD SOME INVOLVEMENT WITH SOMEONE NAMED STARR?
YEAH...
...WHY?
WHEN THE HOURGLASS IN OUR TIME WAS DESTROYED, THE TIME VORTEX BROUGHT US BACK TO A TIME WHEN A VERSION OF THE HOURGLASS FROM THE PAST WAS IN USE...
...AS THIS ONE WAS WHEN IT WAS USED TO ACQUIRE THIS FUTURE WEAPONRY!
AND IF THERE'S A VERSION OF THE HOURGLASS HERE, THEN WE MAY HAVE FOUND OUR WAY HOME!
NEVER MIND. IT'S TIME TRAVEL. IT'S COMPLICATED.
THE IMPORTANT THING IS, WE KNOW THE IDENTITY OF OUR ENEMY. WE KNOW WE FACE--

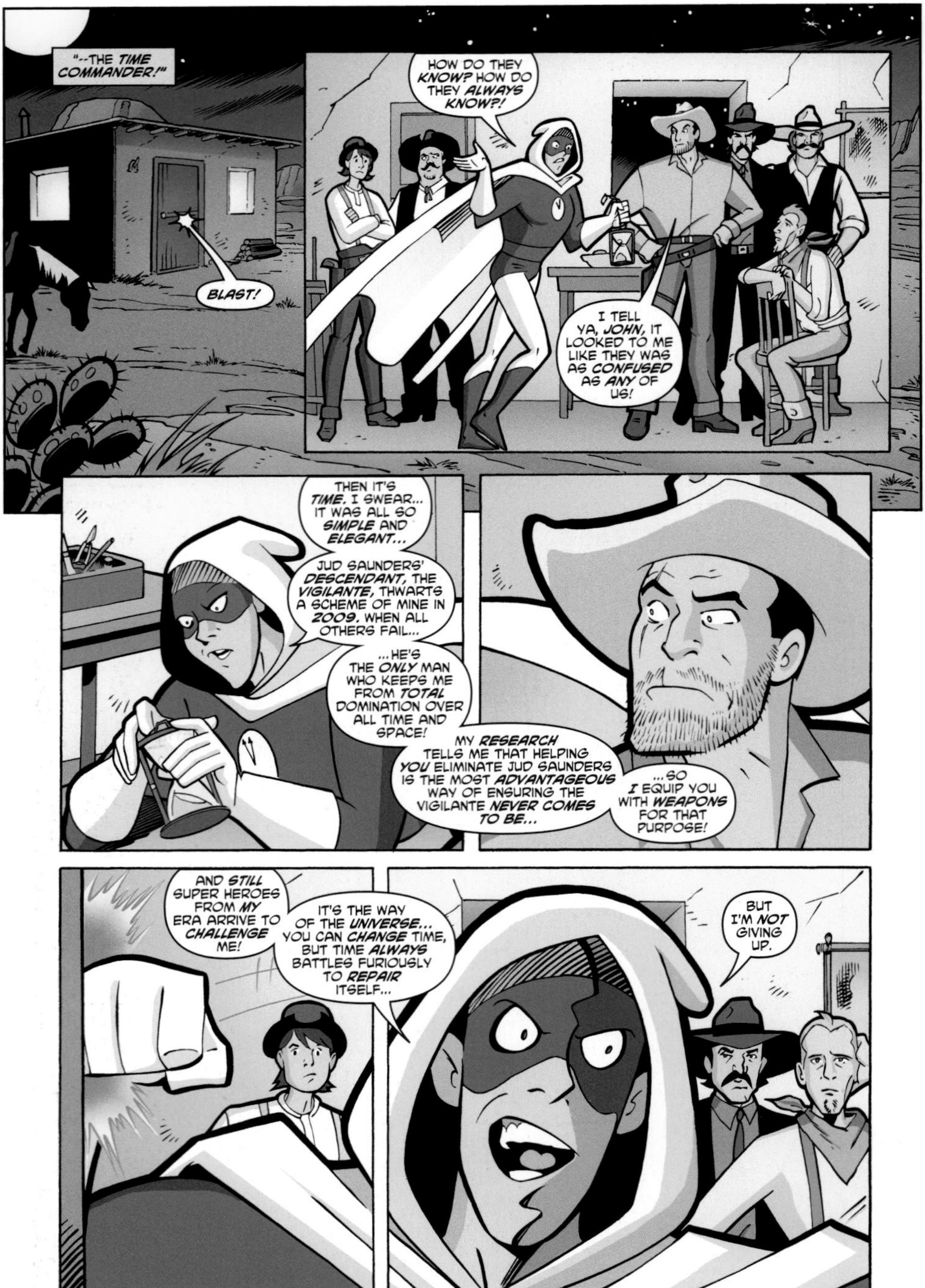
"--THE TIME COMMANDER!"
BLAST!
HOW DO THEY KNOW? HOW DO THEY ALWAYS KNOW?!
I TELL YA, JOHN, IT LOOKED TO ME LIKE THEY WAS AS CONFUSED AS ANY OF US!
THEN IT'S TIME. I SWEAR... IT WAS ALL SO SIMPLE AND ELEGANT...
JUD SAUNDERS' DESCENDANT, THE VIGILANTE, THWARTS A SCHEME OF MINE IN 2009. WHEN ALL OTHERS FAIL...
...HE'S THE ONLY MAN WHO KEEPS ME FROM TOTAL DOMINATION OVER ALL TIME AND SPACE!
MY RESEARCH TELLS ME THAT HELPING YOU ELIMINATE JUD SAUNDERS IS THE MOST ADVANTAGEOUS WAY OF ENSURING THE VIGILANTE NEVER COMES TO BE...
...SO I EQUIP YOU WITH WEAPONS FOR THAT PURPOSE!
AND STILL SUPER HEROES FROM MY ERA ARRIVE TO CHALLENGE ME!
IT'S THE WAY OF THE UNIVERSE... YOU CAN CHANGE TIME, BUT TIME ALWAYS BATTLES FURIOUSLY TO REPAIR ITSELF...
BUT I'M NOT GIVING UP.

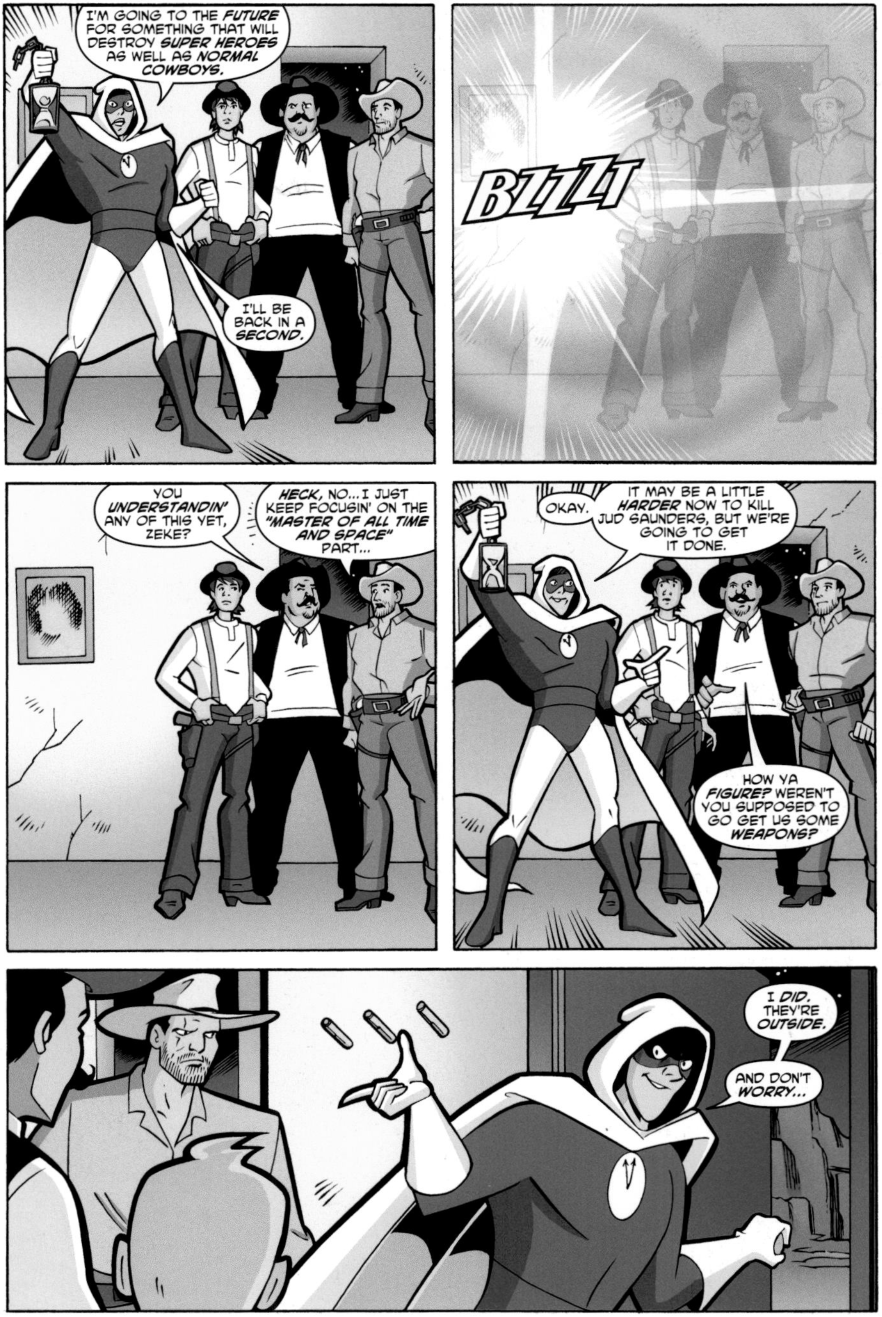
I'M GOING TO THE FUTURE FOR SOMETHING THAT WILL DESTROY SUPER HEROES AS WELL AS NORMAL COWBOYS.
I'LL BE BACK IN A SECOND.
BZZZZT
YOU UNDERSTANDIN' ANY OF THIS YET, ZEKE?
HECK, NO... I JUST KEEP FOCUSIN' ON THE "MASTER OF ALL TIME AND SPACE" PART...
OKAY.
IT MAY BE A LITTLE HARDER NOW TO KILL JUD SAUNDERS, BUT WE'RE GOING TO GET IT DONE.
HOW YA FIGURE? WEREN'T YOU SUPPOSED TO GO GET US SOME WEAPONS?
I DID. THEY'RE OUTSIDE.
AND DON'T WORRY...

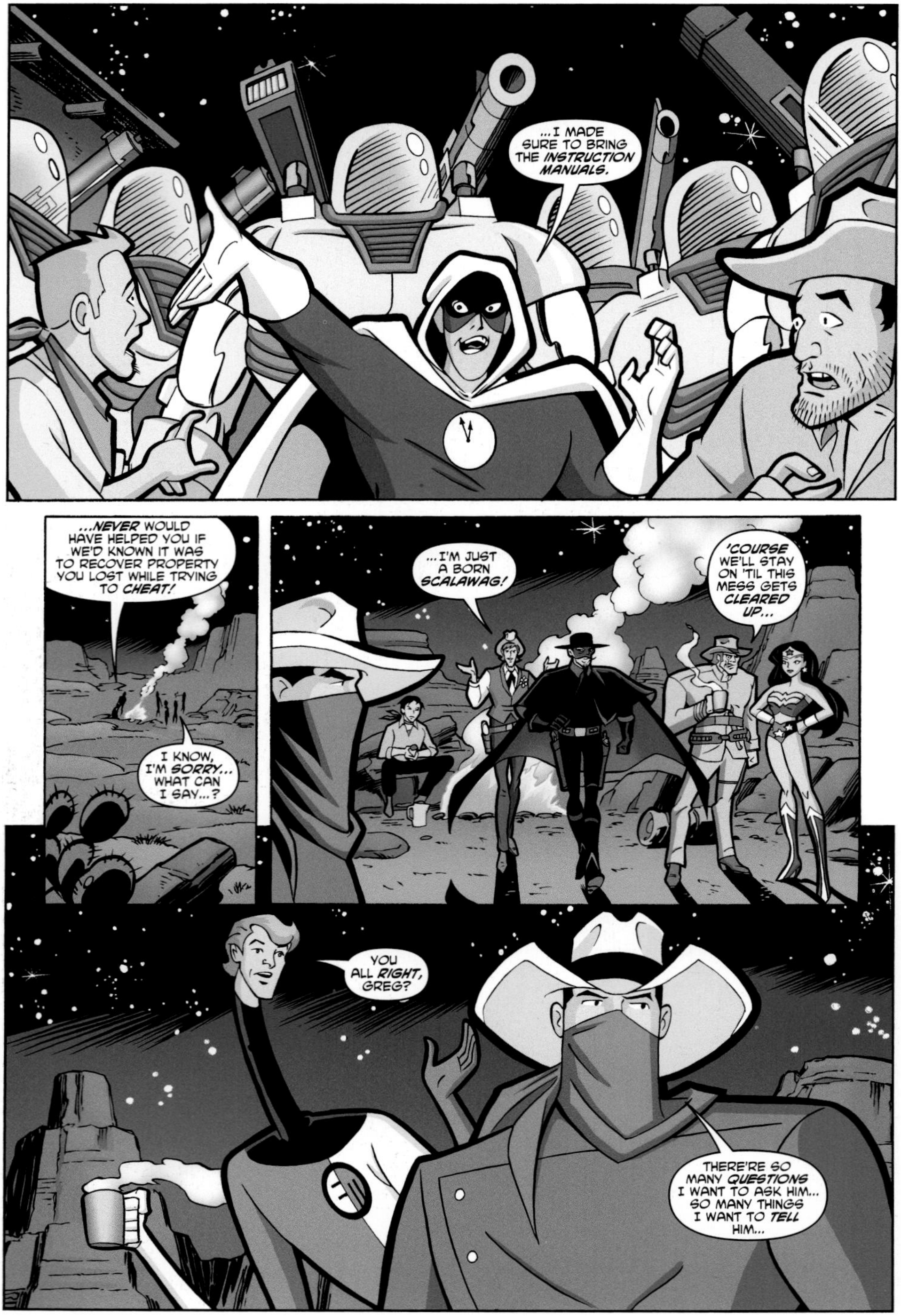
...I MADE SURE TO BRING THE *INSTRUCTION MANUALS.*
...*NEVER* WOULD HAVE HELPED YOU IF WE'D KNOWN IT WAS TO RECOVER PROPERTY YOU LOST WHILE TRYING TO *CHEAT!*
I KNOW, I'M *SORRY*... WHAT CAN I SAY...?
...I'M JUST A BORN *SCALAWAG!*
'COURSE WE'LL STAY ON 'TIL THIS MESS GETS *CLEARED UP*...
YOU ALL *RIGHT,* GREG?
THERE'RE SO MANY *QUESTIONS* I WANT TO ASK HIM... SO MANY THINGS I WANT TO *TELL* HIM...

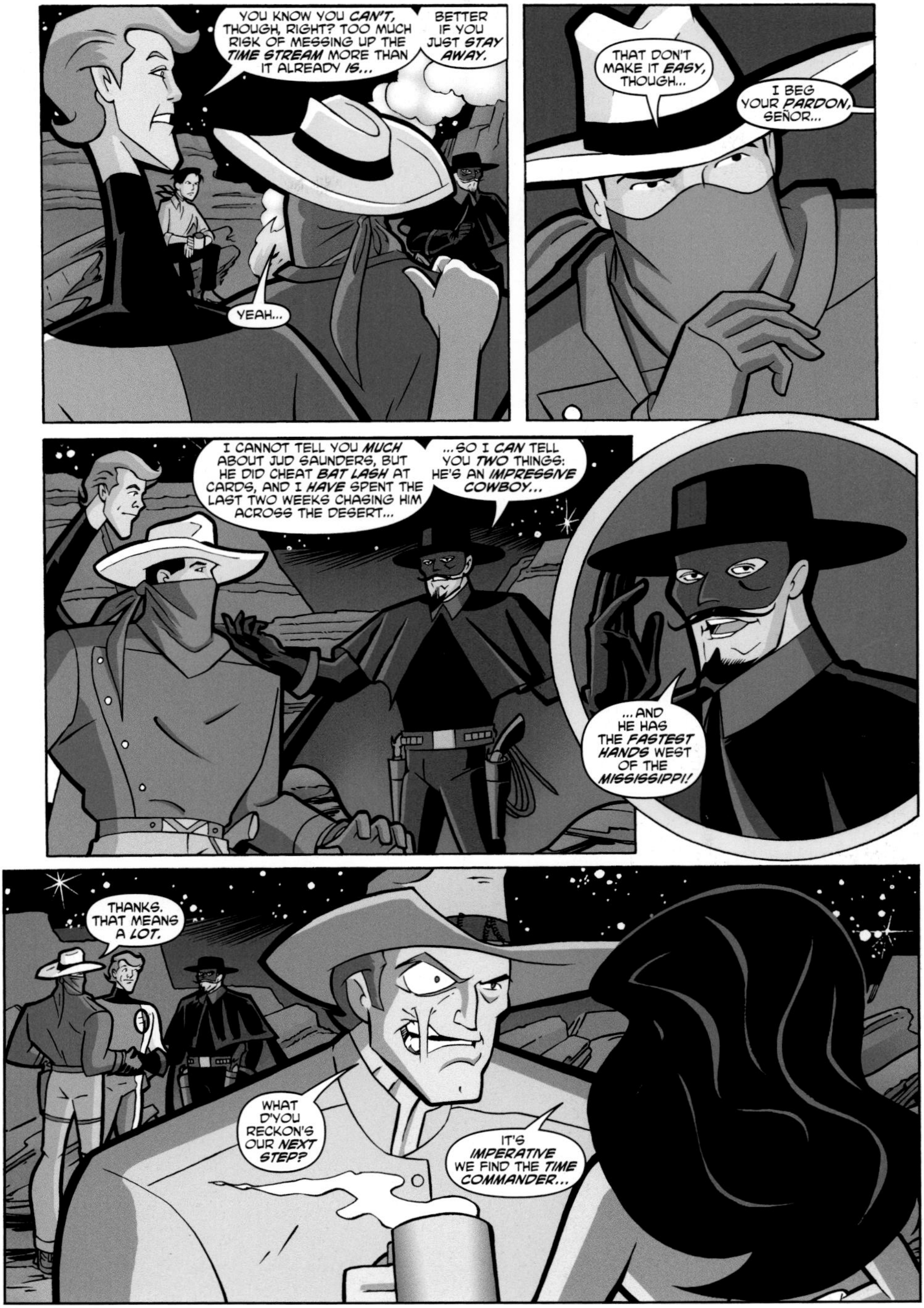
YOU KNOW YOU CAN'T, THOUGH, RIGHT? TOO MUCH RISK OF MESSING UP THE TIME STREAM MORE THAN IT ALREADY IS...
BETTER IF YOU JUST STAY AWAY.
YEAH...
THAT DON'T MAKE IT EASY, THOUGH...
I BEG YOUR PARDON, SEÑOR...
I CANNOT TELL YOU MUCH ABOUT JUD SAUNDERS, BUT HE DID CHEAT BAT LASH AT CARDS, AND I HAVE SPENT THE LAST TWO WEEKS CHASING HIM ACROSS THE DESERT...
...SO I CAN TELL YOU TWO THINGS: HE'S AN IMPRESSIVE COWBOY...
...AND HE HAS THE FASTEST HANDS WEST OF THE MISSISSIPPI!
THANKS. THAT MEANS A LOT.
WHAT D'YOU RECKON'S OUR NEXT STEP?
IT'S IMPERATIVE WE FIND THE TIME COMMANDER...

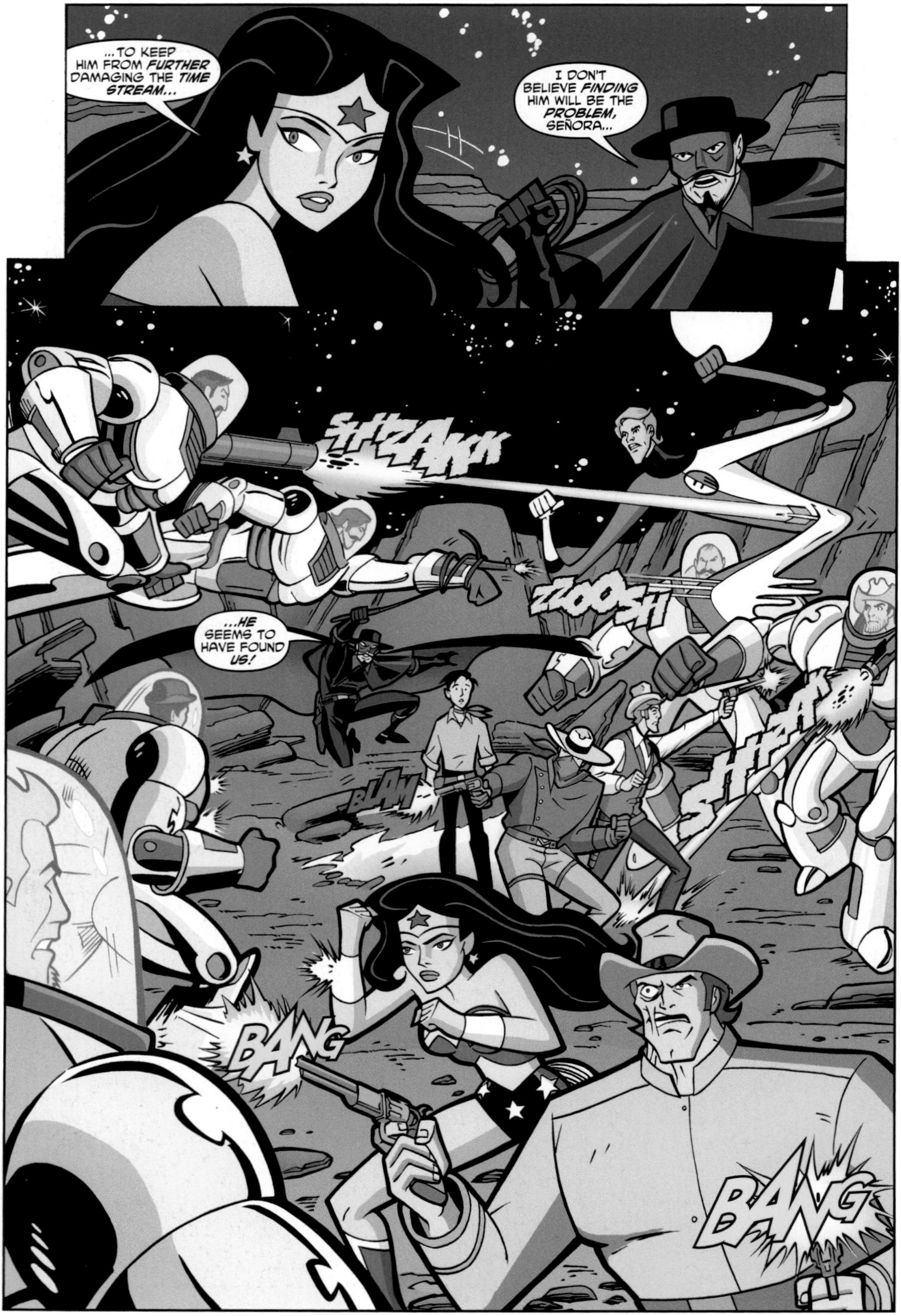
...TO KEEP HIM FROM FURTHER DAMAGING THE TIME STREAM...
I DON'T BELIEVE FINDING HIM WILL BE THE PROBLEM, SEÑORA...
SHRAKK
...HE SEEMS TO HAVE FOUND US!
ZZOOSH
BLAM
SHRAK
BANG
BANG

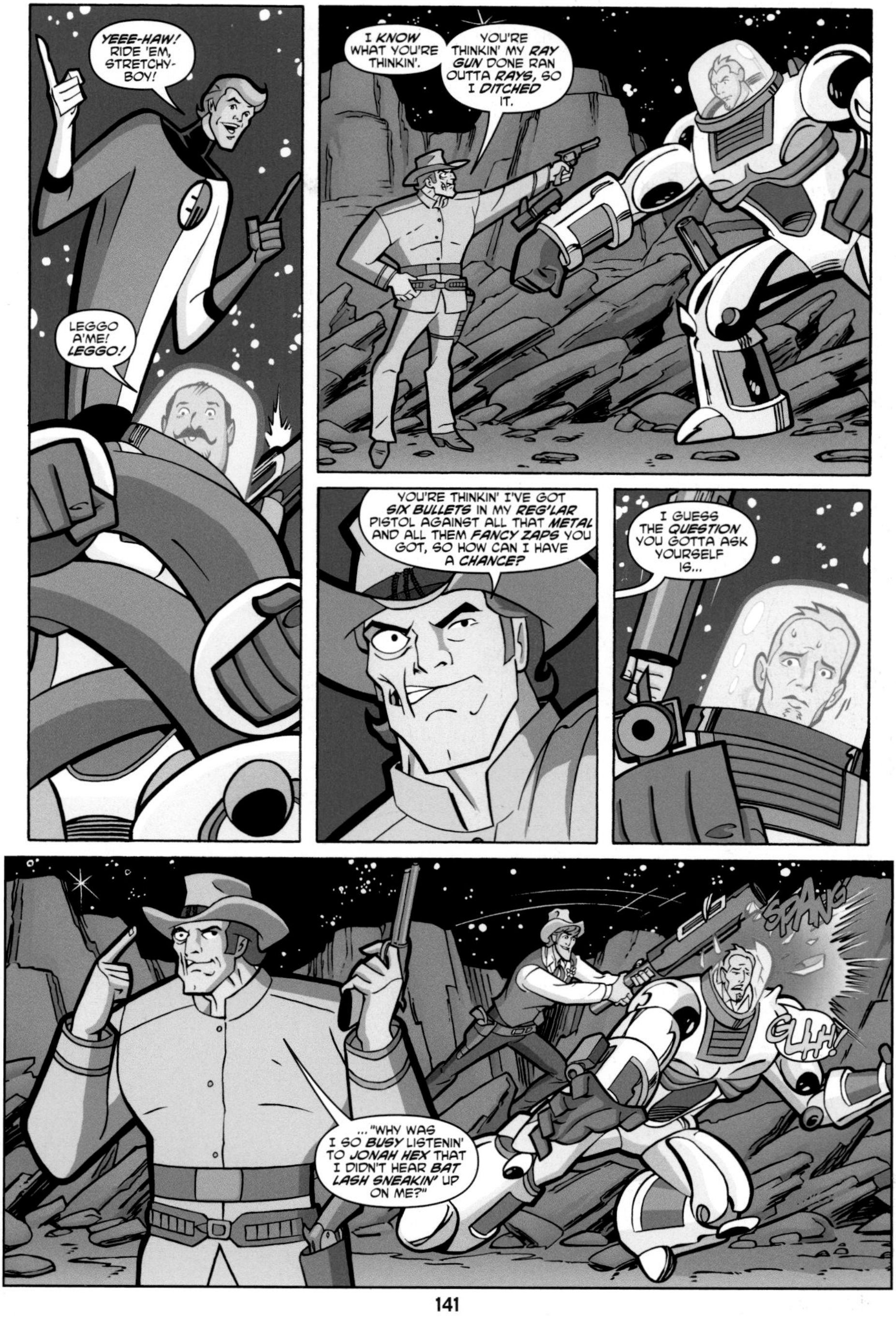
YEEE-HAW! RIDE 'EM, STRETCHY-BOY!
LEGGO A'ME! LEGGO!
I KNOW WHAT YOU'RE THINKIN'.
YOU'RE THINKIN' MY RAY GUN DONE RAN OUTTA RAYS, SO I DITCHED IT.
YOU'RE THINKIN' I'VE GOT SIX BULLETS IN MY REG'LAR PISTOL AGAINST ALL THAT METAL AND ALL THEM FANCY ZAPS YOU GOT, SO HOW CAN I HAVE A CHANCE?
I GUESS THE QUESTION YOU GOTTA ASK YOURSELF IS...
SPANG
GLHH!
..."WHY WAS I SO BUSY LISTENIN' TO JONAH HEX THAT I DIDN'T HEAR BAT LASH SNEAKIN' UP ON ME?"

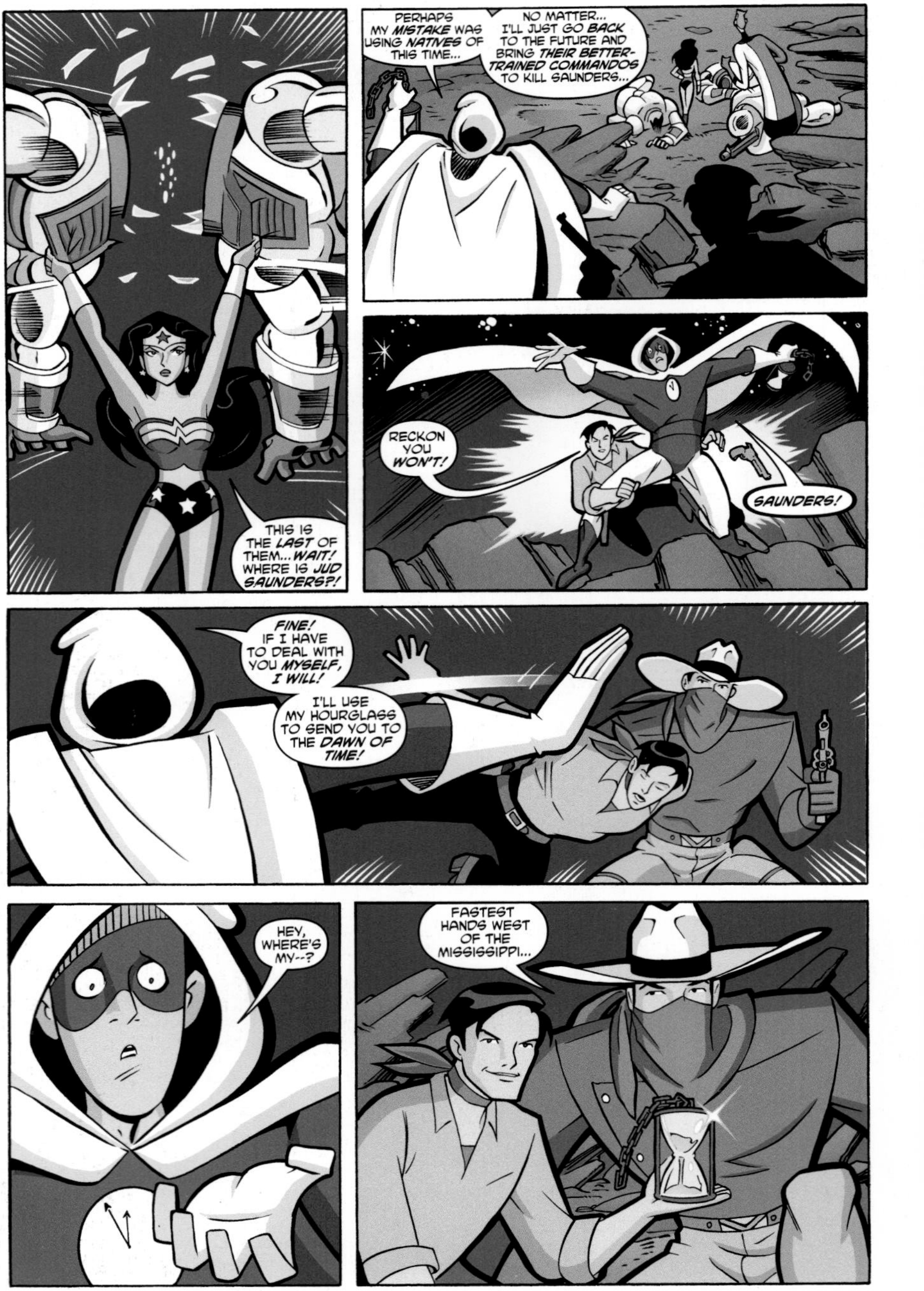
THIS IS THE LAST OF THEM... WAIT! WHERE IS JUD SAUNDERS?!
PERHAPS MY MISTAKE WAS USING NATIVES OF THIS TIME...
NO MATTER... I'LL JUST GO BACK TO THE FUTURE AND BRING THEIR BETTER-TRAINED COMMANDOS TO KILL SAUNDERS...
RECKON YOU WON'T!
SAUNDERS!
FINE! IF I HAVE TO DEAL WITH YOU MYSELF, I WILL!
I'LL USE MY HOURGLASS TO SEND YOU TO THE DAWN OF TIME!
HEY, WHERE'S MY--?
FASTEST HANDS WEST OF THE MISSISSIPPI...

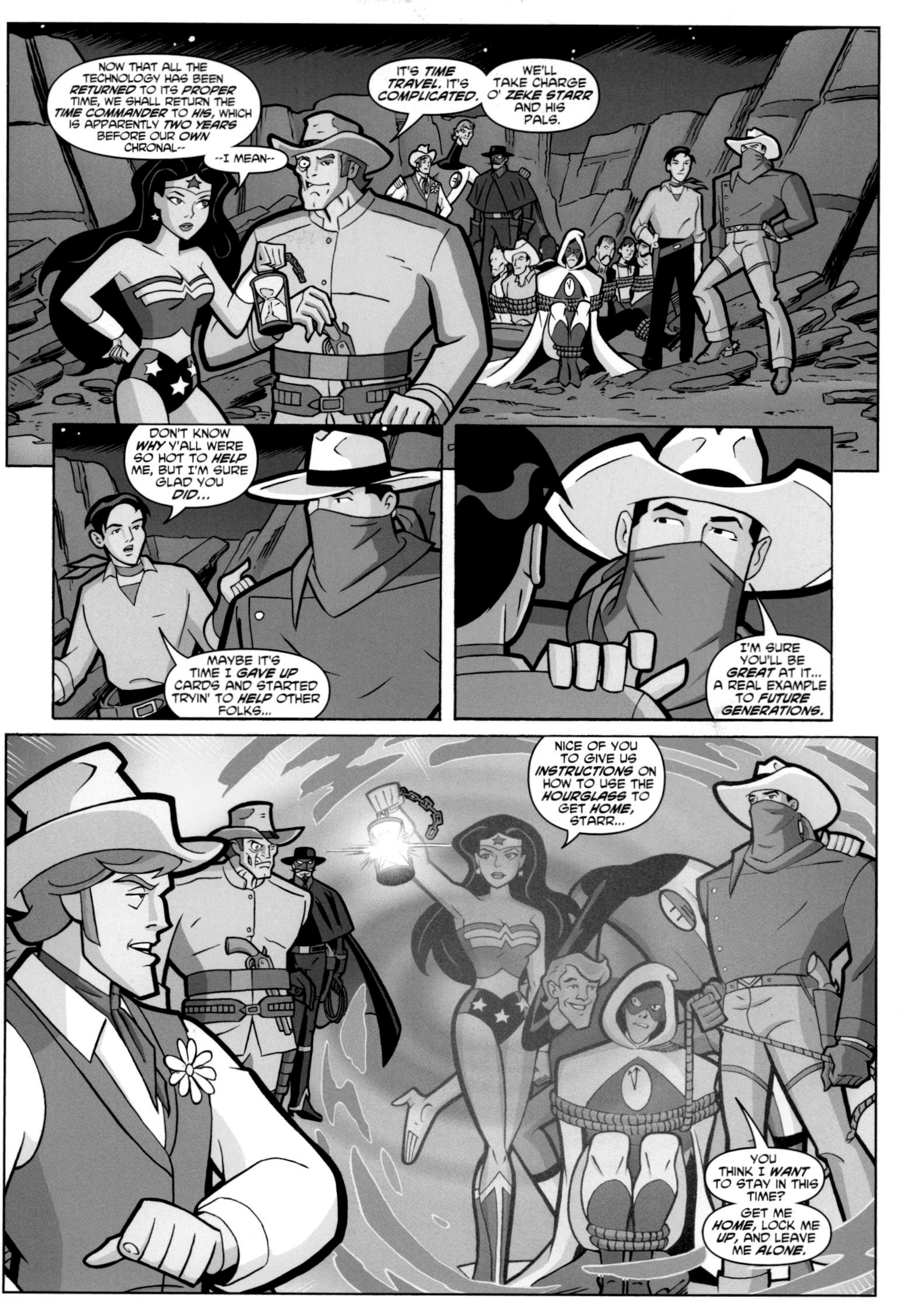
NOW THAT ALL THE TECHNOLOGY HAS BEEN RETURNED TO ITS PROPER TIME, WE SHALL RETURN THE TIME COMMANDER TO HIS, WHICH IS APPARENTLY TWO YEARS BEFORE OUR OWN CHRONAL--
--I MEAN--
IT'S TIME TRAVEL. IT'S COMPLICATED.
WE'LL TAKE CHARGE O' ZEKE STARR AND HIS PALS.
DON'T KNOW WHY Y'ALL WERE SO HOT TO HELP ME, BUT I'M SURE GLAD YOU DID...
MAYBE IT'S TIME I GAVE UP CARDS AND STARTED TRYIN' TO HELP OTHER FOLKS...
I'M SURE YOU'LL BE GREAT AT IT... A REAL EXAMPLE TO FUTURE GENERATIONS.
NICE OF YOU TO GIVE US INSTRUCTIONS ON HOW TO USE THE HOURGLASS TO GET HOME, STARR...
YOU THINK I WANT TO STAY IN THIS TIME?
GET ME HOME, LOCK ME UP, AND LEAVE ME ALONE.

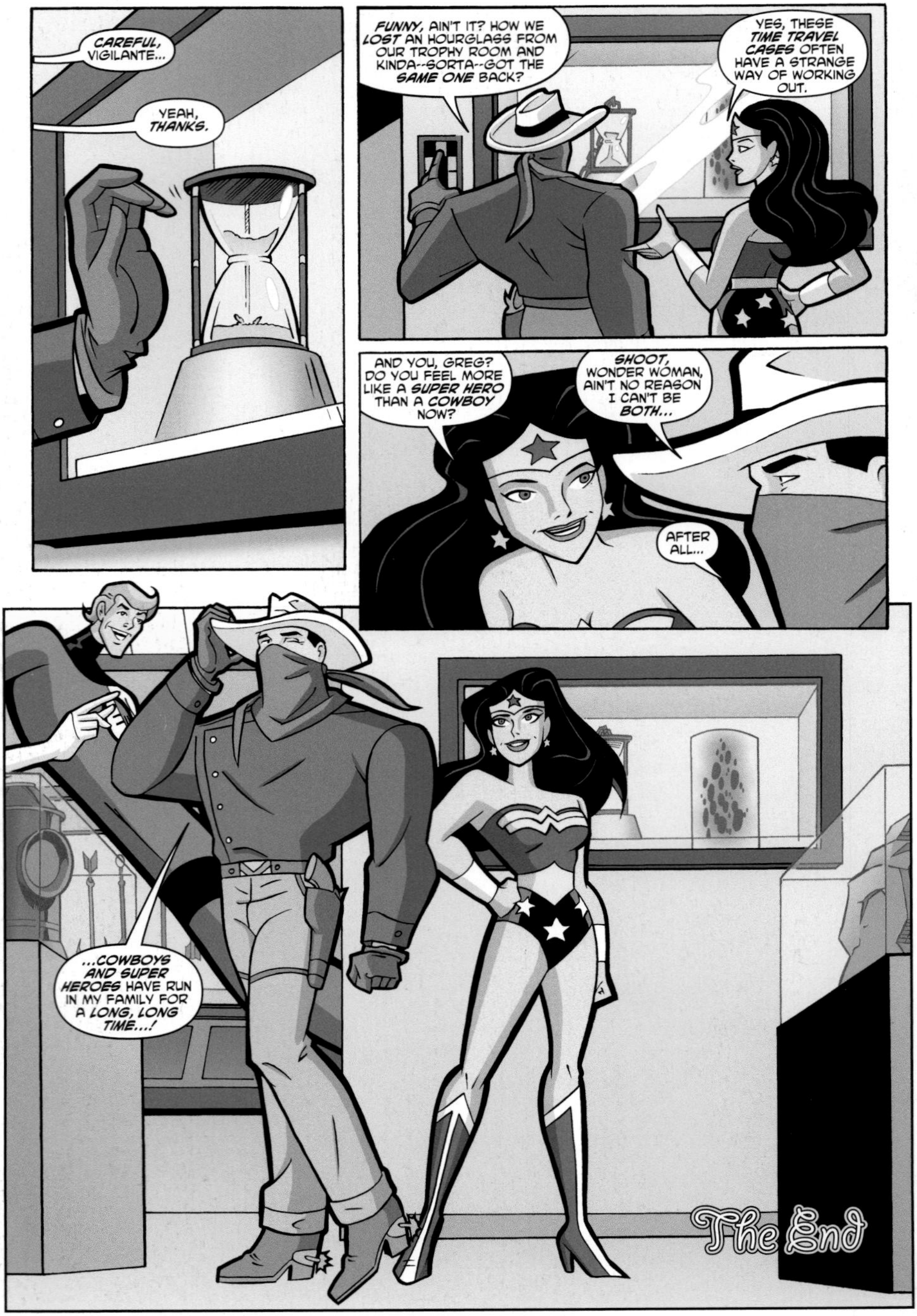
CAREFUL, VIGILANTE...
YEAH, THANKS.
FUNNY, AIN'T IT? HOW WE LOST AN HOURGLASS FROM OUR TROPHY ROOM AND KINDA--SORTA--GOT THE SAME ONE BACK?
YES, THESE TIME TRAVEL CASES OFTEN HAVE A STRANGE WAY OF WORKING OUT.
AND YOU, GREG? DO YOU FEEL MORE LIKE A SUPER HERO THAN A COWBOY NOW?
SHOOT, WONDER WOMAN, AIN'T NO REASON I CAN'T BE BOTH...
AFTER ALL...
...COWBOYS AND SUPER HEROES HAVE RUN IN MY FAMILY FOR A LONG, LONG TIME...!
The End

CAN'T GET ENOUGH DC HEROES?

Roll the dice on a new game of *Basements and Basilisks* as Robin reminds his teammates of all the fun they had on their last B&B quest—and this time, he promises they won't get sucked into any alternate dimensions!

Join the epic tabletop adventure from acclaimed talents **Heather Nuhfer, P.C. Morrissey, Sandy Jarrell,** and **Agnes Garbowska**—coming in Fall 2020!

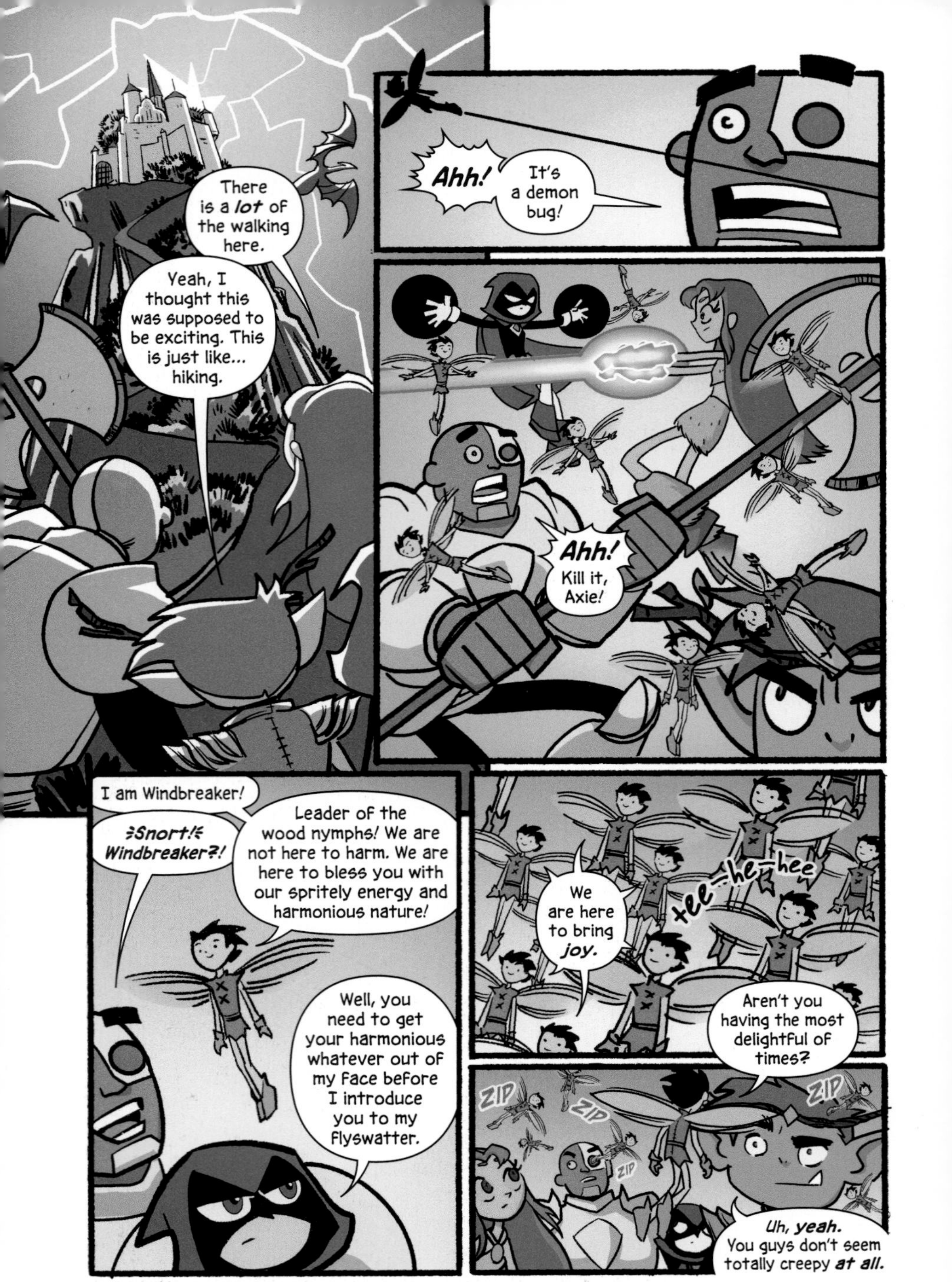
There is a *lot* of the walking here.
Yeah, I thought this was supposed to be exciting. This is just like... hiking.
Ahh!
It's a demon bug!
Ahh! Kill it, Axie!
I am Windbreaker!
Snort! Windbreaker?!
Leader of the wood nymphs! We are not here to harm. We are here to bless you with our spritely energy and harmonious nature!
Well, you need to get your harmonious whatever out of my face before I introduce you to my flyswatter.
We are here to bring *joy*.
tee-he-hee
Aren't you having the most delightful of times?
ZIP
ZIP
ZIP
ZIP
Uh, **yeah.** You guys don't seem totally creepy **at all.**

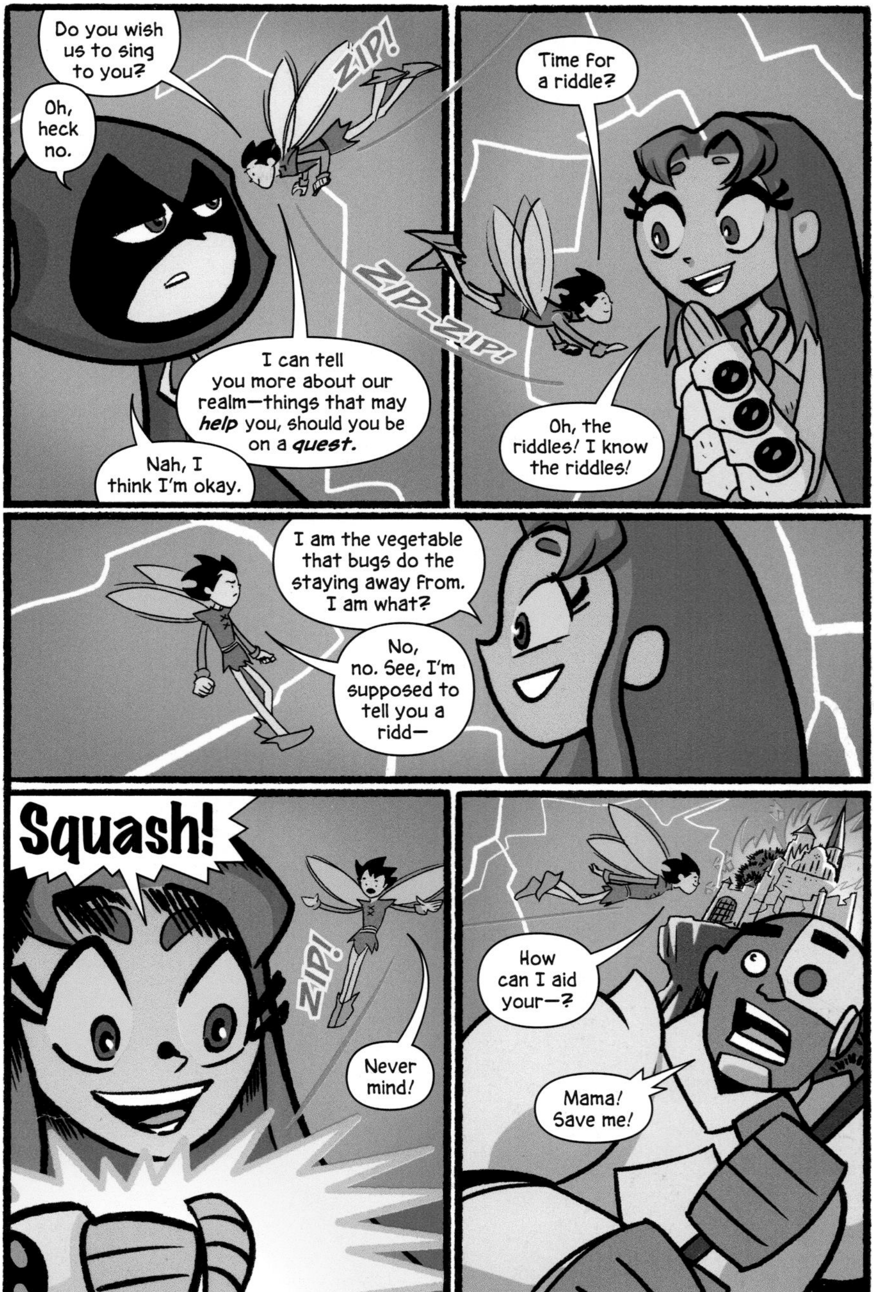
Do you wish us to sing to you?
ZIP!
Oh, heck no.
I can tell you more about our realm—things that may *help* you, should you be on a *quest.*
Nah, I think I'm okay.
ZIP-ZIP!
Time for a riddle?
Oh, the riddles! I know the riddles!
I am the vegetable that bugs do the staying away from. I am what?
No, no. See, I'm supposed to tell you a ridd—
Squash!
ZIP!
Never mind!
How can I aid your—?
Mama! Save me!

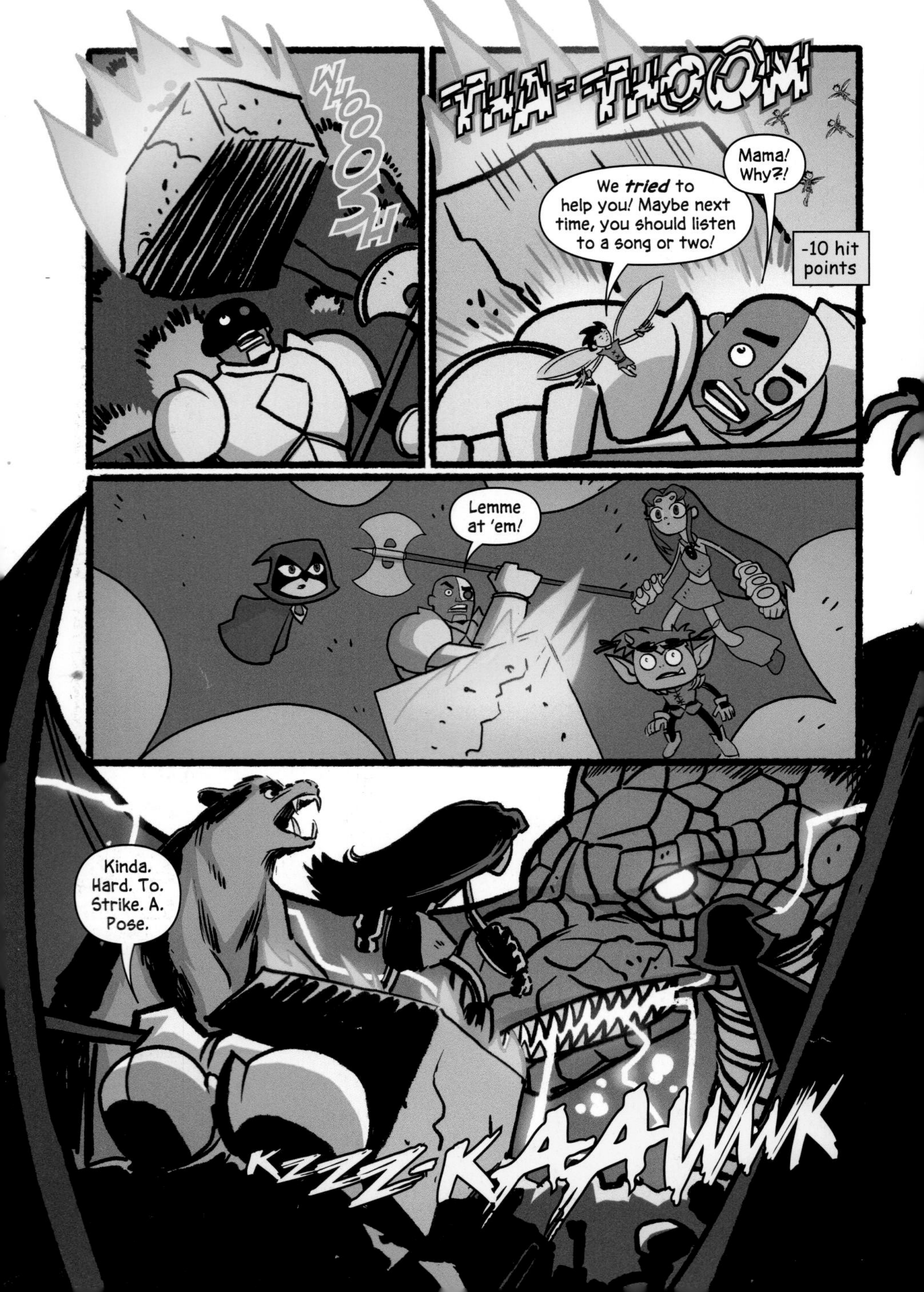
WHOOOOSH
THA-THOOM
Mama! Why?!
We tried to help you! Maybe next time, you should listen to a song or two!
-10 hit points
Lemme at 'em!
Kinda. Hard. To. Strike. A. Pose.
KZZZZ-KAAWWK

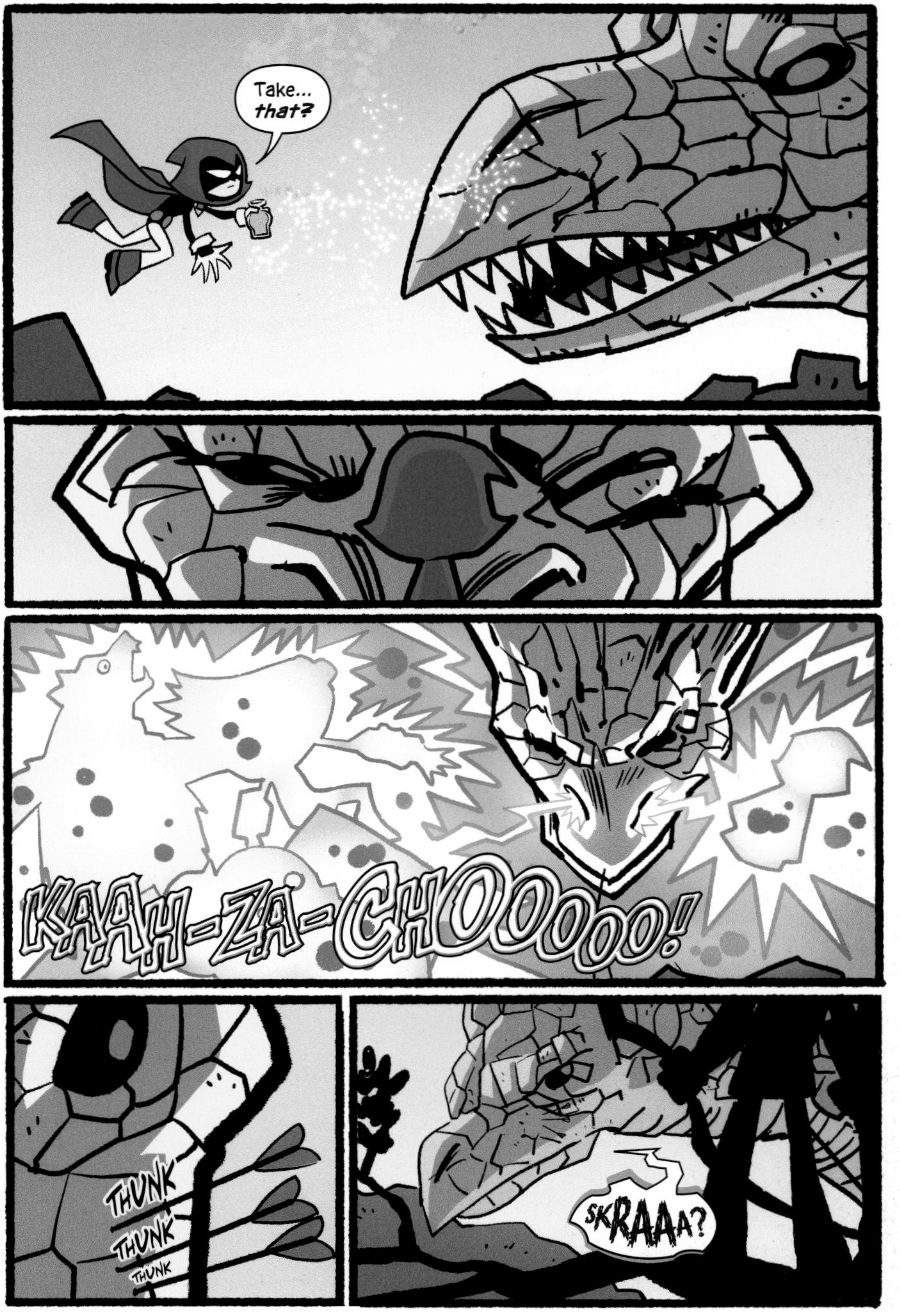
Take... *that?*
KAAH-ZA-CHOOOOOO!
THUNK
THUNK
THUNK
SKRAAA?

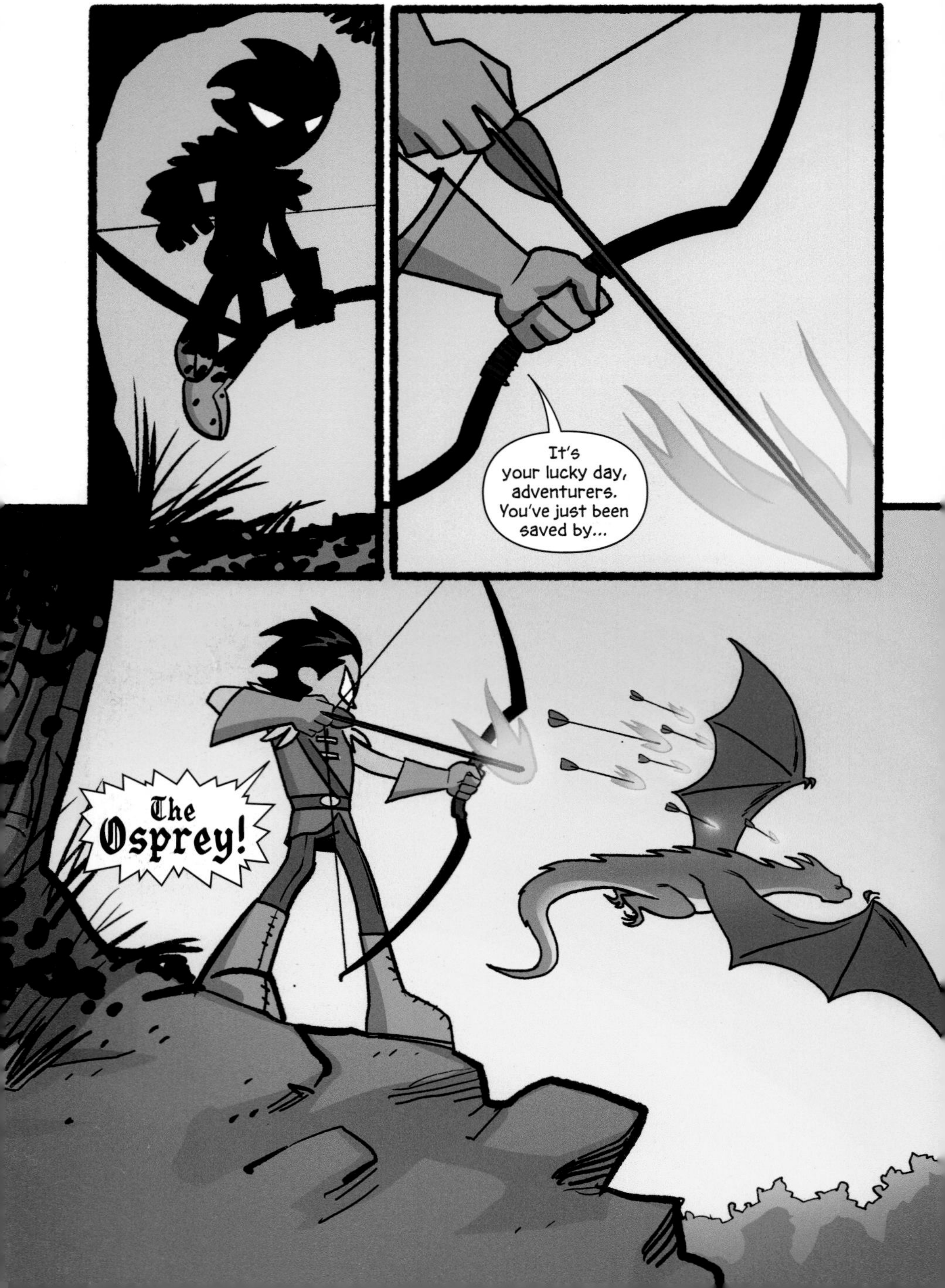
It's your lucky day, adventurers. You've just been saved by...
The Osprey!

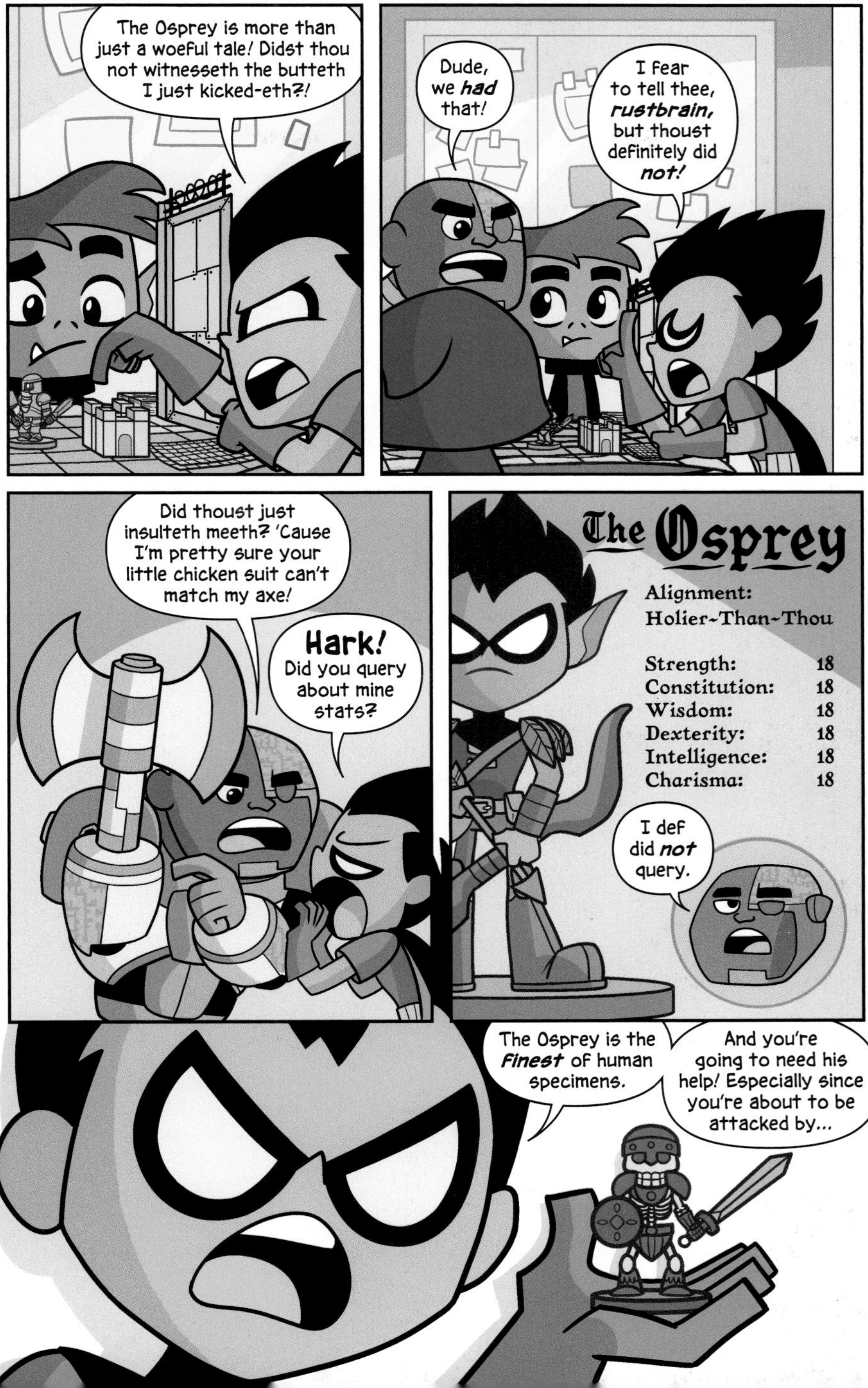
The Osprey is more than just a woeful tale! Didst thou not witnesseth the butteth I just kicked-eth?!
Dude, we had that!
I fear to tell thee, rustbrain, but thoust definitely did not!
Did thoust just insulteth meeth? 'Cause I'm pretty sure your little chicken suit can't match my axe!
Hark! Did you query about mine stats?
The Osprey
Alignment: Holier-Than-Thou
Strength: 18
Constitution: 18
Wisdom: 18
Dexterity: 18
Intelligence: 18
Charisma: 18
I def did not query.
The Osprey is the finest of human specimens.
And you're going to need his help! Especially since you're about to be attacked by...

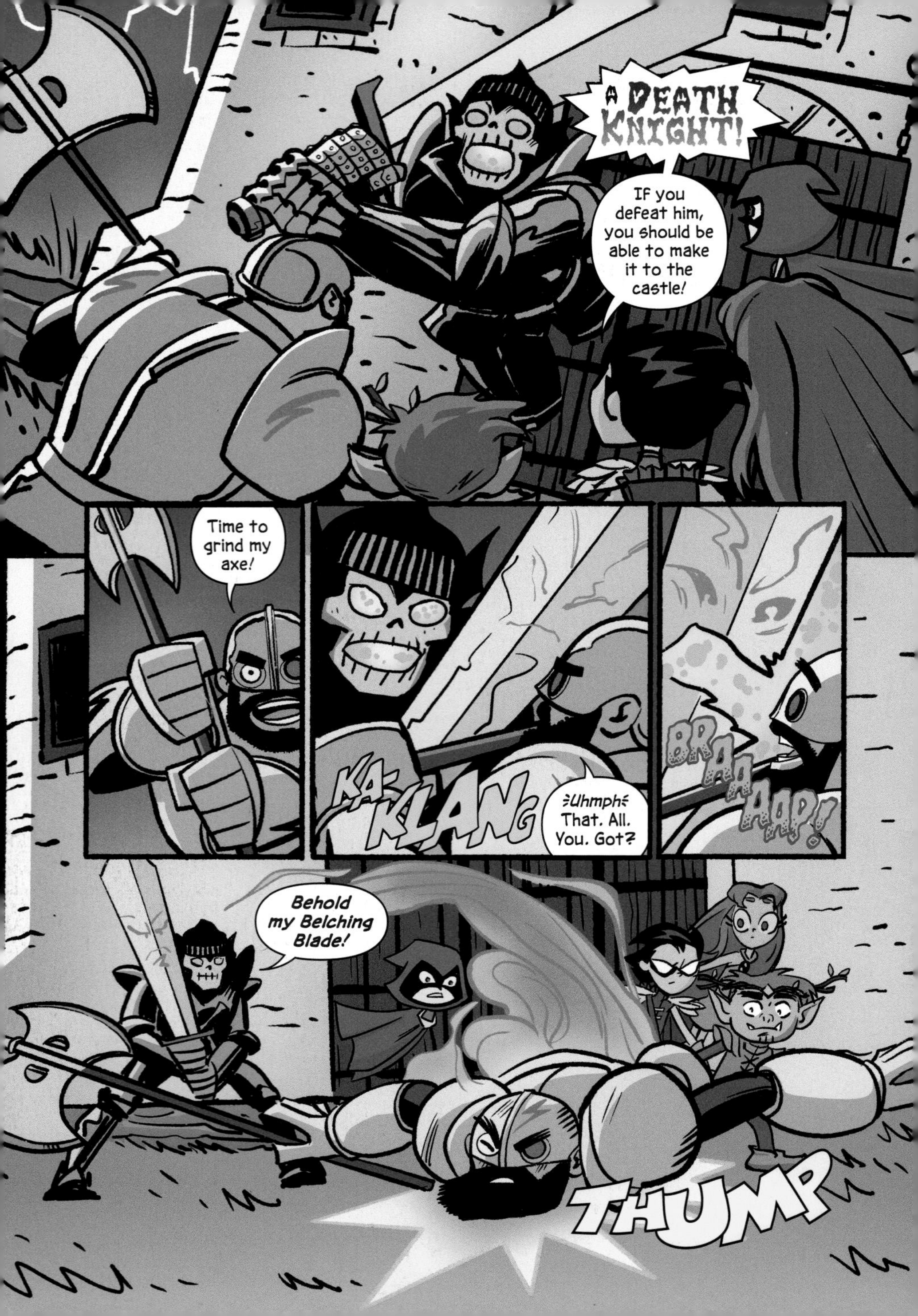
A DEATH KNIGHT!
If you defeat him, you should be able to make it to the castle!
Time to grind my axe!
KA-KLANG
Uhmph That. All. You. Got?
BRAAAAP!
Behold my Belching Blade!
THUMP

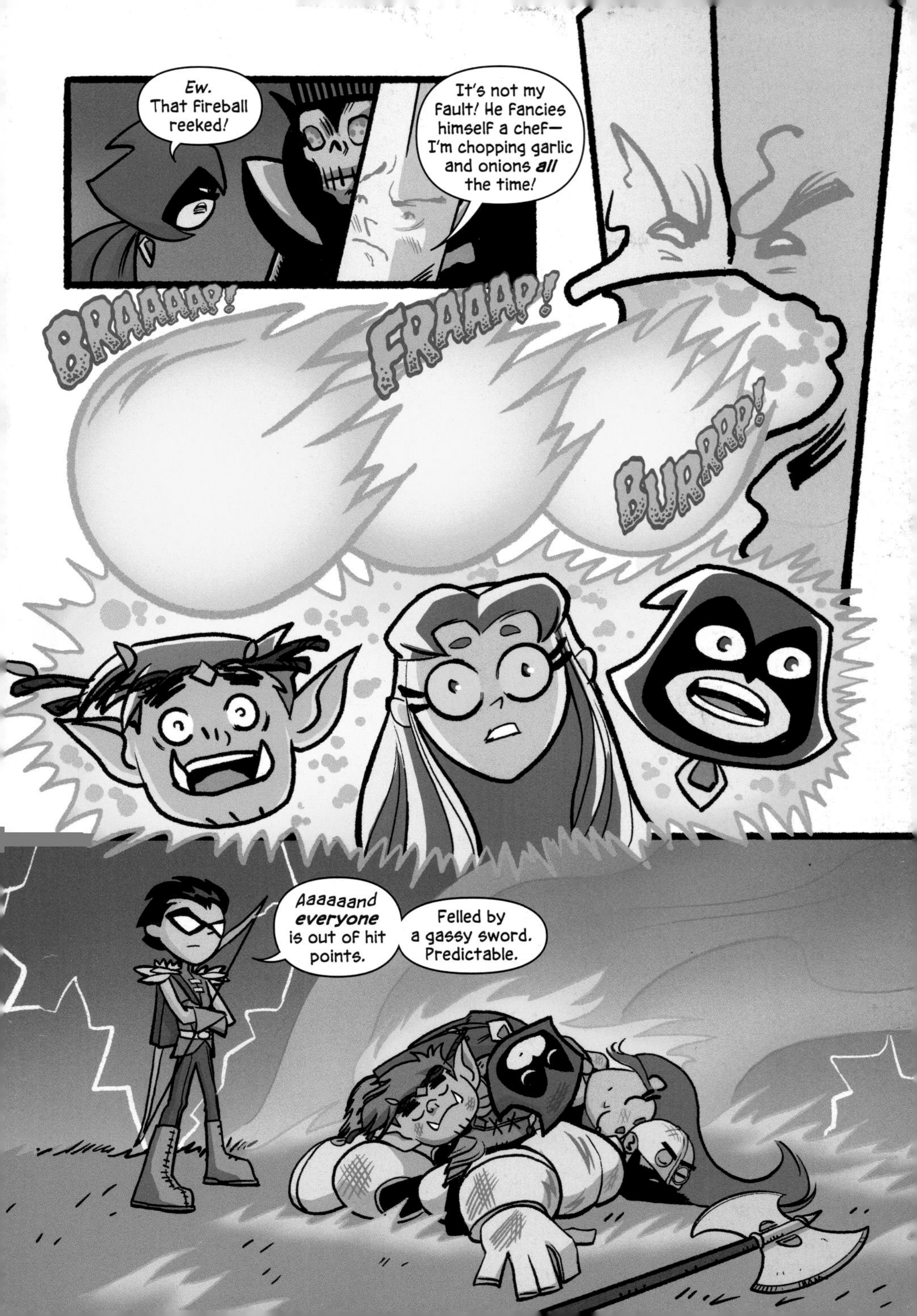

Ew. That fireball reeked!
It's not my fault! He fancies himself a chef— I'm chopping garlic and onions *all* the time!
BRAAAAAP!
FRAAAP!
BURRRP!
Aaaaaand *everyone* is out of hit points.
Felled by a gassy sword. Predictable.

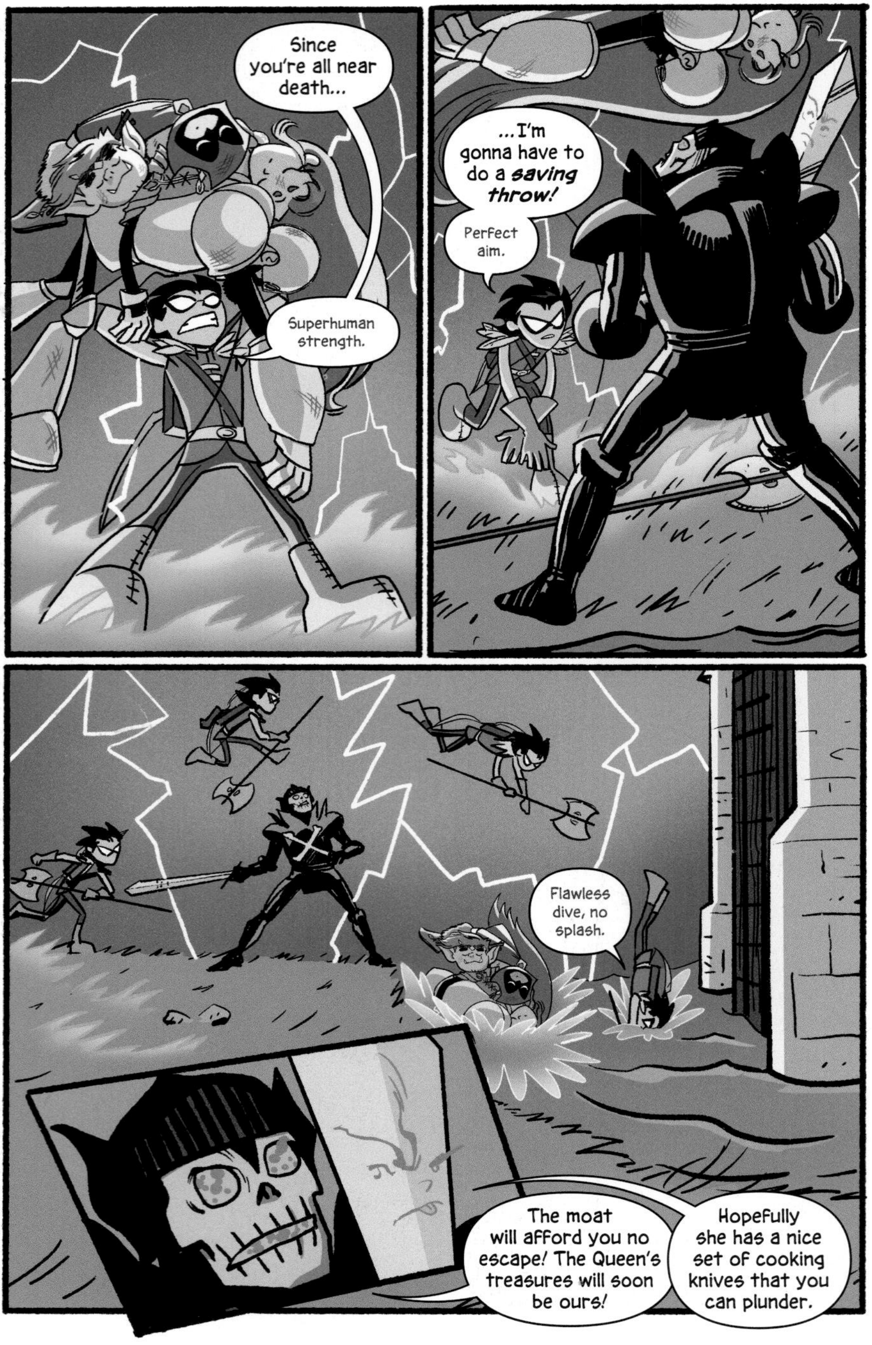

Since you're all near death...
Superhuman strength.
...I'm gonna have to do a *saving throw!*
Perfect aim.
Flawless dive, no splash.
The moat will afford you no escape! The Queen's treasures will soon be ours!
Hopefully she has a nice set of cooking knives that you can plunder.

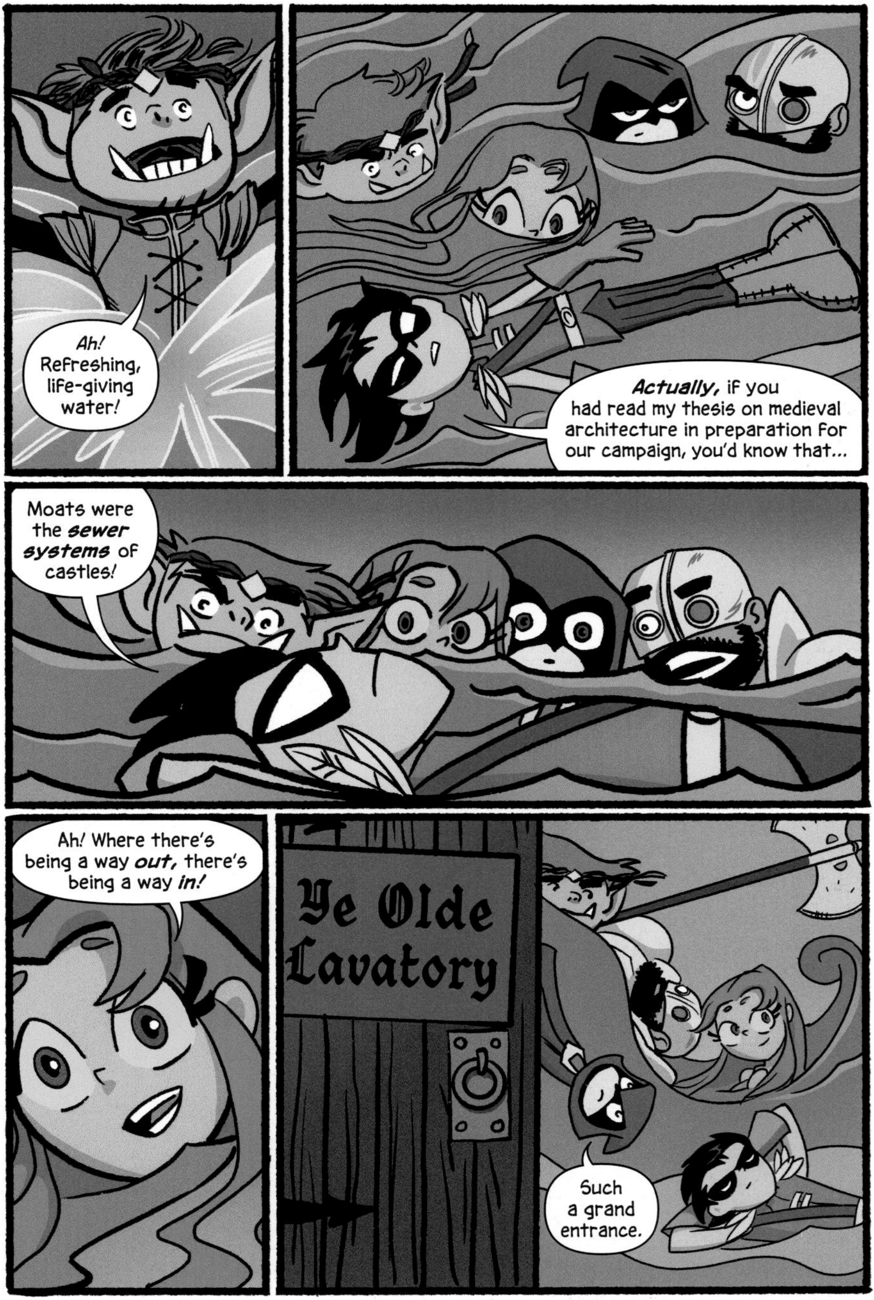
Ah! Refreshing, life-giving water!
Actually, if you had read my thesis on medieval architecture in preparation for our campaign, you'd know that...
Moats were the sewer systems of castles!
Ah! Where there's being a way out, there's being a way in!
Ye Olde Lavatory
Such a grand entrance.

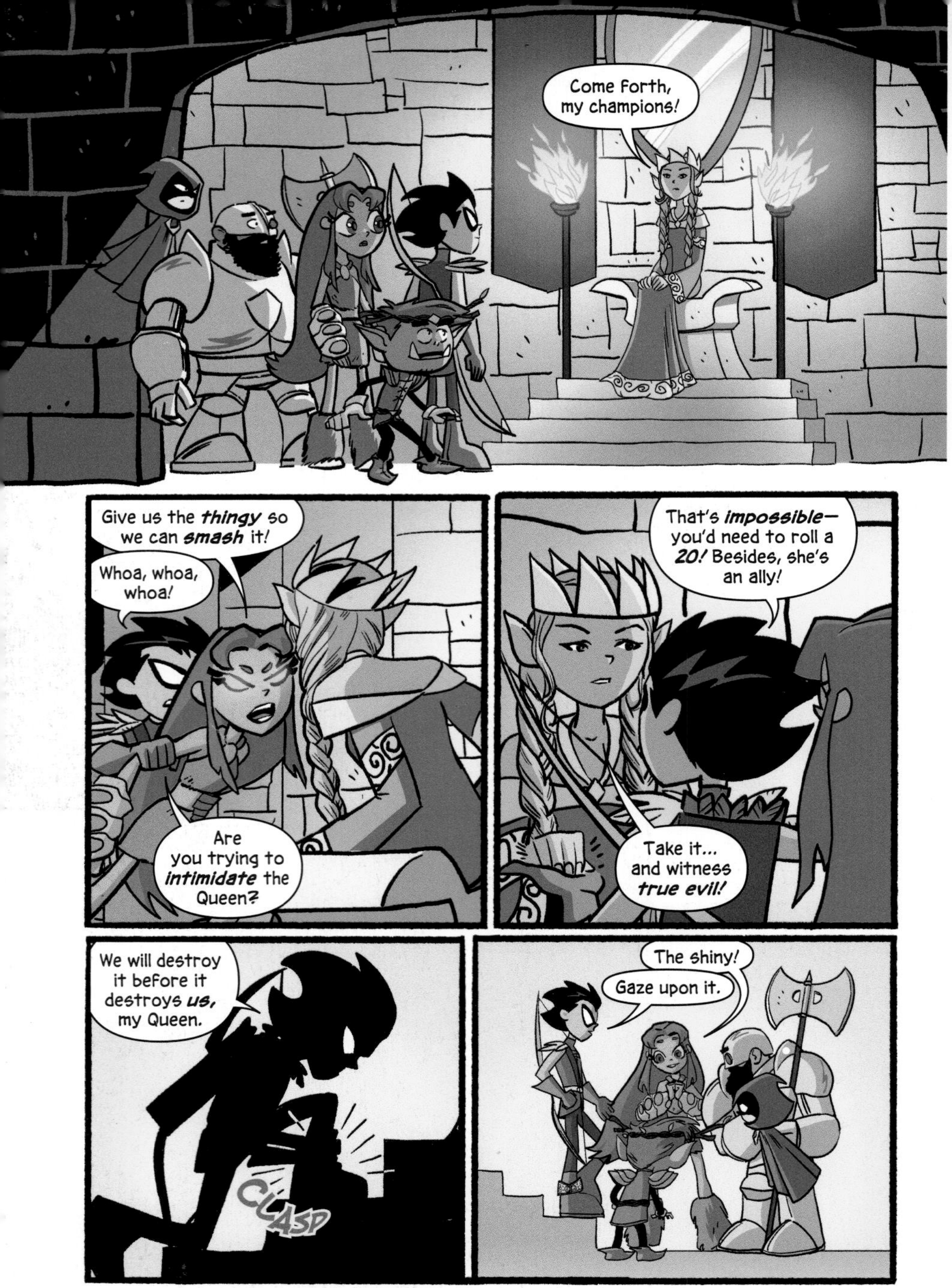

Come forth, my champions!
Give us the *thingy* so we can *smash* it!
Whoa, whoa, whoa!
Are you trying to *intimidate* the Queen?
That's *impossible*—you'd need to roll a *20!* Besides, she's an ally!
Take it... and witness *true evil!*
We will destroy it before it destroys *us,* my Queen.
CLASP
The shiny!
Gaze upon it.

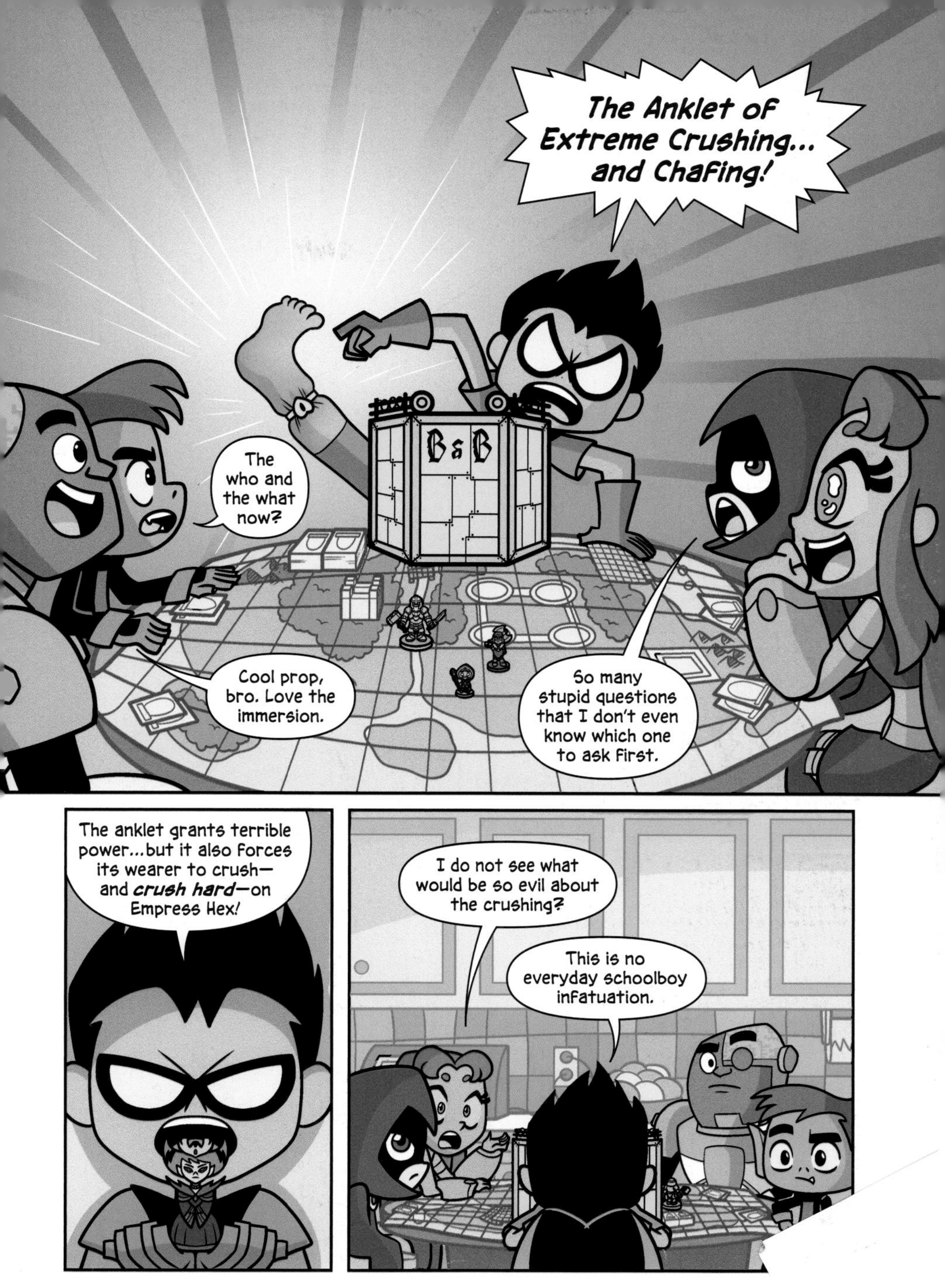
The Anklet of Extreme Crushing... and Chafing!
The who and the what now?
Cool prop, bro. Love the immersion.
So many stupid questions that I don't even know which one to ask first.
B&B
The anklet grants terrible power...but it also forces its wearer to crush—and *crush hard*—on Empress Hex!
I do not see what would be so evil about the crushing?
This is no everyday schoolboy infatuation.

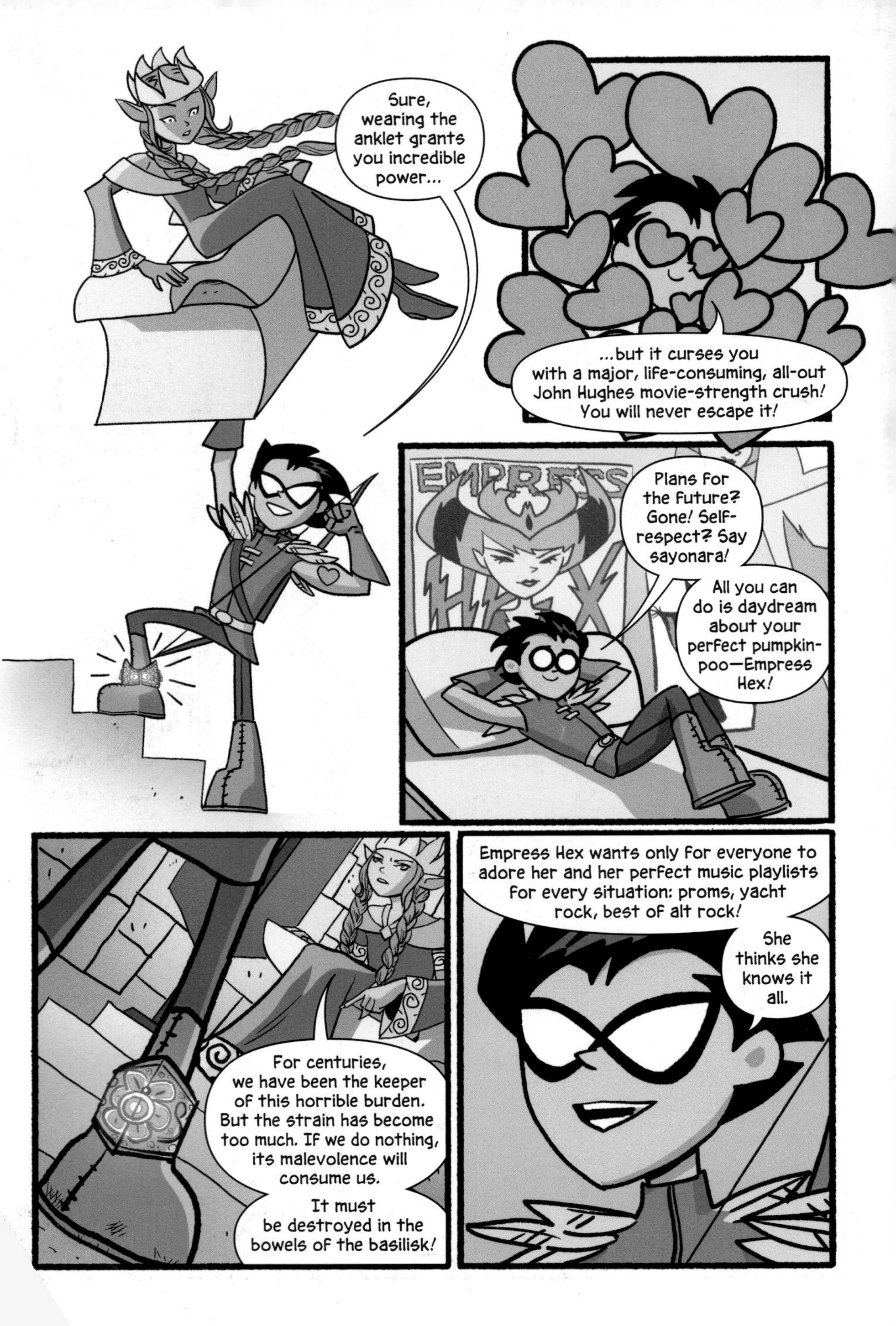
Sure, wearing the anklet grants you incredible power...
...but it curses you with a major, life-consuming, all-out John Hughes movie-strength crush! You will never escape it!
Plans for the future? Gone! Self-respect? Say sayonara!
All you can do is daydream about your perfect pumpkin-poo—Empress Hex!
For centuries, we have been the keeper of this horrible burden. But the strain has become too much. If we do nothing, its malevolence will consume us.
It must be destroyed in the bowels of the basilisk!
Empress Hex wants only for everyone to adore her and her perfect music playlists for every situation: proms, yacht rock, best of alt rock!
She thinks she knows it all.

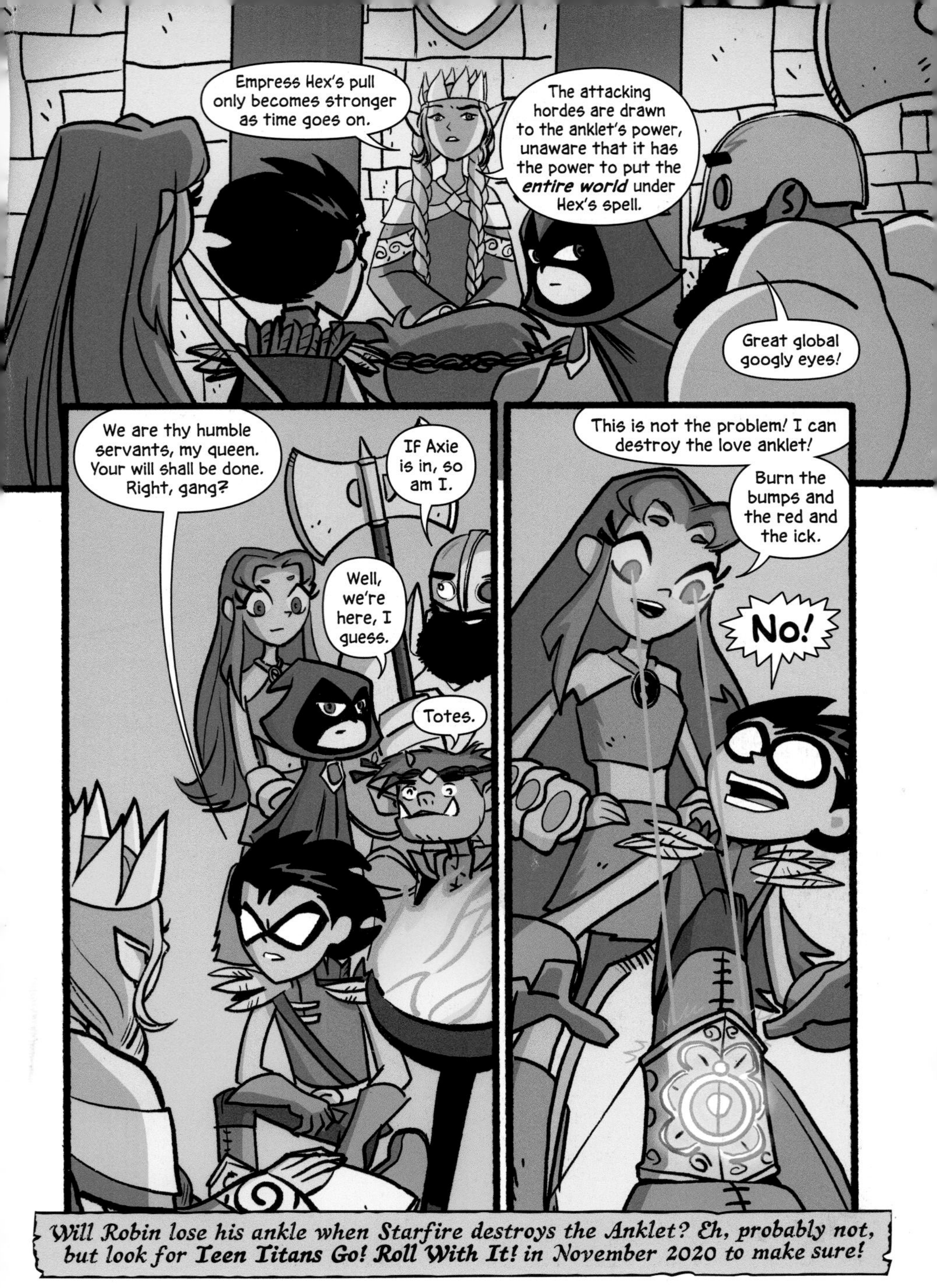
Empress Hex's pull only becomes stronger as time goes on.
The attacking hordes are drawn to the anklet's power, unaware that it has the power to put the *entire world* under Hex's spell.
Great global googly eyes!
We are thy humble servants, my queen. Your will shall be done. Right, gang?
If Axie is in, so am I.
Well, we're here, I guess.
Totes.
This is not the problem! I can destroy the love anklet!
Burn the bumps and the red and the ick.
No!
Will Robin lose his ankle when Starfire destroys the Anklet? Eh, probably not, but look for Teen Titans Go! Roll With It! in November 2020 to make sure!

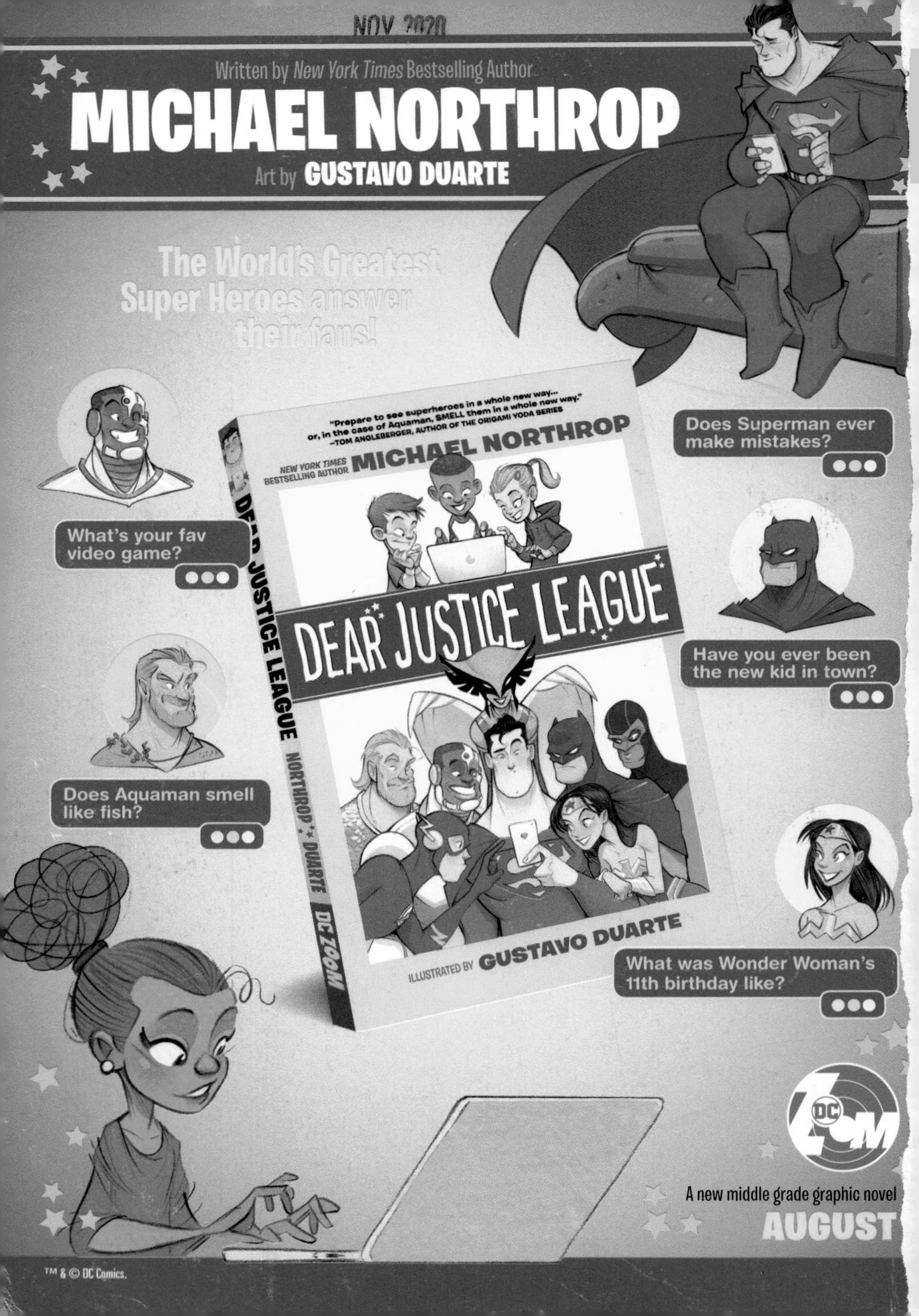
NOV 2020
Written by New York Times Bestselling Author
MICHAEL NORTHROP
Art by GUSTAVO DUARTE
The World's Greatest Super Heroes answer their fans!
"Prepare to see superheroes in a whole new way... or, in the case of Aquaman, SMELL them in a whole new way."
—TOM ANGLEBERGER, AUTHOR OF THE ORIGAMI YODA SERIES
NEW YORK TIMES BESTSELLING AUTHOR MICHAEL NORTHROP
DEAR JUSTICE LEAGUE
ILLUSTRATED BY GUSTAVO DUARTE
DEAR JUSTICE LEAGUE NORTHROP DUARTE DC ZOOM
What's your fav video game?
Does Aquaman smell like fish?
Does Superman ever make mistakes?
Have you ever been the new kid in town?
What was Wonder Woman's 11th birthday like?
DC ZOOM
A new middle grade graphic novel
AUGUST
™ & © DC Comics.